LAZARUS
ENMITY'S EDGE

More Warhammer 40,000 from Black Library

• DAWN OF FIRE •
BOOK 1: Avenging Son
Guy Haley

BOOK 2: The Gate of Bones
Andy Clark

BOOK 3: The Wolftime
Gav Thorpe

BOOK 4: Throne of Light
Guy Haley

BOOK 5: The Iron Kingdom
Nick Kyme

BOOK 6: The Martyr's Tomb
Marc Collins

BOOK 7: Sea of Souls
Chris Wraight

BOOK 8: Hand of Abaddon
Nick Kyme

• DARK IMPERIUM •
Guy Haley

BOOK 1: Dark Imperium
BOOK 2: Plague War
BOOK 3: Godblight

LEVIATHAN
Darius Hinks

THE LION: SON OF THE FOREST
Mike Brooks

HELBRECHT: KNIGHT OF THE THRONE
Marc Collins

SILENT HUNTERS
Edoardo Albert

URDESH: THE SERPENT AND THE SAINT
Matthew Farrer

URDESH: THE MAGISTER AND THE MARTYR
Matthew Farrer

THE SUCCESSORS
Various authors

• VAULTS OF TERRA •
Chris Wraight

BOOK 1: The Carrion Throne
BOOK 2: The Hollow Mountain
BOOK 3: The Dark City

LAZARUS
ENMITY'S EDGE

GARY KLOSTER

BLACK LIBRARY

A BLACK LIBRARY PUBLICATION

First published in 2024.
This edition published in Great Britain in 2024 by
Black Library, Games Workshop Ltd., Willow Road,
Nottingham, NG7 2WS, UK.

Represented by: Games Workshop Limited – Irish branch,
Unit 3, Lower Liffey Street, Dublin 1,
D01 K199, Ireland.

10 9 8 7 6 5 4 3 2 1

Produced by Games Workshop in Nottingham.
Cover illustration by Akim Kaliberda.

A CIP record for this book is available from the British Library.

ISBN 13: 978-1-80407-668-2

See Black Library on the internet at

blacklibrary.com

Find out more about Games Workshop
and the worlds of Warhammer at

warhammer.com

Printed and bound in the UK.

To Lucah and Camille. For getting me started.

For more than a hundred centuries the Emperor
has sat immobile on the Golden Throne of Earth.
He is the Master of Mankind. By the might of his
inexhaustible armies a million worlds stand
against the dark.

Yet, he is a rotting carcass, the Carrion Lord of
the Imperium held in life by marvels from the
Dark Age of Technology and the thousand souls
sacrificed each day so his may continue to burn.

To be a man in such times is to be one amongst
untold billions. It is to live in the cruelest and
most bloody regime imaginable. It is to suffer an
eternity of carnage and slaughter. It is to have cries
of anguish and sorrow drowned by the thirsting
laughter of dark gods.

This is a dark and terrible era where you will
find little comfort or hope. Forget the power of
technology and science. Forget the promise of
progress and advancement. Forget any notion of
common humanity or compassion.

There is no peace amongst the stars, for in the grim
darkness of the far future, there is only war.

CHAPTER ONE

Lazarus stood on the stony shore, staring up at a sky that was the bruised blue of a corpse's lips. Thin black lines marked the horizon, harbingers of what was coming. The vox-channels assigned to his Scouts were silent, but the Master of the Fifth saw those rising plumes of smoke and knew. The orks were approaching, their crude war machines racing across the scarred face of this toxic world, and they were heading straight for him and his gathered Dark Angels.

'Good.' The word echoed in his winged Spiritshield Helm, a comment for himself, not for cluttering up any of the vox-channels currently being used by the Fifth Company. Those channels were busy enough, filled with the deep voices of his brothers as they worked together, fortifying this wretched strand.

Lazarus turned, and the ceramite soles of his armour ground the brittle stone beneath his feet to dust, which slowly rose and hung in the air around him. This planet was called Husk, a good name for an ugly place. It was cold and barren, poisoned by ten thousand years of industrialisation. The sea beside them was the colour of diseased phlegm, its turgid surface barely rippled by the wind. The shore it pressed against was composed of crumbling slabs of dark red rock that made the ground look like a badly healed wound. Those stones rose abruptly into a ridge, a line of sharp-peaked mountains that were topped with dirty ochre snow. They looked like bloody gums, crowned with the splinters of shattered teeth.

This rough shore between those mountains and the sea was the fastest path to Varpitt, the hive of humanity that lay half buried in the desert beyond. Hundreds of millions of humans dug into Husk's crust, eating, sleeping, breeding, dreaming. The beating heart of the Emperor's vast galactic empire, and given the chance, the orks would rip them out of their city like a beast tearing marrow from a bone.

Lazarus and his Fifth were the hard denial of that destruction.

'Command squad, report.' Lazarus did not speak the words aloud. They were a subvocalised order that ran into the black carapace that had been implanted beneath his skin during his long, painful transformation into a Dark Angel. That sacred gene-seed organ was fused with his nervous system, its long strands of artificial neurons wrapped tight around his brain and spine, the interface between Lazarus and his power armour. It made the suit's systems extensions of his body and his senses, and controlling the built-in vox-unit was simply a matter of wanting to do it, requiring no more effort than breathing.

The silent order opened a channel that connected Lazarus with the heart of the Fifth. Brother Demetrius, Interrogator-Chaplain, the man who had saved his life countless times, and his soul at least once. Brother Asbeel, the Apothecary responsible for his second life. Brothers Amad and Zakariah, his lieutenants. Brother Ephron, most senior of the Fifth's Tech-marines. And finally Ancient Jequn, the bearer of the Fifth's standard and the only man in the company who might match Lazarus' abilities with the blade.

'Brother Ephron,' he began, his words reaching the systems now linked through their armour's vox. 'Fleet status.'

'*Status depiction.*' The Space Marines in Lazarus' command squad had picked up on his clipped speaking style long ago. Ephron, more comfortable with his machines than men, had no issue with staying succinct. The Techmarine transmitted a pict, a schematic of the space around Husk.

'*Battle-barge* Unrelenting Fury *has entered geosynchronous orbit directly above,*' Brother Ephron continued, labelling the orbital paths. '*Strike cruiser* Sword of Caliban *shields her while strike cruiser* Death of Mercy *targets the remaining ork fighter craft that fled to the ring system of the third gas giant.*'

Lazarus stared at the chart, satisfied with the placement of the bright dots, then wiped it out of his vision. 'Brother Deme-trius. Ancient Jequn. Brother Asbeel. Fifth status.'

'*Fortifications substantially complete,*' Jequn began. The Ancient also had no issue with keeping his reports short. He much pre-ferred to inspire his brothers with what he did rather than what he said. '*Reapers are dug in, as are the Rhinos. Overlapping fields of fire have been established with our Venerable Dreadnought brothers.*'

'*Here is the placement of the company, Master Lazarus, with vehicle emplacements and squad deployment.*' It was Interrogator-Chaplain Demetrius' duty to inspire the Fifth with both words and deed, and in battle his words were weapons as potent as the deadly crozius arcanum that he held. But for now, he limited them to emulate his commander's succinctness, and like Ephron, he used a pict to convey his report. The detailed image came to life in Lazarus' vision when he acknowledged it, a high view that showed the dug-in vehicles and the neatly carved lines of trenches and fortifications. The placement of each squad was noted with neat runes, and Lazarus looked it over, sketching in the fields of fire with his thoughts.

'Good,' Lazarus said. 'But strengthen the left flank. The orks will race their vehicles up that cliffside to get over our lines.'

'That would be suicide,' Brother Zakariah said. The lieutenant was newly promoted, the youngest member of the command squad and the only Primaris Marine in the group – besides Lazarus, post-resurrection. Zakariah was a deadly fighter, but his experience was still limited in some ways, which included understanding the madness of xenos.

'Agreed,' Lazarus said. 'But the orks will not see it that way. They will see a chance to fly over us, guns blazing, and the wreckage of their attempt will rain down on our lines. Shift Squad Invis fifty yards closer to that side, and order them to destroy anything that comes close.'

'Understood, Master Lazarus,' Demetrius said. *'Brother Asbeel?'*

'Ammo and other supplies have been set back safely.' The Apothecary didn't have to struggle to keep his speech short. Asbeel was always precise, and he marked the locations where he'd cached the supplies with quick ticks made on the pict. Lazarus studied the map carefully, noting all the marks they had added and his change. It was all stone and static runes and lines, but in his head he could see the battle unfold as the orks approached, the fire zones, the choke points, the kill boxes. Everything was as it should be. His men knew their work.

And so should the ones that weren't his. 'Lieutenants. Scout reports?'

The Fifth had two Scout squads from the Tenth Company attached to it for this mission. Not Lazarus' men, but Dark Angels nonetheless, and right now their work was at its most critical, so the Master of the Fifth had given one squad to each of his lieutenants for oversight, so they could closely coordinate the Scouts with the rest of the company.

Lieutenant Zakariah spoke first. *'Squad Jotha has surveyed the valley behind us, and the second narrowing along the shore. They have mapped it in detail, including ice thickness and strength.'* The data appeared in Lazarus' vision, a complicated topographical map of the land behind their current position. Numbers and paths indicated the places where heavy equipment like the Reaper tanks and Rhino troop transports could move without becoming bogged down or breaking through the ice covering the wide river that entered the sea behind them.

If something went wrong and they had to pull back, they could do it fast.

'Have them establish possible positions on the second narrowing.' With the Emperor's favour, and enough ammunition, the ork force would break on the wall they had built here and bleed out into that ugly sea. But the strongest foundation of a plan was another plan, and Lazarus would work out as many possibilities as he could. If the Fifth did have to pull back from this killing field, that second choke point between the next ridge of mountains and the sea would be where they would go, to bleed the green xenos again.

'Lieutenant Amad?'

'Scout Squad Daral has pulled back.' Brother Amad liked to talk, sometimes too much, but he had served under Lazarus for a long time and his words were clear and quick. *'They are staying as close as possible, but the orks' front is disarrayed, as always. They will lay eyes on the main column when they can.'*

When they can. Lazarus looked again towards the horizon. The plumes of exhaust had grown thicker, and at their bases was the first hint of the dust cloud being thrown up by the orks' war machines. That dust, filled with heavy metals and rad particles, was wreaking havoc with the auspex sensors mounted on the ships orbiting high overhead. The data they were sending Lazarus was almost useless, the ork army a shifting mass of magnetic anomalies and bright thermis colours. He needed the eyes of those Scouts.

He opened the reports Amad had sent him, the readings Squad Daral had gathered. The orks were racing across the plains on warbikes and battlewagons, but there were other things hidden in the swirling dust, things hinted at by the bright colours of the thermis images. Lazarus could only guess at what they might be. He needed more information.

You have what you have. Plan accordingly. Master Balthasar, the man who led the Fifth before Lazarus, had told him that, and it had become another litany that Lazarus would repeat to himself when he wanted more information. Which turned out to be every battle, because in the blood and the noise, there were always surprises.

'Same battle plan,' he told his command squad. 'We stop the orks here, on this shore. Then we will bring our wrath down upon them.'

'For the Lion!' they called out in response. 'For the Emperor! Forever!'

The cold wind whined around the hard angles of the Gladiator Reaper as Lazarus stood on top of the massive impulsor tank and watched the horizon. The approaching enemy was a storm now, a swirling dust cloud rolling over the stony red-brown wastes towards him and his men. That cloud was vast – the gravity on Husk was less than half standard, and the polluted grit kicked up by the ork army went high into the air and hung there like a poisonous fog bank. Still, Lazarus could pick out the occasional flashing reflection at the dust cloud's base: the gleam of Husk's dull orange sun shining off the spikes and armour of the smaller, faster vehicles that ran before the rest of the ork army.

They had no discipline. The orks' strategy was numbers, their tactics ferocity. The fastest vehicles, the warbikes and the jouncing four-wheeled machines, would be in the lead, hoping to smash through whatever enemy appeared in front of them. The Fifth would have to shatter those outriders while waiting for the slower-moving bulk of the army to arrive.

When they did, the orks would pack themselves in tight, concentrating their strength into one heaving mass of blades and guns, all striking into the waiting Dark Angels. The green xenos horde would hit them like a tsunami, a bellowing torrent of muscle and rusted metal. It would be a vicious fight and the orks would bleed rivers as they pushed forward, but they would likely break through. The xenos had the vast weight of numbers to back their ferocity.

But Lazarus meant to change those numbers.

He looked up at the clear, ugly sky. Somewhere behind that bruised blue, the *Unrelenting Fury* waited, weapons ready. The ork army was spread out and half hidden behind a cloud of dust that frustrated the machine spirits of the battle-barge's targeting systems. But the Dark Angels would gather the orks together and make them a perfect target, stopped before their lines. The *Unrelenting Fury* might not be able to use its most powerful weapons, not without obliterating the Fifth along with the orks, but it had many others. When Lazarus called for it, a double handful of hell would fall and there would be nothing left of the ork invaders but a vast crater of glass, just one more scar on Husk's battered hide.

'Master Lazarus,' Brother Ephron called. 'Brother Domitius on the vox. Urgent.'

Think of the daemon, and they are invoked, Lazarus thought. Domitius was commander of the *Unrelenting Fury*, which explained why his transmissions were coming in through Ephron's more sophisticated vox. The cloud of pollution kicked up by the orks wasn't any kinder to long-range vox transmissions. Lazarus could feel the channel that Ephron had opened for him and activated it with a thought, letting Domitius' voice fill his ears.

'*Master Lazarus.*' The commander's words snapped through the vox. '*I am pulling the* Unrelenting Fury *out of orbit and preparing for a jump into the warp.*'

'Repeat,' Lazarus said, his voice suddenly hard.

'Unrelenting Fury *is leaving geosynchronous orbit. Now. I have orders of highest priority, given by Supreme Grand Master Azrael himself. The* Unrelenting Fury *is needed, and so I go.*'

It was needed. Here. The orks would be on them soon, and without the *Unrelenting Fury* and its weapons–

Lazarus cut through the angry spiral of his thoughts. They were slowing him down, and time was always an enemy. 'My gratitude for your service to us, brother-commander. Go, and serve the sons of the Lion that need you most.'

'*Gratitude to you, Master Lazarus. May the Emperor guide your blade, and the Lion walk with you.*'

'And with you,' Lazarus replied. The vox-channel went silent, and Lazarus stood on the scabrous shore, staring at the wall of dust rising before him. The orks were coming, and without the weapons from on high, he wasn't sure he could stop them. Not like this.

Time was his enemy, but so was rage. Lazarus ran the Litany of Focus through his head, until his mind was clear, his hand on the hilt of Enmity's Edge, the ancient power sword that hung from his hip. Thoughts spun through his head, plans replacing plans, and he turned his back on the growing storm and stared at the valley that stretched between the mountains, and the ice-covered river that rolled down its centre into the sea.

'Command squad,' he said, his voice clipped and calm. 'The plan has changed.'

CHAPTER TWO

The Fifth Company had become an explosion of activity. Ammunition and supplies were being loaded into six of the Rhinos, the armoured vehicles ready to haul it all back to the second choke point on the other side of the valley. The other vehicles were staying where they had been dug in, but the trench lines made for the squads of Space Marines were being adjusted. Lazarus watched his men work, redrawing the overlapping fields of fire in his mind.

Two Gladiator Reapers. Four Rhinos. Two Dreadnoughts. Forty Dark Angels. Less than half the force he had been working with the last time he laid out the kill-zones on this rocky shore, but it was the most he dared leave. The Master of the Fifth raised his eyes to the approaching army moving like a storm across the plain. Time was almost up.

'Lieutenant Amad.'

'They are ready, Master Lazarus,' Amad answered. 'Shall I–'

'No,' Lazarus ordered, and opened the vox-link to the Scouts hidden out on the wastes before him. 'Squad Daral.'

'Master Lazarus. Sergeant Javan, Squad Daral.'

'Report, sergeant.'

'We are dug in. First warbikes passing us now.' Javan was sending picts as he spoke, of a plain of broken red stone, ochre snow and grey dust. Orks were tearing across it in a motley assortment of two- and three-wheeled cycles, all sporting guns. *'There are more bikes and light vehicles coming. We have not seen anything bigger yet, but we hear their engines.'*

'Wait for the first line of vehicles,' Lazarus told him. 'Then blow your charges and move.' It wouldn't save them. Lazarus knew that, and so did Javan. But the longer the Scouts lived, the more time it bought the rest of the Dark Angels. He had to give them something for their sacrifice, though. 'When they catch you, hold your ground and take as many xenos as you can with you.'

'Understood,' Sergeant Javan said. *'Thank you, Master Lazarus.'*

'The Lion walks with you, Squad Daral. You will be remembered.' Lazarus cut the vox. He stared out at the warbikes charging out of the roiling dust, mere dark marks now but growing fast. There were shadows behind them, small ork vehicles half hidden by the dust trail raised by the first wave. Then there was a distant boom, and a ripple of fire through the dust, and through that ochre curtain something came cartwheeling across the wasteland, a shattered ork fast-attack buggy. It crunched to a stop, one flaming tyre bouncing free and rolling into the sea. The other vehicles and some of the warbikes turned, tyres ripping up dust, and then they streaked off, chasing the Scouts who'd set up those improvised mines.

They'd run them down all too soon.

'They do their duty.' Interrogator-Chaplain Demetrius stood next to him, the polished skull mask of his armour turning towards the enemy. His right eye glowed red, like those of the other Dark Angels, but the left was green, the colour of the cybernetic that replaced the one he'd lost to plasma almost two centuries ago.

'They do,' Lazarus answered. It bought them time. But not enough. The loaded Rhinos were pulling out, tracks churning up rock dust and fans of ugly snow, but over the roar of their engines came the crack of bolters and the ugly thump of ork guns. 'We will use whatever their sacrifice gives us.' He looked back to the Interrogator-Chaplain as the distant bolters began to fall silent. 'Are you ready?'

'To serve and die for the Emperor? Always,' Demetrius said. 'To tell Ancient Jequn that he must retreat? That will be a more daunting task.'

'He will listen,' Lazarus said. 'And guide Amad, as you have guided me.'

'I will.' Demetrius set his mismatched eyes on Lazarus. 'But he needs guidance from you most, now.'

'Time,' Lazarus said.

'Your plan depends as much on him as it does time.'

Lazarus frowned but nodded, the great gold-and-white wings on his helm shifting with the motion. He moved away from Demetrius to where Lieutenant Amad was watching Scout Squad Jotha working on the cliffs above.

'Finished?'

'Soon, Master Lazarus. I know you need them, but–'

'But I need this too,' Lazarus said. 'I have no intention of sacrificing you and the ones gathered here like Squad Daral. I need you to hold the xenos here as long as possible, but it is just as important that you fall back when you need to. That is why I left you to command.'

'And Interrogator-Chaplain Demetrius, and Ancient Jequn.'

'No,' Lazarus said. 'I left them to inspire. Jequn with banner and blade, Demetrius with words. You I left to lead, which means knowing when it is time for inspiration to end and calculation to begin. You have to hold here, but more importantly you have to hold that second line. When the time is right, you will pull back. You will despise it because you are a Dark Angel, but you will do it because you are my lieutenant, and you know that we serve with our minds as much as our blood. The Lion's way of waging war was our inheritance, when we lost him on Caliban long ago. It is in his name that we do as we do.'

'Master Lazarus,' Amad said. 'Thank you.' Behind him, a Reaper opened up, its gatling cannon filling the air with thunder.

'The enemy comes and I must go,' Lazarus said, just as Squad Jotha began to jump down from the cliff, armour barely flexing as they hit the stone in the light gravity. They nodded to Lazarus as they ran by, speeding towards their next assignment in the valley beyond. 'The Lion's legacy walks with you, Brother Amad.'

'The Lion's spirit walks with us all,' the lieutenant said, and moved to the lines, already barking orders.

'*Well done.*' Demetrius' voice rolled through Lazarus' helm.

'It took time.' Lazarus was moving, striding fast over the stone, his robes flowing around him.

'*It gave confidence.*' The crack of the Interrogator-Chaplain's bolt pistol came over the vox. '*We are without fear. But that does not mean we are without uncertainty.*'

Lazarus grunted. He'd spent a long time learning that lesson after his rebirth. 'I thank you for your guidance, brother.'

'*We are guided by the Emperor,*' Demetrius intoned, the low roll of his voice cutting through the thunder of the autocannons, the roar of bolters. '*We are guided by the Lion. We are guided by those who came before. We follow the path they have made for us, and we will know victory!'*

Lazarus increased his pace, long legs stretching out as he raced over the rough stone, away from the battle, towards the war. 'I understand you, Brother-Chaplain,' he said to himself as he ran to join the rest of the Fifth. 'But the path we make now is one to ruin.'

Dim, murky light surrounded Lazarus, and cold, and silence. But inside his armour, he was wrapped in light and fury.

'–three more vehicles moving in–'

'–are His hands, we are His weapons, we are the salvation of mankind. We are the Dark Angels, and–'

'–two survived the jump. Ancient Jequn moving to engage–'

Voices crowded his helm, and his vision was filled with the pict relays and auspex readings of every squad sergeant, Ancient Jequn, Interrogator-Chaplain Demetrius and Lieutenant Amad, along with those of the Reapers and the Rhinos and the two Dreadnoughts still on the line. It was a chaos of sight and sound, but Lazarus breathed slow and deep, his body relaxed as he absorbed the data and spun strategies through his head.

The orks were hitting the Dark Angels he'd left behind hard. Lazarus could see them through the eyes of his brothers, monstrous spiked shapes careening through the dust, engines roaring, tyres and tracks tearing up the ground. The ork vehicles were shrouding themselves in an opaque screen of drifting grit that interfered with eyes and auspex. The xenos were less bothered by it, their standard tactic being to throw a wall of slugs across the battlefield and assume something would hit.

Half blind and outnumbered, Amad and the squads Lazarus had left with him were still acquitting themselves well.

Wreckage piled up before them and ork bodies lay littered across the wastes, smashed apart by bolter rounds. But the odds were shifting. The orks were pushing closer as their army came together before the thin line of the Fifth. And that line was growing thinner. Already there were two brothers down, killed by the xenos' wild shots, and one more who had to drag himself back to the Rhinos, both of his legs gone thanks to a missile that had corkscrewed out of the dust storm.

Amad had to pull back soon – the equations of battle were always merciless, and the numbers were shifting slowly but steadily to the wrong side. But Lazarus had left that decision to him, to the man standing in the midst of that storm of fire and steel, and he had to trust the lieutenant to know when the time was right.

'Xenos mobbing up for another wave.' Lieutenant Amad's voice was steady over the vox, even as he stomped on the belly of a huge ork, pinning it down as he pulled his power sword free from the green-skinned warrior's chest. Lazarus focused on his pict feed and it grew, filling his vision. Amad snapped his sword to the side, xenos blood sizzling and dissolving in the flickering purple field of disruptive energy that sheathed its blade, then turned his head to stare down the strand of stony shore, filled now with the bulky silhouettes of ork fighters and the bigger, faster-moving shadows of vehicles. Straight ahead of Amad was something that wasn't a shadow, though. It was light, sparking and flickering like an electrical arc, but green, and it made the drifting grit sparkle like gemstones. Then the light flashed out, flaring through Amad's auspex, and everything was lost in emerald for a moment.

Miles away, Lazarus' muscles tensed as a memory went through him of bright-coloured flames, burning – but he breathed the Litany of Horrors Past and shoved the searing agony of that flashback away. The pict feed from Amad was clearing, the machine spirit in the lieutenant's armour compensating for the explosion of light. Light that came not from a weapon but from an ork.

The xenos was thinner than its brethren, and instead of armour it wore a cloak of some rough material that had been slashed and shredded into a mass of ragged tendrils. At the tip of each strip something had been tied – bones and rusted gears, jewels and broken utensils, bits of broken glass and chunks of cogitator boards. The ork was holding its claws over its head, but there was no knife or gun gripped in them, just a staff with painted skulls attached to each end with ragged stick-strip. The staff looked hideous and ridiculous, but the eye sockets of every skull glowed with crackling green light, the same light that blazed in the ork's eyes. A psyker, who had just ploughed a tunnel through the dust with its malign powers so it could see.

So its warboss could see.

The ork commander stood behind the psyker, a massive figure wrapped in black mega armour painted with red flames. It was almost as large as one of the Dark Angels' Dreadnoughts, and it filled the back of the vehicle it stood in, a looted mining machine the orks had converted into one of their wartrukks. The wartrukk was wrapped in so many spikes it would have looked ridiculous, except for the grisly trophies hanging from it – skulls, femurs, severed hands and ears, strings of teeth and long, tanned strips of skin. Victims of this warband's ravaging strike on Husk. A banner fluttered over the warboss, bright red and yellow, showing a fanged sun glowering down on an ocean of blood.

Beyond that banner loomed a huge machine painted rust red. Crudely shaped like an ork, it was all massive head and hunched shoulders with a barrel of a body and piston-like legs. Some kind of war walker, belching fumes and studded with lights that glowed like rabid eyes. The thing raised one arm, and the obscene collection of gun barrels gathered in its fist began to spin. There was a thunderous roar, and a stuttering line of shells stitched across the scab-like stone and crashed into one of the Reapers. The shells hammered dents across the tank's armoured hull and smashed one of the tempest bolters mounted on its side, leaving the gun a smoking ruin. Then the dust swirled in again, closing the brief window the psyker had made.

Somewhere in the murk, the orks howled and began a guttural chant, getting ready to charge.

'Now, Amad,' Lazarus told the darkness in his helm, just as his lieutenant spoke.

'*Squad Shivam, Squad Jerash. To your Rhinos and withdraw. Squads Mehian and Anjou, spread and cover our flanks. Dreadnought Brothers Azmodor and Jehoel, anchor the lines. Reapers, prepare for barrage.*'

Lazarus touched his armour's machine spirit through his black carapace, opening the pict feeds from each sergeant, the two Venerable Dreadnoughts, Ancient Jequn, and Interrogator-Chaplain Demetrius. A welter of views filled his eyes, a chaos of movement and colour, but Lazarus stopped fighting to focus and let it all flow into him as he had been trained. Azrael himself had instructed him in this, and he could remember how the Supreme Grand Master had likened it to fighting with the blade on a battlefield. The ability to broaden one's focus to the whole fight, to track every threat, distant and near, while flowing through your own attacks – that same kind of concentration was needed when guiding troops while embedded in the middle of battle.

Lazarus was not fighting now, and that feeling twisted in him. He didn't like this part of the plan, but what he liked didn't mean anything. What mattered was the plan falling together, and the pieces were moving fast. Squads Shivam and Jerash had loaded up, their Rhinos gunning to life, tracks grinding up more dust as they tore away. The dust would be working with them now, hiding this withdrawal from the orks. Squads Mehian and Anjou were firing fast, picking targets where they could but mostly creating the illusion that the Dark Angels were still stubbornly defending this narrow strait. The two Dreadnoughts had taken their positions at either end of the line, weapons cracking as they picked out targets. The Reapers, meanwhile, had pulled themselves out of their emplacements. Their guns pointed towards the enemy but remained silent, conserving ammunition. The one struck by the ork war machine's barrage was moving slower, its anti-gravitic field stuttering beneath it, but it was moving.

Then the orks came.

They moved in a red wave that pounded through the drifting dust like blood pouring through water. Engines roared and tyres shrieked against stone. Mixed with it all was the guttural chant of the orks, repeating over and over, a thundering crescendo as they surged forward.

'Reapers, full volley!' Amad shouted over the vox, and the tanks opened up with their gatling cannons. The guns bellowed and sent a stream of shells into the charging xenos. A three-wheeled bike shattered, and a scout buggy was hit in one of its front tyres. The explosion sent the crude vehicle cartwheeling, flames pouring out of it, and it smashed into the side of a heavy truck, a human-made mining vehicle that had been looted and modified by the orks. A shower of xenos fell out of it, some of them coated in flames, but they all rolled up and kept charging, though several of them were run down by other ork vehicles. In response to the tanks, the orks began to fire too, blazing away with every gun they had.

'Brothers, all back!' Amad shouted. 'Bleed the xenos as they come!'

'We hear and follow!' Interrogator-Chaplain Demetrius called over the vox, cutting through the thunder of guns, the howl of engines. 'We are the razor's edge of the Emperor's rage, and we will bleed them all!'

Bleed them they did. Lazarus watched it, modified eyes and trained mind taking it all in. The horde of orks raced forward like a tidal wave of blood, and before them a handful of Dark Angels in their green armour moved with machine-like precision. The squads took turns, one withdrawing at speed while the other stopped and turned to pour bolter shots back at the orks. They fell back with smooth purpose, and the Dreadnoughts went with them, matching their pattern of movement and fire. But their well-honed cohesion could only do so much. One brother was down, then another, then two more. Brother Jehoel threw his massive form in front of one of the injured, scooping him up with a huge claw, but as he stepped back a blazing laser lit up the dust and carved a line of slag across the heavy armour of his lower body. The Dreadnought stumbled, almost falling as one leg buckled, but he staggered to the Rhinos, waiting as the others threw themselves inside. Loaded, the tracked vehicles started to move, the guns mounted on their thick hulls chattering as they tore away, and Jehoel layed down fire as he limped along with them.

The Reapers were pulling back too, anti-gravitic generators howling, but the orks were almost on them now. One of the tanks gunned its engines, its cannons going quiet as it shot forward, but the other, the damaged one, ground its armoured hull against the stone as its anti-gravitic field faltered and failed. The orks were almost there, warbikes already spinning in circles around it. The Reaper's surviving tempest bolter opened up, shattering one of the bikes, and the gatling cannons swung to face the onrushing orks and fired. The tank poured out a torrent of fire, thundering away until a missile caught it and sent it spinning back, its hull blackened and staved in on one side as though the heavy ceramite armour was nothing more than wood. But after a second of silence, the turret moved again, jerking slowly as it shifted back towards the wave of bigger vehicles getting ready to enter the narrow pass between mountain and sea.

The gatling cannon fired, a ragged, stuttering cough. But the shells still flew, catching an ork wartrukk and making it swerve crazily, smoke boiling out of the hole smashed in its side. Then a storm of shots hit the dying tank, heavy shells shifting it, shoving its immense weight back. There was a moment, and then the deadly machine exploded, tearing itself to pieces in a whirling storm of shrapnel, fire and dust.

'Go to the Lion, my brothers,' Demetrius intoned. 'You now walk with him in death.' And that was all the time they had to mourn the destroyed Reaper and its crew. The orks were boiling past the wreckage, their vehicles leaping over the fortifications the Dark Angels had made, intent on chasing down the last Reaper and the Rhinos racing away from them. Racing, but not fast enough to escape the horde. They'd be pulled down like prey, ripped apart by the xenos, an ugly, shameful end for the Emperor's chosen.

Which is why that would not happen.

'If they strike you, return the blow a thousandfold,' Lieutenant Amad said over the vox. 'The words of the Lion.' And then the cliffs overlooking the shore exploded. Sheets of rock split and fell, thundering down and smashing into the orks, spilling a wall of shattered stone across the narrow strand. Through his men's eyes Lazarus saw the ork army falter, careening to a stop before this new, jagged barrier. Then the view was gone, wiped away by dust.

There was a rumble overhead like distant thunder. Lazarus could hear it through the ice, and through Lieutenant Amad's eyes he could see what birthed the noise: a column of vehicles, red with paint and the dust of shattered stone the colour of old blood, moving across the frozen river that lay in the valley between the two lines of mountains.

The orks were insane, in their xenos way, but they weren't stupid – at least not terminally so. After they had cleared the rubble of the cliff face that the Dark Angels had dropped on them, they had taken off in pursuit of Lieutenant Amad and his troops. They had fanned out at first, charging across the valley, but when the orks reached the ice-slicked river, they drew together again. The trukks and battlewagons formed a line, following the tracks of the Fifth's heavy vehicles, knowing that was where the ice was thickest, since the Dark Angels had made it across. It was the fastest way to follow, with at least a vague nod to caution.

It was a mistake.

Lazarus activated the vox, connecting him with Amad. 'You did well, brother.'

'"Well".' The lieutenant's voice was now bitter. 'I lost a Gladiator Reaper and a dozen brothers. Four more are in the care of Brother Asbeel, and Brother Jehoel cannot walk. I wouldn't call that "well".'

'I would,' Lazarus said, his voice hard. 'And I am the master of this company, lieutenant. I gave you orders and you followed them through. You did as I told you, and you did well, brother. The cost of it all is mine to pay.'

'Yes, Master Lazarus.' The bitterness had at least lessened in his voice, if not completely vanished. *'What orders now?'*

'Hold,' Lazarus said. The main column of heavy ork vehicles was sticking to the path the Dark Angels had laid for them. But the smaller ones, the warbikes and the fast-attack buggies, had taken their chances and spread out to move faster across the ice. They'd lost a few to thin spots, but most of them had made it across and were now circling in front of the Dark Angels' fortifications that had been thrown up at the next narrow strand of stone between cliffs and ocean. 'Keep the outriders from flanking you. Some of the heavies will reach you. Keep them from breaking through.'

'By the Emperor's blessings, it is possible. By the Lion's example, we know we can prevail.'

'By the strength and courage of my brothers, I know victory is ensured,' Lazarus answered. 'You have done the Dark Angels proud this day. Hold, for just a little more, and we will triumph.'

Lazarus cut the vox-link but let the pict feed linger long enough to watch as Amad swept his gaze one more time across the army driving towards him again, the army that had almost destroyed him once already, before he turned to work out troop placements with Interrogator-Chaplain Demetrius and Ancient Jequn, who held aloft the banner of the Fifth.

Then Lazarus closed it and reached out for another.

'Sergeant Asher, Squad Jotha. Are you in position?'

'One minute, Master Lazarus,' the Tenth Company Scout answered.

Lazarus selected the Scout's pict feed, and his helm filled with the orange light of Husk's star. The view swung as Asher bounded up the cliff face above Amad's new position. The rest of his squad were with him, all climbing the rough cliff in scrambling leaps. The view steadied when Asher reached the top. From the height, looking through the optics built into the Scout's visor, Lazarus could see the whole army of orks below, the outriders buzzing Amad's emplacements, and the column moving across the ice. The first of the heavy trukks had just reached the edge of the river, their tyres going from dirty ice to gravel. The rest of the column followed close, engines roaring as the orks gunned them, impatient to get to the sure traction of the stony ground to speed towards the Dark Angels, eager to smash into them again.

Soon. The word ran through Lazarus' mind as he watched the rough vehicles lurch forward. The view shifted as Asher moved, pulling out the Mark III Shrike-pattern sniper rifles the Primaris Scouts trained with. They were deadly things at a distance, and were the second reason Lazarus had ordered the Scouts up the cliffs. The first was so he could have this view, to know when the time was right.

Soon. The orks moved forward, the vehicles still on the ice crunching into each other as they jostled for position. The warboss' trukk was towards the back, the huge walker moving beside it. It was going to be a balancing act, trying to catch those and most of the rest, but Lazarus set aside uncertainty and doubt. He bided his time, waiting, and then the moment came for him, the same way it did when he was fighting with his blade. With a thought he reached through his black carapace and activated the ring of melta bombs he had ordered Squad Jotha to attach to the underside of the ice.

Melta bombs were meant for armour. Place one on an enemy tank or fortification and set it off, and it would unleash a directed blast of thermal energy capable of melting holes through the thickest armour and reducing everything on the other side to slag and ash. Used against ice, the result was devastation.

The bombs went off, and Lazarus felt a pulse of heat from the blasts, even with all the frigid water that lay between them. Then a pressure wave struck, making the water around Lazarus swirl, enough so that he had to shift to keep his footing. An instant later came another pulse, followed by a second wave of pressure which made the roiling water surge around him again.

It was the view from Asher that let Lazarus understand what was happening. From high above, he could see the hell that the bombs had unleashed. When they went off, a great white cloud of steam exploded up as tons of ice suddenly converted from solid to gas. The bombs had been the first wave of heat, the massive expansion of the steam slamming against ice and water the first shockwave. But even as the cloud of vapour rushed towards the cliffs where the Scouts crouched, light had begun to grow in it. The heat from the melta bombs had cracked the water molecules into their basic elements, and the heart of the steam cloud became a volatile mixture of hydrogen and oxygen that exploded again, causing the second wave of heat and pressure.

'Emperor's wrath,' Asher breathed over the vox, right as the steam swirled over him, swallowing up his view. Lazarus dropped the pict feeds so that all he saw was the chaos of murky, boiling water that surrounded him.

'Dark Angels!' he shouted, his voice filling the vox. 'Rise and reap!'

His men heard and obeyed. Metal cables hidden beneath the river went taut as six squads of Adeptus Astartes hauled themselves up from beneath murky water. It took only seconds before they were smashing through the shallow ice near the polluted shore. They rose, dark green armour dripping toxins, bolters in their hands, eyes glowing red through the steam that filled the air.

'Auspex,' Lazarus ordered as he reached the surface and his vision changed. The swirling cloud of hot steam made normal optics useless, but the keen sensors of his armour gave him what he needed – targets.

Blobs of colour and neat lines formed before Lazarus, magnetic sources and moving things. He could pick out orks thrashing in the river, trying to swim in superheated water while wrapped in armour. Dense with muscle and bone already, the xenos didn't seem to be having much success. Lazarus could see the bodies that already littered the muddy bottom, mixed with the wreckage of the wartrukks and battlewagons that had plummeted down when the ice below them transformed into steam.

But not everything had vanished into the river. Something huge moved through the haze, glowing bright in the magnetic sensors. The walker, Lazarus realised, still upright and lurching towards the shore.

'Squad Bethel, with me,' he ordered. 'All other squads, move in. Crush the xenos between you and Lieutenant Amad. Forward, for the Lion!'

'For the Lion!' they shouted back, and Lazarus shifted his perception, putting the placement of his troops in one corner of his mind as he focused on the squad before him.

'Squad Bethel. I want–' Lazarus stopped. Something was happening near the ork walker, a gleam of emerald light that was growing bright enough to penetrate the cloud of steam. The light flashed out, washing the world away with green, and then it was gone, and with it the mist. The air was suddenly clear, a huge bubble of visibility centred around a chunk of ice floating on the river beside the giant ork war machine. Balanced on that sheet of ice was a wartrukk, its engine rumbling. The ork warboss stood on its back, glaring across the corpse-strewn water at Lazarus, and on the roof beside it crouched the psyker, the creature's face spotted with blisters from the scorching steam.

'Squad Bethel,' Lazarus said. 'We have our targets.'

'For the Emperor! For the Lion! Forever!' The squad moved, spreading out as they raised their bolters. Though the walker and wartrukk were both at long range, they began to fire, explosive bolts picking off the orks clinging to the walker. But the distance wasn't far for Brother Silas, who carried the squad's heavy weapon, a massive plasma cannon. He swung it up, the air hissing around it as it charged, then sent a bolt of superheated matter out to scorch a crater into the walker's armoured back.

'No!' Lazarus shouted. 'Destroy the ice!'

Brother Silas nodded, shifting his aim. Slugs screamed through the air around them, the orks clinging to the walker firing their crude guns back at the Dark Angels. Most of their rounds hit the mud on the bank or buzzed overhead, but a few found their mark, whining off green armour. One hit Lazarus' shoulder, barely scratching the heavy ceramite before ricocheting away. But the orks had other weapons than guns.

Silas was lining up his shot when the ork psyker spun its crude staff of skulls and pointed at him, bellowing. A mote of green launched itself from the ork's claw, streaking through the air. It caught Brother Silas in the chest, slipping through his thick ceramite armour as if it were nothing but gathered shadow. Silas went rigid, his body spasming as the gleaming optics covering his eyes cracked and broke, shattered from the inside. Thin trails of poisonous green smoke rose from those cracks and Silas fell to his knees. The plasma cannon hissed and fired once, the blazing matter scorching across the surface of the river and striking one end of the ice floe. The sheet cracked and spun, spilling orks into the water.

'Silas!' Lazarus shouted as he dived forward, scooping up the plasma cannon from his brother's dead hands. The name echoed in his head as he lifted the heavy weapon, aiming it at the ork psyker. It joined all the rest, the long list of brothers Lazarus had seen cut down by the unnatural powers of enemy psykers over the long years that he had fought. That list rattled through his head, name after name repeating themselves, and woven through them all the searing pain and multicoloured light of the flames that had killed him. He let the pain wash over him, the names roar through him, and pressed the trigger studs on the cannon.

Nothing happened, the heavy weapon staying silent in Lazarus' hands. There were cracks in the plasma cannon's rugged casing where Silas had gripped it, a rough print of the dead Space Marine's convulsing death-grip.

Lazarus barely had time to see the damage before another green mote flashed towards him from the psyker. He saw it coming, a tiny piece of the warp that would burn his soul to dust, flung at him by the blistered, howling ork. Then he felt his Spiritshield Helm grow cool, the power vested in it long ago reaching out, surrounding him like a balm. The killing mote came within an inch of his faceplate, then frayed apart, became smoke, and was gone.

'Brother Ephron!' Lazarus snapped. The Techmarine had helped him do the calculations for the placement of the melta bombs, then stayed close by when Lazarus and all the rest had hidden themselves beneath the ice. Ephron was at the Master of the Fifth's side before Lazarus even finished speaking his name. He took the heavy weapon and cradled it, his hands running over the damage.

Lazarus straightened up, looking across the dirty brown water. The psyker was still there, perched on the wartrukk, arguing with the warboss, who crouched over its underling. The big ork in the mega armour waved a claw at the sheet of ice holding the wartrukk out of the water. It was cracking, damaged by the heat and the plasma strike. The psyker threw its arms up, snarling, and the warboss swiped, making the scrawny ork scurry down to hide in the shelter of the wartrukk's cab.

The warboss bellowed at the walker, which had been struggling to shift its feet out of the muddy river bottom without toppling over into the deep water. The machine turned its great head to stare down at the boss, joints shrieking, then reached out with a massive claw. It grabbed on to the wartrukk, its talons crunching into the metal sides.

'Weapon, Ephron,' Lazarus said, reaching out. He could see the psyker, barely, through the dirty armaglass at the front of the wartrukk, and the names were still running in his head.

'Here!' The Techmarine handed the plasma cannon over, and Lazarus felt its revitalised spirit touch the one in his armour. He lifted the weapon, aimed it at the wartrukk and fired.

The plasma bolt shot out as the walker lifted the warboss and its vehicle off the chunk of ice. The motion made the super-heated plasma strike the walker's arm instead of smashing through the wartrukk's window. The walker's claw twitched, almost dropping the vehicle, but it held on just long enough. When the claws parted, the wartrukk fell onto the riverbank and bounced on its oversized tyres. A shower of gretchin, the snivelling little cousins of the orks, fell out of the thing, screeching and cursing as the warboss bellowed again and the wartrukk gunned its engine, tearing away.

Then the walker turned towards the Dark Angels.

Its gun had started spinning after it dropped the wartrukk, and it brought the arm that bore the ludicrous mass of barrels up and fired a stream of shells across the bank, blasting up a wall of mud and smoke. One shell caught a Space Marine, flinging him back to smash against a boulder, then the stream crashed across Lazarus. Shells flew at him, a torrent of death, but he stood his ground, gambling that the gift given to his Chapter long ago by the war masters of Mars would protect him and the men behind him. And it did. The Iron Halo built into his armour, a relic from the Dark Age of Technology, hummed to life as the shells streaked in. The ancient device took the shells apart and spun their lethal kinetic energy into a storm of photons and neutrinos, turning sure death into a storm of light and unfelt wind. The roaring gun cut off, and Lazarus was standing in the mud and the smoke, hidden from the thing, but alive and impatient.

'Take this,' he said, passing the plasma cannon back to Ephron, who had ducked behind a rock to avoid the barrage. 'Keep the beast busy.' Then he charged forward into the river.

The water closed over his head, burying him in murk. In that darkness, Lazarus relied on his auspex to pick out the walker. It was moving through the mud towards the bank, heading towards him. The thunder of its guns shook the water around him, and Lazarus put part of his attention on Brother Ephron's pict feed, watching as the Techmarine moved from boulder to boulder, shooting at the walker and taking cover as shells and rockets smashed after him. Ephron was surviving, and drawing the war machine's attention, which was what Lazarus needed. The water in front of him was black with old pollution and new, and still swirling with the last traces of heat from the melta bombs. But each leg was a glowing magnetic mass, clear to him as a beacon, and Lazarus moved towards them, drawing out his blade.

It felt like a sin to use Enmity's Edge for what amounted to scrapyard work, but Lazarus' anger was rolling through him. He touched the stud on the hilt of his sword and energy flowed over the adamantine blade, a flickering corona of dark power that cracked apart the molecules of water flowing around it, making its edges fizz and glow with the same thermal destruction that sent this walker falling into the mud. He pulled back the sword and cleaved a path of fire and steam through the water, tearing into the thick armour covering the walker's ankle joint.

The orks built crude but tough. The first blow dug chunks of metal away but did little damage. The second only dug in a little more. But Lazarus knew how to use his blade, and even in the murk, with the walker stumbling forward, he could hit the same mark again and again. He chopped at the joint until it suddenly snapped, and the massive war machine lurched, almost falling.

That was when the pilot finally noticed something was happening. The walker stopped, fighting for balance, and the great gun-arm swept around, firing shots wildly into the water. Lazarus moved next to the machine and waited, letting its own armour absorb any shells that came close. When it stopped firing he stepped back and hit the leg one more time, driving his crackling blade into the broken joint until it finally severed, and the leg slipped free of the massive foot. Heavy, ungainly, the walker couldn't keep its balance with that much damage. With a groaning crunch it listed to one side, then fell face first into the river.

Lazarus moved back as the giant fell, staying away from its thrashing limbs. He circled in, moving towards the thing's exposed back. There was the spot that Silas had struck, and Lazarus could clearly see the crater in the thing's armour. He climbed the body, and his helm broke the water. There were cheers on the vox, what was left of Squad Bethel praising his kill, but he ignored them. This beast wasn't slain yet.

'Squad Bethel! Move to back your brothers! I will be there soon.' He stood over the hole in the walker's armour and felt the itchy crawl of electricity from severed power cables sparking in the water. He raised Enmity's Edge and drove the sword down, letting its field tear through struts and wires, piercing deep towards whatever heart he could find. Then the tip broke through, into an open space.

Lazarus pulled out the sword, and for a moment he could hear the enraged bellows of the ork pilot. He had found not the heart but the snarling brain of this metal monster, and the water, cold once again, was pouring into it, filling it. A stream of bubbles rose, and the walker shuddered and thrashed beneath him, convulsing like the dying thing it was. Lazarus engaged the mag-locks in the soles of his armour, waiting until the thing grew still.

Then he cut his mag-locks, jumped down into the shallows of the river and started towards the last piece of the battle, his sword crackling in his hand.

At the final line of fortifications, the orks made their last mad stand.

Lazarus watched them through a dozen different pict feeds, views of the battle streaming into him from his brother Dark Angels. The explosion of steam had cooled and frozen, and now the air was full of snow, filthy ochre flakes drifting down to coat the bodies that covered the clot-coloured stone of the shore. The flakes obscured Lazarus' view, but not nearly as much as the dust and the steam had. He could see the orks smashed against what was left of Amad's men, most of their vehicles reduced to scrap, but the xenos were still fighting, still trying to break through the line even though they were surrounded, being slowly ripped apart by bolter fire.

And through the middle, engine roaring, the wartrukk carrying the ork leader was charging forward, heavy tyres crunching over an ork warrior as it drove straight into the centre of the Dark Angels' line. Right to where Lieutenant Amad was waiting, his bolt pistol snapping shots into its armoured windscreen.

That's where Lazarus headed.

He vaulted the burning wreck of a battlewagon, the grisly trophies hanging from its spikes charring into ash. An ork, missing both legs, rolled out from under the remains of a warbike and shot at him, the first two slugs from its huge gun cracking off the Master of the Fifth's armour, and then his Iron Halo flared again, blocking the others. The light from it blinded the ork, and Lazarus took the xenos' head with his blade as he ran past. He pared down his vision as he charged forward, until he was only seeing with his own eyes and Lieutenant Amad's. The wartrukk was still ploughing forward, its armoured windscreen spider-webbed with impacts, only twenty yards from the lieutenant and moving fast. Amad held his ground, firing until one of his rounds finally broke through and exploded in the cab.

'We are the Dark Angels!' Amad's voice roared over the vox, vicious with triumph. 'We are the First! We are the wrath of the ruler of all mankind!'

The wartrukk swerved, twisting to the side as its driver pawed at its face, suddenly full of shattered glass and molten shrapnel. The heavy vehicle's tyres twisted and the trukk flipped, cartwheeling over and over. Amad moved, slipping out of the way just as the disintegrating vehicle tore through where he'd been standing. But as he dodged, the ork warboss hurled itself out and smashed into the lieutenant. They rolled together over the ground, and the pict feed Lazarus was watching from Amad became a blur of black and red and green, the huge ork bellowing at the lieutenant as it slammed the Dark Angel's head into the ground.

Lazarus ducked a blade swung at him by a gut-shot ork, leapt a line of boulders that had been shoved together to make a wall. He was almost there, but the warboss was pulling back its arm, the heavy power claw that covered the xenos' hand opening, the energy field covering its blades snapping and buzzing with pulses of sickly yellow light. The warboss drove it down, trying to rip away Amad's head, but the lieutenant pulled his power sword up, driving it between the blades of the claw and blocking it. The ork leaned in, snarling, tusks dripping foam, and two claw tips tore across the faceplate of Amad's helmet, ripping it away.

The pict feed flared and died in Lazarus' vision, but that didn't matter. He could see them ahead, could see the bright red of Amad's blood as the tip of one claw scraped across his forehead, the disruptor field around it tearing through flesh and scoring a line in the thick bone of the lieutenant's skull. Lazarus could see that he was going to be too late, that the warboss was going to tear Amad's skull open, but then with a flash of green and white another figure slammed into the ork leader from the side.

The massive armoured ork rolled across the ground, away from Amad, and Ancient Jequn stopped by the lieutenant, the banner of the Fifth snapping over his head. Wrapped in his deep green armour and white robes, relics swinging from his belt, raising the massive power sword he bore with two hands, Jequn was the perfect angel of war. Then he charged forward, blade falling, and the warboss barely raised its power claw in time to block the blow.

Lazarus stomped to a stop at Amad's feet, reaching out to catch the lieutenant's gauntlet, and hauled him up.

'Let us finish this,' Lazarus told him.

'Our Ancient will not like it,' Amad said, smiling through the sheet of blood that covered his face.

'There is enough fury there to share.' He let go of Amad's hand and began to turn, Enmity's Edge snarling as he snapped the sword through the air, and then it hit them: a mote of green, ugly and familiar, and again Lazarus felt the blessed cooling touch as his Spiritshield Helm protected him. The mote spun away, dissolving, but through its dissolution Lazarus saw another poison-green flash of light touch Amad. It vanished beneath his breastplate, and Amad went rigid, his back arching.

The lieutenant's mouth opened far, too far, and Lazarus heard the jawbone snap. Green light flared through Amad's mouth like emerald lightning, forking and splitting as it wrapped around each tooth. Then they exploded, every one of them smashing like glass, the shrapnel of white enamel digging furrows in Amad's tongue and lips and gums, adding more blood to his face, before finally his skull followed. It broke in Amad's head, shattering into a thousand pieces that sent splinters of bone out through his skin. Amad's face crumpled, his whole skull deforming, then it disappeared, sliding down into his armour as his vertebrae popped and fractured. All the bones in the Dark Angel's body came apart, until all that remained was his armour, standing upright, the blood-marked helmet empty. The man who had filled it, the man who had been so much more than a man, was gone, shredded from the inside, now a liquid slurry that slid down into the legs of the armour he once wore.

Lazarus stared at the empty helmet, then turned. Behind him, the ork psyker had dragged itself out of the ruins of the

wartrukk. The xenos' face was a mask of injury, ruptured blisters criss-crossed with cuts from shrapnel and glass, but its eyes
were still intact, and they stared balefully at the Master of the
Fifth, flickering green sparks flashing in their yellow depths.
Lazarus raised Enmity's Edge and the black corona of power
licked at the blade, hissing and snapping as the dirty flakes of
Husk's snow disintegrated against it.

'Amad,' Lazarus said quietly, but in his helm, in his head, the
name echoed. Another name. Another damn name. The list of
them ran through his mind like a litany as he walked across
the blood-coloured stone, sword in his hand, rage in his heart.

CHAPTER THREE

There were birds outside her window, in the tangled hedge that surrounded Wyrbuk House, and Ysentrud thought she was already at her desk. So when Heze shook her arm to wake her, she rolled away, muttering, 'I'm already etching, Learned Thiemo. Leave me be.'

'Learned Thiemo?' Ysentrud recognised the tone in that voice and snapped awake, trying to move, but it was too late. Heze had already grabbed the thin sheet tangled around Ysentrud and jerked it up. She tumbled off her narrow bed onto the floor, where she banged her knee hard against the worn tile.

'Emperor's teeth,' she moaned, clutching her knee.

'First off,' Heze said, stepping around the end of the bed, 'if Learned Thiemo hears you blaspheme, he'll whip the soles of your feet and then fill your slippers with salt. Second, what is that even supposed to mean?'

'You don't understand swearing,' Ysentrud said, and Heze sniffed, offended. The girl was four years younger than Ysentrud's eighteen, with only black lines tattooed onto her coppery-red hairless scalp and face, but she hated the idea that anyone anywhere might understand something she didn't.

'You don't understand getting up.' Heze spun, her white robe flaring out around her. Ysentrud had caught the girl practising that, but then all the Wyrbuk did at some point, didn't they? If they were stuck in these robes forever, best make them dramatic. 'It's a quarter past, and you're going to miss breakfast. Again.'

Ysentrud stuck her tongue out at the girl, and Heze made the same face back, then flounced out of Ysentrud's tiny room. Ysentrud shook her head as she got up. Heze might be her best friend – well, her only friend really – in Wyrbuk House, but she was still a little brat sometimes. Especially when she was right. Wincing, Ysentrud straightened her leg and stared at the clock. Quarter past all right. She sighed and went to the washstand, picking up her cloth then pausing for a moment to look at the ink embedded in her skin.

It surrounded her eyes, a black so dark that it absorbed almost every bit of light, and made her bright red eyes look as though they floated in pits. Nose, neck, ears, around her lips and jaw, the ink had been driven into her, so her smooth, hairless head looked like a crimson skull floating above the simple shift she wore to bed. The full mask of a Wyrbuk, the mark of a Learned, freshly completed, the culmination of all her studies here, the reward for her survival.

Supposedly.

But Wyrbuk House was not done with her yet, was it?

Ysentrud shook her head and scrubbed her face, then wrapped herself in her white robes, the plain cloth scratchy against her skin. If she walked fast, she might have time for a little porridge before Learned Thiemo started cramming more history into her brain.

* * *

44

'Are you ready?'

Learned Thiemo leaned over Ysentrud, all jutting bones, red skin and black tattooing. Wyrbuks were all gaunt, which fit with their skull markings. It was the red pall poisoning. It did something to a person's gut, among all the other things. But Thiemo was tall too, and so he looked like some kind of predatory waterbird, staring down at her with the stycher hanging from his long-fingered hands.

'Yes, Learned Thiemo,' she said, and bowed her head. He strapped the stycher to her scalp, adjusting it carefully until the sharp glass points of it found the sockets hidden in the dark ink at the base of her skull. Ysentrud breathed out a long, hissing breath as the little machine buried clear fangs into her, the pain of its bite never dulling, no matter that she had been doing this every day for years.

Nausea came next, as the device found its home in her brain, and Ysentrud kept up her breathing, right on the edge of memen state. Thiemo socketed the cord that ran down from the stycher into the heavy black desk where Ysentrud sat, then reached into the pocket of his robe and brought out a long holo-crystal, which he also socketed into the desk.

'*The Compiled History of the Lesser Archipelago and Surrounding Reefs*, years 9.223.181.M36 to approximate present.'

Great, fishing stories and promethium drilling, Ysentrud thought, keeping her head down and her annoyance hidden. When Learned Thiemo moved on to the next desk, she slipped another holo-crystal out of her pocket and socketed it in behind his. An outraged sniff came from beside her, and she looked to see Heze glaring at her. The girl's eyes were wide with worried outrage.

Ysentrud leaned closer to her, careful of the cable that connected her stycher to the desk. 'More gris stories,' she whispered.

'You shouldn't etch that trash!' Heze hissed.

'Trash?' Ysentrud said. 'What do you have?'

'Starport shipping manifestos,' Heze said, making a face. 'Half a millennium old.'

'That's trash. Gris stories are fun.'

'They're–' Heze broke off when Learned Thiemo cleared his throat. The tall man had finished handing out crystals and was standing in the centre of the desks. Fewer than a quarter of them were occupied. The emptiness of the room was a constant reminder of the Wyrbuks' decline, but that slip in status had made the elders like Thiemo cling ever tighter to the strictures. He glared at them until they straightened up at their desks, then began the ceremony of the etching.

Candles were lit, incense was spread and chants were intoned, and Ysentrud sat through it all, bored out of her mind until Thiemo finally reached the end and grasped the switch mounted on the pillar in the centre of the room. She took a deep breath and closed her eyes, waiting. She heard the *thunk* of the switch being thrown, and suddenly her head was full of music and agony.

The Wyrbuks might all look the same on the outside – gaunt, with their strange crimson skin, tattooed to look like skulls floating over their white robes, only the differences in their height to really set them apart from one another – but inside their skulls they were as varied as every other member of humanity, and each of their brains accepted the massive flow of information pouring into them from the stycher differently.

Heze had told Ysentrud that being etched was like being surrounded by a whirlwind of stained glass, a beautiful storm that cut and cut and cut. For Ysentrud, it was birds. When the switch was flipped, they came for her, a dazzling flock of birds, feathers of every colour. They swirled around her, and music flowed sweet from their throats as their claws raked her skin and their beaks tore her flesh.

This was the song of etching, the beauty and the pain of having all that knowledge carved permanently in her head. Of becoming a Wyrbuk, a living volume of knowledge. It was a feeling that she loved and hated in equal measures, ecstasy and agony that burned through her on and on and on. Every etching was an eternity, and Ysentrud sometimes felt as if she'd lived for millennia instead of less than two decades. But like always, it eventually did end. The birds went silent, flew away and left Ysentrud hunched over the black desk, tears streaming down her face, blood running from her ears and eyes and nose. She reached automatically for the basin of warm water and soft rag which had been placed on her desk by one of the children adopted by the house.

She cleaned her face of blood and tears and then reached up to carefully remove the stycher.

'Bring up the crystals,' Learned Thiemo intoned. By the Emperor's holy hands, Ysentrud hated hearing him say it – he'd only said it every time she'd done this for almost a decade now – but she kept her mouth shut. He wouldn't whip her feet for making a comment, probably, but it was best not to risk it. Especially when she was filling her head with illicit content. She clicked out both crystals, carefully slipping the one about the gris into her robe. It wouldn't do to let Thiemo see that, no, not at all. Then she got up and walked to the centre of the room, setting the crystal Learned Thiemo had given her in a velvet-lined tray.

'Wait, Ysentrud,' Thiemo said as she started to step away, and she felt her heart skip a beat. He'd seen the second crystal, or noted how it took her longer than it should have to absorb the information he'd placed in her.

'Yes, Learned?' she said, trying hard to keep her voice steady, nonchalant.

He waved her to silence, waiting for the rest to turn in their crystals. Heze was last, and she gave her a worried look and furtively held out her hand. Volunteering to take the crystal hidden in her robe, Ysentrud realised. She felt a sudden flash of gratitude towards the girl, as intense as the pain of etching, but she gave a tiny shake of her head. She'd deal with whatever consequences this brought. Heze sighed and moved on, disappearing out of the chamber, leaving Ysentrud alone with Thiemo.

'Contraband?' he said, looking up at her, and Ysentrud's heart stuttered.

'I– What? Contraband?' she stammered.

He held out his hand, waiting blank-faced until she finally handed over the crystal. Flipping it over, Thiemo read the glyphs etched in its bottom. 'Gris stories,' he said, shaking his head. 'Thousands of years of history here on Reis, plus all the great works from the Imperium, and you fill your head with the ghost stories of ignorant fungus farmers. Stealing dirty pictures would be more dignified.'

Ysentrud couldn't care less about Thiemo's snobbery. She was worried about his authority. 'What will you do?'

'Do?' He blinked up at her. 'Oh. You're worried about being punished. Don't be. If I spent my time punishing young fools for stuffing their heads with idiocy, I'd wear out my whipping arm. I wanted to tell you that you have been assigned.'

Assigned. Ysentrud's fear gave way to excitement. 'Has it been decided that I am finally ready to serve the Regent Prime?'

Learned Thiemo folded his hands. 'It has been decided that you are ready to serve the Regent Next.'

'Sebastian?' Ysentrud said, incredulous.

'Regent Next Sebastian Halven.'

'Regent Uncaring Sebastian Halven!' Ysentrud ran a hand over her smooth scalp, wishing for the first time in years she had hair to tear out. 'He *hates* the history of Reis. He *hates* Reis. Why would you give me to him? Seven years of etching, my brain filled with every bit of this world's history, for what? He'll throw me in a cellar to gather dust!'

'That Regent Next's feelings are not your concern,' Thiemo said. 'The Wyrbuk belong to the Regent Prime. He is the one who had you made, and where you are assigned is up to him. He believes that having you might encourage Sebastian to take more of an interest in the world that he will someday control.'

Ysentrud slid her hand down over her eyes. 'Emperor's' – she changed the word before the blasphemy slipped out – 'blessings.' She'd spent years getting used to the idea of being assigned to the Regent Prime personally. The man was strange, but what noble-born wasn't? He at least was obsessed with history – military history – and would find value in all the things Ysentrud knew. Being stripped from her family, the pain of her poisoning, the years of etching, all of that would have a purpose. But being sent to his son… She would be a book unread, discarded on a shelf to rot, and all that history in her head might as well have been left in its crystal, which at least didn't care if it was never taken out of its box.

'I should have stolen more gris stories,' she whispered to herself. 'I don't have enough to last for a lifetime in the cellar.'

CHAPTER FOUR

The strike cruiser *Sword of Caliban* cut through the immaterium, a bright splinter of reality stabbed deep into the mad eye of the warp. In the ship's prow, wrapped in the protective layers of Geller field and adamantine hull, Lazarus sat in a plain chair in a triangular cabin making notes in a heavy leather-bound book with an electro-quill. Before him, a servo-skull bobbed in the shadows that gathered at the intersection of the room's two longest walls, the bone of its cranium a dull grey in the thin red light that shone from the optics in its eye sockets.

'...and so the beast came to Droslin, and beneath its claws the walls did fall and the red blood ran, until the fields that surrounded the town became a welter of gore that drowned those who tried to flee. Word of this horror spread across the land like sparks of terror borne on the beast's hideous breath, until it reached the Fortress of the First Day, and the knights gathered therein did–'

'Cease.' At Lazarus' command the skull went silent, and the

Master of the Fifth stared at his notes. *Sparks of terror borne on the beast's hideous breath.* How did that translate from the rough tongue of ancient Caliban into High Gothic? It was a puzzle that had stumped the cogitators responsible for the first translation of this tale, and no answer came to Lazarus now as he sat in the dim room.

Sparks.

For a moment he could see them, crimson and gold, drifting through the air like jewelled dust, then they faded, all but one that dimmed... then flared back to life, bright and poisonous green.

'No,' he said as he stood, his deep voice echoing through the cabin, but the spark didn't listen. It drifted over him to the shorter of the three walls, where the Chapter badge of the Dark Angels was painted, the bare wall's only decoration. It was a sword that stretched from ceiling to floor, with two wings spreading out from the hilt. The mote touched the sword, right where the wings joined it, and suddenly the whole thing was in flames, flames of green and purple, red and orange, blue and gold, every brilliant colour of the rainbow. The heat of them blazed across the room, and Lazarus could feel it in every nerve, searing into him.

'No,' he said, ignoring the heat, ignoring the pain, closing his eyes and filling his mind with the Litany of Horrors Past. The familiar words ran through his mind and through his lips, and the heat faded, taking the pain with it, and when he opened his eyes there was nothing but the wings and the sword, bright and pure, untouched by flames.

It had been a long time since the fire had come to him like that.

Lazarus spoke the litany one more time, bowing his head before the winged sword. On one side of its painted blade was his weapon rack, bolt pistol and grenades carefully arrayed around the length of Enmity's Edge, the weapon gleaming in the soft spotlight of a lumen. On the other side of the badge his armour rested, the heavy pieces hanging from an intricate stand. Another lumen shone there, making the dark green ceramite plates glow. All of it had been cleaned and repaired after Husk, but in that light it was easy to see the subtle mismatch. The Spiritshield Helm, with its great white wings rising from each temple, was newly forged but unique compared to the rest of his Mark X armour. Within the helm was a relic of the Chapter, a sacred thing blessed by countless battles – a shard of one of lost Caliban's stone guardians.

His old armour had burned on Rimenok, when the sorcerous minion of the Ruinous Powers had wrapped it in unnatural flame. It had burned, and he had burned, and died, and been reborn.

Resurrections, like everything in the galaxy, came with a cost.

A cost Lazarus had thought he'd paid. But nothing was ever that easy, was it? He shook his head and picked up the book and electro-quill, settling himself back in the chair. He made a note about the difficult translation of the spark metaphor, neat, tiny glyphs spilling from his huge hands, and left it at that for now. 'Resume,' he said to the servo-skull, which had been waiting patiently, its dull red eyes watching everything and seeing nothing.

'And the knights gathered therein did prepare for war, and for death, for the beast was great and terrible and they knew that many of their number would fall. But honour and blood forge chains of responsibility, so–'

The door chimed, and the servo-skull automatically silenced itself. 'Open,' Lazarus said, rising. Interrogator-Chaplain Demetrius stepped in, wrapped in a hooded white robe, much like the one Lazarus wore. On its breast the same badge of the Dark Angels was sewn, and below it the number five had been embroidered with golden thread, the careful work of one of the thousands of Chapter-serfs living on the Rock.

'Master Lazarus,' Demetrius said. He looked past his shoulder, to the silent servo-skull. 'Am I interrupting your work?'

'This work is always interrupted,' Lazarus said. 'If the Chapter wished it in a timely manner, they would have given it to a scribe, not to one of their masters.'

'But it is tradition for you to do it.' Demetrius walked into the shadowy room, towards the floating skull wrapped in its cybernetics. An ancient relic, the cranium of some honoured servant of the Dark Angels transformed after death into a repository of lore. 'Master of the Fifth. Keeper of the Unseen Ritual.'

'Translator of overwrought metaphors. Attempted translator.' Lazarus stared at the servo-skull, avoiding looking at his brother. Demetrius had lost the left side of his face to a plasma blast long ago. Muscle and skin had been regrown, though they didn't quite match – the new skin was a deep black colour, darker than the warm brown of the rest of Demetrius' skin. But his eye had been replaced with a cybernetic implant which glowed green in the dim. It wasn't the same shade as the motes that the ork psyker had flung at Lazarus, but it was close enough that he had been avoiding staring at it. When he realised what he was doing, Lazarus forced himself to look back. It was a weakness, to let worry over a possible flashback direct his eyes, and weakness was something to be faced, addressed and removed as soon as he found it. That lesson was the anvil against which a Dark Angel's training was forged.

'It is a title and a task that suits you, Master Lazarus. You would have been a good academic, in another life.'

It suited the Dark Angels that Lazarus did this task, and not just because the ancient stories were instructive in history and tactics. The translation of the lore from Caliban fell to the Master of the Fifth not because he was skilled at it, but because he was part of the Inner Circle, the shadow council that was the true heart of the Dark Angels. He knew the secret sin committed by his Chapter so long ago, and one of the principal parts of his work was to find anything in the old stories that might have grown in the telling to hint at that secret, and to bury it.

To hide the treason that had almost seized them and dragged the Dark Angels into the service of madness.

'I had another life, before this one,' Lazarus said. 'It comes back to me at night sometimes, when I dream of hunting saw-snakes and men in the swamps of the world that birthed me.' He tilted his head, looking down at the Chaplain. 'What brings you here, brother? It is not to discuss my translations.'

'No,' the Interrogator-Chaplain said, shaking his head. He looked at the chair and Lazarus waved a hand. Demetrius moved book and quill and sat. 'If I have to look up at you, I would rather an excuse. After being taller than you for a century, this change still discomforts me.'

'You did not come to talk about that either,' Lazarus said.

'I did,' the Interrogator-Chaplain said. 'In a circuitous way.'

'You know my love for indirect speech.' Lazarus was happy to have given up the chair. This conversation was making him uncomfortable already, and he began to move, pacing back and forth. If it had been any other brother from the Fifth than Demetrius, he would have had them checking and rechecking the ammunition inventories as a lesson about wasting time. But Demetrius was another member of the Inner Circle, his closest friend and the Fifth's Interrogator-Chaplain, their spiritual heart. There was nothing they couldn't say to each other, but right now that knowledge was only disquieting. Lazarus turned and stared at Demetrius. 'Why are you here, brother?'

Demetrius raised his hand. The Interrogator-Chaplain would never admit defeat on the battlefield, would keep going as long as both his hearts beat, but he would give in to the head of his company. 'I would discuss your resurrection. Your crossing of the Rubicon Primaris, and what that journey has left in you.'

'We have already had that conversation,' Lazarus said. 'My death and rebirth in a new body… troubled me.'

'Troubled' was a word for it. The battle on Rimenok had been a disaster, the Fifth Company facing a foe that not only vastly outnumbered them, but also commanded unnatural forces that seared and burned their way through the ranks of his men. In the end, it was only his strategy and the enemy's manic overconfidence that saved them. Lazarus had charged them, driving into the heart of their lines to find the traitorous sorcerer laying waste to his forces, and with his strength and the sacrifices of his brothers he had been able to defeat the psyker. But that victory had been bought with the coin of his own life. Lazarus had cut to the heart of their enemy and killed the sorcerer, but he had paid for that win by burning.

His men hadn't let him go easy, though. Demetrius had told him the story, of how Jequn had led them through claws and flames to find him, and how Amad had carried him back, his body a charred ruin in the husk of his shattered armour. He'd been alive, in a way. The sorcerous fire had ripped through his body, but it hadn't touched his head, whether because of the warding built into the Spiritshield Helm or some twisted aspect of the spells that had charred him. His hearts had been burned out, his lungs ruined. His muscles were grease and ash wrapped around cracked, blackened bones. But fitful activity still stirred in his brain. Part of him still fought for life, because of the sacred surgeries that had been done to him as a child. He contained the blessings of the gene-seed, which had forged new organs in his body and made him into an Adeptus Astartes, a man beyond men. Death could not take him easily. So his brain lived on, and Lazarus' spirit, chained in that flesh, did too. But that tenuous connection to life was already beginning to falter when Lieutenant Amad handed his body to Brother Asbeel.

The Fifth's Apothecary could only conceive of one possible salvation. To stimulate the massive regeneration Lazarus would need to survive, Asbeel implanted the gene-seed-wrought Primaris organs that had been crafted by Archmagos Dominus Belisarius Cawl over ten thousand years. The belief was that it would kill him, and it did. For hours, what was left of his body had gone silent, dead. And then the new organs had meshed with the old, and Lazarus was reborn. He rose, an even more potent weapon to inflict the Emperor's will upon the galaxy. Yet he almost fell again.

The operation had seemed a success, but like his armour and helm, Lazarus had been subtly mismatched, the new body unable to mesh with his memory of what he had been. That mismatch had made him slow, had made him weak, and when he tried to tear that weakness out... what was he to grab? Asbeel could find no flaws. Lazarus had crossed the Rubicon Primaris, the name for this terrible, dangerous procedure, and come out the other side not only alive but stronger than before. So he suffered with this feeling of being changed, diminished, struggling to force mind, body and spirit back together through sheer force of will. And failed.

Until he finally spoke to Demetrius about it. And the Interrogator-Chaplain gave him the key to bringing himself together, to becoming whole again. Even if he could still feel the flames sometimes.

'You helped me through, brother. Your counsel led me to a truth in these stories.' Lazarus waved at the servo-skull. 'One that gave me a purpose, that made me whole. I thank you for that. But that is done.'

'Is it?' Demetrius leaned back in the borrowed chair. 'I saw you fight. You are one with yourself. But I saw you after. I saw your rage.'

Lazarus stopped pacing, and his robes swirled around him. 'My rage? You worry about me because of that? That rage was righteous. That was the rage you seek to inspire in all of us when we battle the enemies of the Imperium.'

'I know my purpose. How I serve my company and the Emperor. And I know how little it touches you.' Demetrius smiled. 'You are not fire, brother, you are ice. When you are angry, you wrap yourself even tighter in the armour of your will. You are no berserker – you control your anger, leash it, use it. But at the end, there on Husk, after Amad died, I saw your anger control you.'

'I slew the psyker. I helped Jequn slay the warboss. I finished that fight,' Lazarus said. 'What wrong did you see?'

Demetrius stared at him from the depths of his hood, his mismatched eyes gleaming. Lazarus stared back, fighting the urge to turn away, even though the green gleam of Demetrius' eye kept wavering into a spark, into a flame.

'I was angry,' he finally said.

'Angry because of the battle. Because of what happened to our brothers. Angry about what happened to Amad.' The Interrogator-Chaplain's deep voice was calm, level. The sound of it, usually so welcome, grated in Lazarus' ears.

'All those, yes. And more. You know how I feel about psykers.

About the names that run through my head. I added two more, and I was angry.'

'And more,' Demetrius repeated.

'And what?' Lazarus snapped. 'What is this? You are meant to help make us rage, to make our anger a whetstone that sharpens us for the fight. Not to question it, not to blunt it.'

'My purpose is to sharpen anger and direct it. And more. Who else?'

Lazarus' hands tightened into fists, and the green glow of Demetrius' eye had become a torch, its heat reaching him. But he made himself stare at it, and ran the Litany of Horrors Past through his mind until it was just the soft glow of Demetrius' eye, floating like a star in the darkness of his hood.

'I was angry at Azrael, my Supreme Grand Master, commander of the Dark Angels and Keeper of the Truth.' Lazarus opened his hands, letting the tension go as he spoke. And when he did, he felt it, the anger he had buried inside, that had fed the flashbacks as much or more as the murderous powers of that ork psyker. 'I am angry at Azrael for pulling away the *Unrelenting Fury*, and for everything that happened after. And I am angry for Amad.'

He looked at his brother. His words were insubordination, and it would fall well within Demetrius' duty to report him to the Supreme Grand Master. The thought didn't trouble him though. That anger... not acknowledging it, pretending it didn't exist, was another weakness, and it had to be drawn out, like shrapnel from a wound.

Demetrius raised his hands and lowered his hood. 'To know thyself is to know the first enemy. The words of our primarch, Lion El'Jonson.'

'The words of the Lion,' Lazarus repeated.

Demetrius held out his hand, until Lazarus took it and

pulled the Interrogator-Chaplain to his feet. 'Come, brother. Let us go to the sparring halls and scourge our feelings out with fist and blade. We have only days until we return home, and you need to pour a measure of that anger out before you meet with the Supreme Grand Master again.'

'You are wise, Chaplain,' Lazarus said. 'But what rage must you scourge?'

'The same as yours,' Demetrius said, nodding solemnly. 'The rage of one brother versus another. Prepare yourself, Master Lazarus, for my anger is with you for daring to grow taller than me.'

CHAPTER FIVE

'And so they came to Droslin, and saw the ruin of the town, the shattered walls, the fields of blood. And in those fields they saw the marks of the beast, the great webbed prints of the monster, sunk deep into the gore-rich mud, and they knew that their doom was upon them.'

'Cease.' It was as good a time to end as any. The book and electro-quill sat unused beside Lazarus, and his eyes were on the pict caster hanging beneath another servo-skull drifting beside the one that had been speaking. On it, the image of the Rock was growing fast as the *Sword of Caliban* approached. The vast citadel of the Dark Angels was eating up the stars, and soon there was nothing to see on the glowing screen but that massive chunk of bedrock. It was all that remained of Caliban, the doomed home world of Lion El'Jonson, primarch of the Dark Angels.

It drifted in space like an asteroid, but this close it was clear it was not just another chunk of star-wrought dust, clumped together by gravity over aeons. The Rock had once been part of a mountain called Aldurukh, which meant 'the Rock of Eternity' in one of the ancient dialects of Caliban. On its steep sides had been built the fortress-monastery Angelicasta, where the Lion had taken the Dark Angels as his own.

Lazarus looked at the rough peak of the great mountain. There, beneath shields that flashed with light as though caught in a storm, were the crumbling ruins of that fortress. So much history, and so much of it bound under lock and key. 'Lore and secrets. Secrets and lore.' Lazarus said the words almost silently, adjusting his balance as the *Sword of Caliban* fired its thrusters, slowing its speed to slip through the Rock's vast void shields. This close, Lazarus couldn't see all the fortress at once, but he could pick out details, the great towers and domes and buttresses of the mighty cathedrals that covered huge areas of the Rock, interlaced with titanic carvings of scenes from the Dark Angels' history. Armoured knights charging huge beasts on horseback, chainswords raised over their heads. Vast fleets locked in battle over ringed gas giants. Space Marines, standing their ground against a horde of xenos monsters with standards raised high and bolters blazing.

This was it, this was home, and Lazarus could see the docking area growing in front of them. The guide lights glimmered like home fires beneath the tip of a gigantic sword, the Chapter badge of the Dark Angels cut into a canvas of raw rock miles long and miles wide. Home. Lazarus stared at it until the pict feed from the hull of the *Sword of Caliban* went dark, the strike cruiser overshadowed by stone and plasteel as it slid into its dock. A shudder went through the ship as the docking clamps grasped it, and they were back.

The Fifth Company had returned, living and dead, to its rightful place. But Lazarus had learned long ago there was no peace anywhere in this burning galaxy, and wherever he went, war would meet him. Turning from the dark pict caster, he shed his robe.

'Armour,' he said, and the door to the cabin opened, Chapter-serfs silently filing in as the intricate stand began to move, reaching out to him like a great metal spider. Together, serfs and machine wrapped him in a cocoon of adamantine and ceramite, of tradition and technology, of honour and secrets.

Lazarus' boots echoed on the stone of the huge, vaulted hallway – a tunnel carved through the granite heart of the Rock. So many armoured feet had walked this way over count-less years that the stone floor was worn with their tread, even though the Chapter-serfs maintained and replaced it every few millennia.

Those serfs moved around him like ghosts, mortals wrapped in grey robes, part of the force of thousands that laboured with the throngs of servitors to keep the Rock floating serenely through the void. All of them kept clear of him though, step-ping silently out of his way and bowing their heads, a silent show of respect to the towering figure moving with purpose down the corridor.

They had been in the Rock for days. There had been the ceremony of returning, the blessing of the Lion, and then the sombre gathering for the fallen. Their progenoid glands had been solemnly returned to the Chapter, to await their use in creating the gene-seed for the next generation of Dark Angels, and then they had been committed to the consecrated plasma flames of the Rock's crematorium. They had burned in seconds, and afterwards Lazarus had carried the reliquaries of their ashes to the vast columbarium that held the last remains of count-less generations of his kind.

The reliquaries had seemed far too light for all the lives they contained. They always did, but this time the feeling seemed stronger. Surely there was too much loss to fit in a box of golden cylinders that Lazarus could hold in one hand. He kept thinking of it when, after the ceremonies, he went through the rituals of reconciliation, going over in detail everything that had happened on his mission, every triumph and every loss, so that it could all be meticulously recorded.

Every loss.

Lazarus came to a stop in the centre of a circular chamber at the intersection of two corridors. Their arched roofs rose into a dome high overhead, the stone polished and glowing with reflected light. A skeleton was embedded there, a great beast that had been entombed in the Rock for millions of years, long enough for its bones to turn to stone. It and countless others had been found when the Rock had been hollowed out, and their ancient bones were common decorations in the halls. This one was particularly striking, all claws and teeth and spines, a twisted thing that coiled overhead like the corpse of a nightmare. He stared up at it, tracing the stone bones of the monster, and the serfs moving up and down the passages paused and put their backs against the curving walls of the chamber. They kept silent, staying out of his way, but Lazarus could see their furtive movements beneath their hoods as they turned their heads up, following his gaze, trying to see what he was seeing.

'Doom,' he said, and moved on, leaving them staring after him.

The bones were too old, in reality. That beast had lived and died long before humans had come to Caliban. But the sketchy outlines of the body those bones would have supported seemed similar to that of the monster in the story he was currently translating. That skeletal thing might not be the Doom of Droslin, but it brought that mournful story to his mind.

Not that it had been distant from it, not since his talks with the Interrogator-Chaplain of the Fifth.

Lazarus moved through lifts and corridors, down spiral stairs and through cathedral-like halls. The crowds of serfs thinned around him until he was walking alone down a hall whose walls and floors were covered in polished black onyx. It ended in a door made of dark wood, richly grained, carved with the familiar Chapter badge of winged sword. When Lazarus approached, the door swung silently open, revealing how thick it was. The wood was a veneer over adamantine, an ornate mask over an armoured bulkhead. Like the man who occupied these quarters, a thin veil of polished civility over iron resolve, and that thought didn't make what Lazarus was about to do any easier. The rooms beyond were sacrosanct, and the privacy of the man that dwelled within them was meant to be kept absolute. Lazarus didn't alter his pace, but the hard crack of his footsteps changed as he stepped over the threshold and onto the green malachite and black onyx floor of the private chambers of the Keeper of the Truth, Azrael, the Supreme Grand Master of the Dark Angels.

'Master Lazarus.' Azrael set aside a data-slate and rose from his chair, his robes swinging around his ever-present armour. This was his reception room, a hexagonal chamber panelled in dark wood, the four side walls each carved with the likeness of one of the great native trees of lost Caliban. Heavy chairs were arrayed before them in clusters, meant for talking, with stands in between bearing thick books which detailed the deeds of the Chapter from the First Founding over ten thousand years ago. Each one of them was a hand-lettered work of art crafted over centuries by Chapter-serfs.

The deeds were all carefully curated by previous Keepers of the Unseen Ritual.

The wall behind Azrael held another door, mirroring the entrance. It was carved with the figure of a winged angel in a hooded robe, one hand holding up a sword, its point down, the other hand raised, palm out. Its face couldn't be seen, but there was a gleam of eyes in the dark hood. The wood had been carved deep enough to let the door's adamantine core shine through.

Lazarus had never seen what lay beyond that door. To his knowledge, no one but Azrael and the Supreme Grand Masters that came before him had. Them, and the Watchers in the Dark.

There were two of the diminutive humanoids in the room, flanking that inner door. One held the Lion Helm, the red-plumed helmet of the Grand Master. The other carried the Sword of Secrets, the venerable blade that was both deadly weapon and badge of office. The robed and hooded creature carried the sword easily, even though the blade was almost twice as long as it was tall. How it could hold up the sword at all, much less for hours, without weakening, without moving, was a mystery. But that was nothing compared to all the questions surrounding these little creatures. Were they a species of xenos native to Caliban? A mutant strain of humanity? Or some kind of servitor, a cybernetic creation like the servo-skulls? No one knew. The unnatural darkness that gathered in their hoods defeated the eyes and auspexes of even the Space Marines. And their hands, when they slipped from the sleeves of their robes, were tightly wrapped in strips of cloth, making gloves which covered them completely.

You could only see their robes, robes that looked like the ones Lazarus and Azrael wore over their armour. Robes that were taken from the knights of Caliban known as the Order, from whom the Dark Angels had inherited so many of their traditions. Were the Watchers imitating them? Or had the Order imitated the Watchers? There were stories of them that went back that far. It was a question Lazarus itched to ask, but no one spoke to the Watchers and the Watchers spoke to no one.

They were one more enigma, another secret even Lazarus, member of the Inner Circle, had no answer to.

He stepped into the room, and the door swung shut behind him as he bowed his head to his leader. It felt strangely wrong to be taller than Azrael – the Supreme Grand Master had only been slightly taller than him before his rebirth – but staring down at his Firstborn commander was still something Lazarus was not accustomed to. He made himself brush the feeling aside and straightened, reached up and took off his helm, and suddenly there was another Watcher in the Dark in the room, standing beside him, arms outstretched. Lazarus checked his honed reflexes and kept himself from smashing the thing with one of his gauntleted fists. Not that it would have connected – the Watchers were infamous for their ability to simply not be there when something struck at them. Instead, he handed over his Spiritshield Helm, then took Enmity's Edge from his hip and gave it to another Watcher that appeared on his other side. He was certain neither one of them had been there before – he'd neither seen nor heard them, nor caught a trace of their cold, dry scent. But they were there now, taking sword and helm and then stepping back to flank the entrance door, mirroring their twins on the other side of the room.

'Sit, brother,' Azrael said, gesturing to one of the chairs on the side of the room, near a small table set with a pitcher and delicate glasses. When Lazarus sat, the Supreme Grand Master poured from that pitcher, filling each glass with a pale golden liquid. The pouring was a gesture of respect, the greater honouring the lesser. Lazarus took the glass and held the delicate thing carefully in his hand, the sensation of its smooth, cool touch passing through the sensors built into his armour, through the black carapace and into him. He could smell it, a mixture of sharp and sweet. The neuroglottis organ gene-seeded into his mouth labelled it as mildly poisonous but edible. Some kind of strong alcohol then, fermented from a fruit he didn't know.

'It's called iceburn,' Azrael said. 'From Styx. The tribes there drink it to keep warm in the cold.'

Lazarus took a sip and felt the burn of it in his throat. But the sensation went away quickly when the drink hit his preomnor, the gene-seed organ implanted over his stomach. It took apart the toxin in seconds, rendering the iceburn harmless. A Space Marine could drink pure alcohol by the barrel and never approach getting drunk. Sharing drinks like this was a ritual, something that connected them to the people they had come from, to the ones they were dedicated to defend.

It also wasted time.

Lazarus could feel the anger inside him, coiled in his chest like that fossilised skeleton had coiled in that granite dome. He'd expected it to be there, to flare up again when he had this meeting, no matter how many practice bouts he'd fought over the last few days. But it was stronger than expected, far hotter in him than the iceburn. He took another swallow from his glass, using the time to run the Litany of Focus through his head. When it was done, and the anger was firmly chained, he silently thanked his Interrogator-Chaplain. If Demetrius hadn't made him confront the rage that lay buried inside him, it would have exploded out now – here, with Azrael – and the shame of that would have haunted Lazarus forever. Anger was a part of being a warrior, another weapon that had its uses. But losing control was another kind of weakness.

So when he spoke, his voice was as controlled as it was cold. 'Is this meant to celebrate my victory?'

Azrael stared at him for a long time from his chair, his dark eyes sharp beneath his close-cropped black hair. 'It could be,' he said finally. 'I could argue that it should be. Unlike most reports from the mortals we protect, the authorities on Husk underestimated the strength of their invaders. Both in the number of orks and in how well armed they were. They would have been a challenge for two companies, and you eradicated them with one.'

'At great cost.'

'Indeed,' Azrael agreed. 'A cost that I incurred but made the Fifth pay.' He finished his glass and set it down on the table. 'You were succinct in your reports as always, brother. But I know how to read them. I could see your battle plan, and how it was broken when I recalled the *Unrelenting Fury*. You made up for that loss, pulled victory from what could have been a rout, but your company suffered for that change. Lieutenant Amad dead and four squads' worth of Dark Angels killed or in need of extensive regeneration. One Venerable Dreadnought which will take months to rebuild. A Gladiator Reaper and two Rhinos destroyed, the other Reaper and three transports heavily damaged.' It was a grim recitation, and at its end Azrael fixed Lazarus with hard eyes. 'How much of that was because of my orders? What would have been saved if you had been able to carry out your original plan?'

'Impossible to know,' Lazarus said. 'There would have been losses, no matter the plan.'

'Would the losses have been fewer?' Azrael said, without pause.

'Yes.'

'Significantly fewer?'

'Yes,' Lazarus said again.

'You know that,' Azrael said. 'And that truth wears at you, as it wears at me. The death of every one of our brothers wears at me. But it had to be done.'

It had to be done. Lazarus set down his glass, turning those words over, and the anger in him went cold. 'I understand death, Supreme Grand Master. I understand sacrifice. You did not name Scout Squad Daral, of the Tenth Company. They were lost too, at my order. They died, all of them, just to buy me a few minutes more. I understand giving orders that bring death to our brothers, but you are right, your decision troubles me. The way you say it *had* to be done troubles me.' Lazarus set his eyes on Azrael's. 'You sent the *Unrelenting Fury* to hunt the Fallen, didn't you?'

Azrael nodded, and though his confirmation was no surprise to Lazarus, a storm of emotions still swept through the Master of the Fifth. The Fallen. They were the secret sin of the Dark Angels. Ten thousand years ago, when the Imperium was split by civil war, entire Chapters of Space Marines, the hope of mankind, the incorruptible, were corrupted. They turned against their people and their leader, joined forces with the monstrous daemonic minds that dwelled in the warp, the Ruinous Powers, and declared war on the Emperor of Mankind. The Fallen were Dark Angels that had done the same.

They had rebelled against the Lion, the Primaris Angelus Mortis, their leader, and tried to kill him. The ensuing battle devastated Caliban, and then, when the loyal Space Marines were triumphant, the planet had been engulfed by a warp storm, an act of revenge that shattered the Dark Angels' home world and let the surviving traitors escape across space and time.

They were known forever after as the Fallen, but only to the Dark Angels, and not even all of them. The Lion was struck down in the fighting, an incalculable loss, and leaderless, homeless, the Dark Angels that were left chose to bury their shame. They hid what had happened from all outsiders, hid it too from their own brothers. The betrayal of the Fallen became a secret, and keeping that secret became as important to the few who knew about it as hunting down every surviving Fallen that remained, so that they could be dragged screaming back into the light, where they would admit their treachery and their mistake before they were executed.

The Fallen were the secret at the heart of the Dark Angels, the reason for the existence of the Inner Circle, who controlled every aspect of the Chapter. They had become, in a way, the reason for the existence of the Dark Angels themselves, and that truth was the root of Lazarus' anger.

'I did,' Azrael said. 'Four Fallen were in the Pentel System, hidden aboard a ship that had stopped there to refuel. I knew they would not be there long, so I ordered the closest ship to be sent after them. The *Unrelenting Fury* was that ship.'

'The *Sword of Caliban* and *Mercy Never* were there,' Lazarus said.

'Neither of which had the armament of the *Unrelenting Fury.*'

'I know.' Lazarus kept his voice soft, but Azrael's face was growing hard. The Supreme Grand Master was a wise man who listened carefully when making decisions, but once those decisions were made he had little patience with being questioned. Still, Lazarus kept on. 'And the commanders of those ships were not members of the Inner Circle.' But Domitius had once been a member of the Deathwing before the toll of a thousand injuries had made him shift to command of one of the greatest weapons in the Chapter's fleet. Brother Domitius understood at least a small portion of the truth. He knew the importance of the Fallen.

Lazarus could sense the suspicion growing in his leader, and he knew he was about to call him out, but he kept going. This was what he needed his anger for. Leashed, controlled, it kept him going, even though he knew what would follow.

'The last few days, I have made some enquiries. About where the *Unrelenting Fury* was, and what other ships were near that system. It was not hard – the *Unrelenting Fury* is on its way home, following a slow, careful jump plan. Which means they did not find the Fallen.'

'They did not. Nor any sign of where they had gone.' Azrael leaned against the arm of his chair, and the heavy wood groaned beneath him. 'That failure upset me. It upset me more, knowing what it cost the Fifth. Those men may be your company, but every company in the Dark Angels belongs to me. I invited you here, brother, to commemorate their loss. But instead I am faced with… this. Whatever this is. Tell me, Brother Lazarus. What is *this?*'

Staring into those dark eyes, so sharp and focused on him, *this* felt like suicide. But Lazarus held on to the core of cold anger inside him and spoke. 'You made me Master of the Fifth. Leader of one hundred battle-brothers, one-tenth of the greatest fighting force ever forged to serve the Emperor. But with that you also made me Keeper of the Unseen Ritual. Historian of our Chapter. You know that saved me.'

He had told Azrael what had happened to him, after his death. After he had crossed the Rubicon Primaris and been reborn. After he had pieced himself together again, he had gone to the Supreme Grand Master and reported how he had been weak, and how he had become strong again.

'Our history saved me, Supreme Grand Master. I was lost in the pain of death and resurrection, my strength was taken from me, but the stories of the knights of Caliban showed me my path. They made me understand our purpose as the sons of the Lion. As the defenders of humanity. We are the Dark Angels, we are the Knights of Caliban, we are the slayers of the monsters that would destroy mankind.'

'You have told me this story before,' Azrael said. 'I told you then I was pleased you had found a way forward through our past. But I had my worries then, worries I left unsaid that I now think I should have voiced. We have at times had some among us, Lazarus, who doubted our purpose. Our dedication to the eradication of the Fallen. Has this new purpose of yours made you doubt the oath you took when you joined the Inner Circle? To cleanse this evil from us?'

'No.' Lazarus shook his head. 'What are the Fallen but monsters? The traitor's fate is the same as the xenos', and the daemon's. Death.'

'I did not think so. I give my thanks to the Emperor that I was correct in that.' Azrael frowned at him, still angry, but curious now too. 'I ask you again. What is this, Lazarus? Something troubles you, something more than the deaths of your men, and I feel you want to trouble me with it too.'

'I do,' Lazarus said. 'It is a story, Azrael, from our history. It is called *The Doom of Droslin*.'

Azrael frowned, but he waved a hand. 'Proceed then. But cleave to the succinctness you are known to value.'

Lazarus nodded, and folded his hands before him, gauntlets clicking together. '*The Doom of Droslin* is a warning, like the stories we learned when we first joined the Inner Circle, when the Interrogator-Chaplains began to teach us our secrets. Like most of the stories of the knights of Caliban, this one is about a beast. A great monster that rose up and destroyed a fortress town called Droslin.

'Droslin was guarded by the Knights of the First Day. At that time, they were among the greatest of the knightly orders, feared and respected for their strength and skill, and they took a fierce pride in that. When Droslin fell, they took up arms and rode out to face the beast the handful of survivors had named Doom. But when the Knights of the First Day saw the devastated town, saw the vast beast curled in the smoking ruins, they were suddenly faced with a truth they could not accept. This was a task which was beyond them, a monster they could not defeat. They saw the Doom of Droslin, and they knew that charging forward to attack it was suicide. But that is what they did. The Knights of the First Day rode out, swords and pistols raised, and fell to tooth and claw, destroyed to the last man. Because the fear of death could not touch their fear of being thought of as weak.'

Lazarus reached for the pitcher, looking at Azrael. The Supreme Grand Master nodded, and Lazarus poured them both more. The alcohol might not touch him, but drinking it could still wet his throat, and give him time to think through what he needed to say.

'The lesson of the story is the vanity of pride. The Knights of the First Day could not accept the thought of failure, so they let themselves be destroyed, and in the process they failed the very people they had vowed to protect. The Doom lived on, killing and feeding until more than a dozen knightly orders of Caliban came together and went against it. And won, at terrible cost. A cost that would have been much lower if the Knights of the First Day had been there to fight with them, instead of dead on the broken stones of Droslin.'

'I remember something of this story now,' Azrael said. 'The fight shattered many orders, but they rose from that disaster, stronger.'

'Yes. And became our predecessors.' Which brought them back to the Dark Angels, and the Fallen, and he was supposed to be succinct. He took another drink, then spoke.

'If you want to know what troubles me, it is this. I listen to this story, and in the Knights of the First Day I see ourselves. Proud, noble warriors who came face to face with something in themselves that they couldn't accept, so they made a choice. A tragic one.'

Azrael set down his glass with a firm click. His face was growing hard again, with anger or suspicion or both. 'And what tragic choice do you think we have made, my brother? You have already said that the Fallen are our monsters who must be destroyed. What mistake is there then, that connects this story to them and to the losses you have just suffered?'

'The mistake of pride,' Lazarus said. 'We are the Dark Angels. We are the first of the Adeptus Astartes. That fills us with pride, and that pride fills us with rage at the fall of our brothers. Because of our pride, we risk having the oath we made to destroy the Fallen become an obsession. And obsessions have the power to distract. To distort. To destroy.'

'Obsession.' Azrael's voice was low. 'Do you believe we go too far in our fight against the nest of traitors that we birthed in our ranks?'

'Yes,' Lazarus said.

'The traitors that cost us an entire world, *our* world, Caliban, in a battle with our own brothers?'

'Yes.'

Azrael stood, his chair skidding back across the black and green tiles. 'And you come to me with this, now, because of a revelation that you gleaned from a *story*?'

Lazarus looked up at him, facing the anger in his eyes, in his face, in the set of his body. 'Yes.'

Azrael stared down at him, his armoured hands clenched in tight fists. 'When you returned from Rimenok, after Apothecary Asbeel had saved you by forcing you across the Rubicon

Primaris, there were some who feared what your death and that strange resurrection might have done to your mind. I championed you, Lazarus, because I believed in you. In your intelligence, in your resilience, in your steadiness. I believed they would see you through. And I thought I was right, even with your troubles, after. But now you come to me with this madness.'

'It is not madness, Master Azrael.' Lazarus stayed seated, but he could feel the cold anger in him again, strengthening him. 'It is strategy. We *must* fight the Fallen. They are not just our enemies, but the enemies of all the Imperium, and of the Emperor who protects it. But we must not be so obsessed with them that we lose sight of everything else. We are surrounded by enemies, my lord, all eager to tear us down, to destroy us, and if we let our battle against the Fallen become our everything, our only thing, it will weaken us. We will make ourselves easier prey for *all* our enemies, and for what?'

'To atone for our shame!' Azrael snapped out the words, his deep voice filling the room. 'To redeem our honour! To prove that we are worthy to serve the Emperor as his first, his oldest, his greatest Legion!'

'All of those,' Lazarus said, his voice hard and cold. 'And because we were afraid of having the Imperium, and our brothers, and the Emperor, know that despite our history, our gene-seed, our strength, we are still human, and flawed, and that we can fail.'

Azrael moved to him, a blur of motion, and Lazarus had to fight his reflexes to keep himself still. The Supreme Grand Master grasped Lazarus' armour, ceramite grating against ceramite, and hauled him up so that Azrael was glaring straight into his eyes.

'We are Adeptus Astartes. We are His chosen. We know no fear.'

Lazarus looked back at him, eye to eye, unwavering. Silent. Until Azrael finally let him go.

'You are one of my best, brother. And one of my most challenging.' Azrael had a leash on his rage, but it was still there, coiled beneath the suddenly smooth mask of his features. 'Our strategy, *my* strategy, will not change. The Fallen will always be our first target, our greatest goal. Ten thousand years of hunting, of toil and pain, will not end because you lost four squads and one man. Do you understand me?'

'I do, Supreme Grand Master,' Lazarus said, his words stiff and formal. 'And I shall serve your will.'

'My will,' Azrael said, 'and the will of every Supreme Grand Master who came before me.' The anger suddenly faded in Azrael's eyes, and there was a flash of something else, something that might have been a bone-deep exhaustion. 'You have no understanding of what you say, brother. These days are our darkest, and we are surrounded by evil of a strength not seen since the Heresy. You don't understand the strength and treachery of the forces arrayed against us now.'

I do not, he thought. *Because of secrets wrapped in secrets.* But Lazarus kept his tongue and nodded. He turned, and the Watchers in the Dark raised his helm and sword for him to take, the darkness beneath their hoods as vast and empty as the void beyond the walls of the Rock. They watched him go, silent, more secrets, more mystery, and though Lazarus had truthfully expected nothing else from this meeting, he still felt the cold anger begin to melt into a burning rage.

CHAPTER SIX

'Straighten up.' Learned Thiemo's bony hand slapped Ysentrud on the small of her back, and she jerked upright. 'Shoulders back. Head down.'

'How am I to see where I'm going if my head is down?' Ysentrud muttered, exasperated. Thiemo had been fussing at her all morning, and she was sick of his constant comments and prodding.

'Watch the hem of my robe,' he snapped. He moved to straighten Ysentrud's collar, and she stepped back, pushing his hand away. The moment she did it, Ysentrud felt a flash of panic, but she smothered the feeling. Her last etching session had been two days before, and then she had been raised up, a true Wyrbuk now, sanctioned by the Regent Prime. She was now Learned Ysentrud, and Thiemo couldn't whip her for disobedience any more.

Head down, she felt her lips stretch into a smile. She should have slapped his hand away, instead of pushing it.

The door to the tiny antechamber they were waiting in swung open. Thiemo instantly turned his back to her, straightened up and began to slowly walk forward. His strides were still long, though, and she had to hurry to keep up. Without looking as if she was hurrying.

The Hall of the Fallen was a huge space, walls and ceiling made of polished white wood. Mounted on its walls were giant broken weapons and twisted pieces of armour plate, and from the high beams of its ceiling hung gears and struts and pieces of cogitator boards, soot-stained control panels and broken actuators. All that was left of the Knights that had fallen so long ago, in the Redwash War. Ysentrud jerked her head back down when she realised she was looking up at the pieces hanging above, silently naming the parts and to which long-dead Knights they had belonged, and stared back down at the hem of Thiemo's robe.

The hall was almost empty this afternoon. The air processors were acting up again, and the huge room was hot and humid and full of drifting spores that sparkled in the sunlight slanting through the long, slitted windows. There were only a few of the more desperate courtiers, sweating in their bright-coloured suits, and a lone Wyrbuk etcher, sitting in his niche at the back of the room, helplessly memorising every boring moment. The Regent Prime himself was seated in his broken throne. The complicated chair had once been a Throne Mechanicum, the seat where a Knight's pilot would interface with their war machine, and it too had been salvaged from one of the Knights lost during the Redwash War. Learned Thiemo led her to it, and then bowed low, a movement which she hastily copied, if not as gracefully.

'Regent Prime Oskaran Halven,' Thiemo said, straightening back up. 'I present to you Learned Ysentrud Wyrbuk, holder of the complete history of Reis, from settlement to present. As you wished, so have the Wyrbuk provided.'

Ysentrud risked a look up. The Regent Prime was almost three centuries old, but rejuvenat drugs gave him a thin veneer of youth and health. He was of average height, with the build of a man who had once been athletic, muscle padded now with a layer of fat. His complexion was the light brown common to Reis, and his hair was deep black, cut very short and shaved on both sides so that the neural sockets set behind each ear were clearly visible. The protective plugs in those sockets were set with gleaming sapphires to match the glittering blue powder applied to his eyelids. That and a little rouge on his lips were all the face paint he wore. His yellow suit stitched with crimson thread was beautifully made but sedate compared to most of the courtiers' outfits. He did not look up as Thiemo spoke, ignoring the Learned with a thoroughness that would have given Ysentrud a kick of petty pleasure if she wasn't also included in that dismissal. The Regent's attention was fixed instead to the screen of a pict caster set to one side of his throne. Ysentrud couldn't see what was on it, but she could faintly hear someone shouting, and the pop and sizzle of heavy weapons. Was it a report from the interior of Sudsten? There had been rumours of fighting, of another rebellion, even of a resurgence of the gris. But when the Regent Prime finally looked over to them, he seemed almost jubilant as he muttered to himself.

'Fools. They thought they could ignore those Armigers, but they cut them down from behind.' He blinked, seeming to finally realise they were there. 'Ah, the Wyrbuks. Is this him then? The history?' he asked, pointing at Ysentrud.

'She is,' Thiemo said, a thin note of nervousness to his voice at making even that slight a correction to the Regent Prime. 'Learned Ysen–'

'I don't need the name.' He frowned at Ysentrud. 'I need–'

He stopped, his expression slipping to a frown as he looked past them. There was a ripple through the courtiers, their whispers dying away to silence as they all turned to look at the man who strode down the hall towards the throne. He wore a green suit with cuffs and vest in shining gold, bright enough to blend in with the courtiers, but his black hair was much longer than fashionable, pulled back tight into a tail that hung halfway down his back. His handsome young face was also bare, which would have been scandalous if he were not the Regent Next. It was still probably the subject of many of the whispers springing up again among the courtiers, along with speculation about the woman who trailed him like a shadow.

She was middle-aged, with short dark hair that framed a narrow, determined face that was also bare. But it was her clothing that made her stand out the most. The woman was dressed in the uniform of a lash officer of the Reis Home Levies, its sombre black contrasting with the bright colours of the rest of the court. Petra Karn, the Regent Next's aide, and lover, as the gossip went. Ysentrud cut her eyes to Thiemo, not sure what to do, and the tall Wyrbuk looked back at her and slid as silently and unobtrusively to the side as he could. She followed, thankful, and barely got out of the way before the Regent Next drew up before his father.

'Regent Prime Halven.' Sebastian's voice snapped across the Hall of the Fallen. 'We must speak!'

'Must we?' Oskaran leaned back in his throne, still frowning. 'The evidence of that is hard to find. The Hall of the Fallen has been open for hours, with me and my ears in it, and where have you been? Not here.'

'I've been in the headquarters of the Reis Home Levies. Again, the grey motley stalks the jungles, and its numbers grow. The gris rise, and they won't stop until they destroy you and me, and everyone else in Kap Sudsten.'

'So dramatic,' Oskaran said dismissively. 'It's a pack of mouldy farmers.'

'The mouldy farmers, as you call them, have seized the Redwash Gate.'

The bored whispers of the courtiers went silent, and then rose, arguing about the fighting and how far away the gate was. Ysentrud could have told them, to the inch, but it didn't matter. The Redwash Gate. Nowhere was safe on Sudsten if that was ever opened.

'The gris are meaningless, mindless,' Oskaran said, his voice rising over the fearful muttering. 'And the Redwash Gate is sealed. It does not matter that they overrun the outpost there. We'll just take it back.'

'We know nothing about the gris, except that they are tied to the daemons. And we won't take the gate back that easy, not with the numbers of gris that–' Sebastian's voice was buried beneath Oskaran's snarl.

'I am Regent Prime of Sudsten and all the south of Reis. If the gris were such a threat, I would have been the first informed.'

'You were,' the Regent Next said, each word harsh. 'The moment the reports came in this morning, they were sent to you, here, marked with greatest urgency.' Sebastian pointed to the pict caster hanging beside the throne. 'You ignored them. And when messengers were sent here, in person, you had them turned away. *I* had to come just to make you listen. Tell me, father, what was so important? Which ancient Imperial Knight training record did we interrupt?'

Was that the pict recording he'd been watching? Ysentrud wondered. It fit the sounds, and the Regent Prime's interest in the great war machines was really better called an obsession.

An unsurprising obsession, considering the role those giant war machines had played in the history of Reis and in his family. What was it he'd said? *Armiger.* Ysentrud closed her eyes, put her hands together and triggered memen. It came to her instantly. Armigers were a type of Imperial Knight, smaller, faster and more lightly armed. More information waited, images, diagrams, configurations, tactics... She hadn't been etched to be a military expert, but Knights were so much a part of this world's makeup the information was there. Ysentrud pushed it away, though, and willed herself back to the moment.

'–if you'd been here in the hall at the open!' Oskaran was still standing, and had raised his voice to almost a shout. 'I was expecting you, waiting for you. That's why I wasn't responding!'

'And waiting for me is so difficult that you couldn't respond to a message coded urgent? Couldn't bother to see that half the messages were from *me?*' Sebastian snapped.

The courtiers all flinched back, then leaned forward as one, waiting breathlessly. The lash officer was perfectly still, her face a blank mask, but Ysentrud thought she could read something new in her eyes. Something that seemed like eagerness. Meanwhile, Oskaran's face was growing darker and darker.

He stepped forward, until he was standing inches from his son. They were the same height, and this close it was easy to see the similarity of their features. 'Always you push,' he finally said. His voice was quieter, but it was a growl and Ysentrud desperately wished Learned Thiemo were on her other side, between her and the Regents.

'Always think you know better,' Oskaran went on. He reached out and grabbed his son's hair. Anger flickered across Sebastian's face, but he stayed still as his father shoved strands away, until the neural sockets hidden by the long hair showed through, a gleam of metal around the black plugs that protected them. 'You ignore the past, sneer at your heritage, your *birthright*, and think that makes you smart. Smarter than me.'

'I don't let my view of what's happening in the present get blocked by the past,' Sebastian said. 'The Knights are gone, a thousand years gone – the daemons of Redwash saw to that. Or hadn't you noticed the pieces of their corpses hanging around us?'

'I know well the ruin of the Redwash War,' the Regent Prime said. 'I know our history far better than you. And I know too that the Knights of House Halven may yet rise.'

'As poisoned, rusted wrecks from the bottom of the sea?' Sebastian reached up and touched his father's hand. For a moment Oskaran seemed as if he might keep his grip, might tear his son's long hair out, but in the end he let go.

'I know our past,' Oskaran said. 'I thought you did too. But you know nothing.' He waved his now free hand behind him, towards Ysentrud, and she had to fight not to flinch. 'I prepared a gift for you, to address what you lack. Why don't you make acquaintance with them, while I settle these pathetic gris.' The Regent Prime walked away, leaving the hall to the whispering courtiers, his son, the silent lash commander and Ysentrud and Thiemo.

'What do I do now?' Ysentrud whispered to the tall Wyrbuk.

'Now?' Learned Thiemo said. 'You follow him.' He pointed to the Regent Next, who was also leaving the hall, the lash commander still with him. 'He is your keeper now. The Regent Prime presented you to him.'

'That was a presentation?' Ysentrud had been afraid of being stuck in a cellar, abandoned. Could she be abandoned if she was never even acknowledged in the first place?

Learned Thiemo shrugged, his skull face impassive. 'What else is there for you? You were made for him. Go.'

She frowned, then stared back at the Regent Next. He was moving through the door, disappearing. She cursed silently, picked up her robe and followed.

Outside the hall she saw Sebastian walking into a side corridor with the Reis Militarum officer and hurried after them. But they were moving fast, and Ysentrud's years of training had been universally sedentary. They pulled ahead of her, and by the time she reached the end of the corridor they were outside, disappearing into the gardens that lay beyond the Regent's Palace. She cursed again, but started down a path, hunting for them.

In the bright late afternoon, the Night Garden was unimpressive. The different fungi cultivated there grew in great vines and huge sporing bodies all around, but they were pallid shades of grey and white and brown. When it was dark, they would glow with dozens of colours, a spectacular display of bioluminescence, but now they looked like the vast, puffy corpses of giant slugs.

Ysentrud wandered the paths, looking, listening, wishing she could go back to her room in Wyrbuk House, the place she had waited years to escape. Finally, she caught the sound of voices, and hurried to find them.

The Regent Next was standing with the lash commander beneath a dead tree that was draped in great white sheets of fungus.

'I can't believe it,' the officer was saying. 'You told me, but how could he ignore urgent messages like that?'

'This is Reis, Petra. There hasn't been anything really urgent for him to answer... ever, I think.' Sebastian shook his head, and Ysentrud held back, keeping to the shadows gathered beneath the wide hoods of the giant mushrooms surrounding the courtyard. Listening.

'Well, something urgent has happened now,' Petra said. 'So will he do it?'

'No,' Sebastian said, and his mouth twisted into a sneer. 'The daemons of the warp are a legend in his head. The Space Marines are very real, and the thought of them here, where they might upend his carefully curated life – that terrifies him much more.'

'He's a fool,' she said, frowning. 'Then how will we get him to–'

'Activate the beacon?' Sebastian asked. 'We won't. But that doesn't matter. It's done. I did it right before I came over here.'

'You–' The woman stared at the Regent Next. 'Your father will rage.'

Sebastian shrugged. 'Let him. It's too late.' He moved towards her, as if he were going to embrace her, but Ysentrud cleared her throat and stepped out into the courtyard, making her presence known before they touched.

'Regent Next,' she said, bowing. 'I am Learned Ysentrud Wyrbuk, holder of the complete history of Reis, from settlement to present, and I am yours by your father's hand.' She looked up in time to see him stepping away from the lash commander. She looked angry, but he appeared amused.

'Of course you are, and of course he did.' He straightened his suit, then started moving. 'Time to get back to the base. Father should have found out what I've done by now, and hopefully screamed himself hoarse.' As he passed Ysentrud, he patted her on the top of the head, and she had to fight not to duck away. 'I don't have time for your history now, Learned, but stay with us. We'll show you that history is something to be made, not memorised.'

CHAPTER SEVEN

The mission room's walls were sheathed in stone, basalt brought in from the Rock, carved with the curling forms of monsters from long-dead Caliban. That same stone formed the table that sat in the middle of the room and the benches flanking it, both scratched and worn by the touch of armour that was significantly harder than it. In the air over the table a system chart drifted, a single sun surrounded by the looping orbits of six planets in the midst of a vastly simplified star chart. The Fifth's command squad was standing around the table, silently examining the chart, when Lazarus walked in. Interrogator-Chaplain Demetrius, Ancient Jequn, Apothecary Asbeel, Lieutenant Zakariah, Techmarine Ephron – and a stranger. A man who wasn't Amad.

Lazarus' eyes swept across them all. He didn't pause to stare at the new man. He didn't have to. He'd already memorised his face, the sharp features, the deep-set eyes, the dark hair, short but still longer than anyone else's in the command squad.

Raziel. Librarian Raziel, Lexicanium class. The Fifth had been smashed on Husk, had lost a lieutenant and enough men for four squads, and Azrael had sent them out again with this one man, this psyker to fill that gap. Was he that desperate, Lazarus wondered, or was he that angry? He didn't know. After their private meeting, the Supreme Grand Master hadn't spoken to him. Azrael's orders for the Fifth had come three days later, delivered by a servo-skull.

Anger was at least part of it, Lazarus was sure.

'Brothers,' he said, and waved them all to sit. They did, their armour clicking against the stone. On the walls behind them their helmets rested in alcoves, lurking in the shadows like the faces of sleeping gods. 'Reis. Our next duty.' His gauntleted hands touched the controls of the holo-slate built into the table, and the chart above it changed. The second planet grew until it filled the field, a network of lines drawing a globe dominated by water. There were only two continents, and they were as far from each other as they could get, one in the northern hemisphere, one in the south. Glyphs of data swam into the air around the planet, indicating that it was a Terran-type world with a temperate climate, settled at least thirteen thousand years before, lost during the Horus Heresy and then reclaimed by the Imperium six thousand years ago.

'Reis was a Knight world when it was rediscovered,' Lazarus told them. 'House Halven controlled the war machines that protected and pacified its population, though they were in bad repair. As part of the process for rejoining the Imperium, an Adeptus Mechanicus forge was established on the northern continent, Norsten.

'Reis has had a relatively peaceful existence for the standards of this sector, and the attention of Space Marine forces was not needed there for millennia. Not until just over one thousand years ago, when a previously undetected flaw in reality opened up on the southern continent, Sudsten. This portal to the immaterium, the Redwash Gate, spilled out an army of daemons that overwhelmed House Halven, destroying their machines and causing significant loss of civilian life. The planet would have been lost but for the arrival of the First, Fourth and Seventh Companies. The Dark Angels destroyed the daemons, sealed the gate, and left behind a signal beacon to be activated if it should ever open again.'

Lazarus tapped the controls, and a red mark appeared on the southern continent, pulsing like a bloody pinprick. 'That beacon has been sounded.'

Interrogator-Chaplain Demetrius stared at it, frowning. 'A portal that unleashed a horde of daemons requiring three companies of Dark Angels to contain, one of which was the Deathwing, reopens, and only we are sent. I am flattered by the Supreme Grand Master's faith in the Fifth.'

Especially a Fifth that was reduced, that had only been home long enough for some basic repairs and partial replenishment.

'Astropathic contact was made with Reis after the Rock received the beacon,' Lazarus said. 'The Regent Prime of Reis, descendant of the destroyed Knight house, claims that the beacon was activated by an overzealous underling in response to some kind of plague. At least, that is the meaning our astropath divined from what was sent through the warp. But the Supreme Grand Master is concerned. We have been sent to examine the Redwash Gate ourselves, to make sure its seals stand. If they do, we are to remind the Regent Prime and his overzealous underlings that the Dark Angels are not to be summoned except in ultimate extremis. That reminder is meant to be harsh.'

Lieutenant Zakariah nodded, but his eyes were on that red

mark. 'And what if the gate is not sealed? If these reassurances are lies, prompted by some trick?'

'Then we will gauge the situation, communicate with the Rock, and begin to prosecute our assault on whatever enemy we find.'

Lazarus let them consider that in silence. The mission might be deadly – anything that dealt with the denizens of the warp was. But that wouldn't give them pause. They were Dark Angels, and their entire purpose was to win the battles that would shatter any other force of humanity. The troubling thing about it was that it might *not* be deadly, that it might result in nothing more than a chastisement of a few local officials, a duty far below them.

Was Azrael that angry? Or did the Supreme Grand Master think it best to throw him and his Fifth into another battle to wrench his mind away from the ideas he had voiced when they spoke last?

No. Lazarus pushed the thought away. It was useless. Worse than that, it was weakness. He trusted his orders because he trusted his commander. He might not agree with Azrael on everything, but they agreed on this – the Ruinous Powers were the greatest threat to humanity in the galaxy, and any hint of their presence was to be burned out of reality like an infection.

'Because of the nature of this threat, Supreme Grand Master Azrael has provided us with a new brother.' Lazarus looked to Raziel, who nodded. The man was tall, as tall as him and Lieutenant Zakariah. A Primaris Marine, something that until recently had been unheard of within the Librarium. 'Librarian Raziel will make sure the flaw is sealed. I welcome him to the Fifth.'

'Welcome, brother,' the others intoned, staring at him speculatively. Librarians were invaluable, but they were different, even more so than the Techmarines. They were psykers, and despite the ribbons and badges of purification set on Raziel's armour, they still drew their strength from the same source as the Ruinous Powers, and no one ever forgot that.

Especially Lazarus. He didn't see the flames when he looked at Raziel. But he felt the ghost of their heat in the man's presence.

'I thank the Emperor that I might serve.' Raziel's voice was smooth, even, but his eyes looked to Lazarus as he spoke. Curious, not challenging, as if the man was turning over what he had heard about the Master of the Fifth's enmity for psykers.

Lazarus nodded back to him, schooling his expression, but he could feel his hand touch the hilt of his sword as the remembered pain of burning twisted beneath his skin.

He ignored that heat as he gave them each their orders, establishing how the company would function now without Amad. When they were done he sent them off, but Demetrius lingered.

'It is a strange mission, brother,' the Interrogator-Chaplain said when they were alone.

'We have had stranger ones,' answered Lazarus.

'True. But none given to us by an angry Supreme Grand Master.'

'The Supreme Grand Master and I met in his own chambers. How would you know his mood?'

'Have you forgotten what it was like before you were promoted, brother?' Demetrius asked. 'The mood of the Supreme Grand Master rings through the Rock like a bell. Every battle-brother can read the currents that move through the ranks of our leaders as well as they can read the currents of battle. They are,' he said with a thoughtful look, 'often similar talents.'

Lazarus frowned. They were Space Marines. Human but more, inheritors of the gene-wrought might of their primarch, one of the twenty immortal sons of the Emperor Himself. And they were Dark Angels, the masters of secrets. Yet gossip still ripped through them as if they were characters in a pict drama meant for the worker masses of a hive city.

'This mission is not a punishment,' he said, his voice touched with irritation. But he softened it, remembering his own thoughts. 'My discussion with Azrael was… heated. As words between brothers can sometimes be. But the Supreme Grand Master is a master strategist, and a leader with almost no match beyond the primarchs themselves. He would not let a disagreement interfere with his plans for the Chapter. We are here because he needs us to be here.' *And perhaps also to keep me quiet and away from the Rock with my heretical notions,* he silently added.

'Of course,' Demetrius said. 'We are the Dark Angels. Politics are not our battlefield.' But the Interrogator-Chaplain's mismatched eyes were on Lazarus, and his lips held the faintest of smiles. Then it slipped away. 'But this mission feels tainted by the political situation of that planet. A Regent Prime, the descendant of a Knightly house that lost its Knights, controls one half of a world while the other is controlled by the Fabricator Locum of an Adeptus Mechanicus forge. An awkward, unusual way to share power.'

'Awkward and unusual are the usual in the Imperium, it would seem,' Lazarus said. 'That daemonic invasion reshaped Reis' power structure. That's a matter for the bureaucracy. What I care about is that beacon. If the Redwash Gate has opened again, when they claim it has not…'

'Then the population may have been turned. Become collaborators with the Ruinous Powers, or possessed by them.' Interrogator-Chaplain Demetrius shook his head. 'If that proves true, we may be forced to wipe out the entire population to cleanse the infection.'

'We will do what we must,' said Lazarus. 'The containment of the Redwash Gate is our only concern on that planet.'

'Hence Brother Raziel.' Demetrius looked at Lazarus. '*You* concern him.'

'I concern him,' Lazarus said, and Demetrius nodded.

'Just so. You are death to psykers, brother. And a Chaos sorcerer was death to you.'

'He is our brother, psyker or not. And he is needed for this mission. I will make use of him, and value his contributions, the same as I do you and yours.'

'I know. But I am not the one you need to reassure,' Demetrius said. 'He is also Primaris.'

'And what is that supposed to mean?' Lazarus asked.

'It is another layer.' There was nothing subtle or small about the smile that now crossed the Interrogator-Chaplain's face. 'After days of fighting me in the practice halls, you should know how we Firstborn feel about facing men taller than us.'

'Homicidal,' Lazarus said, remembering the furious bouts they had engaged in, pushing each other to their limits.

'A better word, brother,' said Demetrius, 'is fratricidal.'

Reis hung over the mission room's table, glowing like a gem in the holofield. Clouds swirled over the ocean, brilliant blue only interrupted in two places. On one side of the planet was the continent Norsten. It lay near the north pole of Reis, and it was a great blotch of grey and white, the colours of stone and snow, only its southern coast faintly green with plant life. Even from orbit, scars could be seen cutting across its face, the marks of the great mines the Adeptus Mechanicus had carved into the planet. Between those mines, in the centre of the continent, a pall of smoke and a tangle of tiny marks, like ugly glyphs piled atop one another, marked the forge. According to the data files, the Adeptus Mechanicus used the products of their mines to build servitors and other cyborg tools.

On the other side of the planet was Sudsten, a great green splotch that sat just below Reis' equator. Hot and wet, it was lush with flora, a blanket of jungle covering every bit of land except for the highest peaks and the dark scar of Kap Sudsten, the capital city and space port. Norsten was a manufacturing centre, but Sudsten and the rest of Reis were agri, a source of food and botanicals. The oceans were vast farms for fish and kelp, both products hauled in to be processed into nutripaste for export to local hive worlds. The jungles on the land were overrun with fungi, some beneficial, some highly toxic. Both were harvested for various uses, but the main export was a kind of mould that could be processed into a potent variety of stimm. The powerful drug wiped away pain and boosted strength and vigour in its users, making them able to fight no matter how extensive their wounds. This particular variety had a side effect that clouded soldiers' minds, making them almost rabid, homicidal berserkers who could barely be controlled. That made it useless for the Space Marines, but highly prized for certain branches of the Astra Militarum and the Adeptus Ministorum.

A useful world. Reis had met its quotas for the Imperial tithe for the thousand years since the daemonic invasion that had almost overrun it. So it was ignored, its population left to live, breed, toil and die in peaceful obscurity. Until that beacon had been sounded.

Until the Dark Angels had come.

Lazarus' command squad was gathered at the table, staring at that slowly turning globe, waiting. All except for Techmarine Ephron, who was staring blankly at nothing, lost in the streams of knowledge being fed through his black carapace by the

Sword of Caliban, and Librarian Raziel, who had his eyes shut and his hands folded in front of him. He might have been praying, except for the occasional twitch of his body, as if he were fighting to keep from moving. Still, he shifted sometimes as if dodging an invisible blow or striking an unseen enemy. Behind his closed lids, his eyes moved and twitched, never still.

The waiting silence was broken by a deep voice echoing through the ship's vox-system. *'Final thrust in ten seconds. Five seconds. Three. Two. One.'* The strike cruiser shuddered as its massive engines fired. At the table, the Dark Angels barely moved, braced against the change of momentum. Then in a moment it was done, and the ship fell still, silent, the deep vibrations from its engines gone. *'Orbit established.'*

Lazarus waited a moment, then spoke. 'Brother Ephron.'

'System is empty except for a cargo hauler, the *Pride of Texcalca*. They offloaded five thousand condemned mortals to the Adeptus Mechanicus forge for processing into servitors, and are now beginning to lift cargo for distribution.'

A tiny icon appeared in the void over the planet, indicating the cargo ship. It was on the other side of the world from the glyph representing the *Sword of Caliban*.

'We have tied into the noosphere of Sudsten, and have laid our codes of dominion over the local bureaucracy and Militarum.' Ephron shuddered, then his eyes lit up, the Techmarine aware of the room around him again as he pulled out of the hard, angular world of the cogitators. 'Activity on the planet below seems normal. There is fighting around the Redwash Gate, but it is limited to small-arms, congruent with the local government claims of a police action being prosecuted against citizenry.'

Ephron looked to Lazarus. 'I also made introduction to the Adeptus Mechanicus forge. Fabricator Locum Gretin Lan spoke to me herself, and allowed me limited access to their noosphere. All seems nominal there.'

'Limited?' Lazarus asked.

'To exact protocols,' Ephron said. 'But no more.'

The Adeptus Mechanicus were like that. But if Ephron had been troubled by them, he would have said, and Lazarus nodded. 'Brother Raziel?'

The Librarian twitched one more time, then went very still. His deep breathing changed, and his eyes stopped moving behind their lids, then he blinked them open. His pupils, enormous, tightened in the light and he took a long, slow breath. 'Master Lazarus,' he said. His voice was very precise, each word spoken carefully. He didn't sound tentative – it was more as though he considered each word thoughtfully before saying it. It stood out in contrast to the quick, clipped style Lazarus used. 'I have surveyed the local immaterium. I found the scar left by our brothers when they sealed the gate on the planet below, and traced the currents that press against it. As of yet, I can find no breaking of their work.'

'The seal stands?' Lazarus asked.

'As far as I can tell from this distance, yes.'

As far as he could tell. Lazarus frowned, tapping an armoured finger on the scarred stone tabletop. He could not perceive the flows of machine knowledge the way a Techmarine could, the same way he could not perceive the psychic currents of the immaterium like a Librarian. They were both ways of seeing closed to him, but while he had no issue taking Ephron at his word, it grated at him whenever he had to listen to a psyker describe their perceptions of the immaterium. Even if they were a Brother-Librarian. It was a bias, and it was one he needed to acknowledge and accept. But it still grated.

'So far then, the reports received from the Regent Prime have been borne out.' Lazarus' finger still tapped against the table-top, ceramite cracking against stone. 'This may be a false alarm. But we did not come all this way to immediately turn back.' The rock beneath his fingertip went rough, his tapping digging a shallow hole. He stilled his hand, then pushed himself up to standing. 'We are going down to speak with the man our-selves, and then we are going to the site of the Redwash Gate. Brother Raziel will examine its seals, and we will clear the area of all possible hostiles.'

'You mean to interfere in their little war?' Interrogator-Chaplain Demetrius asked.

'I mean to clear the fighting away from that gate,' Lazarus answered. 'If it's undisturbed, we shall make sure it stays that way. And we will then bring judgement on whoever brought us here unnecessarily. They will learn that the Dark Angels are not their dogs to be called whenever they hear a noise in the dark. We are the Knights of Caliban, forged to fight monsters, and fear rides with us.'

CHAPTER EIGHT

'Where are they?' Regent Next Sebastian strode down the corridor ahead of Ysentrud, snapping questions at Petra as he went. He was dressed in a violet suit whose colour was eye-wincingly bright, with a silver vest so shiny it seemed woven together from mirrors. His hair was braided back neatly, and Ysentrud couldn't understand how he'd done it. They had only received word that the Dark Angels were swooping down on Kap Sudsten a scant twenty minutes ago. Sebastian had been sparring with Petra, but when word of the descending ship had flashed through the palace he had cleaned and dressed himself in a flash. Petra, with her simpler uniform, had barely kept up. Ysentrud, who had nothing to do since she only ever dressed the same way, had still felt rushed as Sebastian had got ready and then torn out of his apartments, heading for the Hall of the Fallen.

'Circling into land,' Petra said. She was shrugging as she walked, fighting to make her uniform settle correctly as she listened to the micro-bead set in her ear, relaying the frantic communications of Reis Militarum. They had only become aware of the Space Marine strike cruiser orbiting their world a few minutes before the landing ship had parted from it, spiralling down towards the city. A flaw in intelligence that had set the Regent Prime raging – well, raging more, from what Ysentrud could tell. The man had been apoplectic ever since he had learned the Dark Angels were coming.

There was a sudden boom, a crack of thunder that shook the palace. Ysentrud stopped, frozen by the sound. Was Regent Prime Oskaran right? Were the Space Marines angry for being called in? Were they attacking? But ahead of her, Petra and Sebastian hadn't broken stride, though they looked towards the windows as they passed.

'Sonic boom,' said Petra. 'They're coming down hard and fast.'

'I doubt they know any other way to land,' Sebastian said. 'That probably cracked half the windows in the city. Father will have another reason to be angry.'

Ysentrud started moving again, following them, wondering for what must have been the ten thousandth time what was wrong with them. After that sham of her presentation, she had trailed after Sebastian when he'd let her, which was often. He told her that he wanted her to remember what was happening, even though she had explained that wasn't her purpose. Ysentrud was a Learned Wyrbuk, not an etcher. She didn't remember every single thing that was spoken in front of her, unlike those poor bastards. But Sebastian didn't seem to understand the difference, or care. So, lacking anything else to do, she trailed along behind him as he sparred with Petra, argued with his father and stood around the Reis Home Levies' base, watching as his father's forces fought their sporadic war against the gris in the muck of Sudsten's central jungles. Most of that time, Sebastian had been appropriately sober, thoughtful and engaged. But sometimes when Ysentrud was alone with him, or with him and Petra, his mask slipped, and he seemed to watch everything unfold around him with smug amusement.

It was unsettling, but she doggedly trailed along behind, even though she had no idea what she was supposed to be doing, even though Sebastian spent most of the time ignoring her completely, even though she was tired and annoyed and confused and wished she could just sit somewhere quiet and run through the folk-tales she'd etched into her brain on the sly. Even if the gris stories seemed a bit too close to home right now.

When they reached the Hall of the Fallen, the great arched space was eerily quiet even though it was packed full of courtiers. Every member of Reis' ruling class was there, and the floor was overflowing with colour like a flower garden run riot, everyone wearing their best and brightest suits even though the air processors still hadn't been fixed and the heat was oppressive. The crowd was sweating and swaying, but they stayed crammed together on the sides of the hall, leaving a wide aisle of empty space in the centre for what was coming.

Despite how crowded it was, the courtiers made space for Sebastian, Petra and Ysentrud to pass. The Regent Next barely had to slow his stride as he cut through the throng, heading towards his father upon the throne. Ysentrud was nervous – being close to Sebastian during what was to come could be hazardous. Or at least that was the opinion of Oskaran, who had told his son that the Dark Angels were going to mount his skull next to the beacon as a warning to the next fool who was tempted to touch it.

But she fell into place behind him and Petra, trapped

between them and the administrator of the southern fisheries. The man was in his finest suit, his badges of office slung around his neck, and Ysentrud wondered if everyone had been waiting, fully dressed, ever since the Space Marine ship had appeared. Probably. They were all on edge – terrified, really, by the stink of their sweat. They were the powers on this planet, but now a greater power had appeared, one they had no control over. The Dark Angels might be the heroes in the history of Reis, but right now everyone assembled seemed to be wishing that was where they had stayed, safely in the past.

It was too late though. Outside, there was the sound of engines howling as a ship landed in the plaza before the palace, the distant thump of landing gear upon the stone. The doors at either end of the corridor leading to the plaza had swung open, and infantry of the Reis Home Levies lined both sides in their best dress, the black cloth wet with sweat and dusty with spores. Frustratingly, Ysentrud couldn't see down that corridor, so she kept her eyes on the Regent Prime and his son. She knew when the Dark Angels were out of their ship by the way Oskaran's face paled, the way his hands gripped his thighs, wrinkling the shining gold of his trousers. His son, though… Sebastian looked calm, collected, focused. Keen. He was waiting, and she wondered for what, but Ysentrud's attention was pulled away by a sound, like distant rolling thunder.

The noise came down the hall, growing, echoing, the crunching march of heavy, metal boots grinding against stone. The floor was vibrating beneath Ysentrud's feet, and she could feel her heart beating fast. There was a shadow at the door, and then they were there. One, five, then more than a dozen, they filled the space in the centre of the hall. It had seemed so wide, so empty, but now it was crowded with red-eyed giants wrapped in dark green armour, and Ysentrud stared at them with a mix of terror and wonder.

The way they moved... That was what shocked her. All the stories in her head described them as huge. If she wanted to go into memen, she could have named exactly how tall they were from tactical charts footnoted in the histories. Their size was overpowering, their helmeted heads towering over everyone in the room, and their armoured shoulders seemed almost as broad as the Dark Angels were tall, but it wasn't surprising. Anyone that big, wrapped in armour that thick, should have been clumsy, oaf-like, shambling monsters. Instead, they moved with purpose, graceful and fast. Too fast. Watching them approach was like seeing a predator stalk closer. Ysentrud felt herself going still, absolutely still, as if she were in the presence of a beast that would snap her up in one quick bite if it noticed her.

The one in the lead stopped right before the throne, so close to Ysentrud she could smell the hot metal-and-electric scent of his armour, could see the subtle movement of his great winged helm as he took them all in through his crimson eye slits. Then he stopped, focusing on the Regent Prime. He was so still. One of his gauntleted hands rested on the hilt of the gigantic sword that rode his waist, a blade that must have been as long as Ysentrud was tall, the other hovering a hair's breadth from the grip of the massive gun that hung on his other side. He might have been a statue, except for the swaying of the robe he wore over his armour, whiter than hers even though it showed signs of much use and repair. When he finally spoke, the sudden sound of his deep voice made Ysentrud and most of the nobles jump.

'We have come. The servants of the Emperor, the protectors of the Imperium. We are the First, the sons of the Lion, we are the Dark Angels, and you have called us forth.' The Space Marine waited until the last echoes of his booming voice had gone to silence, waited until Oskaran had finally pulled himself together, ready to speak. Then he spoke one more word. 'Why?'

The Regent Prime was pale, sweating, faint. But he held himself up straight in his throne and kept his voice level, somehow. 'Champion of the Imperium. I say to you with great pain in my heart, there was a mistake.'

'A mistake.' The Space Marine's voice was hard and sharp as diamonds. Ysentrud wanted nothing more than to slink away from him and hide, and she wasn't even the focus of the Space Marine's regard. She made herself take a deep breath, fighting against hyperventilation. In the crowd of nobles, there were already ripples spreading where some had fainted. That would be her victory, she told herself. She would stand up here, and watch what happened, and not pass out no matter how terrifying it was. She might not be an etcher, but this meeting would stay with her forever. But despite that determination, she had to fight to keep her eyes from turning away as the commander lifted his hands to his head.

The winged helm hissed and clicked when his palms touched it, then lifted easily away. The Space Marine tucked it beneath his arm, and Ysentrud could see his face. It was… a face. He looked like a man, handsome but not inhumanly so. He had the smooth skin of youth, but his short-cropped hair was grey. His eyes were grey too, and his cheekbones were wide, jaw square. It was a rugged face, but there was an intelligence in his eyes that made him seem more thoughtful than ruthless. A warrior scholar, not a berserker, and she felt the first hint of something that wasn't fear staring at him. This man was a weapon, but he was forged to fight monsters, not mortals like her.

Or at least that was a nice thing to try to believe.

'I am Lazarus, Master of the Fifth Company, and I say this. I do not suffer mistakes. You have called the Adeptus Astartes, the last defence of man. Explain why, now.'

'Commander Lazarus–' the Regent Prime began, then was cut off.

'Master Lazarus!' The correction came from the Space Marine that stood behind and to the left of Lazarus. He was armoured like the rest, but his suit was painted black and the robe he wore over its heavy plates was dark green. The faceplate of his helmet gleamed like a mirror, and it was shaped like a skull, grim in the shadows of his hood. His eyes were mismatched, one glowing red, the other green, and he held a brutal-looking club that ended in a silver skull gripping a two-bladed sword in its teeth. He was a figure of terror, and the flicker of anger that went through the Regent Prime's eyes at being corrected was gone in an instant, smothered by fear and self-preservation.

'Master Lazarus,' Oskaran said, barely saving himself from a stammer. 'I will explain. A foul infection has touched Reis, and its unclean victims attack my citizens and my forces. The inflicted, the gris as they are called, have overrun some territory in the middle of Sudsten, but it is inconsequential. My Levies are moving to take it back even now.'

'I care nothing for your territory. I care nothing for your afflictions,' Lazarus said, dropping each word like a block of ice. 'The Dark Angels came to this world over a thousand years ago to battle an incursion of daemons flooding in from the Redwash Gate. After they killed the servants of the Ruinous Powers, they sealed that gate and left behind a beacon, to be activated if and only if that seal was broken. So, tell me, Regent Prime of Reis, do the seals yet stand? Or is the Redwash Gate open once again, to spill hell across this world?'

Oskaran tried to stare back at the Space Marine, but he couldn't. Ysentrud saw him fail, saw his eyes drop away from Master Lazarus' face. The Regent Prime stared down, obviously searching for words, and Ysentrud was amazed that he hadn't simply blamed Sebastian yet. But Sebastian apparently had no use for this possible mercy.

'The seals may stand, or not, we do not know,' the Regent Next said. 'But we know they are under attack. Our enemy bears the grey motley, the mark of the gris, and they have seized the land that holds the Redwash Gate. They wish to break it open, so that they may release the evil that created them once again.'

'Sebastian!' snapped Oskaran. 'Silence!'

But Master Lazarus raised one hand and turned to face the Regent Next. Ysentrud, just behind his shoulder, had to fight not to duck behind him completely, to use Sebastian as a shield. Had she thought Lazarus looked like a man? Maybe, in the arrangement of his features. But there was something in his eyes, a light behind those grey irises that scorched through her and made her want to kneel and ask for forgiveness for being so flawed, so human.

'What is this gris?' he asked, his voice low, but so deep it still filled the hall.

'The gris,' Sebastian said smoothly, 'are the mould that creeps. The soft lurkers.'

'Those are names,' Lazarus said. 'Not answers.'

'Of course. Please allow me to explain.' Sebastian reached back, and then his hand was on Ysentrud's shoulder, pulling her forward. She froze, resisting, but he was much stronger, and she found herself stumbling past him. She would have fallen if he hadn't caught her by the back of her robes and held her up, right in front of the Dark Angel.

So close. Emperor's blackened bones, so damned close. She

barely reached his waist, and had to tip her head back to see his face above her. Which she did for only a second, before she snatched her head down to gaze at the toes of his giant green boots. In her mind, though, clear as if it had been etched, she could still see the image of her own red eyes reflected in his. She stared down, trying to breathe, and barely heard Sebastian speak.

'This Wyrbuk knows the history.'

He wanted her to tell him. It was impossible, insane, she couldn't speak to this... this thing that was more than a man. She couldn't, she couldn't, but at the same time she could feel the training moving through her, could feel her breath fall into the patterns she needed to pull herself into memen. The recall state swept over her, and suddenly she was drifting, all emotions pushed back into some far corner of her mind. She did not lift her head, but she folded her hands before her, straightened her back and spoke.

'My lord. The first gris encounter was recorded six hundred and thirty-eight years ago Reis, or 9.411.371.M41 approximated Imperium, though unofficial and partial accounts have been collected from up to forty-six years before that date. At that time, there was believed to only be one gris, and sightings of the creature were scattered and few. Witnesses described a large humanoid, covered in grey mould, moving through the jungle and avoiding contact. At first the gris was considered folklore, but eventually it became clear that the gris was an actual creature, or creatures, of unknown origin. As sightings increased, it became apparent there was more than one, with varied appearance, some appearing almost human with only patches of grey mould. This was called the grey motley.

'Over the years, the number of gris encounters increased, and they became deadly. The gris attacked lone citizens or small groups, killing them and taking their brains, spinal cords, and other parts of their central nervous systems. The purpose for these stolen organic components is still unknown. Three decades after the first official encounter, the gris began mounting raids on towns and stimm farms. At this point, Regent Prime Arin the Third ordered the Reis Home Levies to purge the creatures. The campaign took twenty-seven years, and resulted in the deaths of one thousand three hundred and seventy-eight military, at least eleven thousand seven hundred and twelve civilians, and an unknown number of gris.

'While prosecuting the campaign, the Reis Home Levies took a number of gris prisoner. It was found that they were each once human, now infected with a previously unidentified species of fungus, designated "grey pall" by its discoverers due to morphological similarities between it and the fungal species know as black pall. Black pall is the saprophytic fungus used to manufacture the stimm type known as STX5789-G, also known by the common names Black Ball, Rager, Brain Burn and Fervour Fire. This grey pall affected the nervous system of those infected by it in ways that seemed similar to the stimulant effects of black pall, but there were other effects that were not understood.

'Biological examination was inconclusive. The infected universally died soon after their capture, cause unknown. Interrogation proved fruitless. The infected did not speak, yet somehow they could perform complex, coordinated actions. Theories were advanced for the creation of a group mind among the infected, but were never confirmed.

'The origin of the grey pall was never discovered, nor how the infection began. Since they originated after the Redwash War, it was conjectured that daemonic influence was to blame somehow, their warp energy causing a deadly mutation, but this theory was never-'

'Enough,' Sebastian said, and the stream of words pouring out of Ysentrud cut off. The memen state ended and she took a deep breath, looking up. She'd forgotten what was in front of her and blinked at Master Lazarus for a long moment. Her emotions were starting to bleed back, and she could feel the chill of her fear returning, but for that instant she could look at him almost calmly. *He has a teacher's face*, she thought, *despite those frightening eyes.* Then her composure fled, and she dropped her gaze, hands twisting together, terrified at having his attention.

'You can see my concern over the gris' resurgence.' Sebastian took Ysentrud by the shoulder and moved her back, and she happily went.

'The gris are defeated,' the Regent Prime snapped. He seemed to take strength from arguing with his son. 'There are always a few of the horrible things out in the jungle, attacking the unprotected. This resurgence is just–'

'Enough.' Lazarus spoke the word to the Regent Prime with the same curt dismissal Sebastian had used for Ysentrud, and she smiled at the ground hearing it. 'You have called, we have come, now we will act. We will go to this Redwash Gate and secure it, destroying any who impede us. There, I will judge if you have squandered your call and wasted my time, and mete out any necessary retribution.'

Those words wiped away Ysentrud's smile. Necessary retribution. She fought not to shake, even though she was faultless. She was faultless, right? She was certainly powerless, but that didn't help the anxiety spinning through her brain. If this Master Lazarus decided that Sebastian had earned retribution, how far into his household would it extend? To her? She was standing beside him, and he'd brought the Dark Angels commander's attention to her, and–

'You will come with me.'

Ysentrud's head jerked up. Lazarus had raised one massive gauntlet and was pointing his finger straight at her, and her heart almost stopped. Then, an age later, she realised he was speaking to the Regent Next.

'Your will, Master Lazarus,' Sebastian said, bowing. His voice was crisp and calm. He was sweating, but Ysentrud was sure that was mostly the heat. The Regent Next seemed to be the only one in the Hall of the Fallen besides the Space Marines who still had an ounce of confidence. 'Shall I bring my guard?'

'No. You will cede the field to me,' Lazarus answered.

Oskaran cleared his throat, his face red with a welter of barely contained emotions. 'I'll inform the Reis Home Levies to work with you, Master Lazarus,' he said.

'What part of "you will cede the field to me" did you not comprehend?' Master Lazarus spoke calmly, but the complete lack of care in the way he addressed the Regent Prime seemed a slap in this place. 'Order them to pull back. Anything under arms near that gate will be exterminated.'

'Understood, Master Lazarus,' Oskaran said stiffly. 'May I ask how long they have to retreat?'

'The length of time it will take us to transition to the battlefield in our Thunderhawk. We leave. Now.'

The Regent Prime looked as if he wished to protest, but he shut his mouth and nodded instead. With a hand he gestured to the chief administrator of the Reis Home Levies. She nodded to him and moved away, placing a finger to the micro-bead set in her ear and whispering.

'Now?' Sebastian asked, his voice still smooth. 'I appreciate the need for haste, but might I have a few minutes to change into something more suitable for the jungle?'

'No,' Lazarus said, raising his winged helm. As he locked

it back on, two of the Dark Angels marched forward to flank Sebastian.

'Go,' one ordered, his deep voice turned to a mechanical growl by his helmet.

Sebastian nodded and started to walk away, his hand brushing Petra's before he went. Ysentrud watched him go, and the knot in her belly began to relax, at least a little. If the Dark Angels decided to mete out some kind of discipline onto her keeper, she would at least be far away. And hopefully forgotten.

The Dark Angels were turning, moving out of the hall with that same fluid grace that seemed so at odds with the heavy, rumbling tread of their feet. But as Lazarus turned, his robes flaring around him, he looked over his shoulder. This time, his red eyes were on Ysentrud.

'You also.'

Ysentrud stared at him, all the terror coming back, and her feet refused to budge until Lash Commander Karn gave her a shove forward. Seeing her move, Lazarus turned his back on her and walked away. Ysentrud trailed behind, wrapped in her robes and her terror.

CHAPTER NINE

While Lazarus waited for the last of his men to board their Thunderhawk, he reached through his black carapace and pulled in the reports sent down from the *Sword of Caliban*. Nothing had changed around the site of the Redwash Gate. Continued auspex scans had coloured in the battle maps a little, but the jungle hid a great deal beneath its canopy, heat and overwhelming life signs. Still, there was enough information for Lazarus to piece together one important change on the road to the site – the shifting of the Reis Home Levies. They were moving back, pulling away from their ragged thrust towards the volcanic mountain where the Redwash Gate stood. No longer trying to regain that territory, not after receiving their orders to retreat.

Lazarus eyed their jerky, haphazard withdrawal and compared it to the projected travel time Techmarine Ephron had calculated. Incompetent as they were, the local forces should still be clear when they landed. That was good. There was no point in killing them. With them moving out, it was time to take his forces in, and he opened a vox-channel to speak to the other Thunderhawk he'd left circling far overhead.

'All squads on *Rage of Angels*, hear me. We are proceeding to secure the Redwash Gate. Mortal Levies forces are in retreat. Squad Jotha.' The Scout squad had never been reassigned back to the Tenth Company, and even if this mission looked like it might be a waste of time, there were still enough unknowns about it to make Lazarus happy to have them. 'Sweep the area around the gate. Locate and classify enemy forces, no engagement if possible. I don't want them to know what is coming.' He paused and looked across the landing craft's hold. The woman who had spoken about the gris was there, trying to figure out how to buckle herself into one of the jumpseats, which was much too big for her. 'These heretics are infected by some foul mould, tainted by the Ruinous Powers. Their skin should bear the mark of their corruption, grey patches of fungus.'

'*Understood,*' Sergeant Asher answered. '*Squad Jotha will infiltrate and avoid confrontation.*'

'Squads Lameth and Hazin, await your assignments. Our brothers still aboard the *Sword of Caliban* will remain in reserve.' Lieutenant Zakariah would be disappointed, but in addition to the Scout squad, Lameth and Hazin, Lazarus had Squad Bethel with him and the Venerable Dreadnought Azmodor, plus all the members of his command squad except Zakariah, who he'd left with the three squads waiting on the strike cruiser. This was already overkill.

The hatch to the Thunderhawk shut with a heavy thump, and in the cockpit Brother Ephron was finishing the blessing of beginnings as he cycled the ship's engines, getting them ready.

'Brace for take-off, brothers. *Adamantine Wings* is ready to fly.' The Techmarine's voice echoed through the ship, and Lazarus watched as the man, Sebastian, grabbed on to the straps holding him to his seat. The woman was still fighting with the buckles, each bigger than her hands. Lazarus loosened his straps enough to lean forward and took the buckles from her. He spoke the act of contrition for mishandling to the Thunderhawk and snapped her in.

'Brace yourself,' he told her as the sound of *Adamantine Wings*' engines built to a shriek.

'My lord–' she started, and then the Thunderhawk leapt into the air, tons of armour and weapons pulled up fast by high-powered engines. Momentum tried to crush Lazarus back into the bulkhead, but the strength in his enhanced body and blessed armour kept him still as stone. The mortal, however, was smashed backwards, unable to speak, the bright red skin of her face pressing tight to the bones beneath, making her look that much more like a skull.

Lazarus had walked over hundreds of worlds in his life – the first and the second. He'd seen mortals dressed and adorned in every kind of fashion, from naked, painted skin to vast dresses made with enough silk to craft a drop chute for a Rhino. This woman was not the most extravagant he'd ever seen, not even close, but she was distinctive with her hairlessness, crimson skin and the black tattooing that made her face look like a skull drifting over her white robes.

It was as though they meant her to look like a servo-skull. And that was how the Regent Prime's son, Sebastian, had treated her. Which was why Lazarus had decided to bring her along.

Questioning her now while she was fighting to breathe wouldn't be much use, so Lazarus reached through his armour and tied in to the pict recorders mounted on *Adamantine*

Wings' hull. They were arcing up, away from the city of Kap Sudsten, heading out over the jungle that covered most of the continent. But he focused back on the city, zooming in until he found what he wanted, and froze the pict there. By this time Ephron had levelled the Thunderhawk off and was streaking towards the distant scar in reality that had once been a portal into the warp. The shifting acceleration forces had eased, and the woman was sitting more forward in her seat, breathing hard but breathing. Lazarus reached up and pulled a data-slate from a compartment above, then transferred the pict from his armour to it.

'What is this?' he asked, showing her the data-slate.

She looked at him, frightened, uncertain, but when she focused on the pict, her breathing evened out and she spoke.

'My lord. This image is of the remains of the Knight Paladin *Pride of Reis.*'

Pride of Reis. What an ugly sense of humour fate had. The ancient war machine must have been close to thirty feet tall once, but now it sprawled backwards against a crumbled wall of rockcrete like a broken doll. The only reason it hadn't slipped down that wall into the mud was the massive brass spear that had been driven through the Knight's thick chest, just below its helmet-like head. That spear had punched through the machine's engines, shattering its heart and spilling out the shining, poisonous blood of its fuel. A thousand years later, nothing grew around it, no plant or flower or moss. It was a dead thing, surrounded by poisoned soil, its once gleaming armour coated with centuries of corrosion and dust.

The Knight was a corpse, desecrated by time, daemons and poison.

'*Pride of Reis* was brought down during the Redwash War, the invasion of Reis by daemonic forces that were connected to the Ruinous Power commonly referred to as Khorne, the Blood God.' The woman's voice was precise, calm, even. 'When the daemonic army swept across Sudsten, House Halven set the southern contingent of its Knights before the city of Kap Sudsten, determined to stop their advance. They were defeated, and each Knight destroyed. The city was then sacked, and seventy per cent of the population was slaughtered. My lord, would you like clarification of any of these subjects?'

'No,' Lazarus said. He watched her carefully, saw the shift in her breathing, the way her pupils shrank down, her facial muscles tightened. She had gone from perfectly relaxed back to her state of badly concealed panic in seconds. 'What is your name?' he asked.

'Master Lazarus. This one is just a Wyrbuk. You don't need her–' Sebastian was cut off when Interrogator-Chaplain Demetrius leaned towards him, his red and green eyes glaring out of his skull mask.

'Do not tell the Master of the Fifth what he needs.' It was loud in the Thunderhawk, but Demetrius' deep voice was easy to hear. The Regent Next went silent, looking away. Frightened, but furious too.

'Ysentrud Wyrbuk. Sir. My lord. My lord sir.' The woman's voice was quiet, and far more uncertain than it had been either time Lazarus had heard it before. He turned back to her and saw the wideness of her eyes. But she was sitting up straight, making herself look at him. At his feet, at least. *Good,* he thought. Weakness must be faced, and fear was mankind's greatest weakness.

'Lord is fine,' he told her. 'Explain to me. What is a Wyrbuk?'

Ysentrud folded her hands together, took a breath and... changed. Lazarus could see her muscles relax, her pupils dilate, could smell the fear stink in her sweat lessen and fade. 'My lord. The Wyrbuk are the information keepers of Reis. The term was originally used to refer to storytellers, oral historians who followed much the same pattern of the rest of human history. But a few centuries after the colonisation of Reis, the name began to be applied to those who survived being poisoned by the toxins of the fungus strain called red pall. Like the other pall strains, spores from red pall have a strong toxic effect on the human central nervous system. Its effects are usually fatal, but approximately five per cent of red pall's victims survive. Those survivors suffer substantial changes. Physically, they lose all their hair, and their skin and eye colour become red. Mentally, the survivors are gifted with vastly increased recall abilities, and it is these survivors who bear the name Wyrbuk today. There are two main types. The first, referred to as etchers, have perfect memory for everything they experience after they recover from the red pall poison. They are useful as recording devices, but are limited in that after approximately a decade their brains become saturated with memories, and they begin to experience information psychosis. The second type are called the Learned, and they are able to take in vast amounts of information perfectly and quickly when administered through a neural communication device called a stycher. When properly trained, a Learned Wyrbuk can recall and repeat that information in an organised manner suitable for teaching or query.'

Mutants, Lazarus thought. Manufactured mutants, in a way. Such alterations to the human pattern were strictly regulated, but things slipped through.

'Ysentrud,' he said, and waited. In a moment her breathing shifted, her pupils tightened, and the fear came back. If a little lessened. 'Can you talk to me without slipping into that altered state?'

'Memen state, my lord,' she said. 'That's what it's called. And yes, but I may need to access it for deeper knowledge.'

He nodded. 'Why were you made like this?'

'My lord. You mean a Learned Wyrbuk?' When he nodded, she tapped a finger to her lips. 'For this. To answer questions. To teach, using the information stored in us.'

'There are simpler ways to do that. Data-slates. Servo-skulls.'

'Yes, my lord,' she said. 'But Reis lost the ability to manufacture such things soon after its founding. The colony ship was damaged in passage through the warp, and a great deal of lore was lost. When the colonists realised what red pall could do, they replaced those machines with Wyrbuks.' Ysentrud touched her bare head, tattooed with black to turn her red skin into a skull. 'They remembered the old machines though. That's why we're marked like this.'

'And when Reis was rediscovered, and brought back into the Imperium?'

Ysentrud shrugged. 'By then, my lord, people were used to the Wyrbuks. They'd used them for thousands of years. And… there was a power struggle that started those first days. The Knightly house did not trust the Adeptus Mechanicus, and did not want to rely solely upon their devices, so the traditions of the Wyrbuk were preserved.'

Preserved. Lazarus considered the word. If this red pall killed ninety-five per cent of those it infected, how many had been sacrificed to create these parodies of servo-skulls? Thousands at least. Probably many more. A vast sacrifice of lives because of suspicion. Because of fear.

'What information do you contain, Learned Ysentrud?'

'My lord. I hold the complete history of Reis, from settlement to present.'

The complete history of Reis. Lazarus checked the images spilling in from the pict caster. Trees and fungi, swamp and jungle, stretching from horizon to horizon. He layered a map over the image, tracing the bright arc of the Thunderhawk's route to the red dot of the Redwash Gate. *Rage of Angels* had already dropped off Scout Squad Jotha and was circling over the target, high enough to stay out of sight.

Lazarus didn't want a history of this place. He wanted to know its present and immediate future, just enough to decide how much retribution he needed to distribute with Enmity's Edge, and to whom. But he had always been greedy for information – a bit of knowledge had swung many battles. The past was a guide to the future. This Wyrbuk might yet be useful.

'Why did House Halven mistrust the Adeptus Mechanicus?' He asked the question as he spun through the first reports from the Scouts, the picts from *Rage of Angels*, auspex scans from the *Sword of Caliban* and local maps of the area. Picking out possible places to drop off the Thunderhawks so that the rest of the squads would start with a noose around the gris forces.

'They needed the Adeptus Mechanicus for their Knights, lord. They were in terrible disrepair after all that time cut off from the Imperium, and the Adeptus Mechanicus were the only ones that could fix them. But with every exchange they bound themselves closer together, each oath teased out in trade for necessary repair work another shackle of resentment for the Knights, until the Adeptus Mechanicus demanded a permanent base on Norsten. House Halven did not like sharing their world with another outside force. And then came the Redwash War.'

'What happened then?' Lazarus asked, marking where he wanted each squad to drop and how.

'That's when the Adeptus Mechanicus destroyed the Knights of House Halven.'

CHAPTER TEN

Adamantine Wings dropped hard onto a rocky tor jutting from the bank of a wide, rushing river, and perched there just long enough for Lazarus to lead his men out into the dark.

His command squad was right behind him, Ancient Jequn tight to his back, the banner of the Fifth carefully furled for the trip through the jungle. Interrogator-Chaplain Demetrius was next, the green-and-red glow from his eyes gone for once, blocked by the filters they had all engaged to hide their presence from their enemies. For now, at least. Apothecary Asbeel came next, and last was the Librarian, Raziel. He bounded down the stones, following Lazarus away from the Thunderhawk, but when they reached the gravel bank of the river he stopped, his helmet cocked as if he were trying to pick some sound out of the chorus of insect and animal noises that filled the night.

Squad Bethel was hard on their heels, their dark green armour making them shadows in the night. Ten Firstborn

Astartes, all veterans, the experience of a thousand drops written in every movement. Last off the ship came Brother Azmodor. The Venerable Dreadnought picked his way down the stones with an unsettling grace, moving like some kind of monstrous ape, the arm bearing his massive power fist helping to steady him as he crunched down to the riverbank to join them.

Behind them the Thunderhawk rose into the air, Techmarine Ephron taking *Adamantine Wings* back up to circle above, auspex scanning the jungle below. The mortals stayed with him, strapped into their seats, waiting for the fight to end. What little fight there would be.

'Squad Bethel. Go.' The order was barely out before they had disappeared between the huge trees, following the path Lazarus had drawn on the tactical map. They would deviate from it soon enough – no amount of scans and picts could capture the actuality of a place – but Lazarus knew they would approximate his intention and spiral in towards where the main concentration of enemy lay.

He'd already ordered Squad Hazin to start their spiral. The terrain on the far side of the Redwash Gate was more difficult, and *Rage of Angels* had to drop them further out. Hazin was one of the newest units in the Fifth, but Lazarus was confident they would match Squad Bethel. They were Primaris Space Marines, an Intercessor squad capable of laying down brutal fields of bolter fire. They would spiral in from the other side, and between them the two squads would destroy the defensive pickets that the gris had set up around the gate, or drive them towards it. The Scouts in Squad Jotha would pick off any remnants that tried to escape outward.

Which left one path for Lazarus and his command squad. The rough, muddy road that ran straight to the low mountain where the Redwash Gate was. The Regent Prime's Levies had spent weeks trying to bash their way down this road, only to be stymied by blockades. Lazarus looked at the chronometer in his helmet. There were eight hours left before dawn, and that was when he expected to meet with Squads Bethel and Hazin at the last line of these gris' defence. It was time to move.

'Dark Angels,' he said, looking back at his command squad and the hulking Dreadnought. Clouds had swept across the sky, blocking the stars and Reis' two moons, so that even on the riverbank the dark was almost absolute. But Lazarus could see them clearly, even without the vision filters of his helm. The gene-seed that made him a Space Marine had changed his eyes, melded them with the occulobe the Apothecaries had implanted in his brain when he was just a neophyte and given him sight that could cut through the shadows. 'With me,' he said, and started towards the road they would walk to war.

The missile cut through the night, drawing a bright line from the rusty bulwark the gris had built across the road. It headed straight towards Brother Azmodor, but the Dreadnought pivoted on one leg, moving like a pit fighter slipping a punch, and the missile streaked into the jungle and slammed into a tree, exploding. The tangled ropes of fungus hanging from the tree's limbs burst outward, burning like fuses, and a sparkling cloud of spores spread through the air.

The night was already thick with spores and smoke and the smell of mud and blood. It added to the chaos of the firefight, the flickering red light of flames, the juddering pops and muzzle flash of stub guns, and the deep bass roar of bolters. It was the familiar cacophony of battle, and it didn't touch Lazarus as he took cover behind the twisted hulk of half a Chimera. The armoured troop transport had belonged to Reis'

Home Levies before it had been torn to pieces by multiple missile strikes, the same missiles that had halted Lazarus and his command squad's advance.

They had passed through two roadblocks before this, choke points along the road where recently felled trees had been stacked and muddy ditches dug. They were crude, hasty fortifications, recently abandoned. The enemy had pulled back before them, even though they had moved in silence through the night.

A wave of brilliant blue split the dark as Azmodor fired his plasma cannon, sending a ball of superheated matter smashing into the wall heaped across the road. Molten metal splashed up and mud flashed into steam and flame, and that part of the rough barrier shifted, but didn't collapse. This wasn't a pile of logs, but cargo containers filled with mud, broken military and construction vehicles, and slabs of rockcrete, stacked in layers. In front of it, a ditch had been dug, and it was full of the filthy water that had flowed in from the swamp on either side of the road. The water in the swamp was deep, the mud beneath it deeper, and they would sink halfway through the planet's crust if they tried to walk through it.

'Brother Azmodor,' Lazarus snapped over the vox as another missile streaked past. 'To me!'

The Dreadnought turned and moved to him, plasma cannon still steaming. Sparks danced off his armour as stub-gun rounds struck it and flew uselessly away.

'Take cover. We don't have the time to break them like this.'

'Then how?' Azmodor rumbled as he caught the shattered hull of the Chimera in his massive hand. From the barrier there was a flare of light as another missile was fired, streaking towards the Dreadnought, but there was a thunder of bolter fire from where the rest of the command squad sheltered behind an overturned truck. They had been waiting for another launch, and the explosive rounds from their guns smashed into the wall around the opening the missile had come from, trying to catch the enemy that had pulled the trigger in a hail of shrapnel. Whether or not they succeeded Lazarus couldn't tell, because by the Emperor's will one of their rounds caught the missile itself only a dozen yards out from the wall. There was a dull thump and the puddles of water on the muddy road all shimmered and splashed under the explosive shock wave. Then the light came, crimson and yellow flashing off Brother Azmodor's armour as the Venerable Dreadnought heaved up the broken Chimera, tipping it on its side.

'We are not meant to hide in cover like mortal infantry,' Azmodor said, crouching with Lazarus behind the tipped-up wreck.

'No,' Lazarus answered. 'But I will not lose your strength to mortals with stolen missile launchers. We have done what was needed, brother, and pinned the target in place. Now we pull the trigger.' Over the vox, he reached out to *Rage of Angels*, circling high overhead. The great trees arching over the road made it impossible to call in an airstrike, but the ordnance he wanted wouldn't be affected by that. 'Squad Lameth. Fall.'

The squad sergeant sent his affirmative, and Lazarus tapped into his feed. Squad Lameth were leaping out of the Thunderhawk, dropping like bombs towards the jungle below. There were flares in the dark as they fired their jump packs, not slowing themselves yet but steering their descent towards the coordinates Lazarus had set for them. He watched their fall, timing it, then spoke to his command squad.

'Full suppressive fire. Now!'

Lazarus stepped out from behind the Chimera's wreckage, his bolt pistol cracking. There were no obvious targets in the rough wall ahead, but he'd noted the crevices where the enemy had been firing from and marked them in his targeting system. Now he snapped shots at them, probably striking nothing, but the exploding rounds would keep the enemy from responding.

The others in the command squad were doing the same, sending a hail of bolter shots towards the barrier, covering the places where the enemy was likely to fire back from. In the middle of them, between Jequn and Demetrius, Raziel was staring down the road, his bolt pistol still at his side. He raised an empty hand and pointed it at the wall, and blue-white light gathered around it, the same colour as the glow in the lenses that covered his eyes. The light in his hand shaped itself into a ball, its core gleaming white as it dripped blue flames like tears, and then it shot towards the wall. It struck one of the rockcrete panels and disappeared into the cracked grey surface. An instant later a figure jerked back from atop the wall, a woman whose skeleton glowed through her skin as if her bones were lit with eldritch fire. Lazarus saw her burn from the inside out, and felt his own skin grow hot. He ignored the feeling, and the twist of rage that came with it, whispering the Litany of Horrors Past as the woman plummeted over the wall, hitting the mud and going still, never having made a sound.

There was noise enough, bolters cracking and the sizzle of the air as Brother Azmodor poured plasma into the wall. A lance of fire and smoke speared out from the Dreadnought's armoured shoulder as he fired a missile, and his storm bolter was thundering, the metal walls of the piled cargo containers sparking as his shells chewed great holes into their sides. Given a little time, the venerable warrior would have blown a hole through the wall by himself, and Lazarus and his command squad could have followed him through, mopping up the infected gris. But the risk of losing the Dreadnought to a missile was too high. The Fifth was injured enough before it even came to this world, and there was no need to take unnecessary chances. So Lazarus fired with his men, keeping the enemy ducked behind their defences, until Squad Lameth slammed into them from behind.

The ten members of the Firstborn assault squad had used their jump packs to land behind the enemy, and now they charged into the gris' undefended flank, their bolt pistols thundering. The sound of them was drowned out a moment later by the growling buzz of chainswords revving. Then the squeal of sharp adamantine teeth biting through metal and bone mixed with the booming of the bolt pistols. After that, it was only seconds before Lazarus heard the voice of Lameth's sergeant over his vox.

'Objective secured. Zero casualties. The Emperor protects.'

'And the Lion triumphs.' Lazarus waved to the others. 'Come. One more.'

When the Redwash Gate had opened a thousand years ago, it had torn a hole in reality right over the caldera of a small but active volcano. In the centuries since, the magma had stopped flowing and the volcano had died, its molten heart gone cold and solid. Now it stood above the jungle, a rough cone covered in stunted trees and brush. At its base, Lazarus stood with his command squad and three units of the Fifth staring up the road carved into the extinct volcano's steep flank. It switchbacked up the mountain, then disappeared into a rough crack two-thirds of the way to the summit, a narrow ravine that drove into the mountain's silent heart like a stab wound.

In that ravine, the gris had gathered their forces, waiting to rain down death on the Dark Angels.

'Will you let us have any of them, Master Lazarus?' Jequn

said, staring hungrily up at the trap, one hand on his sword, the other holding up the unfurled banner.

'You will get a few, my brother,' Lazarus answered.

'Scraps,' the Ancient said, shaking his head. 'Your tactics are wise, but my blade stays far too clean because of them.'

'Do not worry. The Emperor always provides.' Lazarus looked up the road, comparing what he could see in the pre-dawn light with the picts and reports the Thunderhawks and his Scouts had gathered. 'Squad Jotha.' The Scouts were still out in the jungle, sweeping through the area they had cleared. 'Anything?'

'*Nothing,*' Sergeant Asher answered. '*All enemies have pulled back. We have found no stragglers.*'

Lazarus frowned at that, still staring at the distant ravine. Squad Bethel and Squad Hazin had both reported the same thing. They had cleared out their first cluster of targets, and then all the others had melted away, pulled back through the jungle to the volcano. In a way it was exactly Lazarus' plan – to kill the gris waiting in the jungle and drive any survivors here, to the Redwash Gate. But everything had gone too quickly, too well. Even with vox, there should have been more confusion. The other squads should have found some of the enemy still in their camps, or at least not far from them. They had fled with an uncanny efficiency, and Lazarus was troubled by the fact that they *hadn't* found any kind of vox-equipment on any of the bodies or in the camp behind the barricade the Dark Angels had taken.

What they had found was marks on the bodies. Patches of grey, growing across their faces and hands, covering any exposed skin. It was thickest around the eyes, forming ugly masks. What the Regent Next had called the grey motley. The grey pall, the infection that turned farmers and soldiers into these silent fighters, these gris. Silent, but somehow not voiceless.

These gris were communicating somehow. Maybe that didn't matter, not for what he had planned, but an unknown like that bothered him. A bit of knowledge might swing a battle, but a bit of ignorance always hit harder, and this felt like more than a bit. He itched to be able to talk to that Wyrbuk, to question her about those unconfirmed theories regarding a group mind shared between the fungus-infected.

No. Leave the questions for the Inquisition, if they ever visited this backwater. His responsibility was to treat the cancer, not diagnose it. So he would, with fire and steel. Quickly, he laid out his orders, then started up the road with his men.

They let the gris watch them come. The Dark Angels walked up the road, banner unfurled, the filters gone from their glowing eye slits. They were armoured giants whose monstrous shadows stretched long before them as Reis' sun broke the horizon and flooded the world with light. They were only half a mile from the entrance of the ravine, striding up the slope like wolves until they hit the spot Lazarus had marked on the tactical map and exploded into action. Squad Lameth hit their jump packs and leapt off the ground, arcing across the slope to the right of the trail. Lazarus headed to the left, with his command squad, Squad Bethel and Squad Hazin following. There was a trail here, rough and narrow, something made by the shaggy brown animals that grazed the volcanic slopes. It marked a winding path that went all the way to the top, through a maze of broken stone and collapsed lava tubes. Lazarus ran fast and easy in his armour, one eye on the pict casts coming from the Thunderhawks circling overhead.

Rage of Angels came first, diving out of the sun towards the dead volcano. The Thunderhawk hurtled through the air like a stone, but it was nearly silent. The transport ships were graceful as bricks, the Techmarines had told Lazarus, but momentum covered many sins. As the ship came close, the engines kicked on, boosting *Rage of Angels* over the volcano's ragged top, right above the ravine's exit. As it passed, the howl of the ship's engines was joined by the thudding boom of its guns.

Heavy bolters fired streams of shells into the rock walls, where they exploded, sending out storms of shrapnel, while the ship's two lascannons drew streaks of light across the sky that ended in scrawling lines of red-hot stone that slumped and dripped down the ravine. But it was the Thunderhawk cannon mounted on top of the ship that did the real damage. When its shells hit the brittle volcanic stone, they carved deep craters and sent avalanches of broken rock pouring down to the bottom of the gorge.

Rage of Angels was there and gone, a terrible miracle of sudden noise and destruction, but seconds after it streaked off to climb again, *Adamantine Wings* came in from the opposite direction. It followed the same plan as *Rage of Angels,* screaming over the ravine, lascannons and heavy bolters blazing, its battle cannon smashing apart stone like a giant's hammer. Then it was gone, climbing away. One lone missile rose from the ravine, trying to chase the ship, but its fuel supply ran out before it was halfway to the Thunderhawk and it tumbled down to explode somewhere in the jungle.

There was a moment of shocking peace in the early dawn, every animal and insect gone silent after all the crashing noise, and all Lazarus could hear was his even breathing and the groaning, clashing slide of stone falling in the ravine. Then there was the distant howl of engines, and the Thunderhawks were streaking back, ready to make their next pass.

They came in again just as Lazarus broke out of the rough jumble of stone that covered the mountain's flank and into a clearing near the top of the volcano. He could see the ships, *Adamantine Wings* hitting one end of the ravine while *Rage of Angels* struck the other. The ravine was collapsing, rock cascading down, burying the road that ran through it under tons of broken stone. Whatever gris were waiting inside for the Dark Angels were trapped now, if they weren't already dead. The Thunderhawks made one more pass, dropping barrel-shaped cluster bombs between the sheer walls. The bombs went off behind the transports, and flames filled the ravine. Then there was just smoke, rising in a great pillar up into the sky, as if the mountain's heart had reignited.

Lazarus watched it rise, and the thought that Squad Lameth were going to be as disappointed as Jequn went through his head. He'd sent them to sweep around and take the gris from the side when the Thunderhawks had finished, disposing of any remaining resistance, but seeing the rising dust and smoke, he doubted they would have anything to do now. Which was just as he planned. With the Fifth wounded as it was, he was taking no chances. Let these gris die beneath heaven's fire, and they would dispose of the remnants.

Lazarus crested the top of the volcano and looked down at the caldera below. It was a steep-sided crater overgrown with lichen. Its bottom was a circle of rippled stone, seamed with pockets of stagnant rainwater and stunted brush. On one side was a building, a rockcrete bunker with a rusty metal roof. As the Dark Angels moved into the crater, leaping over boulders and grinding down rockslides, shots began to crack out from the narrow window slots in the building. They were stub guns mostly, with a few autoguns mixed in, their power low and their aim poor. Most of the slugs thudded into the gravel around them, and when one did find a target, it whined harmlessly off ceramite armour. Then came the light.

The las-beam almost took Lazarus in the chest – would have if he hadn't jerked to one side, having seen the flashing gleam of energy gathering in one of the slit windows facing him. Instead, it streaked past and carved a deep hole in the stone behind him. A mining laser, powerful but difficult to aim. He kept moving, bounding over rocks, and the next shot went wide.

'Brother Azmodor,' he said, but the Dreadnought was already firing, his plasma cannon sending a ball of superheated matter into the wall of the building. It smashed a smoking crater into the heavy rockcrete, almost tearing through, but the laser still fired again and cut a blazing line across the stone beneath Azmodor's armoured feet.

'Destroy the roof,' Lazarus ordered, pulling out his pistol as he kept running. It was barely in range, but he snapped shots as he charged, trying to fill the air in front of the building with dust and shrapnel. Behind him, Azmodor picked his way across the steep slope, firing as he went, burst after burst of plasma striking the building's roof. The first few seemed to do nothing, the metal absorbing the heat and impact, but the steel panels began to glow red with heat, then went white, turning to molten metal that fell like rain into the building. Smoke was soon billowing up, black and stinking, and the shots pouring out stuttered to a stop, laser and guns falling silent as the building became an inferno.

A door set in its corner opened and a line of mortals surged out. The first few were smoking, but the last ones were wreathed in fire, the flames rolling off their hair and backs as they ran forward, power picks and mining drills clutched in their hands. Lazarus stopped, snapping off shots with his bolt pistol, and he could hear the guns of Squads Bethel and Hazin open up behind him. The gris dropped, bodies smashed to bloody ruin by the explosive bolts, until there were only a handful left. Jequn pounded past Lazarus, sword and banner up, and then he was among them. The Ancient moved like a whirlwind, the crackling blade of his power sword cutting through the hard metal of tools and the soft flesh of bodies with equal ease, until there were none left standing.

Lazarus moved forward and turned over the body of a man who'd been run through, his abdomen ripped to shreds by Jequn's sword. He was young, dressed in the black rags of a Reis Levies uniform. Grey marked his face, fuzzy, wet-looking splotches of it around both eyes and dripping down his cheeks like tears. He was dying fast, the blood pouring out of him, but when Lazarus rolled him onto his back he smiled, his teeth coated in red.

'My Dark Angels,' he croaked, blood splattering from his mouth with every word. 'You have come for me again.'

CHAPTER ELEVEN

From Ysentrud's perspective, the flight was a series of brutal lurches, dizzying spins, and the terrifying shudders that went through the Thunderhawk every time it fired its weapons.

The aftermath, by contrast, was much more nauseating.

She stood in the caldera beside Sebastian, trying to look at anything but the bodies lying spread before the burning building that once sheltered the tiny guard detachment posted here. When *Adamantine Wings* had landed she had staggered off the ship, grateful to be on solid ground again, and stared curiously at the red smears on the dirt, wondering what they could be. When she had realised that they were people, bodies shredded by the Space Marines' massive guns, she had to go into memen state and silently recite black pall harvest statistics for the past three centuries to keep from throwing up. It had worked, and her stomach was almost settled when she came back to herself, but the smell of burnt flesh and blood kept threatening to make the nausea return, so she breathed through her mouth and kept her head turned away.

'Is this your grey motley?' Lazarus said, but he was talking to Sebastian, so Ysentrud didn't have to look at him. Which was good, because he was standing in the middle of the gory remains.

'Yes,' the Regent Next answered. He seemed untroubled by the bodies, his face calm and appropriately determined. He'd been that way through the whole battle, though Ysentrud had seen a smile of smug satisfaction cross his face when Lazarus announced that the fight was done. 'The grey around the eyes is common. It often also appears around the mouth and on the hands, then spreads across the body as the infection worsens.'

'You talk of infection,' the Dark Angels leader said, 'but you don't seem concerned to be near them.'

Ysentrud's heart skipped a beat, and she suddenly held her breath, blocking out whatever spores might be in the air with the smoke and the stink. But even as Sebastian spoke, she found the information in her mind and let herself breathe again.

'However grey pall spreads, it doesn't spread easily,' Sebastian said. 'No one has ever got it except those that the gris take. We don't understand how they infect them.'

The Space Marine made a sound, a low bass rumble that from a normal man might have been a 'hmm'. It was followed by a wet, crushing, tearing sound. 'Whatever it is,' Lazarus said, 'it is in their brains.'

Ysentrud felt her stomach heave again as her mind's eye gave her a vivid picture of what the Space Marine might be looking at, and she dropped into memen again, running through all the generations of House Halven from Redwash War to present. When she came out of it, Lazarus was halfway across the crater with most of his men and Sebastian. One Space Marine had stayed behind, the man with the skull mask for a face and the red and green eyes.

'Are you recovered?' he asked. He didn't speak loudly, but everything these giants said came out like a monstrous growl through their power armour.

'I... I just...' she started, then shrugged. What use was it trying to save face to a man like this? 'I needed a minute to not throw up.'

'Are you recovered?' he said again.

'I am if I can move away from... this,' she said, waving towards the bodies without looking at them.

'The Emperor provides.' He pointed towards where the others were gathering near the caldera's centre. She nodded and started towards them, very aware that he was walking just behind her.

The knowledge etched into Ysentrud's brain had little to say about Space Marines. It dealt with them only insofar as it detailed their appearance during the Redwash War, when they destroyed the tide of daemons that was tearing Reis apart. From the little she knew, she thought the skull mask meant the man was a Chaplain. She had no idea what that was, but the name implied some kind of spiritual guide. One that wore a skull mask over glowing, mismatched eyes...

She shuddered, and then felt like a fool for shuddering, wondering if he'd noticed. The useless whirl of her thoughts was interrupted when she reached the others. Master Lazarus had Sebastian standing to one side of him, and another Space Marine standing on the other, wearing armour marked with a horned skull. The rest of the Dark Angels had set up a perimeter around them, half facing in, half facing out, perfectly still except for the slow sweep of their helmets back and forth as their red eyes searched for... enemies? What enemies? They'd killed everything on this mountain. But they were Dark Angels, and they probably never stopped looking for enemies.

That thought made Ysentrud nervous too, and she tried to

focus on what the others were looking at. It wasn't much. Just a darker, smoother circle of stone set in the frozen lava. A disc of obsidian, maybe fifteen feet across, its edges buried in the caldera's floor as if it had been floating in the lava that once flowed here but was caught now and held in the cooled stone. The surface of it was smooth but unpolished, a dull black like a death-hazed pupil. Cracks ran across it, jagged marks that branched like lightning over the surface. They radiated out from a point set about six feet from the centre of the stone. *Is this–* she started to wonder, and then the man next to Lazarus spoke.

'I can feel the ward. Still here, still strong. I feel the will of the men who made it, like scar tissue stitching together reality.'

'Do you sense any weakening, Brother Raziel?' Lazarus asked. 'Any sign these gris were trying to break through?'

'No,' Raziel answered, and Lazarus turned his helm towards Sebastian. How cowardly would it be to tell them that he had called for them before she had been forced into his service? Ysentrud wondered.

Sebastian was still as calm and collected as ever, though. 'They would have,' he said, 'given the chance.'

'They had the chance,' Lazarus said, and there was something in his deep voice that made Ysentrud want to slink away as quietly as possible. But the Chaplain was standing right behind her. 'The gris have been here weeks, and they have done nothing more than hold the place against your army.' The Master of the Fifth loomed over Sebastian, the armour of his gauntlets clicking as he wrapped a hand around the hilt of his sword. 'That beacon–'

'Master Lazarus.' The Space Marine Raziel had raised his hand, but his head was down, as if he could see something in the fractal cracks that ran across the obsidian. 'There is something.'

Lazarus turned, and again the motion was too fast, too fast for someone that big, wrapped in armour so heavy. 'The ward?'

'Is still strong. But there is something.' Raziel shook his head. 'There has been something, something I've felt since leaving the Thunderhawk. A current in the warp. Thin, small, but there.' He looked up at Lazarus. 'It leads to here.'

'The Ruinous Powers?' Lazarus' hand was still on his sword, and the Space Marine's stillness had changed, to something somehow dangerous. 'Is something trying to reach through?'

'No,' Raziel said. 'The flow goes from the material plane into the warp. Something beyond this Redwash Gate is being... fed.'

Fed. Ruinous Powers. Ysentrud stared at them, trying to understand what was going on, what had made these men without fear become so watchful and wary. Suddenly she understood. Raziel was a witch, what the Space Marines called a Librarian. And the Ruinous Powers... That must be what they called the hideous things that had spilled through the Redwash and killed so many centuries ago. 'No,' she whispered to herself. 'No.' For once cursing failed her, and she fumbled through her head for a moment, so overstuffed with so many useless facts, and finally found what she wanted in an account from the Redwash War, a prayer to the Emperor for deliverance from the things beyond the walls of the real, the sane and the true.

The Librarian was still staring down at the cracks, as if he could see through them into another world. 'This is the centre. Where the warp broke through. This is the seal.' He held his hands out, his fingers spread wide over the black rock. 'This was heat, and light, and fire. With the strength of the Lion, they froze it into stone and sealed the wound in the real. But there is a flaw, as thin as a soul, and through it the current flows, like a cold breeze through a crack.'

'What is it?' Lazarus asked, and Raziel finally looked up from the fine cracks.

'Pain,' he said. 'Despair. Misery. That is what I feel, flowing out into the warp. A current of suffering runs through this place, and the longer I stay here, the more I am convinced I feel something else. A shadow of something terrible, crouched on the other side of that ward.'

'A shadow.' The Master of the Fifth frowned. 'Can you mend this flaw, Librarian Raziel?'

'No.' Raziel shook his head. 'Four Librarians wove this seal, working together. To fix this, to stop it, the seal would have to be undone, then woven again. I am not sure I have the strength to break this, but I know I do not have the strength to remake it.'

'What do you sense, Raziel?' Ysentrud couldn't see Lazarus' face, and she was glad. He sounded angry, and she didn't want to see that anger in his grey eyes. 'Will this *shadow* break through?'

'No.' The psyker shook his head. 'The seal could be broken from this side, but in the warp it is quite potent. This door is barred, and the shadow at its threshold is held at bay. But it can feed from this current of misery that is somehow being channelled through the flaw.'

'I told you,' Sebastian blurted out, interrupting the Space Marines. 'It's the gris! Those infected were doing something here!'

'If all you have is conjecture, your voice is unnecessary, Regent Next.' Lazarus' hand had found the hilt of his sword again, and Ysentrud wondered if there was a prayer for telling someone to keep their damned mouth shut. She didn't know it if there was, but maybe sheer force of will was enough, because Sebastian didn't say anything more, and she carefully kept her sigh of relief silent when Lazarus turned his attention back to Raziel.

'Is this the gris' doing?' Lazarus asked.

'I cannot be certain,' Raziel said. 'But that would be my suspicion.'

Lazarus stood perfectly still, staring at the cracked stone. The only motion to him was the sway of his robe in the wind, and the slow tap of one finger against the hilt of his sword. 'I do not like this,' he said finally, and those simple words so calmly spoken in his deep voice seemed to carry more anger than a torrent of profanity. 'Brother Raziel, you will prepare a missive to your superior, Grand Master Ezekiel, telling him what you have found here. He can determine if it is necessary to come back and remake this seal. As for the Fifth, we–' He paused, then shifted, helm turning as he stared out at something Ysentrud couldn't see. 'We are going back to the Thunderhawks. The Scouts have found more heretics, trying to flee our retribution, and I find that I have questions.'

'By the Throne,' Ysentrud whispered as she stepped out of the Thunderhawk. When the Space Marine piloting the ship had said he'd found a clear spot in the jungle to land in, she had suspected what it was. When the smell hit her, she knew. 'Of course,' she said, looking around the open space that had been cleared of trees. A stimm farm. It was filled with low wire cages, mesh barriers covering the bodies that lay rotting in the sun, keeping the scavengers out. The wire mesh was tight, meant to block the bigger insects, but through it Ysentrud could catch glimpses of the things decaying inside. Most were animals or their butchered remnants, but there were human corpses too. Stimm was Sudsten's most valuable commodity, and the black pall it was made from was a saprophyte, a carrion eater which only grew on flesh. Animal flesh and human flesh, the fungus didn't care, so when anyone died their body was taken directly to the farms, to help grow the next crop. In this way, even death had become a duty for the citizens of Sudsten as everyone gave their body into service. Everyone except the obscenely wealthy who could afford to buy themselves a cremation and a clean death.

It was good that the screens were tightly woven and she could only catch glimpses. But those wire cages did absolutely nothing about the stench. Ysentrud stopped at the bottom of the ramp, trying to settle her stomach, wishing this whole trip had involved significantly less nausea.

'Of course?' Demetrius asked. The Chaplain – no, Interrogator-Chaplain, that was what she had heard Master Lazarus call him, and the possible implications of that added title were heavy with dread – wasn't far behind her, but he was far enough that she was still surprised he'd heard her. Space Marines had ears as big as their muscles.

'Rot ranch,' Ysentrud said, using the crude slang term for the farm.

'Apt.' Demetrius swivelled his head, looking around. 'I have smelled battlefields worse than this. But only the ones with orks.'

'You can smell things wearing that?' Ysentrud asked. She'd assumed the armour blocked out such things.

'Far better than you,' he answered. Sebastian walked past them, heading down the ramp, and Demetrius gestured for her to keep moving. Somehow the skull-masked man had ended up their keeper. That fact wasn't helping her queasiness either.

In the middle of the field of corpses, another group of Space Marines were waiting. They were just as huge, but their armour wasn't as bulky, and their heads were bare. Lazarus' Scouts.

There were two people sitting on the ground before them, grey masks of fungus around their eyes and streaking their faces. One was an old man dressed only in ragged pants and boots, the other a middle-aged woman wearing the uniform of a junior lash officer of the Reis Home Levies. The black uniform was stained with mud, blood and smears of spores. One sleeve was ripped away, baring an arm marked with grey streaks, bruises and insect bites. Both of them were staring at nothing, their eyes blank, their faces vacant.

Lazarus stopped in front of them, and his men fell in around him, watching. Demetrius herded Ysentrud along until she was standing next to Sebastian, a little way back from the Master of the Fifth. Then he stepped around her, walking up to join his leader.

'Will you put them to the question?' Demetrius asked.

'Do you think that will be fruitful?'

Demetrius moved over to the man, grasped him by the hair and bent his head back. The man looked up through his mask of grey, eyes wide, vacant. 'I am very persuasive. But to be honest, I believe I would be wasting my time. There is nothing behind these eyes. I did not see anything in any of the others either.'

'Or hear it,' Lazarus said. 'Not one of them gave voice to a word, or a scream, or a curse. None of them made one noise, except for that final man. Your skills are wasted on these.'

'Then why are we here?' Demetrius asked. Ysentrud, waving away flies as she silently watched, wondered that too.

'Because, silent as they are, I think something wants to talk,' Lazarus said.

That's when Ysentrud saw the woman change. Her eyes blinked, and then there was life in them, purpose. The once-officer turned her head and looked up at Lazarus, and Ysentrud almost shouted a warning. Because in those newly aware eyes, there was something ugly, something terrifying. A mix of amusement, bitterness, hate and certainty. But Lazarus had turned his head to meet the woman's gaze the moment she shifted her eyes to him.

'Yes,' the woman said. 'We had so little time before, didn't we, Dark Angel?'

'Death interrupts many things.' Lazarus pulled his sword as he spoke, held it out so that the tip of its dark blade was inches away from the woman's throat. But her eyes never shifted from his face.

'Death ends, death begins.' She raised her hands to that great blade. Ysentrud flinched when she touched it, but the sword's field wasn't active, and her hand wasn't ripped to shreds by its destructive energies. Still, the adamantine blade had a razor edge, and when the gris touched it blood bloomed from her fingers and ran down her wrist to drip onto the ground. 'Death nourishes.' She took a deep breath of the corrupt air that filled the clearing and smiled, her teeth dripping with grey fungus. 'Death is necessary for new life. But do you know something, Dark Angel?' The woman moved her hand up the sword, blood pouring from her as she slit her palm to the bone. Then she drove herself forward. Her throat hit the sword and split, skin and muscle peeling back from that keen edge, and then there was more blood, so much more, pulsing from her severed carotid in time with her heartbeat. The blood splashed across the Master of the Fifth's armoured arm, and a spray of drops speckled his robe, making a pattern of gleaming red on that blank white.

Ysentrud focused on those dots, trying to breathe, trying not to scream, trying not to hear that horrible bubbling noise coming from the woman's throat as blood flowed down her severed trachea and filled her lungs. The Wyrbuk heard the thud as the woman's body hit the ground, and she couldn't stop herself. Ysentrud looked and saw her, sprawled in her own blood, face slack now with death, one of her wide-staring eyes half covered by that puddle of gore.

'Death hurts.' The words came from the lips of the old man, his head still held in Demetrius' hand. His eyes were alive now, filled with the same ugly mix of feelings that had animated the dead woman's. 'You never forget how much it hurts.'

'I know,' Lazarus said, and he snapped his sword to the side, clearing blood from the blade.

'Do you?' the man asked, and Ysentrud stared at him, sick and confused. She'd never seen someone die before, much less like that, so violent, so sudden, so hideously purposeful and purposeless at the same time. Why had the woman killed herself like that? What was she talking about, what were this man and Lazarus talking about?

'Maybe you do,' the old man said. 'And if so, you know why I'm doing this.'

'No,' Lazarus said. 'I know nothing about what you are, or what you want. I just know you are an obscenity, a monster, and I shall cleanse you from this world.'

The man laughed then, and the sound of it grated on Ysentrud's ears, made her want to raise her hands to block it out, but he cut it off before she could so that he could speak one last time. 'You already tried, Dark Angel.'

Then everything exploded.

CHAPTER TWELVE

Everything was dark, and everything was ringing. Ysentrud could taste dirt and smoke and blood. Then someone picked her up and her eyes snapped open. Everything around her was chaos and pain.

There was smoke and dust and spores, all twisting together into choking curtains that blocked out the sun. Through the dark, bright sparks flashed all around, big and small, and with them came a distant sound like someone knocking far, far away. But the high ringing noise that filled her head almost swallowed it up. Ysentrud blinked, trying to understand what was happening, and why her head hurt so much, and her stomach, and why everything was lurching from side to side, and most importantly, why was everything upside down?

Then there was a shadow beside her, looming up out of the smoke, something huge and inhuman. Ysentrud blinked at it, would have panicked, but she was too confused for fear, too confused to do anything but stare dumbly as the monstrous shape lunged forward. Then she recognised it. It was the armoured machine shape of the Dreadnought, the walking war machine that Lazarus had called Azmodor. It was some kind of servitor, part man, part machine, though she didn't see any sign of humanity in all that heavy metal and weapons. There was a piece of humanity gripped in Azmodor's heavy mechanical fist though, a man who was bringing one hand down over and over, chopping at the Dreadnought with a heavy-bladed cleaver while Azmodor fired at something through the smoke. The blade sparked when it smashed into the hand, but that's all it did – sparked and flashed as the man swung until Azmodor tightened his grip.

There was a crunch, soggy and wet, like tramping on a pile of sticks, and a rush of blood burst out of the man's nose and mouth, more than Ysentrud would have expected to be in a person, and she felt nausea again. But it was distant this time, lost amid the pain and smoke, the way the knocking sounds were almost lost in the ringing that filled her head.

Gunshots, she thought, watching as Azmodor threw the crushed body of the man away, then raised his other arm and fired the gun mounted on it. From this close, the knocking was enough to almost break through the ringing, and she could feel the vibrations of the gunfire in her lungs. Her lungs. The smoke and grit that filled the air was in her lungs too, and she coughed, coughed and coughed, and then the nausea finally took her and she threw up, heaving the contents of her stomach down the back of the man carrying her.

Carrying her. She retched again, then pushed against the man's back. It was broad, heavy with muscle, and it was the thick muscles of his shoulder that were digging into her gut. He was holding her legs tight as a vice and running. Running through the smoke, away from Azmodor with the bloody fist and shuddering guns, running for... Ysentrud twisted, shoved herself up and looked over her shoulder. The man was pushing through the smoke, heading towards a crater surrounded by broken wire cages and the shredded, mould-covered remains of what had been under them. Just ahead, she saw a group of at least a dozen men and women in muddy rags running for that same crater, awkwardly dragging something huge wrapped in a blood-smeared tarp behind them. They reached the crater and jumped in, disappearing.

Not a crater. A hole. He was carrying her to a hole. Ysentrud knotted her hand into a fist, raised it up, and brought it down as hard as she could into the man's lower back, right above where her kidney should be.

The man grunted, and his steps stuttered, but he kept running, so Ysentrud kept hitting him. He didn't stop but he shifted, reaching up for her with his other hand. He slapped at her and she twisted, using his motion to grab at his hair on the top of his head. She jerked it back and down, as hard as she could, twisting his head, and he stumbled to one side. Ysentrud kept pulling, putting her weight into it, but he was holding her with one hand and tearing at her with his other, trying to break her grip on his hair. Then his foot slammed into one of the corpse cages that were still staked to the ground and he fell, sprawling into the dirt.

Ysentrud hit the ground and rolled. The world was still ringing, she was still nauseated and coughing, but she lashed out and grabbed one of the stakes connected to the corpse cage and ripped it out of the earth. She held it up as she got to her feet, a two-foot-long piece of corroded metal, thick as her finger with an end that was as blunt as Learned Thiemo's head. But it was something, and she kept it between her and the man as he picked himself up. He was much taller and bulkier when he loomed over her, and his hand went to his belt and pulled out a hammer. He raised it, and on its blunt head Ysentrud could see half-dried blood and hair. She felt the nausea bite her again, but kept the stake up. She could see the grey on his face now, the band across his eyes, the streaks running down from his nose, his ears. The grey motley, and she would fall on this damned stake before she let him drag her away into the dark.

He stepped towards her, hammer starting to fall, and then something slammed into him, tumbling him across the dirt like a broken toy. He came to a stop against a corpse cage, and she could see his hand, still gripping his hammer tight, but the grey on his face was gone, wiped away into red ruin. Ysentrud looked away from his corpse and at the figure in armour and winged helm, standing before her.

Lazarus.

'Stand behind me, Ysentrud.'

She was moving before she could think, which was good. Still clutching the stake, she went behind him, wanting to put all that armour between her and everything else. Lazarus had his sword out and she skirted wide around it, but still felt a kind of itching buzz across her skin from the crackling field, jangling flickers of darkness that flashed down the blade like jet-coloured lightning. There was a gun in his other hand, a bolt pistol so large she probably couldn't have picked it up much less shot it, its barrel trailing smoke. Once behind him she realised there were others here. Demetrius, holding his crozius with the massive skull clenching a hilt between its teeth. Two blades ran out to either side from that hilt, both stained with blood, and a field crackled around them and around the skull too, a flickering gold shimmer like reflections of the sun on water. The Interrogator-Chaplain also held a gun in his other hand. Jequn, the one they called Ancient, was there too, carrying a sword like Lazarus', which flickered with flashes of deep midnight blue, and a banner that showed a winged figure holding a sword in one hand, a book in the other, standing on a stone beneath a star-filled sky. Finally there was Raziel. The Librarian carried a sword as well, but his was thinner than the others, slightly curved, and when he moved it didn't crackle but made a mournful sound like wind wrapping around stones. Raziel's other hand was held up high, and between his fingers gleamed blue light, as if he had ripped off a piece of sky and clenched it in his fist. The Librarian's eyes, which had glowed red out of his armour like the other Dark Angels' before, now shone with that same blue, and there was a chill flowing from him as if the Librarian were carved from ice.

'Stay between us,' Lazarus told her, and the four Space Marines spread out, making a circle around her. Then they began to move, pulling back away from the hole, each one of them keeping their distance from each other and from her, steady, perfect.

Stay between them. The ringing in her head was slowly dying away, the quiet knocking of the guns growing into distant thunder, and she could hear his words when he shouted at her. Hear them and obey, desperately happy to put those huge, armoured warriors between her and the carnage. The smoke was thinning and rising, and the dust and grit were settling to the ground. Now Ysentrud could see, even if she didn't want to. There were people everywhere, dressed in rags with grey on their faces, on their limbs, grey streaming from their eyes and dripping from their mouths like vomit.

The gris, wearing their grey motley – and how were there so many? The question rattled unanswered through Ysentrud's head as she spun around, trying to see in every direction.

Grey-smeared farmers, soldiers and tradesmen were pulling themselves up out of the ground, springing from the holes that had been gouged into the corpse field. *Tunnels*, she thought. *Tunnels hidden beneath the ground with explosive charges to blow them open when we came.* A trap.

There were hundreds of gris, each of them clutching a weapon – guns or power picks, rock drills or combat knives, or just metal tools or splintered wooden clubs. It was a riot of them, but every gris was silent except for their hissing breaths and their running, thumping feet. Their mouths were shut tight beneath their blank, empty eyes.

They were terrifying in their silence, in their numbers, in their uncaring indifference as they swept forward to kill, but the rushing horde broke against the Dark Angels like the tide crashing onto stones. The unarmoured gris shattered as they were hit by the exploding shells of the bolters, their fungus-infected bodies flying apart into gore and guts and scattered limbs, falling to the ground in a shower of blood. But they didn't stop coming, and the Dark Angels didn't pause in their slaughter.

In the noise and the confusion, they butchered with a precise, ordered efficiency. The Dark Angels had split into their separate squads again, each group intent on their task. The Scouts climbed to the top of the Thunderhawks, and Ysentrud could see them picking off gris with shot after shot, their exposed faces set and cold as they killed. Below them, in the shadow of the transports' stubby wings, she could see another squad of fully armoured Dark Angels, their massive bolters raised to crash and roar whenever any of the grey-masked gris tried to rush the ships.

The other two squads were in the corpse fields, adding to the bodies sprawled out there. One squad was moving from hole to hole, picking off targets as they went. When they reached an opening, one of the Dark Angels would step forward and blast a sheet of flame down into it. While Ysentrud watched, the Space Marine carrying the flamer stopped pouring fire into the tunnels and stepped back. As he did, two people came crawling up, sheathed in burning promethium, jerking as they were consumed. But still the gris said nothing, stumbling forward, clumsily swinging their weapons at the Dark Angels. The Space Marines blasted them with two quick shots, their huge guns blowing gaping holes in their burning chests, then one of them kicked the corpses back into the hole and tossed a grenade down after. There was a dim thump from below, and dirt and burning gore showered to earth around the Dark Angels as they moved on to the opening of the next tunnel.

The last squad stalking the fields of the dead was the one Ysentrud had heard called an assault squad. They were stalking across the broken ground, their chainswords whirring an almost inaudible scream until they reached another group of gris. The sounds changed as sharp, speeding teeth met flesh and bone and shredded through both. Ysentrud turned her eyes from them, determined not be sick again.

The only other fighters on the field were Azmodor, still crashing his own path through the gris, and the group moving around Ysentrud. She looked around wildly, remembering Sebastian, but he was nowhere in sight. Maybe he was at the ships, where the Space Marines surrounding her were heading. But as they moved, Ysentrud saw that the gris were shifting, closing in on them, pushing forward to cut them off. They came at them in a swirling confusion, running around each other but never colliding, moving like a murmuration of birds, charging in towards the Dark Angels that had spaced themselves around Ysentrud.

The bolt pistols in Lazarus' and Demetrius' hands were thundering, pouring out shots. The huge slugs tore open gaping wounds, sometimes ripping straight through one gris and hitting another rushing in behind. The shrapnel from the exploding shells cut down others, but they were still charging forward, uncaring.

A bolt of blue light flew past her, not touching her, but Ysentrud felt something as it went by, a terrible feeling of cold that came from inside her, as if her bones had changed to ice. Then it was gone, the light striking one of the gris rushing in. He stopped, his breath turning the air white, and for a moment his skull shone blue through his skin, and then he fell. As he went down he lurched into another, and that man fell too, the deadly blue flaring out through his skin.

The Dark Angels killed, but there was still a great crowd of gris left, bloody, muddy, silent, tearing towards them with weapons raised. Ysentrud was moving back, the panic she'd been shoving down rising again to drown her, until a great hand touched her shoulder. She looked back, ready to scream, and Raziel stared down at her.

'Hold your place,' he told her, then turned his back on her again, his sword up, and Ysentrud stopped, remembered where she was, where she should stay, and whipped her head back towards the approaching mob. They were right there now, close enough that she could smell the stink of them, and Lazarus swung his sword, the black flickers of its field warping the air around it.

His movements were so fast, and so strangely delicate. He was huge, the sword was huge, and she expected him to swing it like some giant from the tales, in vast chops that would rip men in two. But his movements were fast, precise. He struck, then pulled his blade back just as quickly, moving to hit another, and another, and every blow left ruin behind. His strength folded men over and cracked bones, but that power was married with the deadly field of energy that wrapped around Lazarus' blade. When it struck clothing, the cloth tore apart, threads igniting. When it hit the flesh beneath, it was worse than the cutting bite of the chainswords. Skin ripped as if invisible hands had seized it and pulled in opposite directions. And beneath the skin, sheaths of muscle shredded, strands tearing away from each other, steaming and hissing as the water in them boiled. Fat burst like bubbles, organs writhed and flailed apart, spattering out of chest cavities, and bones splintered and shattered, their gory shrapnel filling the air.

The others were fighting too, surrounding themselves with piles of dead and gore. Jequn handled his sword like Lazarus, with a little less speed but more bone-breaking finality. The skull-headed club Demetrius wielded was somehow even bloodier than the swords. Instead of tearing open wounds in long slits, it smashed into the gris like a hammer whose blunt, heavy head was surrounded by a swarm of invisible teeth that shredded and tore. Behind her, Ysentrud could hear Raziel battling the gris that wrapped around to him, and she could hear the thud of bodies and something else – a moaning howl that rose and fell, and a chill wind touched her back. She didn't turn to see what the Librarian's sword was doing to those it touched – she didn't want to. It was hard enough watching Lazarus and the others fight. But she kept her eyes open, her head up, to make sure the enemies were falling – and not surging past her Dark Angels protectors to grab her and drag her towards one of their pits again.

The circle of those protectors grew tighter. As fast as Lazarus and the others were cutting them down, there were always more, more, a surging flood of grey-masked people driving forward. They were smashing into the Dark Angels with whatever they had, some of them grabbing on with bare hands, trying to slow the Space Marines with their numbers, to drag them down with their weight. They drove in, and right in front of her Lazarus was forced back a step, then another, his massive, armoured body pushed towards her by a tide of silent fanatics. Then one of them slipped past.

The man was dressed in rags, coated in mud. A patchy beard spread across his face, the hair growing through the splotches of grey fungus that coated his skin. One arm was bleeding, the skin ruptured open where Lazarus' sword had passed close, but in the other hand he held a knife, which he was swinging at her, the blade cutting through the air at her face. Ysentrud made a noise, a growl, a whimper, a denial, and raised the stake she still clutched. Somehow, by the grace of the Golden Throne, she got that rusty piece of metal between her and that falling knife. The blade clanged off the stake and banged painfully against her knuckles, then the tip hit her forearm, carving a furrow in her red skin. She barely felt the cut, but the blow had slammed her arms down, stripped away the meagre protection of the rusty stake, and the bearded man was driving in again, stabbing the knife straight at her belly. Ysentrud tried to pull the stake back around to block, but she was too slow and the man was right there, the stink of his breath on her. In that endless moment as the knife drove forward, she found herself staring at the grey mask that covered his eyes. It was moist, shining in the daylight, and made up of circles of mould that overlapped each other, covering the skin beneath, and she could see grey threads of the fungus striating the white of the man's eyes and marking the brown of his pupils. Then those eyes went wider as a wave of blood suddenly smashed out in a great halo around the man's head.

Ysentrud blinked, then the blood splashed against her, sticky and surprisingly hot, and the man sank to his knees, the knife falling from his hand. Beyond him, Lazarus was bringing his sword back around, its heavy pommel dripping blood from where he had smashed it into the back of the man's head, crushing his skull like an egg. Part of Ysentrud wanted to vomit again, but she was too busy falling to her knees, scrambling for the dropped knife while never taking her eyes off the Master of the Fifth.

He hadn't turned his helm. He'd struck the man down with his backhand blow without looking, and now he was turning that motion into the start of a swing, a great two-handed cutting arc like the ones she had imagined him giving. It ripped through the gris that were rushing in, cutting apart limbs and torsos, barely slowed by its tearing path through muscle and bone. At the end of the arc, Lazarus stopped the huge sword, holding it across his body at the height of his waist, and then he drove himself forward. He slammed into the crowd as they crashed into him, and for a long moment he was still, an armoured stone being pounded by a tide of silent, dead-eyed humanity. But his sword crackled, its energy field biting and tearing into the front rank of attackers, splitting chests and rupturing ribs, cutting throats and tearing through collarbones and jaws. The gris fell apart against that terrible blade, held still and unmoving by the Dark Angel, and then he took one step forward, shoving into the crowd, rippling them back. Then another, and another, and now Lazarus was forcing them back, breaking them. His boots were crushing over bodies, the dead and the almost dead, and then suddenly they shattered.

By bolters and blades the gris had been torn apart, killed in masses that left drifts of corpses on the ground, their blood making gory puddles out of the dirt. A few of them still moved and twitched, but for the most part the bodies were shattered red smears, barely recognisable as having once been human. Ysentrud held the bloody knife in front of her in both hands, staring at the man Lazarus had killed with his pommel. His head was lopsided, deformed by the blow, and through the tangled mess of hair and bone that was the back of his head she could see the smashed remnants of his brain. White and grey, the strands of fungus mixed in with it weren't immediately obvious, but they were there, a net that ran all through the dead man's cortex. She stared at it in silence, clenching the knife tight, her face sticky with drying blood, then she turned her head and retched again.

CHAPTER THIRTEEN

Lazarus cleaned Enmity's Edge on the body of one of the dead, waiting for the mortal to finish vomiting. When she was done, he sheathed his sword and held a hand out to her. She stared at it for a long moment, then dropped the knife she'd been clutching and reached out, letting him help her up.

'Can you walk?' he asked, and she nodded. She followed him back to the ships, where the other Dark Angels had formed up. 'Brother Asbeel.' The Apothecary finished stapling shut a jagged cut that ran down one of the Scouts' necks and came over. Lazarus gently pushed Ysentrud towards him, and Asbeel took her hand, turning it to expose the bloody gash on her forearm. The scanner servo arched over his back and whirred and clicked, its glass eyes staring, sensor wands stroking the air over the wound like an insect's antenna.

'Minor, even for a mortal,' the Apothecary said. 'Hold still.' Ysentrud looked as if she desperately wanted to move, but Asbeel took hold of her arm as his narthecium whirred into place over the wound, and the mortal shut her eyes, waiting. There was a sharp click as a needle stabbed out of the complex medi-pack, and then Ysentrud relaxed as the drug wiped away her pain. 'It will take just a moment to stitch up.'

'Casualties?' Lazarus asked him.

'One of the explosions that blew open the tunnels was right under Squad Bethel,' Apothecary Asbeel said as tiny servos in the narthecium whirred, stitching the mortal's delicate flesh back together. 'Two have minor injuries, but Variel lost most of his left arm. It will need replacing. Scout Squad Jotha came under heaviest attack at the start, before they could pull back to the ships. Two of them have injuries that will degrade their combat abilities for the next few hours. Two are missing. Dead or alive, I do not know.'

'They do that,' Ysentrud said, almost a whisper. She had turned her red face away from the work the Apothecary was doing. 'My lord. In the histories and the stories. The gris take people. They take bodies. Sometimes just the brains. We don't know why.' She frowned, looking faintly queasy again. 'I saw a group of gris, dragging something big and bloody. They took it into one of the holes.'

Two Dark Angels missing. Lazarus stared at the still-smoking holes surrounded by the shredded dead. A hundred of them for every missing Scout, at least, and that wasn't nearly enough. But his men hadn't been the only targets. 'They take the living to infect,' Lazarus said. Infection was not something that could happen to a Space Marine. That did not mean the gris would not try.

Ysentrud nodded, then shuddered. 'Yes.' She looked around, suddenly realising something. 'The Regent Next. I don't see him!'

'Taken,' Lazarus said, and Ysentrud stared at him, her eyes wide in the red skull mark of her face.

'What are we going to do?' she asked.

'Do?' Lazarus said. He reached up, and his winged helm hissed softly as he pulled it off. 'These gris laid a trap. Wounded my brothers. Took two of them. We will do what must be done. We will slay every last one of them.'

'*For the Lion!*'

The shout echoed up from the gathered Dark Angels, so deep and powerful Lazarus felt it in the heavy bones of his chest. But the shout seemed to rattle Ysentrud, and the mortal trembled after it had ended, her thin body shaking beneath the filthy robes wrapped around her. She clutched them tight to her, standing next to him with her head down, eyes on the ground. A frail thing, even more so than most mortals, but there was information locked behind her strange red eyes that he needed.

My Dark Angels. You have come for me again.

There was something here, on this world, something behind these gris, and it knew them, and it wanted them dead.

Yes, he needed to know more about this world, and the Emperor had provided. He looked at the mortal, still trembling in his shadow.

'You did well, Learned Ysentrud.'

'I did nothing, my lord,' she said, and he could smell the fear in her sweat, read the exhausted tension in her body.

'You survived,' he said.

She looked at him again, uncertain, but she nodded and her shaking went away. Mostly. Good enough.

Lazarus looked away from her and called his command squad to him, and the sergeants of each of the squads. 'We have fought the first true battle of this war,' he said when they had gathered around him. 'There will be more.' He turned to Sergeant Asher, whose face was hard, anger tensing every muscle. 'What did you find?'

'We went into the tunnels the gris made – the ones we had not destroyed. They all converged into one passage, less than half a mile from the edge of this farm.' Asher pointed to the thick jungle lying to the west, away from the volcano. 'That tunnel was larger than the others, older, deeper. But it was a dead end. The gris brought it down behind them, collapsed it to keep us from following.'

Of course they did, Lazarus thought. He looked to Ephron. 'Can we divine these tunnels with auspex? Map their nest out from above?'

The Techmarine shook his head. 'The earth here plays havoc with auspex scans. We will not get more than a few yards without our readings becoming unreliable to the point of uselessness.' Ephron paused, and Lazarus could hear him whispering to himself in the strange, buzzing private language of the Techmarines. 'It may be possible to divine them using acoustic waves. We have the explosives to send out a pulse, but I would need equipment from the *Sword of Caliban* to build a receiver, and time to set it up.'

From the ship. Time to set it up. Time, and what would the gris be doing while Ephron did his work? But it was a start.

'Contact the *Sword of Caliban*. Claim what you require.'

'Master Lazarus,' Ephron said, his voice sharp. 'I do not have to. The *Sword of Caliban* has contacted me. They have received an emergency transmission from the Fabricator Locum. She states that the Regent Prime has sent Reis Home Levies troops to attack her forge on Norsten.'

Adamantine Wings shifted and lurched, the Thunderhawk's powerful engines roaring as the ship fought the savage crosswinds kicked up by the storm they were tearing through. Lazarus barely noticed the movement, the sudden jerks nothing compared to the evasive manoeuvres he'd felt in hundreds of combat drops, but he unconsciously shifted with the craft's movements, keeping his face centred in the sights of the holo-caster clinging like a spider to the ceiling of the transport's hold.

'This is Lazarus, Master of the Fifth. What is your need?'

In the narrow aisle that ran down the centre of the hold, a hissing cloud of light took shape, cast by the myriad lenses of the holocaster. The light brightened and dimmed, then snapped suddenly into place, pale motes forming together into a woman's face. The face was beautiful, smooth, unblem-ished, perfectly symmetrical. Too beautiful – it was a mask the colour of ivory, still and unmoving except for the mane of white hair that framed it, and the eyes. They were the deep colour of wine, unmarred except for a dark circle in their centre, like a pupil. But this pupil split into two, then three, the black points moving around each other like shifting stars, then merging again into one, before splitting again. A shift-ing, distracting dance as she stared at Lazarus.

'Precision.' Fabricator Locum Gretin Lan's voice was clear, but with a rippling sound like faint music behind the words. '*Master Lazarus, you and your Dark Angels were summoned to fight a threat that my own auspex could not detect. Now my holdings are assailed by members of the Regent Prime's Levies. Schedules have been disrupted. Personnel have been lost. Quotas are endangered. Precious technological fabricants have been damaged. All of this occurred without signal or provocation. I respond to the situation but seek elucidation to root causes. Communication with the Regent Prime has been unfruitful. Thus, I reach out to you, Master Lazarus of the Fifth Company.*'

The Fabricator Locum might want precision, but she didn't seem to care about conciseness. Lazarus decided to offer her both. 'You have pict data of the attack?'

'*Of course. I shall offer.*' Her face faded from the holofield, ivory and white becoming a cloud of static, and then the light redrew itself into a flat pict of a bulbous air transport ship sitting on a snow-covered field, rough mountains rising behind it. The pict shuddered, lines of static dancing across it, and then resolved again. The static was snow now, heavy flakes drifting across the pict, dusting the transport's pitted metal hide. On the edge of the image something moved, a wavering blur that resolved into a mob of servitors trundling towards the ship, their tracks churning the snow. They were cargo units, and the scarred and wrinkled torsos of what had once been men and women stuck out of heavy mechanical bases, metal braces holding them up and wrapping around their arms, making them into heavy clamps or nests of jointed tentacles like twisting spinal columns. Their heads bobbed, mouths wired shut or flopped open, drooling, but they oriented on the ship, blank eyes shifting. Then a hatch popped open on the transport's curved side. Light flashed out of the dark interior, and the drifting snow splashed up from the ground in neat lines until they reached the servitors. The bullets pouring from the ship smashed into flesh and steel, and blood and electrical sparks arced through the air.

The servitors muddled to a stop, bumping into each other as the ones in front lurched to a halt and tried to back up while the ones behind still ploughed forward. The gun, some kind of heavy stubber, raked back and forth, smashing metal and tearing through flesh. It left behind a ruin of broken machines and bleeding bodies, all of them still except for a lone servitor that turned a slow circle on its damaged track, its human head lolling, blood leaking from the wound in its temple. Beyond the broken cyborgs, figures had started to run out of the transport, men and women dressed in the black uniform of Reis Home Levies, running through the snow with guns raised, their eyes–

'Cease.' Lazarus snapped out the word, and the holo froze, hovering in space before him. Almost in its centre glowed the face of a woman. A black rebreather covered her mouth and nose, but her upper face was bare. Her brown eyes were dull, empty, and surrounded by a shiny grey mask of fungus. 'Do you know these marks?'

'They are unfamiliar,' the Fabricator Locum said. The pict dissolved and was replaced again by the holo image of her face, perfectly still, pale lips shut and fixed in a tiny, enigmatic smile even as she spoke. *'Assumption was made that this was a form of cosmetic camouflage.'*

'It is not.' Lazarus looked at the forge leader, watching as her pupils split and circled and moved. 'Are you aware of the uprising, the enemy that seized the Redwash Gate? The people of Sudsten call them the gris.'

Gretin Lan blinked at him, a flicking of half-translucent nictitating membranes that moved sideways across her eyes. *'My databases indicate they are mythical figures central to a kind of terror fable told by the civilian population of Sudsten. A supernatural, lurking horror whose purpose is to frighten children and the naive.'*

Six hundred years ago. That's when the Regent Prime at the time had declared war against the gris. And in all that time they had never informed the Adeptus Mechanicus forge that the gris even existed. Even if he had believed they were no threat, it was unconscionable to keep their existence hidden. Lazarus sat in his jump seat, his face set, one finger tapping against the hilt of Enmity's Edge.

'You require information,' he said. 'This one will provide it.' He waved a gauntleted hand at Ysentrud, and the holocaster's sights followed his gesture, framing the stylised red skull of her face.

'A *Wyrbuk*.' The Fabricator Locum's voice was filled with disgust. '*An infected organic system, a contemptible copy of an elegant cogitator. A mutant.*'

'And the person you will be listening to while I review all information you have collected on the disposition and placement of the forces attacking you,' Lazarus said, his deep voice a breath away from a snarl. 'The soldiers that attacked you are gris, and I have made a promise to burn their infection from this world. We come, now.'

'*Master Lazarus.*' The pupils in Fabricator Locum Lan's eyes spun apart fast, then jerked themselves together. '*When I contacted your ship, it was not a cry for martial aid. The only reason my forces have not rooted out these attackers is because of the sensitive nature of the area where they have taken shelter. We will be able to–*'

'We come. Now.' Lazarus looked towards the mortal. 'Learned Ysentrud. Please inform Fabricator Locum Lan about the gris.' The young woman blinked at him, her red eyes wide, but then she nodded. She turned to face the ivory-coloured mask of Gretin Lan, and her crimson face went smooth and mask-like itself as she slipped into her teaching trance.

'The first official gris encounter was recorded...' she began, and Lazarus picked up a data-slate, shutting her voice out as he began poring over the information coming in from the Adeptus Mechanicus.

'What is going on?'

The holocaster in the Hall of the Fallen must have been ancient and badly maintained. The Regent Prime's face was barely recognisable, an orange caricature hovering in the air in front of Lazarus, when it wasn't flickering incoherently, threatening to fray apart into meaningless static. But Oskaran Halven's voice came through strong, his frustration clear over the muted roar of *Adamantine Wings'* engines.

'War,' Lazarus said, leaning forward. He was trying to keep his anger well leashed. He had spent the last few hours looking over the information from the Fabricator Locum, interspersed with sending orders to Lieutenant Zakariah on the *Sword of Caliban.* He was busy, and had little patience for this man.

'The Redwash Gate?' The Regent Prime's eyes went wide, then his image dissolved and slowly re-formed, the mortal's fear evident even as the lines of his face sketched themselves back into place.

'If the daemons of the warp were wreaking ruin on this world again, do you believe I would take the time to discuss that with you?' Lazarus asked. He ignored the contortions of the Regent Prime's distorted face and went on. 'The gate is sealed. We destroyed the gris that were holding it. But they moved against us, ambushing us. Two Dark Angels and the Regent Next were captured.'

'Captured?' Halven's face twisted, then relaxed, but his expression was still hard to read. *'By the gris. Damn him.'* The Regent Prime looked at Lazarus with orange, static-filled eyes. *'You must get him back!'*

'I *must?'* Lazarus leaned forward, making sure the hard features of his face were clear to the mortal, no matter how bad their equipment was. 'There is an issue with your transmission, Regent Prime. I feel I am hearing things that I would not were I standing before you.'

The Regent Prime's face frayed yet again, but when it re-formed his expression was clear enough despite the static. Frustration, fear and anger thwarted by unfamiliar impotence.

'That boy has betrayed the heritage of our house and is a faith-less fool who has abandoned everything we've ever stood for. But if the gris contaminate him...' He paused, his face twisting. 'They must not.'

'Then you should have killed them off long ago,' Lazarus said. 'Instead, you let them grow in your shadow. Now they strike from their hidden places and endanger your people and the Adeptus Mechanicus. Who were never warned of the gris, by your ancestors or you.'

'Traitorous machine men,' Halven snarled. 'They deserve nothing from us. Nothing! They squat on half our world, worshipping their false god, and we allow it because we were commanded to by your ancestors, Dark Angel. Your forebears saved those soulless monstros-ities from the justice they deserved after the Redwash War and bid us to let them continue in what was by all rights our lands. And we did, for we are bound to serve the Emperor and His servants. But we give them nothing more than the tithe we were ordered to one thousand years ago. Nothing more!'

'You've given them your Levies infected by the enemy you failed to destroy, loose in their forge,' Lazarus said. 'Too many of the gris we have fought were once soldiers in your army. There is an intelligence behind this infection, one that recog-nises me and mine. One that has wormed tunnels beneath your lands, stolen your soldiers, your equipment, and launched an attack on the other side of your world. There is a plan here, Regent Prime, and a mind directing it, and I mean to destroy both. To that end, you will keep your silence and listen.'

With a tap on the data-slate, Lazarus sent the orders he had prepared to the Regent Prime. 'I am calling down the rest of my forces. Lieutenant Zakariah, with Squads Revir and Nabis, will be sent to Kap Sudsten. You will follow his instructions until I return from cleansing the enemy from this forge.'

'*But–*' Halven stammered, then recovered, putting together at least an attempt at proper humility. '*Master Lazarus. The Adeptus Mechanicus have soldiers of their own. My son–*'

'Questioning my actions wastes my time and patience,' Lazarus said, his words a rumbling growl. 'I will deal with your son.' The other squad that had been with Brother Zakariah, Invis, was dropping down to the planet with Techmarine Cadus. They would assemble with Ancient Jequn and Squad Jotha, who had stayed at the ruined stimm farm in the shadow of the dead volcano. Brother Cadus would compile the equipment Techmarine Ephron had requested and begin mapping the gris' tunnels, so Jequn could begin the search for their lost Scout brothers and the Regent Next. It was a plan Lazarus might have explained to the Regent Prime if he wasn't tired of wasting time with the fool. 'I will deal with the gris. Then I will deal with you.' The fraying orange face in the holofield started to open its mouth, but Lazarus cut him off. 'What will you do?'

For a long moment the Regent Prime was silent, his features flickering, the sound buzzing with static. When he finally spoke, his lips didn't match the words, and they were distorted with feedback. But they were understandable.

'*I will follow the instructions of your lieutenant until you return.*'

Lazarus nodded. 'The Emperor protect you, and all who serve Him here.' He cut the transmission, and the glitchy holofield collapsed into sparks that faded into shadow.

'Apologies, Master Lazarus,' Ephron called from the cockpit. 'There is interference on all bands. It may be the storms we passed through. My prayers are having little effect.'

'Understood, brother. How much longer?'

'Thirty minutes until touchdown.'

Time enough. Lazarus looked at the mortal sitting beside

him, a canteen clutched in both hands. It was the size of her head, and she was struggling to drink from it without spilling water everywhere. When she lowered it from her lips, he took it from her. 'I have questions.'

'My purpose is to answer, my lord,' Ysentrud said. Despite the water, her voice was harsh. The Fabricator Locum may have regarded her with disdain, but she had questioned her closely once the Wyrbuk had laid out the history of the gris. All the questioning seemed to make Ysentrud calmer, wiping away, perhaps, the shock of the battle and her wounding. Even with her rasping voice, she seemed happy to face more. But she hesitated, just as she was about to draw a breath. 'A moment, and I shall enter into memen state.'

'Your trance? Do not bother, unless it is required,' Lazarus said. She had been in that unemotional trance while answering Lan's questions, and the Fabricator Locum seemed to appreciate it, but to Lazarus it felt like an unnecessary affect, a mortal trying to imitate a servo-skull. He dealt with those necrotic machines enough. And for what he was about to ask, some emotional nuance might be useful. 'What transpires between the Regent Prime and the Fabricator Locum? From what wound did this bad blood spring?'

'A very old one, Master Lazarus,' Ysentrud said. 'A thousand years old. But too big to heal, even in that time.' She frowned and shook her head. 'It began before that, though, with jealousy and economics.

'When the Imperium returned to Reis, the planet was controlled by House Halven. Halven ruled through the might of their Knights, with a contingent on each continent, but their power was slipping as their war machines grew more decrepit. Being cut off from the Imperium degraded most of the technological knowledge on Reis, and House Halven was unable to maintain its machines. Rebellions were becoming more common, and grew increasingly difficult to put down. The house might have fallen, but then the Imperium returned.'

The Learned paused to take a deeper breath. She sounded much the same as when she was in her trance, but Lazarus could see the way her eyes and head shifted as she spoke. She was considering her story as she told it, instead of just repeating facts. 'The Imperium was happy to affirm the rulership of House Halven over Reis, after they had sworn their oaths to the Emperor. They sent the Adeptus Mechanicus to provide the needed repairs, but the Adeptus Mechanicus... wanted more than loyalty. They bargained for control of Reis' mineral wealth, and eventually got it, along with territory for a forge on Norsten. But House Halven hated the bargain. They wanted their Knights whole, but they wanted trained techs who were beholden to them. The Adeptus Mechanicus denied that desire and kept their secrets. Halven had to accept their terms if they wanted to keep their Knights functioning, but they fought back in what ways they could.'

'Fought?' Lazarus asked. 'They brought battle to the Adeptus Mechanicus?'

'Not the way you do, my lord,' she said, shuddering. But she quickly went on, pulling strength from speaking. 'They made the supplies they provided for the forge costly and refused to take as much tech in trade as they could. In the centuries without Imperial support, they had learned to make do without many of the tools available to most citizens. Or they made replacements for them.' She tapped her tattooed scalp. 'Wyrbuk like me, or stimmed workers instead of servitors.'

'They limited themselves,' Lazarus said. 'Out of spite.'

'And pride,' Demetrius added. The Interrogator-Chaplain was cleaning his bolter, but listening.

'Yes, my lords,' Ysentrud said. 'And fear.' She looked at Demetrius' skull mask and then quickly away. 'House Halven didn't trust the devices of the Adeptus Mechanicus. They thought the technology could be used to spy on them, or turned against them.'

'They feared that, and yet they let the Adeptus Mechanicus maintain their Knights?' Lazarus asked.

Ysentrud nodded. 'They had no choice. The machines were falling apart. They needed the Adeptus Mechanicus, and that made them even more fearful. Then came the Redwash War.

'When the daemons began to pour from the Redwash Gate, House Halven moved the southern contingent of their Knights out to defend Kap Sudsten,' Ysentrud continued. 'But when they met the daemons in battle, they were beaten.' She went silent and frowned. 'My lord, excuse me. That information is accurate, but not true. When these records were etched into me, I was given extensive cautions on how to speak about them. But you are not of House Halven, so I will tell you this. The Knights of Sudsten were destroyed by the daemons in a battle that lasted barely minutes, a battle which barely touched the army that had spilled through the Redwash Gate. Half the Knights of House Halven were beaten so badly and so quickly that a great deal of Kap Sudsten's population was lost, run down by the daemons as they tried to flee.'

'And so the continent of Sudsten and half the forces of House Halven were lost,' Lazarus said. Part of him wondered what use this was, if he was just indulging his penchant for gathering history and knowledge. But the voice of the grey-masked man kept coming back to him. *You have come for me again.* There was some history here that was secret from him, and secrets scraped at him like knife edges. He had some time, now, and he would spend it on this. 'What then of Norsten, and that half of the house?'

'The northern portion of House Halven had moved to assist

the moment the threat was known,' Ysentrud said. 'Though they needed the Adeptus Mechanicus to move their Knights across the ocean to Sudsten. By the time they arrived, the southern Knights had already fallen and the daemons were sacking Kap Sudsten. The northern Knights were unloaded, their pilots boarded them... and then they died.' She cleared her throat, and Lazarus poured a little water into the canteen's cap and handed it over. Ysentrud seemed shocked by the gesture, and tried a little curtsy while taking the cap, almost spilling it. Safely seated, she said, 'My thanks, lord,' and drank.

'They died, each and every one,' she continued. 'The remaining Knights of Halven stood by the sea, nothing more than tombs. And so the doom of Reis seemed sealed. But then at the last, the Dark Angels came and saved this world.'

The way she said it made her sound as if she were uncertain of the world's worth. Lazarus ignored it, concerned with the story she had laid out. 'What happened to the northern pilots of House Halven?'

'Treachery, my lord,' she said. 'One of the enginseers assigned to the repair and maintenance of House Halven's northern Knights, a man named Heris Amis, had been corrupted by the daemonic forces. He sabotaged the Thrones Mechanicum of House Halven's northern Knights, so when the pilots linked to their machines they were poisoned, their nervous systems ravaged, sending them into delirium and then death. The other enginseers detected the changes only after, but they were able to determine the culprit.'

'What happened to him?' Lazarus asked.

'Dealt with by the victorious Dark Angels. Along with all the others who had gone mad and joined the daemon army.' Ysentrud frowned. 'There were many, apparently. I never understood that.'

'Madness and despair are paths to ruin, and to the Ruinous Powers,' Interrogator-Chaplain Demetrius said. 'That is why we guard against them with faith and righteous fury.'

'Truth spoken, brother,' Lazarus said. He looked to Ysentrud. 'What happened to the Knights then? I assume the scrap in the Regent Prime's hall is what is left of House Halven's southern machines, along with the wreck with the spear through it. But what of the Knights from the north continent?'

'Lost, my lord,' she said. 'After the battle, after the findings and the executions, House Halven wanted to declare war on the Adeptus Mechanicus. They refused to believe it was just one enginseer who had caused their ruin. But the Dark Angels stopped them. They separated them, told the Adeptus Mechanicus to return to Norsten, and told House Halven that they would rule Sudsten only now. Then they ordered the Adeptus Mechanicus to repair the Knights and undo the damage their enginseer had caused. That made the survivors of House Halven howl. They didn't want the Mechanicus to touch their Knights any more, but the Dark Angels overruled them. But when the Knights were taken back to Norsten to be repaired, a storm hit the ship carrying them and it sank into one of the deepest parts of the ocean. Both the Adeptus Mechanicus and newly named Regent Prime blamed each other for that disaster, but it didn't change the fact that the machines that had been the heart of Halven's power for untold generations were gone.' She shook her tattooed head. 'But not forgotten.'

Lazarus thought of his meeting with the Regent Prime, in that ill-named hall hung with the crumpled pieces of destroyed war machines, thought of the man seated in that broken Throne Mechanicum, his useless implants glittering in the hazy light. 'The Regent Prime believes they may be found?' It was a foolish notion, after a millennium gone, but mortals embraced many foolish things.

'He does, my lord,' Ysentrud said. 'There are legends that the Knights of Halven will rise again. Ambiguous, contradictory legends, but they exist, and the Regent Prime seems to believe in them.' She paused and took a deep breath. 'Master Lazarus. If I... I mean, may I offer...'

'If you have some knowledge that bears on the question, speak it,' Lazarus said, and she ducked her head but spoke.

'Yes, lord. During my training, I occasionally partook of knowledge that was not officially sanctioned by the Regent Prime. Mostly folklore. But one of the more dangerous histories etched in me is the theory pushed forward by the leaders of a small, quickly crushed rebellion that occurred four centuries ago. The rebels claimed that these tales of the Knights' return were made up by House Halven to justify their rule over Sudsten. I... believe there may be truth to that. But I can tell you that the Regent Prime... He is a true believer. To him the Knights of his house are lost but not destroyed, and someday they will return to his house.'

'Is he a fool then?' Lazarus asked. The woman hesitated, and then finally nodded. There was a tinge of fear in her scent, and tension in the muscles of her neck and face. She feared speaking these truths, but she had, because she thought Lazarus should hear them. 'What about his son?'

'Master Lazarus, Sebastian does not believe,' the Learned said. 'He was given the implants as an infant, as all the heirs of House Halven are, and as a child he trained with his father on the simulator the house brought to Reis centuries ago. It is the one piece of technology that they've ever embraced. But as he grew older, he rejected his father's... dreams. Even questioned them, just publicly enough to draw his father's ire, but not his censure. He didn't risk that until he summoned you.'

And so Azrael sent me, Lazarus thought. *Because I confessed my doubt about our secrets, I am ordered to this place, and find myself battling with the secrets of these mortals.* 'Was there anything more to the tension between House Halven and the Adeptus Mechanicus?'

'No. Yes. I mean… your pardon, my lords. There was a thousand years of hate between them, but it was cold hate. The Adeptus Mechanicus and House Halven split this planet, but they try as hard as they can to pretend that the other doesn't exist, except as targets for petty slights.'

The Thunderhawk lurched, and Ysentrud clutched at the huge straps that half covered her. 'That's it, lord, except for arguments over boundaries and raw-material exchanges. I can go into great detail about all of them, if you wish.'

'No.' Especially when Lazarus could see Ephron running through the rituals of landing. They were almost to the Adeptus Mechanicus forge. 'Thank you, Learned Ysentrud, that will be all.' He meant the words but wasn't sure what he should be thankful for. He understood the feud between the planet's powers better now, but he didn't care about that. It didn't matter in this battle with the gris, who seemed completely unrelated to those events. Lazarus frowned, thinking, but in a way he was actually pleased. History was like a battle. It seemed like chaos when you were dropped into it, but as you looked around you could draw the lines, see the tactics, understand the goals. Eventually. If you weren't killed.

'Landing in ten, brothers,' Ephron called back.

Lazarus picked up his helm and snapped it into place. The displays inside lit up, picts of the compound below overlaid with maps and plans provided by the Fabricator Locum. Battle reports from each squad listed their readiness, and he could see the trajectories of the other Thunderhawks arcing down from the *Sword of Caliban* to the surface of this troublesome world.

History could kill in its own way, just as quickly as battle. But in battle, at least, Lazarus knew he could return the violence.

'Interrogator-Chaplain Demetrius!' he shouted, and the warrior raised his crozius arcanum, the fell weapon's skull gleaming in the hold's dim light.

'Brothers!' Demetrius shouted. 'Ready yourselves! We go to fight these unclean things again, these infected, monstrous gris, traitors to the Imperium! We have marked them, and from our hands the only mercy they will find is the release of death!'

'Death to the mutant! Death to the rebel! Death to the unclean!' the Dark Angels answered, in the hold and over the vox from *Rage of Angels*.

'For the Lion. For the Emperor. For our brothers.' Lazarus spoke the words slowly, his voice almost quiet after the shout. 'We are the Dark Angels. The shadow of our wings is death.'

CHAPTER FOURTEEN

Adamantine Wings' landing struts were just touching down when the door to its hold fell open, spilling pale sunlight and a dry, bitter wind into the ship. In her seat, Ysentrud flinched away from the rush of air. It *hurt*. Born and raised in the jungles of Sudsten, she was used to atmosphere that was heavy with heat and moisture and spores, rich with the scents of teeming life, the perfume of flowers, the reek of rot. The frigid air of Norsten was like razors in her lungs and across her skin. It pulled the heat from her and made her ache. A convulsion went through her, and she was shaking again, but it wasn't anything like the trembling of battle shock. This was a shuddering of her whole body, and it made her teeth click. Then the smell hit her. Acrid, harsh, it was the bitter smell of metal and electricity and chemicals, and it made her cough as her body shivered and shook.

By the time she recovered, the Space Marines were gone. They had rushed off the ship, out into the bright daylight, and she was alone. Should she stay? She had been meaning to ask if she should – if she could. She had no interest in being part of another battle. But she had got so wrapped up in answering questions for the Master of the Fifth that she had never got around to asking.

She probably could. They had left her behind, after all. She probably should. She was useless in a fight, more than useless, a liability, and the thought of hiding behind the armoured walls of this Thunderhawk was tempting. But the hatch was open, and the whisper of wind coming through it felt as if it was made of knives.

If she stayed here she was going to freeze to death, a possible termination she was familiar with from the histories etched into her brain but one she had never considered likely for herself. Now it seemed almost certain. Teeth still chattering, she wrapped her inadequate robes around herself, slipped off her seat and went outside.

It immediately felt like a mistake.

Outside was huge. There were no towering trees, no jungle to cut off the sky which stretched forever overhead, pale blue and marked by a few bands of white clouds. The horizon was interrupted by mountains, sharp-peaked and tall, but they were far, far away. The Adeptus Mechanicus had built their forge on a vast plain of stone – and snow. That must be what all the white, gritty stuff on the ground was. Snow. Ice that had fallen from the sky, so much of it that it made piles all around them. The snow gleamed under sunlight that seemed to carry no heat, but there were vast patches of it coloured grey and black and red, marked by the fallout of the factorum's squat vents. Those protruded out of the snow everywhere around them, a stunted forest black with soot or red with rust. Intermixed with them was a vast warren of pipes that popped up and then disappeared again, along with bundles of wires, some slung on poles, others just running along the ground. There were clusters of storage tanks painted a bewildering array of colours – some round, some square, some high, some low, huge and small. But of the forge's factoria themselves there was no sign. Except for the huge doors that were built into a low hill, tilted back against the ground so that they opened into a tunnel that dived down below the frozen earth. A tunnel that blazed with light and steamed with noxious exhalations. Sounds rolled out, a distant rattling like chains, a low grinding like the surf pounding rocks, and the occasional shrill trilling like the call of some giant, mad bird. The Adeptus Mechanicus factoria were buried, a vast underground warren that ran beneath stone and ice and snow.

Ysentrud stared at those gates as they flickered with strange lights, and she thought of some of the folklore she had absorbed. Most of it was ghost tales and gris stories, but some of it had been about daemons and their home in the warp, which had been universally described as a place of fire and smoke. The gates into the Adeptus Mechanicus' holding resembled those descriptions, but right now all she could think of was that it was probably warmer down there.

'Master of the Fifth.' The voice cut through the wind and the sounds spilling out through the gates. It was high and sweet, the words lyrical, and it distracted Ysentrud from the pain of the cold. She moved away from the ship, looking past its bulk to see where Lazarus and his men were standing in neat lines, their deadly weapons slung but inches away from their gaunt-leted hands. Before them stood a squad of... things.

They were roughly shaped like humans, and about the same size. They wore hooded ivory cloaks which were plain except for a red badge over the place a human's heart would be. The badges were shaped like the delicate skull of a long-beaked bird. Under those cloaks and hoods, lenses gleamed and metal flashed. Long tubes of something flexible and leathery coiled and shifted, some of them expanding and contracting as they moved air or liquid through them. Tiny brass actuators swivelled and twitched, and silver-plated joints flexed. The things may have been human once, but they had been so altered by bionics and cybernetics that now not a bit of humanity showed in the faces and claws that their cloaks didn't cover. These weren't like the monstrous cyborg servitors that Ysentrud had heard of. These were something else, as was the thing standing before them, speaking to Lazarus.

The thing's voice identified her as Fabricator Locum Gretin Lan. Her still, perfect face was recognisable too, but it was different, so different in the light of the sun than when it was woven together by a holocaster. It was still a perfectly symmetrical ivory mask of delicate features, but now Ysentrud could see its intricate filigree, the tiny openings in the ivory giving glimpses of something shining crimson below her face. She was all white of different kinds, except for those wine-coloured eyes and that almost hidden red. Her hair was long, but it wasn't made of strands. It looked more like narrow feathers arcing back from her face like a sweeping headdress. Her shoulders and arms were bare, and they were the same ivory filigree as her face, but the finely tooled holes here were large enough to reveal what lay beneath. It was striated bundles of flesh, crimson muscle stitched with strands of silver cable and gleaming white nerves. They stretched and moved beneath her ornate shell, as beautiful at a distance as they were hideous up close.

She wore a dress of eggshell-coloured silk. It clung to her breasts and belly, covering the disturbing filigree, but at her waist it flared out into a great skirt divided into hundreds of panels of slippery cloth that somehow clung together, hiding her legs completely. Legs that must have been extraordinarily long, because while the Fabricator Locum's torso and head were about the size of Ysentrud's, she stood almost as tall as Lazarus.

Her guard, as Ysentrud guessed the machine things must be, carried long guns over their shoulders – guns with heavy stocks and barrels that seemed to glow faintly in the sunlight. Gretin Lan carried no weapons, but a mechanical bird clung to one of her arms. It had wings, a beaked and crested head, a body made of metal bone and banded crimson muscle, and intricately jointed legs, but its tail was three times the size of its body, a great length of narrow feathers like the ones on the Fabricator Locum's head. All of its extravagant plumes were varying shades of white, and it was difficult to tell where the bird ended and Fabricator Locum began, but the talons on its feet were silver, shining, and wickedly sharp-looking, while its eyes were the same wine red as Gretin Lan's. A pet? A decoration? A tool? Ysentrud couldn't begin to guess.

There was something else about the Fabricator Locum that caught Ysentrud's eye, something easily seen but hard to identify. There were things moving around her, small things looping through the air in smooth orbits centred on her. They were skulls – not human, like the servo-skulls that Ysentrud was tattooed to resemble, but bird skulls. Small, delicate things, their beaks like thin spears. In each wide eye socket there was a spark of red, and there were at least a dozen of them, bobbing and circling around Gretin Lan, never still.

Ysentrud took all of it in, a flood of information so fast and strange it was almost like being etched. She watched and she listened as the Fabricator Locum continued speaking in her strangely harmonious voice.

'Dark Angels. Be welcome to my forge. Your offer of assistance is a gracious boon that we must discuss.' The music of her voice made her words sound grateful, welcoming, but there was a darker melody beneath, a strum of warning. Lazarus heard it too, judging by the hard edge in his deep voice.

'We offer nothing. We are here to slay the monstrous unclean. I will tell you what we require as we move towards the gris incursion.'

The Fabricator Locum's mask never changed, but the way she rose a little and tilted her head to look down on the Master of the Fifth conveyed volumes. 'This is *my* forge, noble Space Marine. It will be my circuits that are flayed if my quotas are not achieved. I will not have you and your weapons wreaking their ballistic havoc on my factoria.'

'And I will not allow my orders to be challenged.' Lazarus' voice was as cold as the air burning across Ysentrud's skin. 'Killing these unclean things is *my* purpose, the purpose for which I was created by the Emperor Himself, and I will pursue that purpose as I see fit. You have one choice, Fabricator Locum. Do as I say, or face the wrath of the heirs of the Emperor and the sons of the Lion.'

Her delicate arms folded across her chest and her head tilted, the colour of her eyes darkening as her pupils grew in shape and number. But she dropped herself down into a graceful bow, and when she rose, she stood just as tall as Lazarus again, no higher, no shorter. 'I give welcome to the Dark Angels to Forge Norsten, and greet you in the name of the Omnissiah, may They bless us in our production.'

'And in our destruction,' Lazarus said curtly. Gretin Lan blinked at him, then spun away, the hem of her skirt flaring just a little. Beneath, Ysentrud had a glimpse of her legs. There were four of them, enormous bird-like things roped with raw red muscle. They ended in feet with splayed toes bearing stubby claws, except for the central one. That toe carried a long, sickle-shaped claw, gleaming silver with an edge that looked sharp enough to cleave through stone. Each of those claws was cocked back, held up off the ground, just waiting for the Fabricator Locum to kick out and cut someone in twain.

'Everyone and everything here is a weapon,' Ysentrud whispered through lips gone numb. 'And I can barely move.'

But move she did, stumbling into almost a run, as the Fabricator Locum led Lazarus and the Dark Angels through the gates into the lights and smoke. Forge Norsten looked terrifying, but it also, praise the Emperor, looked warm.

It was warm.

There was a rush of wind as Ysentrud passed through the gate, a gust that came from fans buried in the tunnel's walls. The fans made a curtain of air that blocked out the cold, and when Ysentrud moved through it, she almost fell to her knees in relief. It was hot here, maybe not as hot as home, but warm enough that she no longer felt as if death was steadily pressing in on her, like shadows growing at sundown. But she had little time to appreciate the heat. A few steps beyond the invisible, turbulent curtain, she took her first real breath, and the flood of caustic gases that filled the air seared into her lungs like acid. She did fall then, knees banging on the stained rockcrete floor as her body was wracked by great, heaving coughs.

'Your mutant is suffering respiratory failure.' Ysentrud could barely hear the Fabricator Locum, but she felt the huge hand on her back, grabbing her robes and lifting her up to her feet.

'Hold your breath and close your eyes.' Lazarus' deep voice rumbled through her, and she tried to do as he said, but she couldn't stop coughing. 'She requires a rebreather.'

An eternity passed while she fought to stop coughing and tried not to inhale any more toxic air. Then something pressed over her face, and she felt cooler air hiss across her skin. She took a breath, and it was dry and flat and dead, but clear of the harsh toxins that had been rasping through her alveoli. After a few more coughs, she got herself under control. She reached up and tapped the giant armoured hand holding the mask to her face, and it pulled away, leaving her to hold the rebreather. She took it off for a moment, holding her breath while she used her grubby sleeve to clean the tears and snot from her face. Then she put the mask back on, wrapping the straps around her head.

'Are we now ready?' Gretin Lan asked. 'You are eager, I believe, to bring your destructive cleansing.'

'We are,' Lazarus said, his voice low and flat, and Ysentrud wondered how the Fabricator Locum could stand having it directed at her. Being mostly machine must have its advantages, she thought. 'Continue,' he told Lan, and then looked down at Ysentrud. 'We require celerity, Learned. Brother Asbeel will take you.'

Before she could respond, Ysentrud felt something grasp the back of her robes. She was hoisted into the air by the Apothecary, who set her on his shoulder, a servo-arm holding her in place. It wasn't comfortable, but with their long strides Ysentrud knew she would never have been able to keep up on her own. Too small, too weak, compared to these transhumans in their armour or the cybernetic fanatics of the Machine God. Forget keeping up, she couldn't even breathe down here, unlike all of them.

'And they call me mutant,' she muttered to herself. She just had some mould in her brain that made her remember things better, took her hair and made her red. They–

'Do you require something?' Asbeel asked her.

'No, Lord Apothecary,' she said quickly, her voice still harsh. They had transhuman senses too, which she best remember with her mutant powers. She frowned behind the clear mask of her rebreather, annoyed at her sulking. But at least it was a distraction from what they were heading into. There would be another battle, and she wasn't sure if she could stomach that again, despite the fact that her belly was hollow, emptied by time and vomiting.

They took a turn off the entrance tunnel, down another, turned again and went down another, always moving deeper into the earth. The massive tunnels dwarfed Gretin Lan and the Dark Angels, and even the Dreadnought looked small pacing down the rockcrete halls. They were brightly lit by huge white lumens that hung from the ceiling like regularly spaced stars. The light pouring from them was as harsh as it was bright, washing out colours and making everything ugly, except for the Fabricator Locum in her varied whites. But the brightness made the tunnels sterile and endless, their grey walls perfectly flat and even except for two bands of carvings, one about ten feet off the ground, the other around sixty. The higher band was a line of pictures, of machines and parts of machines, of mathematical equations and chemical formulas, of dense lines of text in a language she couldn't read. It seemed more like some kind of text or instruction manual than art. The lower carvings were just dots and dashes, repeating endlessly with no pattern she could discern. Ysentrud had no idea what they meant until she saw a servitor moving down one of the tunnels that intersected with theirs. A thin line of red laser light sliced out from the cyborg and traced over the carvings as the servitor passed, and from hidden speakers a low, musical chant came, mixed with a strange mechanical hissing. The noise changed tempo as the cyborg slowed down to dodge around a cleaning machine, then increased again as the cyborg sped back up. The carvings were like a music box she had once seen, their shapes pulling these chants from the servitors as they passed.

Prayers? Music? Directions? All three, possibly. Directions of some sort would be needed. They'd only made a few turns, but they'd passed innumerable other tunnels running off in every direction and Ysentrud knew she was hopelessly lost. She would have to have been an etcher Wyrbuk to remember their route. But the Fabricator Locum moved swiftly through the tunnels, until she stopped outside a heavy metal door. It was shut, but twisted in its frame, the metal warped and buckled. Ten more of the machine men waited outside it, their guns in their hands.

'Factorum C-433.' Gretin Lan turned to the door, her dark red eyes focused on it. The bird skulls that flew around her hung still now, their sharp beaks and crimson pinprick eyes all aimed at the damaged portal. 'When the Reis Home Levies, now bearing designate gris, rushed inside, they came straight through the complex to this location and sealed themselves inside.' She pointed at the buckled door. 'Pict casters showed that the doors were damaged by use of low-yield explosives, then blockaded from the inside through destruction of our assembly equipment.' The music of her words seethed with anger.

'There were nine major and seventeen minor ways to enter this factorum on your plans,' Lazarus said. 'Did they seal those too?'

'Each portal was secured,' the Fabricator Locum said. 'Quickly. The hostiles also actioned damage to each pict caster and passive auspex scanner in the factorum, causing malfunction. They were aware of each sensor's location. The gris designates' understanding of the workings of my forge is as puzzling as it is unacceptable. I require knowledge about this.'

'Know later. Now is the time for ending.' As Lazarus spoke, Asbeel reached up and lowered Ysentrud to the ground. The Space Marines were forming up, shifting weapons, getting ready for… something. Ysentrud hesitated. She wanted to put as much distance between herself and whatever the massive warriors were about to do as possible, but she did not want to leave their protection.

'Guards have been set at each entrance, as I commanded?' Lazarus asked.

'The fulfilment of those commands was achieved even before you gave them,' Gretin Lan said. 'A standard base ten of skitarii such as these' – she waved at her cyborg guardians – 'are fixed before each major entrance. The minor entrances are patrol-protected by weaponised servo-skulls. If the gris designates attempt redeployment, I will know instantly.'

'Then we begin.' As Lazarus spoke, the Dreadnought Azmodor moved forward. The Dark Angels cyborg's fist was raised, and the air shimmered around it, snapping and popping as if it were glass beginning to break.

'By the Holy Maker of Machines,' the Fabricator Locum said, and Ysentrud couldn't tell if she was pleading or praying. But she turned and stepped smoothly between the Dreadnought and the doors. 'This course of action you are designating cannot–'

'Wait,' said Lazarus. 'I have read your attack strategies in the information you sent me. We do not have time to wait for their rebreathers to die, or for you to raise the temperature in the factorum enough to broil them. We don't have time for any of your other sanitised, no-confrontation attacks. The gris know your layout, and they took that factorum for a reason. Five thousand reasons, perhaps.'

Five thousand? Ysentrud stared at Lazarus in confusion. What was he talking about?

'You reference the malefactor designates sent to us by the Imperium for processing into mining and Lathe-pattern multi-task servitors. Their preparation is still in first stages,' Gretin Lan said, waving her hand, bundles of muscles flexing beneath the filigree. 'Cryogenic stasis has only been ended for two hundred, and those units were in the midst of surgical conditioning. Such processing renders them functionally useless. Even if gris designates sought to thaw remaining heretical units to infect, such action would require multiple complex operations. Therefore, we have time—'

'No,' Master Lazarus said. 'Your time is done. Brother Azmodor.'

The Dreadnought moved forward, and the Fabricator Locum had to back away or be trampled. 'Assertion acknowledged,' she said, the music behind her voice sharp and fast. 'Please allow me to provide additional pertinent information. I have already had charges set around this entrance to facilitate removal of the damaged doors. They can be activated when you command.'

'I command it. Now.' Lazarus drew his sword, and it pulsed and flickered, its energy field dancing around it like shadows. Behind him, the squad of Space Marines bearing chainswords formed up while Azmodor stayed crouched in front of the door. They had barely fallen into position when the Fabricator Locum spoke a single word.

'Ignus.'

There was a sizzle around the edges of the metal, and white lines drew themselves across the seams. Even through the rebreather, Ysentrud caught the smell of burning metal, and then the great door shifted and fell forward into the hall.

Azmodor didn't step out of its way. He reached up with his

great fist, and its power field made the metal shriek and warp as he caught the falling door by one red-hot edge. He took it and turned, throwing it down the wide hall. It landed on the floor with a sound like thunder, sparks streaking up as it slid across the rockcrete and smashed aside a maintenance servitor which had been scrubbing at a dark smear on the floor. Ysentrud was still gaping at the sliding door when the Dreadnought moved forward and swung his fist into the machinery piled on the other side of it. The tunnel filled with noise, an avalanche of crashing echoes, as the makeshift barrier exploded into debris and flew back into the vast space beyond the door.

Without realising it, Ysentrud had stepped back to the far wall, hands tight over her ears, but she couldn't escape that storm of sound. The Dreadnought pulled back his fist and then pistoned it out, charging forward as he did, crashing through what was left of the barrier. Ysentrud caught a glimpse of the other side, but it was full of shadows, a black hole compared to the brightly lit hall. Then she saw nothing but the backs of the Dark Angels, following Lazarus into the black.

'Remember your assignment!' The deep voice was Demetrius', the Interrogator-Chaplain standing before Gretin Lan, his crimson and green eyes glaring into her dividing pupils. 'Nothing comes through this door, whether it is trying to flee out or rush in. Understood?'

'I am fully cognizant of the task assigned to me,' she answered, matching his gaze.

'By the Emperor you should be,' Demetrius growled. He pointed towards Ysentrud, and only the wall behind her kept her from flinching back. 'Keep watch on her, and keep her safe. The Master of the Fifth commands you.'

Then he was gone, disappearing with the last of his brothers into the darkness. Beyond the broken doors, the factorum was a cavern carved out of stone like the hall, but so much larger. It was dark, its lumens almost all shut down except a flickering few, but the brightness from the hall flashed off vast machines that squatted like strange, still monsters, connected by webs of cables and long conveyer belts. Stacks of supplies sat around them, mounds of materials and boxes and barrels, massive shadows in the dark.

That dark was beginning to split now, cut by flashes of light, the snapping flash of stub guns, the strobing fire of bolters, and with those flares of brightness came the cracking sounds of shots and the screaming whine of the chainswords. Ysentrud flinched from the noise, and then she noticed Gretin Lan. Her cyborg skitarii had arranged themselves into neat formations, most of them guarding the blown-open door to the factorum, standing by to deal with any gris that might try to escape. Others had arranged themselves in the hall, guarding against attack from any other direction. The Fabricator Locum, though, stood in the centre of the hall, her back to the open door, surrounded by her cloud of tiny skulls, arms crossed. Her body was still, as still as her face, but on her arm that great white bird stirred, head shifting, wings spreading a little as its exposed muscles flexed in time with the sounds of the battle. Often in time with Ysentrud's flinching. The motion of the bird-thing made Ysentrud wonder whether Fabricator Locum hated those battle sounds as much as she did.

The bird caught her looking at it and shifted on Gretin Lan's arm, dark red eyes staring at her. Gretin's head turned, following the gaze of her pet. 'Learned Ysentrud Wyrbuk. Your altered mind retains a history of this world. Perform the following query – has there ever been a failure to meet Imperial quota on Reis?'

Ysentrud took a breath. Slipping into memen was tempting. She could leave her fear behind, lose herself in history. But she couldn't make herself vulnerable like that. Not surrounded by allies she barely trusted more than the enemy. So she spun through her memories but stayed present.

'There are two instances shortly after Reis rejoined the Imperium in which House Halven came in just below the tithe requirement. Both times they came within five per cent, and both times they were granted clemency through corporal mortification. The forge of the Adeptus Mechanicus has a separate tithe system, and I have no direct records for them. But...' She hesitated. The rest was speculation, and Learned Thiemo had warned against such things. But she didn't mind making Fabricator Lan squirm. Or at least her bird. 'But seven hundred years ago, circumstantial records indicate that a substantial gas pocket was hit during mining operations on Norsten. Most of the mine itself supposedly collapsed. There is no information regarding whether or not this affected quota, but that seems likely. Months later, after the accident and the quota shipment, the Fabricator Locum at the time was reported killed in that explosion. A new Locum arrived later.'

'Terminated.' Gretin Lan shook her head. 'Their functions ceased as sanction for incompetence. Though perhaps not fully ceased. Analysis indicates that significant portions of his corpus were incorporated into the forge's main cogitation system.'

Ysentrud didn't know how to answer that, so she stayed silent. There was no sound except the distant thunder of a bolter and the hiss of her breath through the rebreather. Then the lights flickered.

Gretin Lan raised her face towards the shining globes overhead, tiny muscles shifting beneath her filigree mask as her eyes narrowed. When the lights flickered again, going out long enough to make Ysentrud blink in the darkness, the Fabricator

Locum moved, backing up towards the broken door of the factorum. The skitarii moved around her, a line of ten remaining between her and the dark interior while the rest split and moved into the hall, half on one side of the doors, half on the other. They formed lines across the rockcrete, the ones in front kneeling down, with their glowing guns raised, the ones behind them levelling their weapons over their heads.

'What's happening?' Ysentrud stepped away from the wall, feeling exposed. There was no cover in this empty tunnel besides the skitarii themselves, or the Fabricator Locum's skirts.

'The forge's noosphere has fallen. Connection with the pict casters and auspex sensors has been lost. But something comes.'

Ysentrud barely understood what the Fabricator Locum was saying, but she could hear something that sounded like fear in the strange music of the machine-woman's voice. She ran across the hall, sliding in behind Gretin Lan. She didn't trust the Fabricator Locum, but at least Lan had been ordered by Demetrius to protect her. Ysentrud moved just in time, because as she took her place between the wide white skirts and the cloaked skitarii, the lights went out again and stayed out. The hall went black as blindness, the only illumination the crimson sparks that shone from the eye sockets of the bird skulls floating around the Fabricator Locum, and the soft shimmer of her guard's guns, blue in the darkness.

'Targets approach,' said the Fabricator Locum, and suddenly there was light, crimson light flaring down the hall. It came from her flock of skulls, their red lumen beams splitting the dark. In the hazy gloom at the reach of the beams there was the gleam of something reflective, then movement. Shapes, bulky shadows at the edge of the light. Ysentrud couldn't understand what she was seeing – pallid skin and red-glowing metal – then she realised they were the ill-made shapes of servitors.

She felt a wave of relief sweep through her, knowing the disturbing, corpse-like things served Fabricator Locum, but that feeling was shattered with a flood of illumination. A spear of brilliant laser light lanced down the hall from the right and smashed through the double ranks of skitarii on that side. Two of them fell, a smoking hole punched through the head of one and into the belly of the other. They had barely hit the floor before the skitarii fired back.

Lightning leapt from their guns, jagged lances that snapped through the red-tinged shadows almost as bright as the lasbeam. They hit the servitor, and metal sparked as flesh sizzled and boiled. The servitor lurched to a halt, but there were more coming up behind it, strangely angled shadows shifting in the dark. There were those with twisted bodies mounted on tracks and spidery legs, but mixed in with them was something else. Four-legged things built like beasts. Maybe they *had* been beasts once, but now they were an amalgam of armoured plates and twisting hoses, sharp-clawed metal limbs and glowing sensors.

Ysentrud gaped at these new monsters, horrified, and then they were charging forward, horribly fast, their claws ringing off the rockcrete. As they closed, fire suddenly roared from their metal muzzles, orange-yellow flames pouring out over the line of skitarii. Gretin Lan's guards fell, buzzing and smoking, the stench of burning synthetics mixing with scorched meat. Then the cyborg beasts were on the skitarii, their claws tearing into the survivors.

'What...?' Ysentrud gasped, then whipped around when flames bloomed across the hall. There were more monstrous cyborgs and servitors gathered there, rushing forward to attack that line of skitarii.

'Sulphurhounds co-opted. Position untenable,' Gretin Lan snapped. The skulls were spinning around her, thin lines of light lancing from them, slashing down the hall towards the servitors. The bird on her arm had spread its wings wide, the edges of its feathers gleaming like razors. 'Fall back into factorum C-433!'

Fall back. Ysentrud barely heard the order in the din, but she knew what it was when everyone moved around her. The skitarii assigned to guard the door were retreating, skittering over the debris left from the Dark Angels' violent entrance. Gretin Lan spun, her skirt flaring to show the murderous claws of her bird-like legs. Ysentrud had to move fast to stay with her, clinging to the Fabricator Locum's skirts as she strode into the factorum. The flying cloud of bird skulls were all around her, zipping through the air in complex patterns, somehow never hitting one another nor anything else as they swung around their mistress. One of them fired a laser as it whizzed by Ysentrud, the bright beam slicing through the air so close to her face she could feel its heat. It vanished into the dark, aimed at some unknown target, and then the skull was gone, flying on. Ysentrud wished she could fly too as she tried to dodge through the chunks of debris, but the corner of her robe snagged on a twisted strut as she ran into the factorum.

Ysentrud was yanked hard to the side as the thin fabric of her robe refused to tear and she fell, landing awkwardly. A broken chunk of rockcrete dug into her ribs, smashing the breath out of her. Gasping, she tried to pull herself up, but as she reached out, the cut on her arm from the stimm farm screamed in pain, and her hand spasmed, and she only got to her knees, trying in vain to scrabble back.

Gretin Lan was gone, her whiteness lost in the red-tinted gloom, and the skitarii were suddenly all around Ysentrud. The cyborgs were moving backwards, nimbly picking their way through the debris like long-limbed bugs. Their lightning guns flashed in their hands, spewing bolts back behind them, but the lenses of their eyes were bright with the las-fire and flames of their attackers. One fell, stinking of scorched metal and flesh, a burning line cut halfway across its chest by a bar of light. Another went down, body jerking as stub-gun slugs slammed into it. Ysentrud was still trying to get up, trying to rip her robe off the debris it had caught on. Trying and failing, and the skitarii were moving on, leaving her behind – until she felt a hand close on her collar.

The skitarius that grabbed her stank of oil and ozone, and the touch of its hand against the back of her neck was like cold leather. Ysentrud flinched away instinctively, but the cybernetic warrior didn't notice.

'Mortal designate will accompany.' Its voice was like harsh static, shaped into words. When it jerked on her collar, the bottom of her robe ripped, coming free, and the skitarius dragged her across the floor behind it. It only got a few steps before one of the sulphurhounds leapt over the debris and smashed into it, clawed limbs slashing the skitarius' back. A gout of blood splattered across Ysentrud as the skitarius fell beside her, and she felt its leg smash into her shoulder as the corpse spasmed and kicked. At least the blow knocked her out of its convulsing grip, away from the bestial cyborg that was ripping Gretin Lan's guard to shreds. But in the red light she could see the thing pause and turn its head, the dull amber glow of its sensors tracking her as she tried to crawl away.

Ysentrud went perfectly still, but the sulphurhound pulled its claws from the back of the ruined skitarius and stalked towards her. She could smell it, the stench of hot metal and caustic chemicals mixing with blood, and the clink of its claws against the floor somehow cut through the sound of battle behind her. Staring at it, breath held, frozen, Ysentrud waited until she saw it crouch and then began to turn, knowing she would be too slow, that it was going to tear her down before she could even get to her feet.

Then a delicate bird skull cut past her through the air, a tiny thing no bigger than her eye. It flew straight at the cyborg, its sharp beak driving into the monstrous beast's chest. It hit and stuck, but aside from causing a tiny trickle of blood seemed to do nothing at all. The sulphurhound twitched, but it ignored the skull and started its leap, claws spreading as it threw itself at Ysentrud – and then the little skull exploded. The violence contained in that tiny weapon was limited but carefully applied, the force directed into the chest of the sulphurhound. There was the hideous wet noise of tissue shredding mixed with the crack of bone, and the cyborg's chest was gone, just a raw red wound threaded with a few metal pieces holding it together. Then those bent, warped, and the bestial thing fell to pieces on the floor.

Ysentrud felt nauseous, but it was almost lost in the static of fear – and the grim determination to survive. She pulled herself up, and the moment she came to her feet Lan's white bird appeared in front of her, wings spread and eyes flashing. Its beak was open, spitting projectiles, thin needles of death.

'Proceed, mutant, or my guarantee to your Dark Angels master will be voided by your hesitation.' It was the Fabricator Locum's voice, but it spilled out of the bird even as it dived around her, its long tail feathers a drifting curtain of white, its eyes flashing as it fired shots into the dark. Ysentrud followed, waiting to feel the pain in her back from some killing blow, but it never came. Seconds later she was dodging skitarii, moving through the ragged line they had formed among the debris, crouching behind cover where they could. The Fabricator Locum stood beyond them, sheltered by a massive stack of copper wire spools.

'If you expect shielding, you must stay with me,' Gretin Lan said. Her face was expressionless as ever, but the muscles behind the filigree were twitching and the music of her voice held a snarled note of irritation. 'Always.' Her bird landed on her arm, and she raised it up, the pupils in her eyes spinning and splitting as she examined her pet for any possible damage.

'I'm trying to,' Ysentrud answered, wishing she sounded angry instead of desperate. A line of light hit a spool overhead, and she moved away from the pile, avoiding the spatters of molten copper. 'What are those things? Why are they attacking us?' First the gris, now these half-machine monsters, and were they fighting together or was this something else, a rebellion of enslaved cyborgs against their makers? And which would be worse?

'Designate *things* are mix of manufactured servitors and newly completed sulphurhounds, cyborg weapons produced for Adeptus Mechanicus forces. Query, why have they attacked – answer unknown.' Gretin Lan's anger was clear in her voice. Around them, the skitarii began to lay down a barrage of shots, not aiming, just flinging a sheet of lightning at the entrance where the servitors now clustered.

'What do we do?' Ysentrud shouted over the roar of the skitarii guns. The Fabricator Locum's answer was to wave one hand towards the door. Four of the bird skulls orbiting her rose up, streaking towards the ceiling. They slammed into the rockcrete above the opening, beaks driving in deep, and then they exploded.

Rockcrete cracked and dust burst out, a dull cloud that covered the door. There was thunder from inside the cloud, the sound of stone falling and breaking. The skitarii stopped firing, and the muzzle flashes from the servitors' stub guns disappeared. The light was now just a dull red glow spilling from two of the Fabricator Locum's bird skulls and a dull white haze from the distant lumens in the factorum. The only sounds were the settling of the stone and Ysentrud's breathing.

Gretin Lan stared at the drifting dust and the pile of broken rockcrete that covered where the door had been. 'The variables of this attack have shifted significantly. We must find the Dark Angels and discuss the strategy of our survival.'

CHAPTER FIFTEEN

The tunnels were narrow, low and damp, and they twisted through the earth like veins, a vast network of foetid passages that reeked of mud and mould. Caught in their grip, hunched over because he could not stand up straight, Ancient Jequn moved through them, shifting his vision with every careful step as he stalked the gris.

'Nox,' he said quietly, subvocalising the word to his armour, and the dark vision of his helmet drew silvery-white lines along the tunnel ahead, highlighting every toolmark carved in the soft walls. It made the ragged puddles on the floor gleam like quicksilver and outlined the hole in the wall ten yards ahead where another tunnel intersected this one.

'Thermis.' Washes of colour replaced white as Jequn's armour showed him the traces of heat that clung to the walls. Mostly faint blue, but there were a few greens and yellows, marks where the gris had passed through and left a bit of their heat behind, a thermal track.

'Ultra.' Most of the tunnel went a dull white, a different kind of blindness, but there were spots that stained the purity. Dark drops marked the floor and sometimes smeared the walls, a ragged trail of blood. This was what Jequn had been following ever since they had smashed their way into the gris' tunnels with an explosive knock.

Ephron's plan had worked. A few hours after Techmarine Cadus landed a Thunderhawk on the muddy ruins of the stimm farm, a network of arcane equipment had been spread out through the jungle, long spikes driven into the ground by members of Squad Jotha and Squad Invis. Invis had come down with Cadus, and with their help and that of the Scouts, the Techmarine had quickly connected all the spikes with nerus cord, a black web of cables that all ran back to a metal box covered in prayers and purity seals. A sanctioned cogitator, its complicated machine spirit was eager to glimpse the world through violence, and they gave the mathematical machine its wish by detonating a demolition charge that Cadus had carefully set in the ground.

'It maps the earth sonically using the shockwaves,' the Tech-marine had said, but Jequn had ignored his explanation and focused on the map the cogitator drew across a flickering holo-field. A rendering of the tunnel network the gris had used to attack the Fifth. A map that let them find a way around the blockage the gris had left, a way to infiltrate their burrow and hunt them down.

But that meant crawling through these warp-damned tunnels.

'Visiblis.' The normal spectrum of light, the one mortal eyes used, and once again, as it had been for so many cycles before, only darkness touched his vision, a view as black as nothing. It was a time to sharpen his other senses, to taste the air and feel the walls, to listen for something, anything, moving towards them. That constant cycle, of switching between senses, between kinds of perception, was a skill he had honed long ago in the Deathwing.

'Nox,' he whispered again, and vision of a sort came back, gleaming lines lancing through the dark, outlining the walls, and for a moment a memory clouded his vision. A narrow corridor of steel, not earth, a black labyrinth twisting through the bowels of a massive ship, a space hulk drifting through the vast dark. A place of silence and darkness and stillness, until the xenos beasts came rushing down the corridors towards them, monsters with gaping maws and reaching claws on too many limbs, things with gleaming eyes and glowing saliva, screaming as they charged, bolter fire bouncing off their armoured carapaces...

No. Jequn pushed the memory away, running through the Litany of Horrors Past, focused on seeing the curving walls of the tunnel before him, not the squared-off passages of the long-dead ship. His time with the Deathwing was a century ago, and whatever these gris were, they weren't genestealers with claws and teeth that could tear through the thickest ceramite.

'Thermis.' He had finally reached the opening in the wall of the passage they were pushing down. The heat marks were brighter here, glowing green and yellow on the wall like bruises, and when he told his vision to move to ultra, he could see the black marks of blood spotting the new tunnel's floor. He activated his vox.

'Brothers,' Jequn said softly. 'This way.'

He followed the blood, moving carefully, and he could sense his brothers at his back. This tunnel was narrower, and he wondered if the Primaris Space Marines in Squad Jotha would make it through. But the Scouts' armour lacked the bulk of the Firstborn Space Marines of Squad Invis, and they all followed

Jequn's lead with only a few small sounds of scraping earth until the tunnel began to widen.

Jequn's vision shifted again to visiblis, and it was no longer dark. There was light ahead, thin but there, so the Ancient commanded his armour to stay on the visible light spectrum. Jequn's keen eyes could see what looked like some kind of crude door ahead, rough wood planks bound together and set over the end of the passage. The light leaked through the gaps between the planks and around their edges, harsh and white. Whatever space lay beyond was lit with lumens, and Jequn moved forward carefully, his sword in his hands, the crackling power field off, but his finger on the activation stud, ready. Yet there was nothing between him and the door – no guards, no sign of traps or surveillance. It was just those crude planks, nothing more, though from this close he could see that the walls changed here. They went from damp soil to stained, broken rockcrete, a good half a yard of it. The opening covered by the rough door was a crack in a heavy wall, thick enough to belong to a fortress.

The Ancient reached out to touch the planks, carefully testing them, and they wobbled like a loose tooth. The door wasn't fixed in place, the boards simply leaned against the broken rockcrete to make a rough barrier. Its weakness was almost disappointing, but Jequn decided to smash it away anyway.

He waited until the rest of his brothers had drawn as close as they could. 'Ready your anger,' he told them, then started to count down from three. On one he raised his boot and kicked the crude barrier. The boards flew apart, and Jequn charged forward, the power field blazing to life around the blade of his sword. The others followed, Squad Invis staying together, their bolters raised, while Squad Jotha spread out, the bolter carbines they had brought into the tunnels at the ready.

Beyond the shattered door was another tunnel, but it dwarfed the twisting dirt passages they had come from. It was a rigid square of rockcrete walls, sixty feet high and wide. The tunnel stretched off into darkness on Jequn's left, but forty yards to the right it ended in a set of blast doors. The thick walls were broken by age, cracked and buckling in places, with dirt, thick roots and trickles of water spilling through. Lichen and mould ran riot over the rockcrete, staining it with ugly patches of green and yellow and brown. The floor was thick with mud that had washed through the cracks – only the blast doors seemed untouched, free of any corrosive stain. Their silvery metal shone in the light that spilled down from a line of lumens running along the centre of the tunnel's ceiling. The ones farthest from the doors were dark, cracked and broken, but those closer began to show some life. Many were dim, their light muted, or they flickered and strobed, flashing between bright and dark with buzzing snaps. The last few still glowed like new, and they cast a harsh, industrial light down onto the blast doors and the death that lay before them.

Jequn couldn't tell how many bodies lay there. The drifts of mould that covered the corpses made them into a sprawling charnel pile. Some of the bodies were animals, but most of them were humans. They had been stripped bare, the fresher corpses on the edge of the mound showing patches of skin through the mould that grew across them. There were ragged splotches of red and black, but most of the mould was grey, the same grey as the ugly masks that covered the gris' faces. Near the doors, where the bodies were piled high, the mould was a thick grey blanket, and almost nothing could be seen of the corpses beneath except for horribly suggestive shapes that rippled the greasy velvet coating of decay.

Jequn saw all of that as he crashed into the tunnel, catalogued it and set it aside, focusing on the immediate enemy. There were gris in the tunnel, filthy figures with mud-caked clothes and feet, their skin spotted with grey growth. They stood in haphazard groups, or sprawled in the mud like toy soldiers abandoned by a child. But when Jequn smashed through the door they all began to move, jerking to life like a single organism, turning to face the Dark Angels with empty eyes and weapons raised. One, a man dressed in the tattered remnants of a Reis Home Levies uniform, was directly in front of Jequn, and he raised his autogun up to point it at the Ancient's chest. The standard bearer of the Fifth swung his power sword up in a massive blow which ripped the gris in two.

'Strength of the Lion!' Jequn shouted. 'Strength of his blood!'

The tunnel was suddenly full of thunder, the sharp hammer blows of the Scouts' carbine bolters and the roar of the plasma incinerators as their crackling bursts superheated the air around them. Mixed with that fury was the lesser crack of the gris' guns and the growling rev of the mining tools some wielded – drills and power picks and shearing blades. Through the din of battle, the only voices were the snap of orders over the vox as the sergeants of both squads organised their men. It was unnerving – Jequn had fought countless foes, and all of them had been loud in their own way, filling the air over the battlefield with their words or roars. But these gris were silent, whether they were charging forward or being smashed back by exploding shells or plasma bursts.

Jequn moved across the tunnel, cutting down every grey-smeared figure in reach. He smashed into a man in coveralls who was swinging a power pick at him, breaking the gris' leg with a stomping kick before the tip of his sword ripped out the man's throat. Another gris rushed him while he pulled the sword back, driving at him with the spinning tip of a rock drill.

Jequn slipped to the side, letting the sharp bit scrape across his armour. He pulled his sword down and it crashed into the tool, shattering its housing. The drill ripped itself to pieces, the spinning shaft flinging away shrapnel that pinged off Jequn's armour and ripped through the gris' flesh. The infected fell without a sound, his blood splashing across the Ancient's breastplate.

The fight was dying out around Jequn, the bodies of the enemy sprawled across the muddy floor. The huge tunnel they had broken into was filled now with a haze of smoke and the stench of burning meat and mould. Most of the gris were shattered wrecks, blood dripping from the walls behind them, splattered there by the shrapnel of bolter rounds. Squad Invis were standing together at the centre of the tunnel, near the edge of the grey-covered corpse pile, the lumens near the door gleaming off their armour. Squad Jotha were moving in the shadows, looking for any survivors.

Jequn reached down and ripped the shirt from a dead gris, then wiped it across his breastplate, polishing the unclean blood from the Imperial aquila set there as he stared grimly at the mound of mould-covered dead. 'Squad Jotha, perimeter,' he snapped as he threw down the cloth. The Scouts moved to obey, circling the tunnel, checking the darkened side for signs of more of the enemy. Jequn began to stalk towards the doors, but as he passed the mouldering pile of corpses, he noticed a line of living mortals chained down among the rotting remains. They were almost indistinguishable from the dead, until one of them raised his head and called out, his voice harsh and desperate, 'Help! Please! Get me away from here!'

There were five of them, dressed in rags, their wrists cuffed and their necks collared. Chains ran through loops on their bindings, holding them down to the floor. Four of the mortals were still, silent, seemingly dead in the mud – but their chests still moved. The fifth rolled to his knees as Jequn approached, trying to rise but stopped by the bindings that held him down. 'Free me!' he croaked. 'Quickly! They're not dead!'

'Who–' Jequn started, but before he could get any more words out, the corpses in the centre of the pile exploded.

Mould showered up and out, a cloud of it rising in the light like a thunderhead, a storm of spores that hid whatever violence had happened beneath. It wrapped around Jequn, blinding him, and poured past to envelop Squad Invis. In the sudden murk, grey forms lunged past, vaguely shaped like men but too big. From the gloom behind him came the thunderous crack of Squad Invis' weapons, and a bolter round flashed by Jequn, missing him by less than a yard.

'Invis, draw knives!' Jequn shouted as he charged through the cloud. Suddenly the fog around him thinned enough to reveal a brother Space Marine, caught in the grip of something grey, a figure almost formless in the haze, its boundaries ill-defined. It was roughly humanoid, two arms, two legs, a torso with a lumpy mass on top that was something like a head, but it was big, the top of its head reaching the chin of the Firstborn it grappled with. Its body was covered in shrouds of grey, fuzzy sheets that wept thick mucus.

Grey. The grey lumps Jequn had thought were fungus covering the bodies. It had been these things instead, feeding, sleeping or lying in wait – he didn't know which, nor did he care. The only thing the standard bearer of the Fifth needed to know now was the line between this gris-born thing and his battle-brother, so he could bring his sword to bear.

The easiest target was the head. Jequn moved in, dropping his blade into the space between his brother's armour and the grey thing's neck. Then he flicked the power sword on as he jerked the weapon back.

The crackling sheath of destructive energy tore through the grey folds, slicing deep. More of the grey fluid gouted out, covering Jequn and the other Space Marine, the thick liquid popping and hissing as it boiled on the sword blade. But halfway through the monster's neck, the sword bucked in Jequn's hand, twisting as if it had hit something as solid as armour in the centre of the soft grey mass. Jequn tightened his grip, but his sword stayed still, snapping and hissing in the midst of the thing, until it finally moved – back, in the other direction, sliding in tiny jerks towards his brother.

'I am a son of the Lion,' Jequn grated between clenched teeth. He set his other hand on the sword hilt, shifting so that the strength of his body and his armour was all focused on the sword, driving it back. It stopped moving, buzzing and crackling where it was, halfway out of the gris' neck, the deadly edge of its field a handspan from his battle-brother. 'His strength is in my body. His will is in my soul!' Jequn wrenched with all his might, the heavy muscles of his back tightening, the servos in his armour straining with him, until the sword started to move where he wanted it to. An inch, then one more, and then with a lurch it was carving through the gris' neck. It was a wretched, ragged cut that was nothing like the smooth lines of death he usually carved through his enemies, but for this it would do.

With a final jerk, Jequn ripped the sword out, and the head of the thing tumbled down its back, trailing long strips of tattered mould. A fountain of grey slime burst from the stump of its neck, viscous and sticky. Most of it showered over the other Dark Angel, but enough clung to Jequn to blur his vision through his helmet. Still, he could see that the decapitated gris' hands still clutched at his battle-brother. Headless, oozing its grey slime, it kept its feet even as the other Space Marine carved great wounds in its belly and chest with his combat knife. They would have to cut this thing to ribbons to make it stop. Or...

With a low snarl Jequn reached out and grabbed the decapitated thing by the stump of its neck. His gauntleted fingers slid inside, and he felt cold slime and twisting, flexing muscles, then something hard, something like bone but different, brittle and thorny, but it was something to grip. Jequn tightened his hand around it and pulled back and down, jerking the thing away.

'Ready weapon!' he shouted as he hauled backwards. The gris twisted, one blunt hand trying to grab at Jequn, but the Ancient stepped back, let go, and slammed his sword into the belly of the thing. The sword ripped it open, spilling slime across the rockcrete floor and sending the gris lurching back another step, but it didn't fall. Headless, gutted, the gris caught itself and started to lurch forward, arms spread.

'Fire!' Jequn stepped back, sword still raised, clearing the shot for his brother. The shrapnel from the bolter rounds might catch the survivors Jequn had found, but he didn't hesitate to give the order. Any information the mortals might have was nothing compared to the life of one of his brothers. The Space Marine raised his weapon and shot, and half a dozen bolter rounds slammed into the grey thing's chest, and then exploded.

Another gout of slime splashed across the lenses of Jequn's helmet, but when they cleared, he could see what was left of the gris on the floor, just an arm and two legs, the stumps smoking. The limbs had been sheared off the torso, and that lump of fungus-infected flesh was gone, ripped to shreds and slime by the exploding shells of the bolter.

Jequn snapped his head around, hearing the vicious crack

of the other boltguns. The haze of spores and mould had cleared, and he could see more of the grey things falling or fallen, hacked apart by knives, then blasted to pieces by bolter rounds. But scattered among the smoking corpses, five green figures sprawled. Dark Angels, their armour unmarred except for a coating of that viscous grey slime. They were unmoving, but when Jequn reached through his vox he did not hear the sombre chorus of grief given by armour whose wearer had died. Jequn went to the closest, knelt down beside him and carefully touched his helmet, tripping the manual releases. It opened, catches ratcheting, but there was no hiss of equalising pressure. Jequn frowned as he stared down at the face of the man inside. His eyes were open but still, staring up at nothing. The double pulse of his heartbeat was there, but it was slow, his breathing steady but shallow. The Dark Angel was alive but unconscious, and Jequn had no idea why.

'What are these things?' He rose, turning, and walked over to the bound man. Reaching down, he snapped the chains that held him, then picked him up. This close, despite the mud, Jequn knew him. He was Sebastian Halven, the Regent Next.

'Gris,' he said. 'Maybe people infected so long they're mostly mould. I don't know. I saw them infect the others.' He pointed at the ones who still lay bound and motionless on the ground. Tiny spots were beginning to bloom on their faces, like freckles but grey and wet, blotting the skin around their eyes.

Jequn stared at the Regent Next, looked hard through lenses touched with slime, but he found no traces of mould growing on Sebastian's face. Still. Jequn reached out and grabbed the mortal, then moved to stand beneath the brightest lumen.

'They didn't infect me!' Sebastian said. His eyes were wide, but he kept his voice level, almost calm even as he hung from the Ancient's hand. 'I told you, I saw them do it. I saw them press their hands over those people's mouths, watched those people fight, heard them screaming and gagging until they fell, their faces covered with that slime. I saw the gris do it, but they didn't do it to me. I don't know why they didn't. Maybe they were saving me for something, maybe… I don't know. But I thank the Throne they didn't. I thank the Throne.'

His words rolled over Jequn, but the Ancient wasn't listening. He leaned close to Sebastian and inhaled the scent of the man. There was the stench of his sweat, harsh with excitement and fear; the smell of his blood, heavy with adrenaline; the acrid smell of the perfume he had put on after his last shower and the faint rot of bits of food caught between his teeth. But there was no smell of mould, no gris scent. None. Jequn turned and dropped the man in front of Squad Invis' sergeant.

'Watch him,' he said. Then he moved down the line of the bound infected, cutting their heads away, breaking their chains and kicking the bodies deeper into the pile. 'And move our injured away from these unclean dead.'

Injured. He finished off the last infected and stared again at his motionless brothers. Space Marines didn't lose consciousness, not for long. They shrugged off concussions with healing and stimm. This quiescence, it reminded him of sus-an, the hibernation state a brother could enter if gravely injured. But they weren't injured. The toxins in the grey pall must have done this, somehow. But it troubled him.

'Yes, Ancient,' the sergeant said. 'Do we burn the gris?'

'Yes,' Jequn answered. 'After.'

'After?'

'After we find a way to open those,' he said, looking past the bodies to the gleaming metal of the sealed blast doors.

Behind him there was a noise, and the Ancient turned. Sebastian stood there, mud-covered, but his back was straight, his eyes shining as he stared at the doors. 'I think I can do that for you.'

The Thunderhawk *Vengeance is Prayer* spun in a wide circle over Kap Sudsten, and Lieutenant Zakariah stared down from it, frowning. The city was a rough blot of rockcrete and glass set in a thick jungle, roads running from it like spokes, some paved, some raw red earth, connecting the city to the stimm farms that pockmarked the jungle. It was all open and unfortified, except for the base belonging to the Reis Home Levies, which stood on the opposite side of the wide landing field that separated it from the city. The fortifications of that place were more pretence than effective defence. Looking down at it, he could calculate a dozen ways the Fifth could take the place in a day.

But he had been sent to defend it.

He would have rather been dealing with the gris that had attacked the Adeptus Mechanicus forge, or hunting through the tunnels for their missing brothers. Instead, he was here, preparing to face an attack that might never come, to protect mortals who were ruled by a fool.

'The Regent Prime is requesting an audience,' said Meshach, the Techmarine encased in the pilot's couch, webs of cables linked into ports buried beneath the plates of his armour, as much a part of the ship as its machine spirit.

An audience. What did the Regent Prime want that couldn't be handled by vox? 'Land where Master Lazarus brought his ships down,' Zakariah said, and the Thunderhawk banked away from the landing field and dropped into the plaza before the palace of the Regent Prime, right on the scorch-marks of the ships that had been here just hours before.

'Squad Revir. Squad Nabis.' Zakariah unclipped his crash

harness and stood, head almost scraping the top of the hold. The Thunderhawk had been designed thousands of years before, with Firstborn Space Marines like Squad Nabis in mind, and the new, taller generation of Primaris Marines did not fit as well within. They were used to it though, and all of Squad Revir ducked their heads instinctively as they rose around him. Primaris squads like Revir were becoming more common in the Dark Angels Chapter, but the Fifth had more of them than any other company, probably because of their master. The Dark Angels, oldest of the Space Marine Legions, were conservative, but a change as big as the Primaris made sense under Lazarus. Not just because he had crossed the Rubicon Primaris himself. The leader of the Fifth had a kind of pragmatism to him, Zakariah had observed, that made him amenable to change if he could see the advantage in it. Other Dark Angels, especially among the Firstborn, tended to have more difficulty with change.

It was one of the reasons Zakariah had become so fiercely loyal to his commander.

'There is no foe to fight out there. Yet. And we may not have one to face at all on this mission.' Which was a bitter possibility, but Zakariah knew he had best lay it out at the start. 'But in everything we do, we represent the Fifth, the Dark Angels and the Emperor. Let us never fail to show why we are the sons of the Lion, and the greatest of the Emperor's own.'

'For the Lion and the Throne!' the men of Revir and Nabis shouted, and followed him down the ramp into the courtyard. They moved down the long entrance passage of the Regent Prime's palace, massive, armoured shapes built for devastation, and the few mortals they saw pulled back out of their way, eyes wide with terror and awe.

The Hall of the Fallen was crowded with people, men and

women in strange, brightly coloured clothes packed against the walls. Lieutenant Zakariah ignored them, focusing on the man seated in the hard-angled throne. Oskaran Halven was leaning back against the worn cushions, his expression one of sullen resentment, like a child denied a sweet. A woman stood beside him, dressed in the uniform of the local Levies, frowning. Despite the sounds of his entrance and the muttering of the courtiers, Zakariah's auspex-enhanced hearing picked up her whisper to the Regent Prime.

'Sebastian. That's all that matters. Where is your son?'

Oskaran waved her away, his expression growing even more sour, and Zakariah carefully smoothed his face to cold disdain as he stopped in front of the strange throne and pulled off his helmet. The air of the room hit him, hot and humid and laden with the scents of sweat and decay.

'Regent Prime,' he said, allowing his disgust at the organic stench of the place to mix with his disdain. 'As ordered by Master Lazarus, commander of the Fifth Company of the Dark Angels, we are here.'

'That is... evident,' Oskaran said slowly. The Regent Prime's eyes were bloodshot, and his breath carried the acrid stink of alcohol. When he stood, he wavered on his feet and had to grab hold of his throne in order not to fall. 'You are here. My son is not. And that...' He trailed off, frowning. Then he looked past Zakariah and the Dark Angels behind him, glaring at the courtiers that lined the walls of the room.

'Get out,' he said. 'All of you. All but the Space Marines. Get out. Now!'

There was a pause, and then with quiet murmurs the courtiers streamed out, staring back over their shoulders. When they were gone, the only mortals left were the woman, the Regent Prime's guard, and a scrawny man seated in a niche to the side of the throne, heavily tattooed so that his hairless head resembled a skull.

'You're dismissed too, Petra,' Oskaran told the woman. 'And take my guards and the etcher.' He jerked his thumb at the tattooed man.

'But my lord,' she protested, 'it is law that the etcher–'

'Take him and go, or I'll have you all hung from these rafters!' the Regent Prime shouted. Petra frowned, anger boiling in her eyes, but she saluted then silently led the guards and the tattooed man away. They shut the doors and it was just the Regent Prime, standing alone before his throne, staring at the floor in front of Zakariah's boots.

'You must get him back,' he said.

'You show a grave misunderstanding of the order of the galaxy when you use that word to me, Regent Prime,' Zakariah said. 'Or to any Dark Angel. We are not yours to command.' The lieutenant stepped forward. Even standing on the dais of the throne, the Regent Prime was shorter than him, and he stared down at the mortal. 'Whatever power you hold through the Imperial bureaucracy, know this. It means *nothing* to us.' His gauntleted hand touched the winged sword painted onto his shoulder. 'We are the Dark Angels. We are the First. And where we are, we command.'

Oskaran's eyes flicked up to him, red with drink and rage, but they couldn't hold his. The mortal looked away, then folded, his body collapsing into the throne like a rag doll dropped by a child.

'I know,' he said softly. 'I know. I have no power here.' He looked up at the broken pieces of the Knights hanging overhead, like gigantic reliquaries. 'My house died a thousand years ago. We are merely ghosts, our bodies buried beneath the earth.'

Zakariah, already sick of the Regent Prime's voice, started to turn, but Oskaran lifted a hand, desperate.

'Master Lazarus sent you his orders, I know. To guard in case the gris appear. But he didn't know. He couldn't know. Only I know, and Sebastian, and that's why he has to be found and killed.'

Zakariah frowned. 'This is not about a rescue attempt?'

'Rescue?' The Regent Prime laughed. 'That Throne-cursed fool? I don't want him rescued – I want him dead. Now. Now!' Oskaran looked up again, and this time his desperation gave him the strength to meet Zakariah's eyes. 'We don't know how the gris works. We don't know what the ones who are taken by it remember. But I can't take that chance. You can't, Reis can't. He knows where they are, and if the gris takes him, it might know too.' His eyes fell, but not before Zakariah saw the horror in them. 'It might know too.'

'What?' Zakariah took two steps and his hand was on the Regent Prime's shoulder, covering it and half his back. Holding him in his grip, ready to tighten if he wouldn't stop speaking in riddles. 'What does your son know that the gris must not?'

'He knows where our bodies are buried,' Oskaran said. 'He knows where the Knights of House Halven sleep, waiting to rise again.'

CHAPTER SIXTEEN

Azmodor smashed through the heaps of machinery set against the doors to the factorum, then charged forward, bulling a path through the pieces that remained. Lazarus paused for an instant, just enough time to let the falling debris hammer onto the floor, then followed after, his command squad hard on his heels, while Squads Lameth, Hazin and Bethel followed close behind.

The factorum was a dark hole compared to the brilliance in the hall, but the auspex sensors in Lazarus' helm married to his hyper-acute senses melted the shadows away. He could see through the dark, and he matched the piles of supplies and the great hulking machines to the detailed schematic the Fabricator Locum had given him. Away from the door, where the gris had taken things apart for the barrier, the map matched the reality of the room – except the map had no notations for where his enemies were hiding. That information was won when those enemies began firing at Azmodor. The gris had taken position on a spiderweb of walkways that hung from the ceiling, and they were using their position to slam slugs down at the Dreadnought. But the fire from their autorifles ricocheted off Azmodor's thick armour, doing no more damage than rain.

'Squad Lameth,' he snapped over the vox. 'Ascend.'

There was the roar of jump packs, the bright flare of their thrusters arcing through the air followed by the thunder of bolt pistols as Squad Lameth raked the catwalks above. The bolt pistols almost drowned out the autorifles and the whining ricochets of slugs smashing off ceramite armour. But then came the screaming whine of the chainswords.

The chatter of blades ripping through bodies came from above. Metal shrieked as a catwalk buckled, and then something was falling down. Lazarus sensed it before he could see it, a disturbance in the air, and dodged to the side as a body slammed into the floor. Lazarus caught a glimpse of it as it smashed into the rockcrete, a man dressed in what was left of a Reis Home Levies uniform, his body split open from shoulder to hip. Blood and organs splattered out, a gory mess spilling across the ground. But in its crimson Lazarus caught threads of grey, strings of fungal infection running through the tissue.

'Squad Hazin,' Lazarus said as he stepped around the mess. 'Outer perimeter.' The factorum was a massive cube gouged out of Reis' crust. Squad Hazin would have to move fast to see if the enemy was trying to flee through another exit, but they knew what to do. Squad Bethel remained with him and the command squad, moving through the equipment at his back, following the infiltration pattern he'd laid out over the schematic. They would sweep the centre of the factorum, blasting from one side to the other, where a great cage was set into the far wall – a barred prison where the mortals damned to suffer as servitors for their sins were roused from their cryo-sleep and made into the living dead, cursed to labour for the Imperium until they finally dropped. Then they would be stripped for parts, their organic bits recycled into nutrients and their souls sent to whatever judgement awaited them – if they hadn't been destroyed already.

Lazarus moved forward fast, dodging the great machines as he charged towards the far wall. He could hear the thunder of his command squad and Squad Bethel, the ceramite soles of their armour ringing off the rockcrete floor. The space was vast, but it wasn't long before he caught the glint of bars. The cage. In his hand, Enmity's Edge crackled and snapped, the edges of its power field cutting through the air, and he remembered the grey fungal lines running through the corpse that had shattered on the floor before him. Whatever this infection was, Lazarus held the cure for it in his hand.

A lance of light split the dark just ahead of him, then another. A laser, firing from where the cage was, and just ahead of him Azmodor was staggering back, his armour smoking.

'Brother, to me!' Lazarus had reached the last machine that lay between him and the factorum's far wall, a gigantic, blocky thing webbed all around with conduits and pipes. It was big enough to shelter Azmodor when the Dreadnought spun back around and returned to Lazarus, blocking any more las-strikes. Strikes like the one that had drawn a line that ran across the front of the Dreadnought's armour, a deep cut that still glowed at its edges.

'Damage?' Lazarus asked. The rest of his command squad were drawing up with him, Asbeel and Demetrius and Ephron and Raziel.

'Nothing,' Azmodor said, waving his heavy hand at Ephron as the Techmarine examined the wound carved into the Dreadnought's ceramite.

'Your skin is thick, brother,' Ephron said. 'They couldn't break it, though they came close. But another strike here could penetrate your sarcophagus.'

'They will not be given the chance,' Azmodor rumbled. The Dreadnought shifted, his auspex arrays aimed at Lazarus. 'The gris have taken shelter behind the bars of that cage, but that will barely slow me. I will begin the breaking.'

'Brother,' Lazarus said, 'your zeal is an inspiration to us. But you are more than a battering ram.' He checked the displays in his helm. Squad Lameth were rooting out the last snipers hidden in the rafters, and Squad Bethel were working their way across the room, searching methodically and finding nothing. Squad Hazin were still circling, but they had seen no sign that the gris had fled. More than likely, the enemy had seized the cage, the most defensible part of the factorum, and were waiting.

Which meant they were trapped.

'Brother Ephron.' When Lazarus spoke, the Techmarine stopped examining Azmodor's damage and turned to him. 'Smoke grenades.'

'I have four, brother.' He pulled them from his belt – smooth oval grenades with pins on their tops. Lazarus took two and handed them to Demetrius.

'You are with me,' he told Ephron. 'We will come in from the right with half of Squad Bethel. Interrogator-Chaplain Demetrius and Librarian Raziel will lead the other half of Bethel in from the left.' Lazarus pointed to the two grenades Ephron still held. 'When I command it, we release these. Two, and then two, and then we charge, Demetrius and I in the lead. We shall cleave through the cage and destroy them.'

'And me?' Azmodor asked.

'Step out after the grenades. Covering fire. If they try to use those lasers, destroy them.'

The Dreadnought flexed his hand into a fist, clearly wishing he was still leading the charge, but all he said was, 'Understood.'

'Master Lazarus.' Librarian Raziel was staring at Lazarus, but it seemed as if his eyes were looking through him, through the great machine they sheltered behind, to whatever lay in the cage beyond. 'That current of misery that I felt at Redwash Gate. It is here too. Drifting in the air, a current of suffering flowing away from our location.'

And what did that mean? Emperor only knew. The pronouncements of psykers only seemed to gain meaning after whatever horror they predicted had already happened, which made them more maddening than useful. But he nodded to Raziel, before moving to the other end of the giant machine, with Ephron and half of Squad Bethel following behind.

'Ready.' He took one of the grenades and pulled the pin, watched the flicker of its activation lights, and saw Ephron do the same as he whispered a prayer to the Machine God.

'Begin.' Lazarus moved away from the machine, just far enough to get a line of sight to the cage. It was a square room carved out of stone, an antechamber attached to the great cavern of the factorum, with bars across its front meant to seal in any prisoners attempting to escape in the brief time between being roused from cryo-sleep and lobotomisation. The cage had no entrances other than the one set in its barred front, making it an excellent spot for a defensive stand. But that also meant it was a kill box, where the gris were all going to die.

Las-beams lanced out from the barred wall, one towards Lazarus, one towards Demetrius, but the hands operating them were far too slow. The powerful weapons did nothing but scar the floor, slagging through one of the conduits leading to the machine Lazarus had already fallen back behind after throwing the grenade. The conduit spilled sparks like a waterfall, bright in the dim factorum, until their light was suddenly wiped out by darkness.

The smoke grenades poured out a cloud of black that rolled across the factorum. Its darkness hid the cage, but Lazarus called out the order and Ephron and Raziel stepped out, throwing the grenades they held. No lasers lanced out at them, but Lazarus waited anyway, until a second wave of smoke flooded the space between them and the cage. If he was going to blind these gris, he was going to blind every one of them, and not chance that the smoke would thin as they charged.

'Dark Angels! For the Lion!' Lazarus shouted, then rounded the corner of the huge machine, Enmity's Edge raised in one hand, bolt pistol in the other. He pounded towards the cage, its steel bars glowing in the magnetic sensors of his auspex. Behind them, he could see the crude metal platforms that had been built to support the mining lasers, and more dimly the metal components of the lasers themselves. They were moving, swinging back and forth as the gris that controlled them hunted blindly for targets.

The gris could not see, but they could hear, and the gunner closest to Lazarus swung their laser towards him as his armoured boots smashed across the rockcrete. A blaze of light punched through the smoke in his direction, cutting a furrow across the floor a few yards to his right and melting through two of the bars of the cage. Lazarus had no intention of giving the gris a second chance and fired his bolt pistol.

He couldn't see the gunner, but he could see the metal of the laser, and that was enough. His pistol thundered in his hand, and the exploding slugs smashed through the weapon, destroying it and spraying shrapnel into the gris that controlled it. Then Lazarus was at the cage, Enmity's Edge swinging.

The sword hit the bars and the metal ripped itself apart as

if fleeing that crackling edge. He cut a great arc over his head, then crouched as he backhanded a blow across the bottom. The cut bars fell, clattering to the floor, and Lazarus was through. He switched his auspex to thermis, and suddenly he could see the gris around him, the heat of their bodies glowing through the smoke.

Great flashes of white came from the other side, where bars were ringing down, Demetrius chanting a litany of destruction as he smashed through them with his crozius. Squad Bethel were hard on Lazarus' heels, knives out, and the antechamber was a crowded swirl of flashing blades and blood. Face set as stone behind his helm, Lazarus pressed forward, leading his Dark Angels in the grim business of slaughter.

'Every one of them is dead,' Brother Asbeel said.

Lazarus set down the cloth he had used to clean the blood from Enmity's Edge and frowned at the Apothecary.

'I do not mean the gris.' The Apothecary waved a hand back at the cage. The last hold of the gris was a silent, blood-filled abattoir. 'I mean the prisoners. The ones the Adeptus Mechanicus were making into servitors. Those they had already taken out of cryo-sleep had their throats slit and were dumped in a corner out of the way. The ones still in cryo-sleep...' He nodded towards the giant machine they had used for cover when moving up on the cage. From this side, Lazarus could see that there were racks built into it, row after row of narrow boxes lined up inside. There was a light on each one, glowing a pulsing red. 'That was the support unit which kept the cryo-coffins functioning. One of the gris' lasers cut the power conduit to it, and they all failed. The remaining forty-eight hundred prisoners drowned in cryo-fluid.'

'A tragedy that they died before they could pay for their

crimes,' Demetrius said. 'But at least it was at the hands of the gris. The Fabricator Locum cannot be angry at us for her lost material.'

'You have too much optimism behind that skull mask, brother,' Lazarus said. He frowned at the great machine, noticing the clear fluid leaking out of it, running down a drain in the floor. It smelled faintly of mortals. In this heat it would soon reek of decay. 'Why did they come here? If they weren't after the prisoners to infect, why fly all the way here, fight their way to this particular room and die?'

'It is difficult to know the minds of the daemonic, the xenos or the rebellious,' said the Interrogator-Chaplain. 'And we don't even know which one of those these things are.'

'All three or none at all,' Lazarus said. 'It doesn't matter. There is some intelligence behind these things, which means some kind of plan.' He slipped his blade back into its sheath, but his fingers tapped the hilt, wanting to pull it free again. 'I am winning every battle, but begin to fear that I may be losing the war. We destroy these gris whenever we find them, but we must rip their roots from the ground. I need to–'

'*Master Lazarus.*' The voice over the vox was from Squad Hazin, who had continued sweeping through the factorum, hunting for any hidden enemy. 'We have found the factorum's enginseers. And something else you should see.'

There was a pit in the corner of the room. It wasn't on the schematics the Fabricator Locum had given him. It had been dug recently – the sides of the shaft were raw and crumbling, the broken rockcrete taken from the floor piled a few yards away, along with a larger mound of earth. The servitors who'd done the work were still there, parked in a line beside the hole, a dozen of them with digging tools gripped in their mechanical claws. They looked dead, their heads bowed, their bodies hanging limp from the harnesses that welded them to their mechanicals, but Lazarus could hear the faint rasp of their breathing, smell their sweat, bitter and tainted with hydraulic fluid. The bodies on the floor next to them were dead though, two Adeptus Mechanicus enginseers. They lay face down, and the backs of their skulls had been ripped open, brains removed. Lazarus frowned at the red, empty hollows of their skulls, studded in places with their cybernetic implants, wires and sockets and studs, all broken, shattered by the violent removal of tissue.

'The third lies here,' the sergeant of Squad Hazin said, pointing to the hole. Lazarus stared down, and ten feet below, he saw the enginseer. He lay on his back, his arms spread wide as if he were reaching for something. Both arms were mechanical, the left almost human in appearance, while the right had three multi-jointed servo-manipulators. He still wore his robes, loose and disarrayed around him, but his boots were gone, his feet bare and strangely human. Wires ran to each toe, the twisted copper ends jammed under the nails. Blood tracks ran from them, clotted mostly, but Lazarus could see a fresh trickle of red running out from beneath one split nail and dripping into the mud below.

More blood-soaked mud surrounded the enginseer's head, which lay beside a junction box that had been uncovered by the digging. The box was stainless steel, unadorned, connecting two cables as thick as Lazarus' arm. The top of the junction box had been cut away, and a tangle of wires ran out of it and wrapped around the enginseer's scalp. Some were socketed into the tech-priest's implants, while others were driven into the few patches of exposed skin still left on his face, surrounded by thick scabs of drying blood. The rest of the wires and cables had been braided into a thick rope and then jammed into the gory socket of his left eye. An implant had once been set there, but it had been torn out, discarded so that the thick line could twist its way deep into the enginseer's head. Tiny lights had been delicately wired into place around the thick braid, and now they blinked and flashed in strange patterns. Their colours reflected off the enginseer's dull brown skin and the grey mask of mouldy growth surrounding his eyes.

'What is this?' Lazarus asked, his bolt pistol raised and pointed at the head of the infected enginseer. Nothing good, he was sure. He wanted to pull the trigger, to smash the grotesque union of brain and fungus and wires, but he looked to Ephron first, wondering what the Techmarine saw in this hideous melding.

Ephron crouched beside the hole, and a servo-arm unfolded from his back and snaked over his shoulder. A bright beam of light speared out from it, aimed into the open junction box. 'These are communication command cables. Part of the forge's cogitation backbone.' His light played over the cables, disappearing into the dirt. 'This junction box is not warded against intrusion, the way it would be if it were in the open. This is why they came here. The gris somehow knew this junction was buried here, and would be vulnerable to… whatever this is.'

'The work of their master.' And who was that? Lazarus thought of the shadow Raziel had said was behind the seal at the Redwash Gate. *What* was that might be a better question. But the memory of the shadow made him think. 'Librarian,' he called, and Raziel turned his head to him. He still held his sword out, the blue-white blade steaming, tiny icicles dripping from its hilt. 'What do you feel?'

'I feel that current, still. It is everywhere the gris are, or have been. At this moment, it is strongest here,' Raziel said, pointing down at the mutilated enginseer. 'But I am feeling it all around us.' He waved a hand, indicating the factorum and the forge that surrounded it. 'It's growing out there.'

'I want to talk.'

The voice was hollow, a low, rasping croak, not loud. But to a Space Marine's senses it was clear, and every Dark Angel arrayed around the hole snapped up their gun. Lazarus, standing at the hole's edge, had never lowered his. Staring down over its sights, he could see the bloodshot eye of the enginseer open and blink at him, the mouth twist into an ugly grin.

'To you, Dark Angel. I want to talk to *you*.'

'Why would I want to talk to you, obscenity?' Lazarus asked.

'Why?' The enginseer's grin broadened. When he spoke again, his voice was a mocking parody of Lazarus'. '"I know nothing about what you are, or what you want. I just know you are an obscenity, a monster, and I shall cleanse you from this world."' Then his voice switched back to his former rasp. 'How prettily you talk of your ignorance. A voice like an angel, a grim, dark angel. But then, there was this.' He switched his voice back to his mockery of Lazarus. '"There is some intelligence behind these things, which means some kind of plan."'

The enginseer's grin went sly. 'That almost sounded like curiosity. Like an admission that there might be something beyond bolter and blade that would advance your cause. Something like knowledge. Do you want to know me, Lazarus, Master of the Fifth? Because I feel like I want to know you.'

'You play for time,' Lazarus said, and pulled the trigger. One explosive round erased the enginseer's head, turning it into a mass of blood, wire, bone fragments and smashed circuit boards. The solid pieces were still ticking down from the air when the few lumens that were still lit far overhead flickered, once and then again, before finally going out. The factorum fell into darkness, absolute, and the visual light bands were gone from Lazarus' auspex. Heat and magnetics still glowed bright before his eyes, but he called for lumens over the vox regardless. Each Dark Angel flared to light, their power armour casting crisp white beams across the factorum.

'Killing the gris enginseer should not have done that,' Ephron said. 'The cogitation backbone forms the forge's noosphere. Which is tied to basic functions like lighting, but not directly. I–'

'Ware,' Demetrius snapped. The Interrogator-Chaplain was looking across the pit at the servitors gathered there. Their bowed heads had come up, dead eyes focusing on Lazarus.

'I don't play, Dark Angel.' The voice spilled from every servitor. 'I've had a thousand years to plot my revenge. All of them spent in pain. If I spend time speaking to you, it's because I have the time to spend.'

From the far side of the factorum where they had entered there came the sound of shots, lascannons and stubbers and the distinctive sizzling crack of the skitarii's arc rifles. Eyes still on the servitors, Lazarus spoke his orders over the vox.

'Demetrius, Azmodor. Back to the doors with Squads Lameth and Bethel. Squad Hazin, with me.' His men thundered away, their lights disappearing into the dark. Lazarus stared at the servitors, then spoke aloud. 'Spend your time dying, gris.' Then he sent the fire order to Squad Hazin.

The Dark Angels raised their bolters, and the guns sang their powerful hymn. The servitors flew apart, flesh shredding, their metal pieces falling to the floor as their human body pieces disintegrated. When the last piece hit the ground, Lazarus turned and led the rest of the Fifth back to the doors.

CHAPTER SEVENTEEN

It was easy for Ysentrud to find the Dark Angels. They came in a rush, Interrogator-Chaplain Demetrius, the Dreadnought and two squads pounding out of the darkness that shrouded the factorum. The Fabricator Locum and Demetrius barely had time to snap at each other before Lazarus joined them, his suit gleaming with lights, the rest of his men at his back.

When she saw him, Ysentrud felt her coiled tension ease. Not that she was sure why. It was this man's arrival which had set off everything that had happened in this disastrous… She paused, bewildered. How many days had it been? Two yet? It felt like an eternity. She felt as though she'd aged an eternity. But still, the relief spread through her when she saw his winged helm and the flowing white robe that covered his deep green armour. Whatever else was happening, this Space Marine, this transhuman, seemed to care that she lived, and that felt very, very important right now. Even though he seemed not to notice her as he strode over to confront the Fabricator Locum.

'Explain,' was his only word to her as he pointed at the rubble-choked door.

The Fabricator Locum drew herself up, her arms crossed, her bird on her shoulder, wings half spread. 'The forge's noosphere has been compromised. Control of critical functions has been appropriated, my own servitors and cyborgs turned against me. My dominion over our sacred system has been seized by an outside agency.'

'The gris,' Lazarus said.

'An assumption,' the Fabricator Locum answered. 'A credible-seeming assumption, but that solution is ultimately non-viable. My forge's noosphere is warded against all intrusion.'

'Expand your definition of "all",' Lazarus replied grimly. When she started to speak, he raised a hand. 'Techmarine Ephron will take you to where it was done. You can examine the breach of your defences there and attempt to reassert your control. While you do, we will secure this space. Go, and may the Emperor guide you.'

Gretin Lan blinked her strange eyes at him, then swept away, her skitarii guards scuttling around her like a cordon of insectile predators. Lazarus turned and looked at Ysentrud. 'Learned. Are you all right?'

All right. Ysentrud pulled herself up as straight as she could, fighting not to wince. She was battered, bruised, cut – no, she was more battered, more bruised, more cut, her whole body ached, she was trembling with an adrenaline hangover, the rebreather mask was digging into her face, and Gretin Lan had snapped at her. She was not all right, not even close. But she just nodded and said, 'Yes, my lord,' a lie of such magnitude that the Emperor probably winced.

'Good,' he said, then spun away to speak with his men, giving orders, sending them out. When he was done, he strode away, the knot of Space Marines that always seemed to surround him orbiting him like Gretin Lan's bird skulls. She watched him go and sighed, starting to walk after them, but one of the sets of lights stayed, and she recognised Apothecary Asbeel waiting for her.

He held out his hand, and when she started to protest, he simply picked her up and set her on his shoulder again. 'We will not leave you in the dark, or make you run to keep up with us.'

Ysentrud shut her mouth. Trying to argue that she didn't need their help was ridiculous, especially as she sat sagging on his shoulder, exhausted and battered. She felt a sudden prick on her back. 'Lord, what was that?' She swung her head around to see his servo-arm folding back in. Something was burning in her shoulder, almost painful, but as it spread through her, the burning became warmth.

'Stimm, mostly.' When she made a noise, he shook his helmeted head. 'Not your black stimm. The Dark Angels do not need or use such things. It's the same stimm we use, merely a much smaller dose.'

Much smaller. The warm sensation swept through her, wiping away her aches and fatigue, along with the dread that had been hanging over her. She knew the sudden elation was nothing more than chemicals, but that knowledge didn't stop her from sighing with relief and sitting up straighter on the Apothecary's shoulder. Her mood was so improved that she wasn't even startled when the lights on Asbeel's armour flashed off a silver skull mask. Interrogator-Chaplain Demetrius had slowed, waiting for them. He held out an arm, and Asbeel reached up and handed her over to him. Even with the boost in her mood from the stimm, being passed like a child was annoying. But kicking her legs and sulking would only make her feel ridiculous.

'Now that my health has been assured, at least for the moment, are you here to attend to my spirit? Lord?'

'In a manner of speaking,' Demetrius said. The green light of his left eye gleamed off her torn, grubby robes. 'Master Lazarus wants to know how you are faring.'

'Tell him I was terrible, but then your Apothecary drugged me with the best of the Imperium and now I'm feeling amazing. I imagine when it wears off I'll spend six months wanting to die, though.'

'It is more like six hours, but it may be worse for mortals.'

'Most likely it is,' she said, but the thought couldn't come close to denting her mood. 'Interrogator-Chaplain,' she said brightly, ignoring the fact that some distant part of her brain was quailing from merely addressing the giant in the mena-cing mask. 'Why does Master Lazarus give a damn about me?'

'You have knowledge about this situation. It makes you a valuable tactical tool.'

'A valuable tactical tool. How lovely!' Ysentrud meant it, too. She had been raised to believe that her worth lay in helping others with the knowledge that had been etched into her. Knowing she was useful not just to a Space Marine but to the leader of an entire company of Space Marines was better than helping some lord figure out the best way to squeeze taxes out of stimm farmers. 'He likes knowing things, doesn't he?'

'He does. The Master of the Fifth is a fell fighter, but more importantly he is a master of tactics. This requires knowing the troops that serve him, the battlefield he fights on and the enemy he faces.'

'That's too bad,' she said. 'All this arguing, and secrets, and lies, all the weirdness with the gris. It must all be driving him crazy.'

Demetrius made a sound that might have been a laugh, cut

off. 'The Master of the Fifth is not fond of such things, no. And I'm sure he would greatly appreciate your concern, Learned. But he has dealt with more difficult things.'

'Like death?' She turned to look down on him. It was the one good thing about riding around on the Space Marines' shoulders – she didn't have to crane her neck staring up at them. 'When the gris was talking to him back at the stimm farm, all that crazy talk about death, the way Master Lazarus answered... What happened to him?'

'The same thing that happens to us all, save our Emperor eternal. He died.' Demetrius' voice went quiet. Sombre. 'He sacrificed himself for us, and fell in flames. Master Lazarus did his duty, the one duty that is required from us all – he died for his brothers and for the Emperor. But duty was not done with him, and he was reborn.'

'Such strange people you are. My lord. Fighting and dying and being reborn.' She shook her head, and for a moment the great factorum spun around her. But that was fine. Everything now was more than fine. 'It seems like so much. Do you ever get a chance to do anything fun?'

'We serve the Emperor. We protect the Imperium. We destroy the enemies of man. We are the sword of vengeance for the helpless and the afraid. We are the Dark Angels.' He looked up at her. 'We are the first of the Adeptus Astartes. That is the greatest honour any man can attain. And, just occasionally, we are capable of experiencing what you call fun.'

'I think you're making fun of me,' Ysentrud said, and swayed as he shrugged. He was, and that made her feel even better. These Space Marines were so serious. But if one of them, one of them as terrifying as Interrogator-Chaplain Demetrius, could tease... Whatever else they were, maybe these Dark Angels were still human. At least a little bit.

'You spoke of secrets and lies.' Demetrius' pace slowed, putting distance between them and the rest of the group. They were walking almost alone, surrounded by the dark bulk of equipment. 'What did you mean?'

'Besides the fighting between the Regent Prime and the Adeptus Mechanicus?' Ysentrud shrugged. 'Or all the folklore about the gris? Like how there used to be only one, a figure all covered with mould, crawling out of the ground to snatch away children? Probably not, no one cares about that. Maybe you meant whatever Regent Next Sebastian was up to.' She hesitated, then smiled. 'I was afraid of saying anything about him to anyone. Sebastian was my keeper, even if he had no interest in me, and he is – was – the Regent Next, one of the most powerful people on Reis. But he's probably stuffed full of mould now, and right now I'm not afraid of anything.' Ysentrud paused, thinking. 'Which is why you're talking to me! You're clever about interrogation. Lord.'

'I have some training,' the Interrogator-Chaplain said dryly.

She nodded. 'I hated Sebastian.' She tried to sort her thoughts and failed. These weren't memories etched into her, and with the stimm flowing, memen state would probably be impossible. But the memories of her time in the keeping of the Regent Next were recent and raw. 'I only served Sebastian for a little while, but… there was something to him. Something smug, and knowing, and sneering. He hid it well in public, but in his apartments, it came out.' She shuddered, remembering the way he would smile, the laughter that would sometimes erupt from him unprompted. 'It made me stay away from him, which was easy since I think he forgot I existed most of the time. So while I wasn't spying, I overheard a great deal I likely was not meant to. Things he said to himself and things that happened between him and Lash Commander Karn.' She shuddered. 'I mean, besides them being lovers. They made absolutely no effort to be discreet.' Especially in his apartments. She shuddered again.

'Everyone knew that Sebastian did not get along with his father. That was no secret either. But I don't think anyone realised how much contempt he had for the Regent Prime. How he thought he was weak, thought he was a fool. Sebastian would argue with his father in public, but in private he mocked him. I would have thought that he was about to declare rebellion, except the only thing he seemed to hate more than the Regent Prime was Reis itself. He spoke to Petra sometimes as if they weren't going to stay here. As if he planned to get off-planet somehow. He wants to go, I know that. He says Reis stinks.'

'It does,' Demetrius said. 'But there are much worse things in the galaxy. What else did you hear from the Regent Next?'

'What else besides treachery and abandoning his position?' Ysentrud asked. 'Little. Treachery, complaints and...' She thought for a moment. 'He spent a lot of time talking with the lash commander about the Reis Home Levies. Questions about their fighting with the gris, but he also kept asking her the dullest things about what forces were where. He wanted to know the location of every patrol, every training camp. I don't know why, and I don't know if it matters, but it was strange that he was so interested in knowing those details, when he cared so little for anything else to do with Reis.'

They came around a mound of supplies, and there was Lazarus with the Fabricator Locum, standing beside a hole that had been ripped out of the factorum floor. There were lumens set around them, bright emergency ones that made monstrous shadows on the walls. Demetrius crouched and tipped his shoulder, letting Ysentrud slide down to the floor.

'The gris are at every door,' Lazarus was telling the Fabricator Locum. 'There is no way out.'

Lazarus scanned the displays laid out before his eyes by his helm, the reports from all the squads he had sent to probe the edges of the factorum. He could see the picts from everyone, the wide halls of the forge crowded with servitors, waiting with dead eyes and raised weapons. Among them were the sulphurhounds, savage weapons that were meant to be skitarii battlefield mounts. Every exit from this place was a kill box, waiting for them to step into it.

'How many servitors belong to this forge?' he asked.

The Fabricator Locum had her arms folded, her perfect mask of a face turned towards the pit where the dead enginseer lay. 'Six thousand servant designate servitors toiled for us. Labour and technical units.' There was an edge of frustration in that musical voice. She had no expression, no heartbeat, no pheromones, none of the usual signals that Lazarus could read off a mortal. There was just her voice, but that was enough now. 'Additionally, one thousand newly crafted mining units, presently under preparation for shipment.'

'How many carry mining lasers?'

'Four hundred units,' she said. 'But Forge Norsten currently holds seven hundred and three more mining lasers assembled and awaiting installation.'

Four hundred ready. Seven hundred and three more that could be used by the gris forces. 'Over one thousand weapons capable of penetrating ceramite armour. And then there are the sulphurhounds. How many of those are there?'

'Two hundred and twelve that can be utilised. Other units are at early stages of assembly.'

'Only two hundred and twelve,' Lazarus growled.

'I possess a keen awareness of the capabilities of all equipment my forge creates, Master Lazarus.' The music in Gretin Lan's voice was hard. 'Understanding of the danger of the weapons and tools we make is integrated deep in my system. These things complicate our present circumstance. However, probability indicates that it is unlikely we will face such odds. The designate gris must have some limit on the sum of entities it can control.'

'Must it?' Lazarus asked. 'You have no idea how this is happening. How can you be sure of that?'

Gretin Lan turned, her skirts swirling, and faced him. 'My comprehension of this attack would have been greatly enhanced if you had not chosen to destroy their implementation.'

'Destroy it?' Lazarus waved to the dark factorum. 'I only destroyed the tool that they used to infiltrate this forge. Whatever implementation that tool achieved continues unaffected. That must change.'

She made a hissing noise, but nodded. 'Concurrence. We must determine a solution for this trap.'

'You do not solve a trap. You break it.' Lazarus tapped the hilt of his sword. 'My squads will probe the doors. Let the gris think we are searching for weakness.'

'Distraction directed at the gris. What is the actual intention?'

'Searching for weaknesses. Just not at the doors.'

She nodded. 'You possess other forces, beyond this forge.'

'I have already tried to reach them,' Lazarus said. 'The gris are jamming us. It began sometime after they seized control of your forge. My Techmarine cannot reach our Thunderhawks. I cannot reach my squads. All our vox communication is gone. My squads can only send back brothers to make reports to me.'

'Omnissiah correct me,' she cursed, the pupils in her eyes shifting and turning. 'My communication functions are also disrupted. Assumption was made that this was due to the gris designate's control of the forge's noosphere. But the difficulty must lie deeper if it also attacks Space Marine equipment.'

'Can you stop it?' Lazarus asked. Ephron had had no answer for him. The gris' jamming was all-encompassing, and nothing the Techmarine could do seemed to touch it.

'No,' she answered, and there was anger in her words. 'I am stripped of my tools, my vestments. Denied the noosphere, I cannot factor out what the gris designate has done, or how to counter it.'

'Do you not have a physical connection to your noosphere right there?' Lazarus pointed at the hole.

'No longer,' she said. 'That node has been schismed, severed from the system. All equivalent nodes to that one lie beyond this factorum.'

She waved her hands, and one of the tiny bird skulls sprayed light through the air. It was a holo-projector, and it drew a schematic of the forge before them. Pinpricks of light lit up on the map, marking spots across the vast facility. A few were close, but all of them were beyond the factorum's guarded doors. Lazarus frowned at the map, at the twisting maze of conduits and vents and ducts and halls.

'Designate the closest to us,' he said. Three of the marks grew brighter on the schematic. One was directly over them, on the surface, through one hundred and fifty feet of stone. Another was on their level but half a mile away, in a conduit less than a yard wide. Too small for any Dark Angel, or even a skitarius. The last was below them and to one side, through almost three hundred feet of rock. Lazarus considered the possibility of digging, then shook his head. That kind of work would be too easy to detect by auspex, even outside this factorum. The gris would have time to react by simply severing those cables.

He looked again at the middle one. 'Your bird is small enough to reach that,' he said.

'Avix Alpha's dimensions would allow it, but her cognition would not. Her cogitators are not sufficiently complex to achieve the actions necessary to tie me into that node.' Gretin Lan stroked the bird's long tail feathers. 'Her potence also lacks. Else I would thread a line of nerus to her and govern her through it. But that burden would be beyond her capabilities.'

'She is not strong enough,' Lazarus said, and turned to look behind him. He had seen Demetrius come back with Ysentrud on his shoulder, but he had paid little attention to the mortal. Now he stared at her, gauging her.

Scrapes marked the woman's red skin and half-dried blood striped the black tattoos that covered her neck. Her once white robes were ragged, dirty and torn, and the rebreather strapped to her face was coated in dust, amber warning lights glowing around its filter intakes. But her eyes were bright, very bright, and she bounced when she realised he was looking at her.

'Master Lazarus! My lord! What's going on?' Her words tumbled over each other, and from the trace of sweat on her skin Lazarus could catch the familiar scent of stimm. 'Oh! Are you going to try getting out through that conduit?' She was staring at the map spread through the air behind him, at the tiny passage he still touched. 'Is there anything I can do to help?'

'Yes, Ysentrud,' he said. 'I think there is.'

Lazarus watched as the Fabricator Locum, with the help of two of her skitarii, wove together a long line of nerus cable, her slim hands moving like spiders. 'This is sufficient,' she said, holding the looped strand in her hands. She had wired one end into a plug, which she slipped into a socket hidden beneath the feather-like fronds of her hair. The other she attached to one of the bird skulls of her flock. The tiny thing's eyes still glowed, but dimly now, pulsing in a slow, steady rhythm. 'Open the conduit box, Learned, and transfix the cable with this.'

'Simple!' Ysentrud said enthusiastically.

She said everything enthusiastically now. When Lazarus had questioned Brother Asbeel, the Apothecary had insisted that he had given the Learned a miniscule amount of stimm. But the mortal was miniscule herself, wasn't she? That lack of size was what they were hanging this plan on, and it needed to work. Lazarus couldn't think of another that didn't involve rushing into those halls under a storm of las-fire.

Space Marines were without fear. The thought of making a charge like that and dying would not slow any of the battle-brothers in his command. But that same lack of fear kept him from rushing into anything that would degrade his forces while there was any other chance. Lazarus watched as Gretin Lan handed the loop of nerus cord to Ysentrud. The mortal staggered under the weight, and was held up by Interrogator-Chaplain Demetrius.

Any chance, Lazarus thought. *Even the slim ones.*

'No, I have it,' she said, straightening. Barely. Demetrius let her go, and Ephron held out a small leather holster to her.

'A cutting laser,' the Techmarine said. 'Small enough for you.' When Ysentrud took the holster, it immediately stopped looking so small. 'It can be used as a weapon if needed, but the range is extremely limited, and you must keep at least thirty per cent of the charge for opening the conduit.'

'She should have a better weapon,' Lazarus said. They had none to offer, though. Even their combat blades would have been huge for her, like great swords with handles she could barely grasp in two hands. But he wasn't talking to Ephron.

Gretin Lan stared at him with her strange eyes, the pupils shifting, then her hand moved, reaching into her skirts and pulling out a small knife sheathed in white with a carved ivory handle. 'Present your hand,' she told the Learned. When Ysentrud did, the Fabricator Locum placed the handle of the blade in it and closed her own hand around the mortal's. Gretin Lan sang something that sounded like birdsong, and Ysentrud's eyes went wide.

'It moved!'

'Weapon bonded.' The Fabricator Locum did not sound happy about that, but she brusquely continued on. 'The blade is adamantine with mono-molecular edge. Do not allow it to touch your corpus – significant damage would accrue. Blade also contains a miniaturised shock energy pack. On successful strike, engage stud in hilt and voltage discharges. Ensure you are not in contact with any part of victim's corpus, or it may arc back. Damage is severe. There is sufficient energy for three discharges.'

'Dangerous,' Ysentrud said, trying to juggle tool pouch and blade while not lurching over from the weight of the nerus cord.

'It is.' Lazarus knelt down, his head still higher than hers. He took the blade Gretin Lan had given Ysentrud and tied it to one of her belt loops with a thin strip of cloth he took from the tattered hem of her robe. 'But so are you, Learned. You are human, the most dangerous species this galaxy has produced, and with faith and courage there is nothing you cannot do.'

She blinked her copper-red eyes at him, then beamed. He grasped her tiny hand in his, then picked her up, moving to the narrow conduit the Fabricator Locum had indicated. A skitarius had cut a hole in it, and Lazarus lifted Ysentrud so that she could crawl inside. She fit, barely, and placed the nerus cord where she could drag it along behind. Clicking on the tiny lumen that hung around her neck, she took a breath and sang softly.

'Into the dark, into the night. Should I lose my way, pray I'll find the light.' She looked at Lazarus and smiled, a little less brightly. 'It's traditional.'

He nodded. 'You will do this. The Emperor protects.'

'The Emperor protects,' she echoed, and began to crawl forward, the cord slowly uncoiling behind her. As her light disappeared, Lazarus started to turn away, but he stopped when he heard a faint whisper coming down the conduit. 'I'm probably going to die in here. Praise the Throne I'm stimmed out of my mind.'

Time crawled like the Learned, but Lazarus busied himself staging probing raids with his squads at one exit then another, testing the defences of each one without wasting his men or ammunition.

'They do not rush us,' Demetrius said.

'They want us contained and alive,' Lazarus said, looking over the schematics again, gauging distances to the surface, marking areas that looked likely to collapse if hit with explosives. 'Otherwise they would have collapsed the ceiling of this cavern from above. Or pumped it full of promethium and struck a spark.'

'Why?' the Interrogator-Chaplain asked.

'To take us over,' he answered. 'Like the mortals in the Reis Home Levies. To make us into gris.'

'Impossible.' Apothecary Asbeel was standing with them, along with Librarian Raziel. 'Our immune systems would destroy that fungus before it could find any kind of purchase in our systems. We are immune to this grey pall.'

'That is how it should work. But in the same way we are

looking for weaknesses in this trap, the gris are searching us. That is likely why they ambushed us at the stimm farm, to claim our brothers from the Tenth Company. They are examining us, the way they examined the mortals here to determine how to take them over.'

'It may have been more than that,' Demetrius said. 'I questioned the Learned earlier about the Regent Next. She told me that he hated his father and this place, treachery that was easy enough to read. But she also mentioned that he was strangely focused on the location and disposition of the Reis Home Levies.'

Lazarus took a long moment to think, letting things fall into place. 'There are too many Home Levies soldiers among the gris. Far more than they should have just from prisoners of war they might have taken. But if a spy was telling the gris where to take patrols, or remote camps...' Lazarus considered it. The evidence was paper thin, but it fit.

'Sebastian working for the gris would explain how the ambush at the stimm farm happened,' Interrogator-Chaplain Demetrius said. 'And how he disappeared so quickly in that fight. It would have been a rescue for him, not a capture.'

'A rescue.' Lazarus twisted his mouth into a cynical smile. 'Sebastian is the one who called us here. Against his father's strict orders. To rescue Reis.'

'So the gris wanted us here,' Demetrius said. 'Why?'

'An important question,' Lazarus said. 'Let us ask someone who might know.'

CHAPTER EIGHTEEN

The vox crackled, meaningless static filling Lieutenant Zakariah's helmet. 'How long has it been like this, brother?' he asked, moving through the bands. There was nothing but noise, the senseless electronic screaming of stars.

'Minutes only.' Techmarine Meshach was seated beside him in the cockpit of *Vengeance is Prayer*, fixing a prayer ribbon to the Thunderhawk's vox-unit as he adjusted its controls. 'I had just received a report from Brother Ephron saying they had engaged with the gris force that attacked the Adeptus Mechanicus forge, and defeated them. And then a moment later, this. I cannot reach Master Lazarus in the north, Ancient Jequn at the Redwash Gate, or the *Sword of Caliban*.' He dropped his hand from the vox, shaking his head. 'This is not a problem with our equipment. Something is jamming us.'

'Something,' Zakariah echoed. 'The gris?'

'They are our enemy here,' Meshach said. 'But to block us so thoroughly shows an affinity with technology which they have not shown before.'

Zakariah nodded. 'Make this work, brother. We must tell Master Lazarus and Ancient Jequn what we have learned.' Knights, a whole company of them, hidden away for centuries. And one of the two men who knew where they were had been captured by an enemy that took its prisoners over from the inside out. 'The Knights of House Halven. What do you think, Brother Techmarine?'

'I know little, lieutenant,' Meshach said. 'The reports I have seen indicate that the interface to the pilots was sabotaged, which may mean that they are mostly intact, and those machines were made to last. Their spirits are fierce. But they obviously have not been functional for a thousand years.'

'Else the Regent Prime would be in one now,' Zakariah said. 'House Halven covets that power, that prestige.'

Meshach nodded. 'I do not understand how they could have given it up for so long. The Adeptus Mechanicus could have fixed their war machines centuries ago.'

'But to do that, they would have had to admit that they had stolen them,' Zakariah said. Once the Regent Prime had admitted that the Knights still existed, that House Halven had taken them in secret from the Adeptus Mechanicus tasked to repair them, he had answered every question Zakariah had put to him, spilling the secret his house had spent a thousand years concealing. 'They would have had to admit that they went against the commandments given to them by our forefathers, the Dark Angels who just saved them, and faked the Knights' loss. Then they would have to admit that they could not learn to fix their own machines after centuries of study to the Adeptus Mechanicus, the rivals they believed betrayed and attacked them. If they did all that, they would risk being judged as incompetent at best, traitors at worst. The heritage they have spent a thousand years hiding and protecting might be stripped away from them by the Imperium. No. Their motivations are base, the actions of cowards, but that is what fear does to men. That is why the Emperor stripped it from us. But this Oskaran, and all his ancestors, they had no such boon, and it is no wonder the Regent Prime is a bitter, angry man. He would rather hold on to the hope that his Knights will rise again through some sort of miracle than risk losing them by doing anything.'

'The Omnissiah works in mysterious ways. But not illogical ones.'

'That is a talent of mortals.' Secrets and lies, stretching back so long. Zakariah shook his head. It was better to be a Dark Angel, and walk in the clear light of the Emperor. 'I will go back to Oskaran and see if I can press any more truth from him. And while I do, I will question the Regent Prime about their communication network.'

Meshach was wrapped in his armour, seated in the couch of the pilot's chair, but still Zakariah could read his disdain. 'I am sure the locals will have an answer,' the Techmarine muttered.

Zakariah smiled, but it was gone before he left the ship. Losing vox was bad enough. Having it taken away was worse. This mission had been a tangle from the start, with an enemy that refused to take the field and fight. It made him almost miss the orks.

He strode back into the palace, turning before he reached the Hall of the Fallen. The Regent Prime had retired to his office, a room panelled in golden wood with an intricate pattern of dark stripes running through it. Ancient holo-picts hung from the walls, depicting the Imperial Knights that had once belonged to the house, striding through battles which took place over a millennium before. How it must dig into Oskaran Halven's soul to stare at them, knowing those Knights lay still and useless, dead to him and his house unless he chose to reveal them – and that doing so risked losing them forever.

The Regent Prime sat behind a desk, staring at nothing. When Zakariah strode in, he managed to push himself to his feet and bow his head, but his skin was pale, his features slack. Giving up his secret had broken something inside him, probably his last hope that his family's heritage might ever be salvaged.

'Have they found him? Have they killed him?' Hope and bitterness were twisted together in his words.

'Not yet.'

'Not yet.' The Regent Prime slumped back down in his chair, somehow looking even more defeated. 'That boy... He went from being more fanatical about our heritage than I to denying it! He stood before me, where you stand now, dread Dark Angel, and told me our prophecy was a lie! He told me once that the only way I would ever ride a Knight into battle was on the bottom of its foot, do you believe–'

'We cannot reach them, Regent Prime.' Zakariah cut off the man's tirade, profoundly uninterested in his familial battles. 'The gris have done something to jam our vox signals. What is the status of your communications?'

'Communications?' the Regent Prime said, confused. 'I... Someone came in to tell me that Lash Commander Karn had disappeared. And that our communications were failing. I told them to get out.'

Orks were definitely better sometimes, Zakariah thought. Their incompetence didn't hurt you, and you could simply shoot them on sight, without wasting time with their blather. 'Get them back,' he said, instead of drawing his plasma pistol. 'And–'

There was a noise, faint in his ears, but one that he was

honed to hear. The crack of gun fire. The Regent Prime made no sign of hearing it. But as the lieutenant turned, he saw a mortal rushing into the office behind him.

'My lord, the Levies–' The man cut off when he saw Zakariah and froze, gaping, useless.

'Are they attacking or being attacked?' the Dark Angels lieutenant asked, and waited a frustrating few seconds while the man tried to find his voice.

'Both? My lord!'

'Of course,' Zakariah said. The ones the gris had taken against the ones that they had not, but he had little faith that the soldiers of the local Levies would be able to tell the difference in battle, even with the grey fungal masks covering the gris' faces. 'Regent Prime–'

There was a sudden squealing from the vox-unit on the corner of the Regent Prime's desk, and in his helm Zakariah saw the alerts bloom. Some transmission had cut through the gris' jamming, and it was flooding every band. A voice transmission, and the lieutenant could hear it spilling from the Regent Prime's vox and who knows how many others from outside the room.

'*Citizens of Reis! This is an emergency warning from the Reis Home Levies. Listen, and attend!*'

'That's Lash Officer Petra Karn,' the Regent Prime said. There was a crackle of static, and then the woman's voice returned. '*–opened. Repeating, the Redwash Gate has been reopened. The Regent Prime has betrayed us. He has sold Reis to the Dark Powers, and now their servants are here. Again, the Regent Prime has betrayed us and is now being hunted by the Dark Angels. Because of him, the Space Marines have declared this world tainted, our population unclean. They are blocking our communications while they prepare to exterminate us.*' Static filled the air again, but this time the Regent Prime didn't speak. He was staring at the vox as if it had become a venomous serpent, coiled on the corner of his desk. Then the static faded again.

'–flee. Make for the shelters in the western mountains, or find a place in the jungle. Repeat, all citizens of Kap Sudsten are advised to flee. The gris are in the city, disguised as Levies soldiers. The daemons gather at the gate to march on us. The Dark Angels have declared us enemy. Your only hope now is flight! Repeating. The only hope you have is–' Then there was nothing but static.

'She lies,' gasped Oskaran. 'She's lying! She's–'

'Destroying the morale of your people,' Zakariah said. 'Many will run now, and be easy prey for the gris to pick off. Others will turn on you, on your soldiers and on us. She sows chaos, and your people will die from it.'

'What do I do?' the Regent Prime gasped.

'Shut up, follow me and listen,' Zakariah snapped as he strode out of the office, moving to meet up with his men and see what bloody order he could sort out of this mess.

Jequn stood before the massive blast doors, silently cursing his vox.

The bands had all gone to static minutes after the fight had ended. He had just contacted Brother Cadus, who he'd left behind to man the Thunderhawk waiting in the stimm farm where they had been attacked, and to send messages back to Master Lazarus using the ship's powerful vox-system. He'd briefed the Techmarine on what had happened so far – the strange, deadlier gris, the brothers who had fallen into torpor, and the recovery of the Regent Next. The vox had been operational then, the occasional cracks and pops of static not unexpected when there was this much distance and dirt between them. But then, right at the end, the vox had fallen apart into static and noise, and Jequn couldn't even use it to communicate with the Dark Angels who stood around him.

Maybe it had been a mistake to leave Cadus up top. The Techmarine might have corrected the issue with skill and prayer. But Jequn threw that doubt away. The vox failing in this way, now, was no malfunction. This was an attack, something the gris were somehow doing to cut them off. Cadus would do what he could from the ship to correct it. Meanwhile...

Meanwhile they would see what this place was, and why the gris had camped on its doorstep.

Sebastian stood before those doors now, staring at them with a hungry look in his eyes. While Jequn had been dealing with the vox, the Regent Next had done nothing but this, silent, impatient.

'You know this place,' Jequn said.

'My father brought me here. Once.' Sebastian flipped a panel open on the doors, showing a dark square of something that looked like smoked glass. 'He told me this place was built when Reis was first settled. The first home of the Knights of House Halven. It was deserted a century later, when a magma plume formed below and the volcano began to rise. Abandoned, but not forgotten.' He pulled a knife from an inner pocket of his suit, a toy of a weapon studded with jewels, and pressed its tip against one finger. When blood began to flow, he pushed his hand against the black panel, smearing the blood against it.

'After the Redwash War, we claimed it again. For our Knights.'

'The Knights that were supposed to be lost,' Jequn said.

'That is the story we told our people, and the Adeptus Mechanicus. That our Knights had been lost beneath the waves, gone forever. But that was just a story.' The dark panel slipped silently aside, revealing a runeboard. Sebastian raised a finger to tap at its keys, but Jequn laid a hand on his shoulder, his fingers almost wrapping around the mortal.

'What lies beyond?'

'My heritage. The Knights of House Halven, hidden for a thousand years. Unbroken, but inaccessible. All our power, within our reach but outside our grasp.' The mortal looked up at him, eyes burning, but then they flashed away. 'The gris were not here when we came before. Obviously. They found this place somehow. They may have been trying to get in. I need to see… I need to make sure that our Knights are still there, waiting and ready.'

Knights were formidable weapons. The gris should never be able to control them – the machine spirits that animated them were fierce things, jealous of their house's honour. But their mould-infected enemy had shown some cunning in their ability to steal weapons and equipment. If they had found some way into this base, they might have stripped the war machines of their deadly armament.

'Open it,' Jequn ordered. 'But I will take the lead.' He raised his voice, so all his brothers could hear. 'Squad Invis right behind, Squad Jotha watching our backs.' He looked back at the mortal. 'Do you understand?'

'I do,' the Regent Next said, and when Jequn lifted his hand, Sebastian tapped a code into the panel. The doors began to rumble, then slid aside, parting down the middle. Behind them was a room, shadowy and vast, a great circle of rock-crete topped with a vast dome. The walls were sixty feet high, and a dome rose another fifty feet above them. Great buttressed ribs supported it, and from these hung huge lumens, most of them dark, their lenses grey and blind as cataracts, but a few still worked, spilling enough light for Jequn to see, even with all the equipment that filled the room.

There was some kind of huge lift in its centre, great rails running from the floor to what looked like a hatch set in the centre of the dome. Around the edges of the walls were gigantic docking stations. In each one stood a figure, tall and still. The Knights, waiting.

They were roughly humanoid, armoured giants with helm-shaped heads set between massive shoulders. They balanced on heavy legs with great clawed feet, made for walking through rubble. Their arms were weapons, huge guns like battle cannons, las-impulsors and plasma decimators. Some had melee weapons like lances, power fists or gigantic chainswords. They varied in size, from twice Jequn's height to more than three times it, but each of them was an imposing, hulking shadow that stood still as stone, gargoyles waiting to spring to life.

Jequn stepped into the room, sword raised, head sweeping back and forth. The docking stations for the Knights were tangles of steel beams, cables, struts and arcane equipment. Much of it seemed to be dead, but around each war machine at least a few panels were working, with tiny coloured lumens flashing and winking, pict screens drawing columns of numbers and runes, or displaying graphs of flowing waves or spiked lines. It was a mix of shadows and light, of vast openness and tight spaces, and a thousand gris could have hidden themselves here. But as Jequn moved he saw nothing but darkness and blinking displays. Heard nothing but the soft scuff of his feet against the rockcrete and the low electronic hum of equipment. Smelled nothing but metal and hydraulic fluid, the sharp stink of electronics and the dry smell of dust, and that awful, sour smell of the monstrous mound of mould that lay beyond the doors. He moved forward carefully, and he could sense Squad Invis right behind him. 'Jotha,' he said quietly, but the Scouts heard, filing in on either side, spreading out through the gloom, moving silently. Jequn walked until he reached the massive lift in the room's centre. At its edge, he stopped and turned a circle, searching again. Nothing. Back at the door, Sebastian waited, a restless shadow standing on the threshold.

'Keep watch,' he told Squad Invis' sergeant. Then he waved over the Scouts, angry again that the vox was useless. 'Anything?'

'Nothing,' Sergeant Asher said. 'This place is a tomb.'

Jequn looked at the silent Knights standing around them. There were a dozen of them, fixed in their docks like crucified corpses, the muzzles of their weapons hanging down, the painted heraldry on their shields dull with dust. The machines looked dead, but he didn't need to be a Techmarine to know that their machine spirits still curled within them, banked but not extinguished. This room might be a tomb, but a dozen drowsing ghosts haunted it. 'Search for other ways in or out.'

The Scout nodded and moved away, and Jequn waved Sebastian over. The mortal started walking, quick and eager, dodging out of the way of Squad Invis as they took their place near the door.

'Is it inviolate?' Jequn asked when Sebastian finally reached him.

'Perfectly,' the Regent Next said. 'Look at them.' He spun in a circle, eagerly staring at each Knight. 'Ever since I saw them that first time, they were all I could dream of. All that power.' He stopped, staring at a massive Knight Valiant, his back to Jequn. 'You don't know what it's like, Dark Angel. To be mortal, and frail, and powerless. But in that...' He pulled back his long hair, revealing the studs set in the side of his head, each one capped with black onyx. 'In that I would be as powerful as your whole company. Can you imagine it? What it would be like to be so weak but so close to all that strength, all that possibility, and not able to grasp it?'

'No,' Jequn said, his voice flat. They had spent enough time here, in House Halven's crypt. It was time to seal it again and move on, to find whatever gris remained and exterminate them so they could leave this stinking world behind. 'I have all the strength I need, through the Emperor and His gifts.'

'I give my thanks to the Throne for what He gives us, and for what He keeps away,' Sebastian said softly. 'That is a prayer that works for you, Dark Angel. Not so much for mortals like me.'

'You tread close to heresy,' Jequn growled.

'You have no idea.'

Jequn heard the words and his sword was up, rising high so that he could bring it down on the man. But as he began to swing, he saw movement from the corner of his eye and spun to face it.

A Knight across the chamber from him was moving in its cradle, the muzzle of the massive flamer hanging from one of its heavily armoured shoulders shifting to aim at him. 'Ware the Knights!' the Ancient shouted, just as the giant fired.

He was expecting flame. A massive gout of it, searing across the room to strike him even though he was throwing himself to the side, trying to get out of the line of fire. But what came instead was a spray of grey slime, thick liquid like the blood of the gris that he had fought in the tunnel. Most of it flew past Jequn and splattered across the floor, but he was still splashed with enough of it to coat his armour. His power sword hissed and popped like a searing-hot pan dropped into water as it burned away the slime that tried to coat it, and Jequn locked his gauntlets around the hilt as he ducked behind one of the lift supports.

He paused for a second, then whipped his head around. The Knight had moved, stepping out from the frame that held it, and twisted so that it was spraying the viscous grey fluid across Squad Invis. It splashed over them, coating armour and weapons, staggering them. But they kept their feet, and as one they raised their weapons. The roaring chatter of boltguns cut through the air – and then they were hit from behind.

Their attackers exploded through the door like a tidal wave, their outlines blending together, a mass of mould and slime. More of the monstrous gris, but with them was something else, something much more horrifying. Armoured forms, Dark Angels, the warriors who had been unconscious, unmoving. They were up now, their dark green armour dripping with grey slime, wading in to grab at their brothers and rip them to the floor with the gris.

'By the Throne, no!' Jequn bellowed. The sight of his brothers mixed with those unclean things, striking out at other Dark Angels, snapped something within him. He charged forward, his sword raised. Caught in his rage, he didn't see the shapes hurtling towards him from the shadows until they slammed into him, almost taking him down, but the Ancient caught himself and kept his feet. He came around, swinging his sword and making his attackers move back, and he saw them. Two of his brothers, one of them the warrior whose helmet he had taken off. There was no mould growing on his face, no grey mask like the mortal gris bore, but his eyes were as vacant, as dead.

'Sacrilege,' Jequn snarled, and he moved towards the infected Dark Angels, sword ripping through the air. There was no hesitation – death was better by far than whatever this was. They had their knives out, trying to stop his blows, but the combat blades were nothing to his power sword. He smashed one of their blades in half, then swung his sword back and caught the one still wearing his helmet in the chest, shearing halfway through. But his blade caught there, trapped by armour and dense bone. Jequn kept moving, turning his body to haul the bound blade out, but the other gris-taken Space Marine slammed into him, grabbing him and knocking the Ancient off his feet.

With a roar Jequn spun in his once-brother's grip, sending an armoured elbow up to smash into the Dark Angel's exposed face, cracking his jawbone. Jequn kept his grip on his sword with his free hand and finally pulled it free, then rolled away, coming back to his feet. The Space Marine he had elbowed came up too, and the one he had cut into still stood, even though Jequn could see lungs and liver, intestine and shredded muscle hanging out of his side. There were no threads of grey in any of it, nothing in the eyes or on his skin, but still Jequn could smell the mould's stench, and rage boiled through him. The gris had taken his own, somehow, had made his brothers turn against him. The obscenity of it gave strength to his strikes as he charged the one he'd cut open, and with a series of brutal slashes, Jequn took his head and hand and leg, dropping the gris-tainted Dark Angel.

He spun away from the body, sword rising, ready to attack the other, but was hit from behind by the stream of grey fluid from the Knight. It made him stagger, his feet slipping on the slime-coated floor. Jequn caught himself on his knees, turning, and saw the war machine standing over him. At its feet was a battle of armoured figures, Space Marine fighting Space Marine fighting gris. But it was almost over. One last brother from Squad Invis fell to the ground, and then the infected Dark Angels turned to Jequn, their red eyes glowing through the grey sludge that covered them.

'By the Lion and the Emperor who made him, this will not be,' Jequn growled.

'You call on the dead to protect you from the risen.' It was a man's voice, innocuous enough, but hard, edged in mocking. Jequn shifted his eyes away from his gris-possessed brothers just enough to see two figures approaching from the side. One was Sebastian, his eyes bright with smug satisfaction. The other was larger, an ugly grey shape like those things they had fought in the tunnels but bigger, about Jequn's size. The foul layers of mould that covered its head were folding back as it walked, opening like some hideous flower to expose a face beneath. A man's – too small for that huge, malformed head. It was a plain face except that it had gone grey in colour, skin and teeth and gums and eyes all the same ugly shade. All except the cybernetic implants that wrapped tendrils around his forehead and over his ears, onto his cheeks. Those were black and flaky with corrosion, probably from the thick fluid that constantly wept from the face's eyes and nose and mouth.

'There is a certain symmetry to that which I like,' the thing went on. 'But it is foolish. Your dead cannot help you here. My risen' – the man's face smiled, the curved, closed lips bubbling with viscous fluid – 'are here to welcome you with open arms.'

Jequn roared, all his battle cries gone, taken by rage and abhorrence, and shoved himself up from the floor. He hurled himself towards the thing, the gris, his sword raised. But when he swung it, the grey monster reached out a hand and caught the blade. It sank in, driving up the heavy arm, buzzing and hissing. But the blade hit a solid core somewhere in all that mould and stopped, and the thing twisted its arm. With a wrench the sword was ripped from the Ancient's grasp, and the gris' other hand slammed into his helmet, cold and thick with slime. It was strong, stronger than the others, stronger than Jequn, and it slammed him down to the ground so hard the Ancient could hear his armour groan, could hear the hiss of escaping air as the pressure seals popped.

'Join us, Dark Angel,' Jequn heard as he felt liquid pour into his armour, running across his skin like icy mucus. It filled his helmet in seconds, pressing against his lips, blurring his eyes, running up his nose and packing his sinuses before streaming down into his lungs. He coughed, choking, and could barely hear the gris' last words to him. 'Be one with my vengeance, and my suffering.'

CHAPTER NINETEEN

Ysentrud crawled down the narrow conduit, surrounded by darkness, walls pressing in on every side. The only sounds were the steady rasp of her breath through her rebreather, the rustle of her robe scraping against the rockcrete and the hiss of the nerus cord. At least that was growing slowly lighter as she moved along.

Which was good, because her spirit was growing heavier.

'Stupid stimm,' she whispered. The drug had lasted long enough to make her happily volunteer for this mission, but it wasn't effective until its end, of course. The sense of invincibility was fading, and she could feel fear waiting. It wasn't on her yet, but it surrounded her like the darkness.

'It's all right. Almost there.' Maybe. The coil of nerus was certainly smaller. There was only a third left, and the Fabricator Locum had given her extra, so she must be close. Must be.

Must.

She wiped the sweat off her hands and reached out, pulling

herself along again until she heard the noise. A distant click that echoed down the tunnel, making her freeze. She frantically fumbled for the lumen clipped to her, found the switch and extinguished it. Everything went black and she went still, holding her breath. A long moment of darkness passed, and then there was a gleam of deep blue light ahead, slowly growing. Ysentrud watched with wide eyes, hoping that light would fade, turn away, but it kept getting brighter until she could see its terrible source.

Fifteen yards away, two sapphire eyes flashed as they passed into the conduit. They glowed from the sockets of a skull, the bone misshapen with cybernetics. The horrible thing drifted from one side of the conduit to the other, then vanished into the shadows there. The blue glow slowly faded, and it was almost gone when Ysentrud realised she was going to die if she didn't start breathing.

Careful to keep from gasping, she breathed in and waited until the darkness was absolute again. Then she started to crawl forward, leaving her light off. After what felt like hours, the walls opened on either side of her, another conduit intersecting this one. She stared around, but there was nothing but darkness. With one hand on her knife, she flicked on the light.

There was nothing but rockcrete, and a heavy pipe that ran down the side of the crossing conduit. Quickly she pushed her way under it, the rough metal scraping through her robe. For a moment she thought she might be stuck, but she braced herself against the walls and shoved herself through, acquiring another abrasion to join the rest. The passage beyond stretched on, and she clicked off her light and started wriggling away as fast as she could. Until something brought her up short. The nerus cord. She had to uncoil more to keep going, but that made her realise she was leaving a clear trail. Would the skull notice? Would it understand?

She had no idea. It was the first servo-skull she'd ever seen. But there was nothing else she could do. Ysentrud kept going, spooling out the coil and hoping – both for the servo-skull to miss her presence and for the stimm not to fade any further.

It turned out that the Fabricator Locum hadn't given her much extra cord after all. Ysentrud lay in the conduit looking at the junction box projecting from one wall, holding the tiny bird skull wired to the end of the nerus cord. It could reach. Barely.

'Praise the Emperor,' she said, pulling out the cutting torch. The Techmarine had showed her how to use it, but she spent a moment looking it over, convinced she was going to burn her face off. That damn stimm really was fading. But the cutting torch was relatively simple, so she slipped on the dark goggles that came with it and clicked it on.

In the tiny space the heat hit her like a wave. If she'd had hair, it would have been charring. As it was, she was very grateful for the goggles, both for being able to see and for protecting her eyes. Carefully, she aimed the torch at the junction box and began to cut, the white flame drawing a black line across the metal. She had cut three sides of a square across the box when she paused to wipe her hands, now slicked with sweat. Then she slid the googles up, staring down the conduit. Was there a glow? It was hard to see – she'd lost all her dark vision to the torch even with the goggles. But no. It was dark. It had to be dark. Sliding the goggles down, she went back to work, making the last cut. The metal sparked and clinked under the torch, and she was almost done when the piece she was cutting away broke almost free, its searing-hot edge falling on her wrist.

Ysentrud yelped and jerked her hand back, the reflexive motion almost making her drop the blazing torch onto her belly. She caught it at the last moment, hissing curses. Fumbling at the controls, she managed to shut the torch off without killing herself. She was gasping in pain and relief, reaching for her injured arm, when she heard a whining, insect-like noise growing quickly louder. Another kind of panic hit her, and she ripped off her goggles.

With the dark glasses gone she could suddenly see the bright blue eyes, shining out from the sockets of the skull rushing towards her. In the second before it reached her, time slowed down and she could see far too clearly. The bone of the servo-skull was the colour of polished ivory. Black enamelled studs sprouted from it, and tiny lumens winked and danced over their dark surfaces, their light reflecting off the glossy bone. The skull's jaw was opening beneath its glowing eyes, revealing teeth of that same enamelled black metal. They gleamed in the blue light, flat and ridged like pliers, teeth made to crush and clamp and hold. Behind them something moved, a tongue white as bone but flexible, its edges lined with tiny blades that moved like the teeth of the Space Marines' awful chainswords. The tongue coiled like a serpent, ready to lash out and strike with all those ripping blades.

Ysentrud clenched her teeth to keep from screaming. Every split second stretched as the skull came towards her, enough for her to agonisingly absorb every hideous detail of ancient bone and deadly technology. Slow as it felt, the skull was on her bare seconds after she'd stripped away her goggles, that terrible tongue ready to tear her flesh apart. But in those seconds she managed to pull her legs up and drag her feet away from the thing, barely keeping its teeth from snapping shut on her toes. Then she lashed out, slamming one foot down. By the Emperor's blessing, she managed to smash her heel into the servo-skull's forehead, knocking the deadly thing back as it lashed its tongue out at her.

Her kick kept the thousand blades from wrapping around her leg, but the tip of the tongue still caught her, ripping away one sandal, and suddenly a terrible rush of cold ran up her leg. Everything was still moving slowly enough for Ysentrud to see the last two toes of her right foot tumble away, severed in an instant, replaced by blood and a sudden jolt of searing pain.

The pain tore across her body, but it didn't freeze her. Adrenaline, or the last of the stimm, exploded through her. Ysentrud jerked her feet up farther, twisting in the tiny conduit, somehow wrenching herself around to face the servo-skull. It had bounced off a wall, bone cracking against the rockcrete, and was starting to charge her again when she raised the cutting torch and turned it on.

The flame roared out, a lance of fire only a few inches long but searingly hot, brilliantly bright. It blinded her, but Ysentrud held it up, her arm locked out, ignoring the heat that was blistering her fingers until the jet of fire stuttered, the fuel going. Then she took her finger off the trigger and sat blinking and gasping in the sudden dark.

Was it dead? Was it destroyed? Those questions overwhelmed the pain in her foot and her hand. Or had it just backed away? Was it even now moving towards her, that cutting tongue lolling out, ready to wrap around her throat? But seconds passed and she didn't die, and her eyes began to adjust again in the darkness and she saw the light. The ghastly blue light of the skull's eyes. But there was just one now.

Ysentrud blinked and held up the little lumen still hanging around her neck. In its low glow, she could see the servo-skull a short way down the conduit. Her flame had caught it on the left side, scorching one eye into a lump of twisted metal and glass, blackening the ancient bone around it, and half melting one of the cybernetic components sticking out of the polished cranium. She'd hit it, damaged it, but it wasn't dead. The other eye still glowed, and the jaws still flexed, showing their awful flat teeth while the bladed tongue shifted. But it wasn't coming towards her. It hung in the air at a strange angle, tilted towards its damaged side, and it shuddered and bobbed, drifting from one side to another, skewing and twisting as it came. It was like watching a sailing boat try to make headway in a storm, and Ysentrud realised she must have damaged the vicious little thing's anti-grav field.

'Spin in place until the stars burn out, you Throne-cursed nightmare.' Ysentrud backed away from it, putting more distance between them. Her foot was beginning to throb, and she could see one of her toes below the skull, nail gleaming blue in its light. Nausea suddenly mixed with pain and she jerked her eyes away. Then she saw the tiny skull that lay beside her, with the dark line of nerus running from it. That. She'd almost forgotten the reason she was in this damned place. Ysentrud grasped the bird skull and, keeping her eyes on the slowly spinning servo-skull, pulled herself back to the junction box.

The metal square she'd cut out of the box's cover was still hanging off by one corner, but it had shifted enough for her to see the thick cable beneath. The Fabricator Locum's instructions had been simple – all she had to do was jab the beak of the little bird skull into the cable's insulation. She had worried she might damage the cable, but Gretin Lan had told her to drive in the beak as hard as she could, enough so it stuck in place. The skull would take care of itself after that. Easy enough. Except…

The cover was open, mostly, and she could wriggle her hand into it, holding the bird skull. But she couldn't swing her arm to strike. Instead, she was lying on her side, digging weakly with the beak into the cable, trying to get it to go in, but it wouldn't stick, it wouldn't stick – and then Ysentrud remembered the servo-skull.

She had taken her eyes off it when she was fighting with the cable, but for how long? Just seconds. But when she looked back, it had moved. It was still awkwardly bobbing and spinning, but as Ysentrud watched, the thing flicked its tongue out as it turned, caught the wall and shoved itself towards her. It was slow – she could crawl away from it – but she had to drive this damn bird skull in first.

'Come on. Come on, you fragging thing. Throne curse you and your stupid fragging beak and your stupid fragging owner and this stupid, warp-cursed, Emperor-kissed, mutant-born piece of fragging xenos crap cable!' Ysentrud pushed the bird skull as hard as she could, twisting the beak against what felt like steel plating, until suddenly it sank in just a little and the red lights set into the tiny skull's eye sockets flashed to life. Hair-thin needles shot out of the beak, piercing the cable's thick insulation and pulling wisps of wire through after them. Ysentrud let go and flopped back, just in time to see the servo-skull manage to catch the wall perfectly and fly towards her, air hissing around the chain of blades that circled the long tongue as it whipped straight at her face.

Without even a chance to scream, she raised the cutting torch and tried to hit the trigger. But as her arm came up, the tongue lashed around her wrist. With a *ting*, the cutting torch hit the floor with most of her right hand still wrapped around it.

She screamed then, screamed in pain and fear and rage. Without thinking she slammed the stump of her arm into the servo-skull's jaw, trying to knock the thing back, but it clamped on to her with those flat metal teeth and she felt the bones of her forearm crunch and pop in its grip. Pain flashed through her, agony piling on agony, and she howled as she swung the terrible thing against the wall, cracking the skull against the rockcrete. Still it hung on, its one eye pulsing as its tongue flicked out and wrapped around her upper arm. Blood exploded where it touched, and it began to sink in, disappearing into her shredded muscles.

The pain was too much. The world was going dark at the edges, shock closing off her vision, and Ysentrud knew she was going to die. This monstrous, necrotic cyborg, this horrible thing she had been tattooed to resemble because of some twisted tradition, was going to cut her arm off and then go for the rest of her, carving her up the way Lazarus had carved up the gris–

Lazarus. Lazarus had tied the blade Gretin Lan had given her to her robe.

Without thinking, she slipped into memen state.

'The Dark Angels are the first division of the warrior transhumans know as Adeptus Astartes, or colloquially, Space Marines.' The words rolled from her, calm and easy, as she reached down with her left hand and pulled the white dagger from its sheath. 'Fell fighters, the Dark Angels are known for over ten thousand years of perfect faith and honour.' The smooth roll of her words was interrupted by a grunt as she swung the blade. The sharp tip hit the servo-skull and sliced across it, gouging a deep line in the bone. The servo-skull jerked and the tongue went tighter, the blades rasping around the bone of her upper arm. The knife slid away just as Ysentrud hit the stud, and she heard the air sizzle around the blade.

Frustration and terror chewed at the edges of her brain, but the emotions couldn't penetrate the memen. 'The Dark Angels are renowned on Reis for their opportune arrival in the midst of the Redwash War.' She pulled back the blade and drove it in again, and this time the tip found the blue gleam of the servo-skull's remaining eye. Ysentrud thrust it in, and the glass buckled and shattered beneath the knife.

The servo-skull twisted, trying to pull away, but its tongue was wrapped too tight. 'Without their arrival,' Ysentrud said, her voice flat and calm in the centre of her trance, 'the people of Reis would have fallen.' Then she hit the stud again.

This time the crackle of the electrical release climbed into a buzzing shriek as the dagger discharged into the servo-skull's eye. Electricity arced through the cybernetics projecting from the bone, making the lights on them flare and then burn out as circuits popped and shattered. The cutting tongue gave one final convulsive clench, the blades on it clattering against Ysentrud's humerus. She felt a buzz of electricity arcing through the tongue, but it stopped when the awful weapon whipped away from her, straightening out – then going limp and still as the servo-skull fell. It rolled onto its back, the eyes shattered and dead, a line of smoke drifting out of the silently screaming jaws.

It was dead, and Ysentrud stopped speaking. She lay on the blood-slicked floor and considered dying. She hurt, Emperor's blood she *hurt*, and she was cold, and she was going to be missing pieces, some pretty bloody major pieces, and just lying here and letting the darkness take her seemed like a grand idea in some ways. But she was stubborn, and damn it, she didn't know what the hell was going on and she wanted to last at least enough for that. Just long enough to know what the hell the gris were doing and why and how and... and damn it, she didn't want to be done yet, not with nothing to show for her life but a head full of history other people had lived through.

Ysentrud wanted to live, but that was going to be complicated. First and foremost because she was bleeding to death.

'Never an Apothecary when you need one,' she whispered.

Then she felt around with her left hand until she found her right, still warm, still gripping the cutting torch. She kept her eyes averted as she shook her right hand off the torch and raised it up. She touched the trigger, just enough for a quick, sputtering flame. It still worked, well enough. The flame itself was far too hot, but the metal torch-tip glowed red for a moment after it passed. She took a breath, looked at the bloody mess of her arm, and aimed for the place where most of the blood seemed to be coming from.

When she pressed the searing-hot tip of the tool to the torn blood vessels, the tiny conduit echoed with her scream.

CHAPTER TWENTY

'Do you think she will succeed?'

Lazarus willed away the schematics he was studying and looked over at Demetrius. The Interrogator-Chaplain was staring at the narrow hatch Ysentrud had slipped through. Two skitarii guards crouched next to it, helping unspool the long nerus cord as it slowly disappeared into the dark.

'She may,' Lazarus said. 'And the cost of failure is low. So it is a chance worth taking.'

The Interrogator-Chaplain's skull mask was unchanging, the red-and-green glow of his eyes unblinking, but Lazarus could sense his brother's dissatisfaction with his blunt answer. 'Have you adopted this strange mortal, Interrogator-Chaplain Demetrius? Did you find some kinship in your shared skull-faced visage?'

'I care for her success,' Demetrius said. 'Your tactics are sound, Lazarus, but the odds are stacked against us and a battle like this is a game of numbers. We will lose many if we must fight our way out of this hole. But...' He shrugged the massive armour of his shoulders. 'I have formed an attachment to our little Learned. Mortals, for the most part, are simply beneath notice. But sometimes their bravery, their willingness to sacrifice themselves, can make an impression. Their fragility can become endearing.'

'Are you growing soft, my brother?'

'It is not weak to care about my brothers,' Demetrius said. 'To pray for their survival. There is great potential in us all, a light I would not see extinguished, so I worry about them. And sometimes mortals have potential too.' He tilted his head, looking at Lazarus. 'You care about our brothers also. After their loss.'

When I can afford to, Lazarus thought, but he left it unsaid. Demetrius knew that truth anyway. He looked away from the slowly disappearing pile of cable to Gretin Lan. She was a pale statue in the dim, beautiful in her alien way, perfectly motionless except for the twisting dance of the multiple pupils in her eyes.

'Before I destroyed its puppets, the gris tried to speak to me,' he told her. 'It said it wanted to get to know me.'

'An inclination you did not share.' She didn't look at him, the still mask of her face enigmatic as always, but the bird on her shoulder cocked its head towards him. 'You forfeited an opportunity to acquire information.'

'As did the gris,' Lazarus said. 'The information it had for me I believe I already know. At least in part. But you can fill in the rest. Tell me what you know about Heris Amis.'

Now she looked at him. 'That enginseer was terminated long ago.'

'A thousand years,' Lazarus agreed. 'That's what the gris told me. One thousand years to plot his revenge. He also told me that he died. Obliquely.'

'There is a high probability that this information is tainted data, from a faithless source.'

'Maybe,' he said. 'But that faithless source had very detailed knowledge of your forge, and the placement of its infrastructure. Have you ever had anyone taken by the gris?'

'No. These gris designates had been limited to Sudsten before this confrontation, and no Adeptus Mechanicus–' She cut off, the music of her words ending abruptly.

'No one of the Adeptus Mechanicus has been to the southern continent for a thousand years?' Lazarus asked. 'Not since the Redwash War. And the execution of Heris Amis. He was the reason for that exile, was he not? A traitor, who sabotaged the Knights of House Halven and killed their pilots before they could even go to battle?'

'Correct,' she said. 'But that incident of treachery was not the product of Adeptus Mechanicus action. It was forged by the isolated actions of a rogue designate who was summarily disposed of.'

'How did he do it?' Lazarus asked.

'Introduction of a toxin into the Knights' Thrones Mechanicum, the system that mediates connection between the Knight's machine spirit and the pilot's mind.' She turned and faced him fully, the panels of her skirt swaying. 'The toxin was manufactured from a mould species endemic to the southern continent. Grey pall.'

'Grey pall,' he repeated, and the Fabricator Locum folded her arms over her chest.

'I am cognizant of the association,' she said. 'However, the fact that Heris Amis has been deceased for a millennium still strongly contradicts your theory.'

'Some things are too stubborn to die,' Demetrius said.

Lazarus frowned at him, but the Interrogator-Chaplain didn't say anything more. So he shifted his gaze to his Librarian.

'Librarian Raziel. At the Redwash Gate, you said you felt some-thing. A shadow. Could it do something like this? Raise the dead? Keep them alive for centuries?'

'I do not know,' Raziel said. 'But that flaw is tiny. I am not sure the shadow I felt could reach enough power through to produce a dark miracle like resurrection.'

'But if he was not dead to begin with?' Lazarus asked.

'Adeptus Mechanicus records indicate that Heris Amis was dispatched when the Dark Angels fired a bolter round through his thorax,' Gretin Lan said dryly.

'It seems unlikely that a mortal, even a member of the Adeptus Mechanicus, would survive that,' Raziel said. 'But if he did, then perhaps the shadow could have healed and sustained him. Though in what state, I cannot imagine.'

'A state of anger,' Lazarus said. 'The Dark Angels judged Heris Amis, executed him, and he was brought back in pain.' For a moment, the Master of the Fifth felt the flames of his first death again. Gretin Lan had a point with her doubt, but this felt true to Lazarus. It made the pieces they had of this plan-et's ugly puzzle almost fit. 'He returned from the death we gave him, and now he seeks to pay us back for his pain.'

Silence followed that, interrupted finally by the low, buzzing voice of one of the skitarii·that were playing out the nerus cord.

'The human has stopped.'

Lazarus looked at the machine man, at the cord that lay on the floor beside him. It was almost all gone. As he watched, it moved a tiny bit, then stopped again.

'Your Learned has reached the node,' Gretin Lan said. 'If–'

The cord moved suddenly, jerking into the tunnel. It wriggled and shook, then went still. For long moments nothing happened, and in the quiet Lazarus could hear the whispered benedictions of Interrogator-Chaplain Demetrius.

Then, with a sound like a bird call, the Fabricator Locum reared up. 'Noosphere connection established,' she snapped, and then she shut her eyes and curled in on herself, the cloud of skulls around her pulling into tight, fast orbits as the white bird spread its wings over her protectively.

'The halls,' Lazarus snapped, heading for the closest entrance. Squad Lameth were watching this one, and as Lazarus ran towards them, cursing the static that filled the vox, he could hear their guns. He ran faster, bolt pistol in one hand, sword in the other. When he reached Lameth, the squad were at the open door, crouching behind makeshift barricades, firing careful shots out into the hall.

'Master Lazarus!' Lameth's sergeant raised his arm, waving him over. 'The cyborgs have fallen back.'

'Back?' Lazarus could see little in the huge hall except smoke and wreckage.

'It started with a charge towards the doors. We opened fire, getting ready to hold, but then they turned on each other, the sulphurhounds attacking the servitors.' The sergeant shook his head. 'We've been picking off any that come close.'

'Good,' Lazarus said, wishing desperately for vox, to see if this was happening at the other exits. But then the steady volley of shots faltered and fell silent. In the hall outside, nothing moved, and then there was a soft *whunk* and the great lumens overhead all came on, flooding the factorum and the hall with light.

A voice filled the factorum, spilling out of the orato system. *'This is Fabricator Locum Gretin Lan. Forge Norsten has been subject to attack, which I have countered. The enemy has been purged from our sacred system. Enginseers, begin immediate damage assessment.'*

'She has countered the attack,' Demetrius said, his voice flat, as he stepped in beside Lazarus.

'It is countered,' Lazarus said. 'Which is what matters.' He turned to the sergeant. 'Prepare your men. We will gather the others, and then we are going.'

'Where?' Demetrius asked.

'Back to where we began. To the place the gris have been pulling us away from ever since we landed. We are going to Kap Sudsten, and we are going to end this.'

Maybe his resurrection had made him soft-hearted too, because Lazarus didn't take the most direct route out of the forge's underground labyrinth. Instead, he took the one that led them past where the Fabricator Locum's servitors were pulling Ysentrud from the conduit.

'Does she live?' he asked as he strode up the forge's wide hall. There was a knot of small, spider-like servitors clustered around a hole carved into the wall. The ugly things, severed heads wired into insect-like bodies with manipulator arms and multi-jointed legs, were grouped around the woman too thickly for him to see her, but he could smell blood.

'Cognitive function has not ceased,' Gretin Lan said. She waved a hand and the spider servitors scuttled back, revealing a body stretched out on a quilted pad, pressed into use as a stretcher. Ysentrud was sprawled upon it, her eyes closed, her ruddy skin dull, and she was barely breathing. Her right arm was a ruin, barely attached, and she stank of burnt flesh and blood. Beside her, set carefully on one corner of the blanket, was a servo-skull. A chainsword-like tongue lolled from between its jaws, and the Fabricator Locum's knife was protruding from the broken lens of one eye. 'She fought,' Gretin Lan said.

Lazarus frowned at the Learned, and waved Brother Asbeel forward. The Apothecary crouched over her, the servo-arms on his back squirming over his shoulders like scorpion tails, whirring and clicking, bringing his narthecium to bear. 'Blood loss and shock,' he said in clipped tones. 'The arm will have to go.' There was an ugly snipping noise, and the hiss of injections and spray. Asbeel leaned back, and Ysentrud's arm was off, but the stump had been coated with liquid integument that became a skin-like covering. The Apothecary did the same with the stumps of her toes and a dozen other cuts.

'I gave her painkillers, regeneratives and stimm – not as much,' he said to Lazarus. 'She will probably live, though with mortals it is hard to say. It would be best if she stays here. She is too weak to do much.'

'I can teach.' The words were little more than a whisper, spilling out through the woman's lips. But she had opened her eyes and was staring at Lazarus, her head raised, unsteady but up. 'All I was ever good for anyway.'

'It seems you are good for more than that, Learned,' Lazarus said.

'Maybe,' she said. 'Just one little skull... Emperor's teeth, I *hurt*.' Then she blinked. 'Apologies, Interrogator-Chaplain. I beg forgiveness.'

'Stimms affect us all,' Demetrius said.

'Not enough,' she hissed, then her head lolled back.

Asbeel looked at Lazarus, waiting.

'Bring her,' he said. 'I will decide what to do with her at the Thunderhawks.'

The Apothecary nodded and collected the woman, carrying her easily in one arm, wrapped in the bloody cover. They started down the tunnel towards the exit and the cold, clear air.

But when they stepped out onto the snow-covered landing field, the Thunderhawks were gone.

CHAPTER TWENTY-ONE

'But it is not possible!'

Brother Ephron stood in the middle of the empty landing field, staring down at the scorch-marks the Thunderhawks had made on the pavement. The dark streaks were cold now, snow blowing across them in thin, twisting snakes of white. 'Our brother machine spirits would never have let the gris in, much less allow them to fly!'

'I am done with hearing what is impossible for the gris to do after they have already done it.' Lazarus was looking around the empty field, taking in the hangars lining its edge. Most of them had their doors open, empty, but two were in flames. 'I do not have time for it. We do not have time. The gris are on the move, and we are trapped here, again.' He spun to face the Fabricator Locum, who was staring at the burning hangars. 'Your other ships?'

'Gris designates have appropriated or destroyed almost all of our air transports.'

'Almost?' Lazarus snapped, and she nodded. A short distance from them, a huge metal disc set in the pavement began to iris open.

'There are nominal advantages to administering this forge. I could at least indulge in two diversions from my standard functions.' Gretin Lan began to walk towards the now-open portal as a graceful white shape rose through it. 'Fabrication and aviation. Because I crafted it myself, *Kestrel* was never appended to the forge's manifests. So its destruction was neglected.'

Lazarus walked past her, barely listening as he stared at the flyer rising out of the ground. It was a dart, slim and long with swept-back wings, a shape that screamed speed. Very different to the blocky, heavily armoured shapes of the Thunderhawks, but those were transports. This thing?

'How many can that carry?' he asked as the lift stilled and locked into place.

'Five of you, with arms and armour.'

Five. By the Throne. Five. 'My command squad,' he shouted, and they pulled in around him, Interrogator-Chaplain Demetrius, Techmarine Ephron, Librarian Raziel and Apothecary Asbeel, still cradling Ysentrud in one arm. 'You are with me.' He spun and looked back at the rest, Squads Lameth, Hazin and Bethel, and the Dreadnought Azmodor. 'Our enemy has outmanoeuvred me. Again.' He felt the anger in him, cold and sharp, a blade slicing through his guts. 'I am sorry, brothers, but for my failure you will suffer. The fight is far from here, and while I rush to it, you will be left behind. Know that I will do all I can to bring you to me, but also know that I cannot guarantee when.' He could guarantee nothing because he still did not know his enemy's plan. Were the gris going to try to turn all of Kap Sudsten? Or force open the Redwash

Gate somehow? The knife of anger in his gut twisted, but he spoke the Litany of Focus and controlled the emotion, kept it in check, and made his decision. 'Watch and ward here. We are the Dark Angels! The sons of the Lion, and we will triumph!' They roared back at him, and Lazarus felt a surge of pride. They were undaunted, despite all their frustrations, and they still believed in him.

He would honour their trust, and see their frustration paid back in blood.

'Sergeants.' He beckoned the men forward and gave them conference, laying out the codes he would give to any Thunderhawks he sent back for them.

Secret codes. Because they couldn't trust their own ships, because the gris controlled at least two of them now. That cold knife of rage was still buried deep in him when he went to the flyer. His cadre were waiting outside its hatch while Gretin Lan worked inside. From the sounds, and the things flying out of the hatch, she was tearing out anything that wasn't necessary for the flight.

'Master Lazarus.' Asbeel nodded down to his arm where Ysentrud lay. Wrapped in her makeshift blanket, she was still shivering. 'Are we bringing her?'

'I don't want to stay,' the Learned said, her voice shaky with cold. 'I'll freeze to death out here, or choke to death in there. Everything about this place is awful.'

'We are going to battle,' Lazarus told her.

'Going, my lord?' she asked. 'We've been in battle since you got here. This whole world is going to be a battlefield soon enough. I'd rather die someplace warm, where I can breathe.'

'The mutant is allowable.' Gretin Lan threw one last chair out of the hatch and beckoned them on board. 'Her weight is negligible.'

'What about you?' Lazarus asked.

The Fabricator Locum turned away from the hatch, moving to the cockpit. Her bird took off, flying to the gates of the forge and disappearing inside. 'I will convey you,' she called back.

'My Techmarine can fly this.' With the Fabricator Locum gone, he could take one more brother. Maybe two.

'No,' she said, fitting her augmented body into the cockpit's strange confines. '*Kestrel* acknowledges only me.'

His anger made him want to argue, but logic said it wouldn't be worth the time. Lazarus boarded with the rest, finding a spot to strap in amid the gutted cabin. The rest of the command squad did the same, but the hatch didn't shut behind them. It stayed open as Gretin Lan flipped switches and whistled something that sounded like a prayer, then suddenly it was full of wings and bone.

Gretin Lan's bird flew through, followed by two more that looked exactly like it. After them came a swarm of bird skulls, which parked themselves in tiny slots in the cockpit. The hatch slid shut, and the flyer began to move.

'Please designate a destination,' the Fabricator Locum said. Her head and hands and legs were buried in the cockpit, wrapped in cybernetic equipment that linked her directly to the flyer.

'Kap Sudsten,' Lazarus told her. All the enemy's actions so far had sought to pull him away from the capital. Instincts built from centuries' worth of battles told him that was where this war would finally be joined.

'Kap Sudsten,' Gretin Lan repeated. 'With haste.'

'By the Emperor and His son, the Lion, yes,' growled Lazarus, and then felt the enormous hand of inertia pressing into him as *Kestrel* shot away, leaving Forge Norsten and half his Fifth behind.

* * *

'How are you?' Lazarus asked, watching Ysentrud as she gnawed a ration bar and sipped at water, a portion of the few supplies that had survived Gretin Lan's onslaught.

'Well, my lord,' she said, setting down the bar and turning her hand palm up. 'On one hand, today was definitely the worst day of my life. On the other...' She moved the stump of her other arm. 'Oh. Right. I guess it was just terrible.'

Lazarus had taken off his helm to wipe his face, and when the corner of his mouth quirked up she seemed almost triumphant. 'What is it?' he asked.

'You smiled.' She leaned back, smiling herself. 'That's the first smile I've ever seen on a Space Marine.'

The Apothecary might not have given her as much stimm, Lazarus thought, but he wasn't sure he had got the dose exactly right yet either. But he was glad Ysentrud was moving and talking. Mortals were so frail, things like losing a limb often ended up deadly for them. 'You have done us a service. That is something that even fewer mortals can say.'

'Yes. Well.' She shifted uncomfortably. 'I did what I had to. Any of you could have done it without losing an arm, if you could have reached it.'

'And so we could not do it,' he said. 'You did well, Learned. And you have done well in your teaching. Because of what you have told me, I think I know the man behind the gris.'

Ysentrud's strangely coloured eyes widened. 'Who?'

But before he could answer, Ephron called out, 'Master Lazarus! There is something on the vox!'

'I have it too,' Gretin Lan said from the cockpit. 'All bands, same signal. Here.'

A voice filled the cabin, spilling out of the flyer's vox. A woman's voice.

'This is an emergency warning from the Reis Home Levies–'

'That's Lash Officer Petra Karn,' Ysentrud said. Lazarus held up his hand, quieting her as he listened to the words. Lies, not very subtle ones, meant to disrupt the civilian population and the Reis Home Levies. They would do well enough, he was sure. They always did. Reason was the first casualty of fear. Lazarus listened to understand how the gris were shaping the battlefield, trying to see how the enemy wanted to guide things. He was distracted, though, when Ephron spoke. Not to him but into the vox, and in the unintelligible crackling pops of the Techmarines' binary cant. He kept it up until the broadcast cut off abruptly, then he went silent too.

'That Throne-cursed–' Ysentrud started, then stopped when Lazarus held up his hand.

'We know. She is working with the gris. With Sebastian.'

'How do you know that?'

'You told us,' Demetrius said. 'Silence now.' His admonition was much gentler than it had been with Sebastian or the Regent Prime.

'Were you able to get through?' Lazarus asked his Techmarine.

'By the Emperor's blessing, I did,' Ephron said. 'The gris could not maintain their jamming of our transmissions while they spoke. I was able to communicate with Brother Meshach and Brother Cadus. I told them what happened to us, what we have learned, and that we are coming.'

'And what information did they have?' Lazarus leaned forward, hungry for knowledge.

'Tidings good and bad. Brother Cadus told me that they were able to find the tunnels the gris had made to attack us at the stimm farm, and that Ancient Jequn led his squads in, leaving Cadus behind with their ship.'

'A good decision,' Lazarus said dryly.

'I told them of the loss of our Thunderhawks. Both he and

Meshach will guard theirs and watch for *Adamantine Wings* and *Rage of Angels*.' Ephron took a breath. 'Ancient Jequn found a nest of gris in the tunnels, and more. He found the entrance to some kind of ancient facility, long abandoned. And he found the Regent Next.'

'Alive,' Lazarus said. It was a statement, not a question.

'Yes,' continued Ephron. 'Jequn reported the gris had taken the Regent Next prisoner, but he showed no signs of being infected. I informed Cadus of our suspicions, and he will relay them to Ancient Jequn, when he can reach him by vox again. Brother Jequn reports encountering a new kind of gris, larger and stronger and completely covered with the mould. Sebastian claimed that those gris infected other prisoners. Sebastian also claimed he could get Jequn into the abandoned facility.'

'A trap,' Lazarus said.

'But what kind?' asked Demetrius.

The Master of the Fifth didn't know, and it was all he could do to keep his anger leashed. The damned vox. He had hoped when Gretin Lan regained control of her forge the interference would fall, but it had not. The gris were not using the forge's technology to cause it, and Librarian Raziel had proposed that it might be a psionic effect, generated by the gris themselves. The psyker had not been able to counter it either though, of course.

'I have a suspicion about that,' Ephron said, answering Demetrius. 'From speaking with Meshach. He had two important pieces of information. The first is that Sebastian's house has been engaged in a lie for a thousand years. The Knights that they claim to have lost never were. House Halven took them, to keep them from falling into the hands of the Adeptus Mechanicus, and hid them in an abandoned facility, hoping to repair them themselves. Though apparently they gave that dream up long ago.'

'What?' The Fabricator Locum's voice crackled with anger and disbelief. 'Omnissiah judge them, they condemned the Adeptus Mechanicus for losing their Knights when they were culpable, appropriating those blessed machines so they might fumble with their repairs?'

'Apparently,' Ephron said. 'They never succeeded.' The Techmarine ignored the disgusted, trilling snarl that came from Gretin Lan. 'The Regent Prime is only one of two people alive who know of the Knights' existence, and where they are hidden. Sebastian is the other.'

'Which means the gris know.' Lazarus looked at Ephron. 'Could the gris control them?'

'You asked me to stop telling you that the things the gris were doing were impossible, Master Lazarus,' Ephron answered.

'Heris Amis was responsible for maintaining those Knights when he lived.' Lazarus tapped the pommel of his sword with his fist. 'Suborning them seems less impossible than most of his accomplishments.'

'It would still seem questionable,' Gretin Lan said. 'A Knight's machine spirit is fundamentally bound to the house it serves, its Throne Mechanicum imprinted with the cognitive patterns of every pilot who has meshed their consciousness with it. Those imprinted ancestors are not easily turned from the principles they held in life. But suspicion indicates at least one member of that house is collaborating with possible antagonist Heris Amis.'

'Sebastian. Who is currently leading my Ancient, Squad Invis and Squad Jotha into some ancient ruin. Which seems likely to be where these Knights are stored.' Lazarus looked at Ysentrud. 'How many Knights did House Halven have?'

'They were a small house,' she said. 'They had twenty-four Knights, half in the south, half in the north. With the southern Knights destroyed, there would only be twelve left.'

'Only twelve.' The words were bitter in his mouth. Two squads and his Ancient weren't enough. All that was left of the Fifth was probably not enough. 'What was the other piece of information?'

'The gris have attacked the Reis Home Levies' base outside of Kap Sudsten. Lieutenant Zakariah was leading his squads to engage.'

Lazarus nodded, unsurprised. He had been almost certain they weren't trying to smash open the Redwash Gate, to unleash another flood of daemons. Heris Amis had already had that chance and not taken it. A framework of the gris' real plan was finally forming in his head. Sebastian and the Knights would take Jequn and his men. Then the war machines would march on Kap Sudsten, where Lieutenant Zakariah would be bogged down dealing with gris-infected soldiers and civilians. And when they were done with that, they would swing back to Norsten and destroy the last of the Fifth's forces.

Divide and conquer, simple as that. But Lazarus suspected that some other, deeper plan twisted below this one. Something that might be even worse than simply wiping out his company.

The thought made him want to draw Enmity's Edge, to savage his way through this fight with the black, crackling edge of its blade. But that was the thought of a neophyte, a Space Marine newly born to his power. He was the master of a company, and he had to draw his strength from more than his blade.

He had to understand his enemy, had to know where Heris Amis was planning to truly strike, instead of chasing his feints. Lazarus sat bowed over his sword, thoughts spinning through his head, making his plans.

Until *Adamantine Wings* fell in behind them, engines cutting a string of fire across the sky.

CHAPTER TWENTY-TWO

A tunnel, dark and twisting through the earth. The rough walls scraped against Jequn's shoulders, and every time they did, the foetid air filled with the stink of mud and mould.

A corridor, dark and close. The steel walls shed rust each time they were touched, adding to the harsh smell of corrosion that filled the abandoned starship, a smell that almost covered the stench of the monsters that hid within the space hulk's metal bowels.

A hall, bright with lumens, the light glowing across the names carved in the stone. The columbarium of the Dark Angels, where the ashes of ten thousand years' worth of the dead were gathered. The hall smelled of incense and dust, and Jequn breathed deep – but there was something else, a thin scent of something acrid, something awful.

The smell of the gris.

The smell of infection.

That stench brought him out of the stupor that had wrapped

him in darkness and delirium, and the Ancient opened his eyes. He *was* in a tunnel, but this one was made of rockcrete, its heavy walls cracked and bleeding mud and roots. It was the same tunnel where they had fought the gris before, the one that led to the Knights' chamber, but this portion was in worse shape, the slanted floor coated in mud and all the lumens broken and dark. There was light though, a glow that grew brighter and brighter, and Jequn realised he was being carried upward. Being taken outside.

He twisted, trying to move, but something held him – a heavy chain, coiled tight around him. Its thick links scraped against his armour, and he could see that one of the purity seals affixed to his pauldron had tangled in the rusty links, its colours stained with grey slime.

He wasn't pure. Not any more. That gris slime was in him, fighting his transhuman immune system, trying to grow through his body and brain so that it could take him as it had taken his brothers. The thought made Jequn rage, and he twisted and bucked, trying to shatter the chain, but the steel was solid beneath its rust, and his movements were jerky, uncoordinated. For the first time since his body had accepted the sacred gene-seed of the Dark Angels, he felt awkward, disjointed, wrong. But still he fought, trying to break free.

'Is he convulsing?' It was Sebastian's voice, coming from somewhere behind Jequn.

'No. Fighting.' It was the low, clotted voice of Heris Amis, and Jequn realised that the monstrous gris was holding him, carrying him despite his size and the weight of his armour. 'I will take him, as I took his brothers. He is strong though, and it will take time.'

'Time?' Sebastian snapped. 'We march out as soon as the Knights reach the surface. What time do we have?'

'What time?' Amis asked. 'I have waited for this moment for a thousand years. Learn some patience, Regent Next. This Dark Angel will be ready when we need him, and for the moment his suffering, so laced with rage and shame, is sweet.'

Amis stepped around a slope of earth and broken rockcrete, through a fringe of ferns and into daylight. The tunnel opening was a rough hole in a bluff that formed one edge of a small algae-filled lake. The stagnant waters gleamed under the sun, and the thick wet scent of decay almost blotted out the stink of gris that filled Jequn's nose. Almost, but not quite. Heris Amis stopped at the edge of the opening, keeping to the shade of the tall ferns that covered the bluff, but Sebastian stepped around him, moving out into the sun to stare down at the lake.

'The longer this takes, the more chance it has to fail,' he said.

'It will not fail, because it has already taken so long.' Amis dropped Jequn, and the Ancient hit the edge of the rock-crete. The jolt did nothing to him through his armour, but he had to roll so that he could see. The motion was ungainly, his body twitching and fighting him as he forced it to move. Shame and rage. By the Emperor and the Lion, yes, Jequn was full of both. But he would use those emotions to burn this infection out of him. He would. The silent vow echoed in his head even as Jequn felt something twisting in his brain like a line of hooks, snaring out memories, pulling at his will. 'One thousand–'

'Years of suffering,' Sebastian cut in. 'I've heard it. But for all that planning, you weren't prepared for everything.' The Regent Next was staring at the green-slicked lake, the tension in his body a silent shout of impatience, but he spared a quick glance down at Jequn. 'This one fights you. And those others beat you.'

'They didn't beat me.' Amis' voice was a guttural roll of thunder, deep and clotted with slime and anger. 'Some of them, the ones they call Primaris, are difficult. But death is not victory. I may not have been able to control them, but I tore their minds apart and ripped knowledge from what was left.'

A flicker of something went through Jequn. He shifted so that he was staring up at the gris, still fighting at the rusty chains that bound his body and the slimy threads that were trying to bind his will. 'Master Lazarus is Primaris,' he growled, the words barely comprehensible.

Amis shifted, kneeling down beside Jequn, his body dripping mould. One thick hand reached out to grasp the Ancient's helmet, and the armour shifted beneath those malformed fingers. It should have been impossible, but the grey monster took his helmet and set it beside him. Then he cupped Jequn's chin, pressed his mouldy flesh against the Ancient's in a disgusting caress that Jequn tried to jerk away from, but couldn't. 'I know,' the gris said. 'I pulled that knowledge from the minds of your brothers. And I will pull the knowledge I need from your master's mind soon enough.' He smiled, his ugly grey face twisting beneath its coating of slime. 'Secrets and codes. The protocols of a Dark Angels company master. I will take him, and they will be mine, and I will use them to wreak such ruin, Brother Jequn.'

'You are not my brother,' Jequn snarled.

'No?' Amis shifted his grip to the back of Jequn's neck, twisting the Ancient's head so that he had to look up at him. 'I will be. Soon, I will be your whole company. And then your whole Chapter. I will be your *brothers*, Jequn. I will be the Dark Angels.'

'No!' Jequn tried to say, tried to shout, but something was locking his jaws shut, keeping him from talking. His whole body trembled and shook as he fought the compulsion, the unspoken order to stay silent that filled him. Fought it, until he finally forced it out. 'No.' A tiny scrape of sound, a whispered denial almost lost in Sebastian's sudden, eager shout.

'There! Finally!'

Amis' mouth twisted into a bitter, mocking smile. 'Cherish that, Dark Angel. It'll be the last word you ever speak.' The gris let go of him and stood, turning his back on him.

Jequn rolled onto his side, glaring at the gris. He tried to shout his defiance, but his throat was shut so tight he could barely breathe. Amis had taken his words, but what use were they anyway? An attack was better defiance, and Jequn planned his strike as Amis and Sebastian stared at the lake below.

The foetid green water was moving, its surface twisting into a dozen whirlpools as the lake began to fall, draining away until there was nothing left but a muddy, shallow depression. In its centre, a huge hatch was opening, metal groaning and mud splattering as it slid off the parting plates. From the space between them, a form began to rise out of the mire. It gleamed in the sunlight, a monster of metal and ceramite, of destruction and death. It was one of the gigantic Knights Valiant, rising from the vault below like a monstrous insect pushing out of the mud. Hunched and massive with armour, carrying enough weaponry to level a city, the machine slowly rose until it towered over them. When the lift beneath it stopped, the Knight moved, stepping out into the mud. The ground beneath Jequn trembled, and somewhere in the jungle a flock of birds took flight, screaming.

The Knight moved to the edge of the vanished lake, the banner mounted on its back stirring and flapping. It was a simple, ugly thing, a great square of blank grey cloth, the same colour as the gris.

'Grey,' Sebastian said. The triumph in his voice had changed to tight anger, muddled with a thread of fear. 'Are you trying to claim them?'

'Only until Kap Sudsten falls,' Amis said, his ugly voice filled with amusement. 'I will keep to our agreement.' He finally stepped forward, out into the sunlight, as the Knight Valiant crouched down on its heavy metal legs before them. A hatch opened in its back and one of the monstrous gris dropped out, like some hideous birth. It landed in the mud with a squelching thud, then dragged itself to one side.

'The Knight *Rovoko* is yours.' Amis waved a malformed hand at the machine. 'With it, you may lay waste to your father's world. Then you can take the rest, and the tithe ship that brought the Adeptus Mechanicus their supplies. Your reward for giving me what I needed to confuse their machine spirits and take them over. Go forth into the galaxy and play at mercenary or pirate or whatever you wish to be. For while I once thought these machines were the greatest weapon I could ever imagine, that was long ago, and my horizons have broadened. Become as vast as my suffering.' The gris turned and looked down at Jequn. 'What are a handful of Knights when compared to my new brothers?'

Jequn couldn't speak, but he could spit, and since Amis had taken his helmet, he was free to do so. The Betcher's gland in his mouth, implanted when he was made a Space Marine long ago, turned his saliva into a wad of acid, and when it struck the gris on the chest it sizzled, dissolving a hole through the thick covering of fungus. But slime poured down over it, and with a slow hiss the acid was diluted and the hole began to close up. Amis barely seemed to notice as he crouched down again beside Jequn.

'Such weapons you are,' he said, laying his hand across the Ancient's mouth. 'I will take all of you Firstborn, all the ones I can. And I will take your serfs, your servitors, your ships and weapons and your fortress itself, and that will just be the start of my revenge. I am going to cut a trail of suffering across this galaxy that will make it bleed tears for a millennium.'

Jequn snarled, enraged, and spat again. But the acid fizzed against the flood of slime that poured out of the monster's hand and into his mouth. The Ancient choked on that slime and helpless rage, until the darkness came again and swallowed him up.

Darkness.

There were no tunnels this time. There was nothing but absolute dark, empty of everything except for Jequn, and the box he held in his hands.

'What is that?'

The thick, guttural words came from the dark, came from everywhere, but Jequn ignored them and held the box tight to his chest.

'You only want to speak when I forbid it,' Amis hissed in his ear, a hideous, choking whisper. 'But I don't need your voice here.' Hands touched the sides of Jequn's head, and pain ripped through him. It was as if that cold, slimy grip had driven a hundred thousand needles through his skin, through his skull, deep into his brain. Each needle teased him apart, ripping his mind open. Memories spun through him, his life before he had been made a Dark Angel, his training, his battles, centuries of life being pulled apart. And there was nothing he could do to stop it.

Jequn was trapped in the black, and Heris Amis dissected him, piece by piece, his mouldy hands peeling away Jequn's life, his mind, until he was nothing but rage and defiance and the box clutched in his hands.

'There is something…' Amis said. He let him go and walked around in front of him, and despite the darkness Jequn could see him, standing before him, staring at the black box the Ancient clasped to his chest.

'Some last secret that you clutch. Something that makes you fight.'

Jequn gripped the box tight. It felt like adamantine beneath his gauntlets, an armoured lockbox, and he could trace the symbol etched in its side. A winged sword, the sigil of his Chapter, and he understood. He was part of the Inner Circle, and he bore a secret that went beyond him. It belonged to his Chapter, his brothers, and he had sworn the deepest oaths to protect it.

You will never have it. Jequn kept the words in his head, sealed inside like this last secret, but Amis stripped them out of him, knew them as if the Ancient had scribed them in his blood across the black.

'I will, brother.' When Amis spoke, slime dripped from his lips, stinking of decay and despair, and the needles in Jequn's head drove deeper. 'You will break, Adeptus Astartes, and you will give me everything. Your secrets, and yourself. But for now...' Amis stepped forward, his terrible grey face growing to fill Jequn's vision, blocking out the black, blocking out everything. 'For now, you will suffer, and–'

The face in front of Jequn froze, then jerked back. 'No,' Heris Amis muttered, his dark grey eyes staring off into the black. 'No!'

With that protest, the pain in Jequn's head lessened, as if the needles had suddenly pulled away. The Dark Angel watched as the gris moved back, Amis' grey face twisting with anger and frustration.

'Gretin Lan, you white-faced wretch!' he spat. 'Slave of false, impotent gods! You've won nothing with this, only stretched out your pain!'

Jequn had no idea what Amis meant, but he understood something had gone wrong. He couldn't talk – he wouldn't – but laughter... That bubbled out of him, low and cracked and awful. Something had gone wrong for the gris. And Jequn could guess what. Lazarus, and the Fifth.

Heris Amis spared him a glance, and the needles came back, driving in, driving deep, and Jequn welcomed them, embraced the pain, and hoped that in his anger Amis would kill him, and he could drag this last secret into the darkness of death.

But that blessing was denied him.

Jequn jerked back to life, head aching, sprawled in the mud at the edge of what had once been a lake. The chain that had bound him lay beside him, a pile of muddy, rusted links. The second he saw it he was moving, rising up to attack – except his body refused to listen. He jerked once, little more than a shiver, but stayed still. Heris Amis had robbed him of his body and his voice, and he could feel the needles in his head still, digging away at him, trying to reach that last secret he held so tight. He shut his eyes and spoke the Litany of Endurance. Heris Amis hadn't taken him yet. And his control had slipped once. It may slip again, and farther. Jequn would hold on until then.

He was a Dark Angel.

He would hold on.

'–knew it! This scheme was too complicated, too dangerous!' It was Sebastian's voice, and Jequn opened his eyes. He managed to turn his head, barely, and saw the Regent Next standing in the mud below the Knight Valiant *Rovoko*. Heris Amis stood close, the grey folds of his mouldy body steaming in the sun. 'We should have raised the Knights, smashed my father then gone, and never involved the Dark Angels!'

'Do you doubt me?' Amis asked, his clotted voice low and threatening, but Sebastian didn't quail.

'Of course I doubt you,' the Regent Next snapped. 'I'm not a fool. You're a pile of mould, resurrected by a daemon! You need me to gain your vengeance, and if I didn't need you to take the Knights, I would have burned you alive!'

'It's good we understand each other.' Heris Amis moved, his long arm whipping out to grab Sebastian by the front of his mud-spattered suit and hoisting him into the air, holding the Regent Next in front of him. The gris ignored the gun that appeared in Sebastian's hand and stared up at him through slime-slicked eyes. 'We need each other, Regent Next. This next part of my plan hinges on those Knights, and so you are necessary to me. But do not think that means I cannot hurt you. Even now, your lover leads a strike against the Reis Home Levies, a feint to draw the Dark Angels out further. I do not need Petra Karn for that. In an instant, I could tell my gris to tear her apart. Or infect her. Whichever I felt like. Whichever I thought would make you suffer more.'

'If you…' Sebastian's words trailed off, and he lowered the gun, frustrated. Heris Amis set him down, and Jequn growled silently with frustration of his own. He wanted to see the gris tear the traitorous mortal's head off.

'What are you going to do?' Sebastian said, frowning at the slime that covered the front of his filthy suit. 'Lazarus has escaped the trap you set him and the Adeptus Mechanicus. What are you going to do?'

'Nothing has changed,' Amis answered. 'I will continue to divide them. Weaken them. Take them. Lazarus is free, but he has left a large portion of his strength in the north. I will speak to him, taunt him, and ensure what few forces he has left are further divided.' The gris turned its body towards Jequn, and the Ancient could see Amis' face, surrounded like some hideous flower by the grey, fleshy flaps of mould that coated him. 'And I know precisely how to do it.'

Amis turned back to Sebastian. 'Prepare the Knights. We will march out soon, with the same plan. I will take the Levies' base, you the city. But you will be taking a passenger with you, and I will take a banner, and we will see to which Lazarus runs. Whichever it is, the Master of the Fifth will be taken alive. Do you understand?'

'I understand,' Sebastian said coldly. 'The same way you understand that my father belongs to me.'

'Agreed.' The word was spoken in a tone that was probably meant to be soothing, but Heris Amis' terrible voice made every statement awful. 'We shall both have revenge, Regent Next. You in full, while mine is just beginning.'

You will have nothing. Nothing but another, final death, when the Dark Angels purge you from this world. But those defiant words only echoed in Jequn's head, a silent vow drowned out by the needles that still dug into him, tearing and pulling and reaching. Inside himself, Jequn wrapped his soul around the last secret left to him and spoke the Litany of Defiance over and over again, waiting for some chance, any chance, to strike.

CHAPTER TWENTY-THREE

'What is it doing?' Lazarus snapped, staring at the images in his helm. He had thrown his Spiritshield back on when Gretin Lan warned them about the approaching craft. The Fabricator Locum had allowed his armour to plug in to the flyer's auspex data, and he could see *Adamantine Wings* cutting through the clouds in their wake, an armoured fist punching through the air behind the *Kestrel*'s white dart shape.

'No weapons systems tracking perceived.' Gretin Lan had not altered the flyer's course or increased its speed, not yet, waiting to see what the stolen ship would do. 'Thunderhawk has fallen into pursuit orientation and… Hold. Contact established through tightbeam signal. Demand made for dialogue with the Master of the Fifth.'

'Insistent,' Lazarus said. He looked at Ephron. 'Are the gris using this tightbeam to keep you from jumping on their transmission again?'

'That would be my calculation,' Ephron answered. 'The gris

do not want us communicating. But it appears they want to talk to you. Very badly.'

'Auspex now identifies tracking. Thunderhawk weapon systems are targeting *Kestrel*.' The Fabricator Locum's voice was calm, almost cold. 'Continued demand for dialogue, threat of attack if dialogue refused.'

Lazarus stared at the image of his stolen ship, the cold anger in his belly threatening to turn hot. If Heris Amis wanted to talk this badly, then Lazarus wanted to refuse. But he didn't have time to play predator and prey with his own stolen ship. And he definitely didn't have time to die. *Kestrel* was more agile, but one hit from the Thunderhawk's main cannon would shred the flyer.

'Pass me command of that channel.'

In the cybernetic nest of her cockpit, Gretin Lan nodded. A rune appeared in Lazarus' helm, and he willed it to activate, opening himself to the transmission from *Adamantine Wings*.

Hissing filled his helm, and then a voice. A rich baritone, almost jovial, but it was strangely thick, guttural. *'Lazarus. Master of the Fifth. Finally.'*

There was a long stretch of silence, the voice waiting for some response which Lazarus didn't give.

'I should have expected silence,' the voice finally said. *'That's the only thing your brothers gave me a thousand years ago, when I begged them to listen, to believe. Silence, broken finally by the crack of a bolter.'*

Lazarus let his silence spiral out again. The main thing he wanted from this exchange was time, time for *Kestrel* to cut through the miles. But the anger of his enemy was another, lesser goal. He drew it out, until he heard a noise like a thick, liquid snarl, and then he spoke, his words even, measured, almost bored except for a thin chill of disdain.

'You are a traitor, Heris Amis. Once that is understood, nothing matters but your extinction.'

There was an angry sound, a precursor to some outburst, but it cut off, and the voice slipped back to its previous joviality, though that seemed thinner now, a mask sitting light over bitter anger. *'Oh, but those Dark Angels didn't understand. They didn't want to, and I couldn't make them listen. But you, undying Master of the Fifth, I can make you listen. And with your history, you might even understand.*

'I was no traitor, Lazarus. My soul was untainted when your brothers executed me for the sin of my people, of the Adeptus Mechanicus.' He laughed, an ugly sound that was thick and liquid as mud. *'You are a clever man. You found my name. But you know nothing of my history, of why I was* sacrificed. *I could tell you, but you seem to abhor the sound of my voice. So I leave it to you to ask the Adeptus Mechanicus about it. Maybe they'll tell you. Maybe a thousand years is enough to loosen even their backstabbing tongues. But this isn't what I came to talk to you about, Lazarus, my brother in death.'*

That made him want to snarl, but Lazarus kept his anger cold, kept it gripped tight, controlled. He was provoking Amis. Not being provoked. 'You spill words like my sword spills blood.'

The laugh this time was harder, forced, and when Amis spoke, his anger cut through his false cheer. *'I speak because you must listen. As I said, you know nothing of my history. You're piecing it together, it seems, with your little Learned friend. Enjoy that puzzle. When I finally take you, it will amuse me to see how many pieces you set correctly. But there is a piece of my life, a key piece that you will never find unless I share it with you, and I so want to share it. Because while I have never believed in anything – in the Throne or the Machine God, in mercy or in justice or in forgiveness – I do admire some things, and one of them is symmetry. What I want to tell you about is my death, Master Lazarus.*

I want to tell you because, like me, you've seen the darkness that lies beyond, the void that swallows all, and have come back from it. We are dead men, my brother, who have both been born into new bodies, new lives, and now we face each other, a Grey Angel and a Dark Angel, deciding between us the fate of this ugly little world and so much more.'

'You are not my brother,' Lazarus said. His voice was still precise, flat, heavy with disdain, his rage still leashed, but barely. 'That word belongs to men of honour, something you would know nothing of.'

'That word belongs to men who are my slaves, brother,' Amis hissed. *'How do you think I know of your rebirth? Your fall into fire, and your resurrection in a body even greater than the one you had before? I ripped those memories from their minds with the touch of my new body. This hideous fungal form lets me live on, and on, and on, forever, the form of a monster given to me so that I can sow suffering and reap pain and retribution.'*

That almost snapped Lazarus, almost broke the tightly held leash he'd put on his anger. For a moment, he saw the flames and felt their touch, but he let the heat and pain wash over him, used that and a litany to help focus himself for once instead of pulling him apart. Letting that remembered pain fill him, he made his rage into a razor's edge, a thing to cut with. 'I died a Dark Angel. I was reborn a Dark Angel. A son of the Lion. A slayer of monsters.'

'You had work undone, and were returned. A spectre, kept alive by hatred and duty. Same as me. As I said, Lazarus. Symmetry.'

In Lazarus' helm, an image formed, passed through the tight-beam. A face to go with the voice, almost human but terribly not. A face gone grey, skin and eyes and everything, marked on its edges with the corroded chunks of cybernetics, dripping with viscous grey fluid.

'I am a monster now. This is the body that I must suffer.' Heris Amis smiled, and fluid dripped from between his grey teeth. *'I suffer, and suffer, and suffer. The wound that killed me never stops hurting. The pain of that betrayal is unending. I am nothing but suffering, and suffering is what I give. That was my bargain. That is what I want you to know, to understand, my brother Lazarus. This is the symmetry. I died, and some spirit from the immaterium, some daemon prince or godling thing, reached through the tiny flaw that you Dark Angels left in the patch of the Redwash Gate. It reached through and found me drifting towards my death, and it remade me. Filled my body with grey pall, my own creation strengthened by the touch of that hideous thing, and it brought me back to life. Because it wanted to feed. On my pain, my hatred, my misery, my suffering. And on all the suffering I would inflict on others. Just the same as you.'*

'You are a sadistic monster, slaved to a sadistic master,' Lazarus said contemptuously. 'There is nothing the same between us.'

'Nothing,' Amis agreed. *'Except that you were dragged back to life, without being given the choice to walk out into the void, so that you could inflict pain, and suffering, and death, for a master that feeds on the same terrible sustenance. And you learned to live with it, didn't you? To justify the monster you had become, the horror that you inflict. Symmetry, Lazarus. Symmetry, brother. We are more the same than we are different. You will understand that when I come for you bearing your banner. When I take you, when I break you. When I make you suffer, brother, as I have. When I make you all suffer.'*

'What… what did they say? My lord.'

Ysentrud's voice was so soft it was almost lost amid the purr of *Kestrel*'s engines. Lazarus' sharp ears picked it up though. But he didn't look up from his helm.

He had taken it off when Heris had broken contact and *Adamantine Wings* had banked away, vanishing into the clouds. Now he held it in his hands and stared at it as his mind turned over the traitor's words.

I ripped those memories from their minds…

They spun through his head, over and over, and the winged helm in his hands became the plainer one worn by the Dark Angels of Squad Invis. The headgear of Squad Jotha. The crested helm of Ancient Jequn.

Jequn. Ancient Jequn. Who had once been a member of the First Company, the Deathwing. Who was a member of the Dark Angels Inner Circle. Who was privy to a portion of the hidden history of the Dark Angels, and the Fallen.

If Jequn was taken, if Heris Amis had him, what did the gris now know?

It was an ugly question, as were almost all its answers.

'How long until Kap Sudsten?' he asked, as if he didn't know the answer.

'Seventy-three minutes,' answered the Fabricator Locum.

Exactly what he had thought. Too long. Too long.

When I make you suffer, brother, as I have.

He finally looked up at Ysentrud. The mortal was leaning against the side of the cabin, swathed in blankets, a copper-red skull staring at him with wide eyes. 'What are the earliest stories of the gris?'

She blinked those strange eyes at him, red lids sliding over the brighter copper of her irises. 'The earliest?'

'The ones that have not grown with the retelling.' Lazarus thought of his work as Keeper of the Unseen Ritual. Of the way stories changed, and meaning was hidden and lost. 'Tell me about the first stories of the gris.'

Ysentrud nodded. 'There's little to them. Just legends of

something the rural people called the *grizen spist*. It's a name from the old tongue, the language that Low Gothic replaced when Reis rejoined the Imperium. The grizen spist was a suffering spirit, a grey figure that wandered the jungle alone, hideous and horrible, constantly weeping in pain. The name became gris when the rural folk came to the Home Levies, begging for help because that spirit had stopped wandering alone and had started attacking people.' She frowned, the expression twisting her skull tattoo. 'It's around that time, when the attacks start, when the name changes, that the more traditional gris stories begin.'

The grizen spist. The gris. The suffering spirit.

By the Throne, he would make Heris Amis suffer.

'Fabricator Locum.' Lazarus looked to the white figure wrapped in cybernetics. 'Why was Heris Amis executed?'

He couldn't see the mask of her face, not that it mattered. But he caught the tiny shift in her shoulders, the tell of movement of the bundles of red muscle beneath the white filigree that would have let him know she was slipping into defence if they were sparring.

'For betraying House Halven and the Adeptus Mechanicus,' she said. 'For serving the daemons of Chaos.'

'Secrets and secrets and secrets,' Lazarus growled. Everyone wrapped in secrets, and now he was tangled in the greatest known to the Dark Angels, forced to factor it into his strategy. 'We clutch them close as armour as the galaxy burns, when most of the time they are just promethium for the flames.' Demetrius looked at him, but Lazarus ignored his Interrogator-Chaplain. 'Gretin Lan. Why was Heris Amis executed?'

She was still, but the white birds perched in the cockpit ruffled their feathers and flexed crimson muscles and silver talons, two of them turning their heads to stare at him with their wine-coloured eyes. When she spoke, her tone wasn't grudging, as he expected, but tired.

'My superiors may bind me on this foetid rock for another century for unauthorised revelation. But one thousand years seems sufficient time, and this situation is dire. Heris Amis was executed because he obeyed orders. Orders that did not originate with the Ruinous Powers but with the Adeptus Mechanicus.'

'So House Halven was right?' Ysentrud said. 'You attacked them.'

'No,' the Fabricator Locum said. 'The malfunction with the Knights resulted from a desperate experiment. Heris Amis was an enginseer who performed the maintenance rituals of House Halven's Knights, but those were not his only duties. Possessing an aptitude for the biologis, and having at one point undergone training as a genetor, a scholar of the disorganised science of life, he undertook study of the life forms of Reis. This research soon focused on one lesser entity, the mould known as grey pall.

'The neurotoxin particular to that strain of mould became Heris' primary focus. The enginseer believed that with certain refinements it could be processed into a pharma capable of amplifying integration between biological and cybernetic systems. Heris Amis had convinced his Fabricator Locum of this immediately in advance of the Redwash War.'

Gretin Lan sighed. 'I have studied the records. The sequence of errors that led up to Heris Amis' execution are obvious in retrospect, and I cannot censure my predecessors for the ultimate unintended consequences. Except their abrogation of their responsibility, and the consequential betrayal of Heris Amis. When the Redwash Gate opened and the hostile warp denizens' designated daemons began their incursion, when the

Knights of Sudsten were destroyed, House Halven prepared its northern forces. But at the time the Adeptus Mechanicus of Forge Norsten knew what the outcome would be. The northern Knights of House Halven would be destroyed also, and this planet would fall. The situation was deemed dire. So the Fabricator Locum proposed a desperate solution. Experiments with servitors using the gene-altered strains of grey pall had resulted in significant enhancement of performance. It was surmised that if these same strains were introduced into the remaining Knights of House Halven, equivalent results would occur between Knight and pilot, resulting in greatly enhanced execution, which might allow the Knights to achieve a victory in the conflict. Or at least reduce the daemons enough so that Adeptus Mechanicus forces could turn them away from the forge.

'According to transcripts, Heris Amis retained doubt, but ultimately agreed to the attempt. But...' Wrapped in her cybernetics, Gretin Lan shrugged. 'The results were regrettable. The strain of grey pall he created in haste for the Knights functioned initially, but then proved toxic, and the pilots' lives were ceased.'

They were ceased, and the people of Reis were completely unprotected. Until the Dark Angels arrived. The rest was too easy to guess. 'Did the Adeptus Mechanicus make up the story about Heris being a servant of the Ruinous Powers?' Lazarus asked.

'No,' Gretin Lan said. 'The situation did not devolve that completely. The Dark Angels accused the enginseer of treachery, and the Fabricator Locum simply retained their silence. They did not deny the accusation, and Heris Amis was executed. Records indicate the Fabricator Locum thought that such a course would simplify the situation and ease tensions with House Halven.'

'It simplified it for them,' Ysentrud muttered, disgusted, and Lazarus raised a hand, silencing the Learned.

'And that was it?'

'Substantially,' answered Gretin Lan. 'The Adeptus Mechanicus laid claim to the enginseer's body, after. Preliminary examination indicated the presence of at least one strain of grey pall in his system, infecting his nervous system and brain. This was considered the result of an accidental exposure during its creation. Further examination was prevented after the corpse disappeared for unknown reasons. I had theorised that the Fabricator Locum cremated it, to prevent detailed enquiries. I now conjecture that Heris Amis may have walked away.'

'That is likely,' Lazarus said. He stared down at his helm again. Heris Amis had reason for his anger, but it didn't matter. There was never reason enough to give in to the Ruinous Powers, to become a monster that feeds on mankind.

'Answer has not been given to the original enquiry proposed by your mutant,' the Fabricator Locum said. 'Concerning what the gris said.'

'Do you think that the Master of the Fifth owes you anything, Fabricator Locum?' Demetrius' voice was low, but the rumbling threat buried in it was clear.

Lazarus caught his eye and barely nodded, but his brother settled back, silent. 'I will answer for Ysentrud. And for my brothers. And for you, Fabricator Locum, for being honest with me. Eventually. The gris is Heris Amis. Heris Amis is the gris. It seems that some power from the immaterium was able to reach out through the flaw in the patch over the Redwash Gate to touch him when he was dying. That power twisted its foul sorcery in with Heris Amis' science, and the strain of grey pall he had created became something foul. Something that brought him back to life and let him infect... almost anything, it seems. He can control people, servitors, the cogitators of the Adeptus Mechanicus forge – and mayhaps Space Marines. He can at least kill us and take our memories. Heris Amis has become a monster not just in his body but in many bodies. He is an infection, spreading across this planet, a disease that will swallow every thinking thing that walks upon it. And when he has done that, I believe he means to spread.'

'Space Marines?' Ysentrud breathed in horror. 'Even you?'

'We must accept the possibility,' Lazarus said. 'Which means he may have taken some or all of the squads I sent to root out the nest beneath the volcano.'

'He may have Jequn?' Demetrius said, and Lazarus nodded. Demetrius' hands curled into fists, ceramite creaking. Lazarus knew he was thinking not just of a lost brother but also of the secrets held by the Ancient. Secrets that if lost would bring Azrael and all the Dark Angels to this world, to scour it in flame.

'I do not believe it.' Apothecary Asbeel shook his helmeted head. 'Whatever this traitor may claim, Master Lazarus, I cannot believe that this gris can affect us. We are not mortals. Our bodies are proof against the deadliest infection.'

'Our bodies may be proof against it,' Ephron said grimly, 'but this creation of the Adeptus Mechanicus, this mutation, was enginseered to facilitate the joining of flesh and machine. The gris may not be able to infect our bodies the way it does mortals', but it may be able to attack us another way. Through our black carapace, the sacred organ that links us to our armour.'

'Sacrilege,' Asbeel hissed, and Lazarus nodded.

'Everything about this, since Heris died, since his grey pall was touched by the Ruinous Powers, is that. Sacrilege. Suffering. Revenge.'

'Revenge.' All three of Gretin Lan's white birds were staring at him now. 'Capacious revenge, you believe. Master Lazarus, you consider that Heris Amis means to spread, which implies that you don't think this revenge will terminate with you. With my forge. With Reis.'

'No,' Lazarus said. 'Heris Amis has had a thousand years to plot his vengeance. I think he dreams of a greater retribution than that. What it is, I cannot say, but I will see it ended. Lazarus stared at the helm in his hands, and for a moment the green and gold of it seemed to burn, but when the flames receded the metal wasn't scorched – it was scabbed with mould, bleeding a filthy grey liquid, thick as blood. His hands tightened on the helm, and he willed the vision away, but in his head he could hear Heris Amis' voice.

A Grey Angel.

What was happening to the men he had left behind? To Jequn, his Ancient, keeper of the same terrible secret that had sent them here, however obliquely? A secret whose shadow warped this mission, even though the Fallen had nothing to do with it.

Dark Angel. Grey Angel.

'I will see this ended now,' he snarled, and his voice filled the small ship. 'I will see my brothers returned, the gris destroyed, and Heris Amis truly, finally, dead.'

CHAPTER TWENTY-FOUR

The Fabricator Locum's flyer bounced and twisted in the air, and Ysentrud sat on the floor of its gutted cabin, clutching a strut with her one remaining hand as the world swung. The armoured giants that crowded around her seemed to spin and dance as up and down became nominal things, suggestions that hadn't been decided on quite yet, and she closed her eyes, hoping darkness would help settle things down.

In fact, it just made it worse.

'Are you all right, Learned?'

Opening her eyes, all she could see was a skull hanging before her, a grinning horror like the one that had attacked her in the conduit, and she flinched back. But this skull was much larger, and its eyes glowed red and green, not blue. Interrogator-Chaplain Demetrius had leaned in so close she could see the reflection of her own red skull face in the polished metal of his mask. She looked like a dead thing, risen to haunt the living with her pain, which felt like an accurate description of her current state, but she just nodded. 'I'm fine, my lord.' Such an enormous lie, but it was all she could say, and the world was slowly coming to a stop around her, up and down finally deciding on their places once more.

'Kap Sudsten is imminent,' Gretin Lan said from her cybernetic nest in the cockpit. 'Rising smoke indicates significant combustion occurrence.'

'Circle,' Lazarus ordered. 'I want to see what is happening.'

The Fabricator Locum nodded, and Ysentrud felt the flyer beginning to bank. A small hatch opened in the cabin's ceiling and a delicate array of gleaming struts unfolded from within. They looked like the thin antennae of insects, each tipped with a cloudy, faceted eye. When they had spread themselves out, the eyes became clear and began to glow, and below them a cloud of light swirled into life. It was a holo-projector, Ysentrud realised as the image of the land below took shape, but its projections were much clearer than any she had ever seen. The apocalyptic image it drew was horrifyingly detailed.

Kap Sudsten was burning.

The city Ysentrud had been born and raised in was a patchwork of fire and smoke and riot. The industrial district was a sea of flame, factoria and warehouses blazing, pouring great towers of black into the sky. The fires were spreading to other districts, slowly swallowing up hab-block after mould-stained hab-block. Where the fire wasn't, the streets were swarmed with people, fleeing the flames and fighting each other.

'All that from one broadcast?' Ysentrud said, staring at the holo in horror. She could see the hall of the Wyrbuk, still far from the flames, but the streets around it were packed, teeming with churning crowds.

'No,' Lazarus said. His eyes, cybernetic and augmented, could pick out details hers could not. 'There are gris in those crowds.

Fighting and taking. They must have had tunnels under the city. Heris has been planning this day for centuries.'

Ysentrud looked away from the surrounded hall, her home for so long. She didn't want to see if its doors were breached, didn't want to know if Learned Thiemo or Heze were fighting for their lives in that mob. Staring at the floor, she whispered a prayer of salvation to the Throne.

'Lieutenant Zakariah is in the Reis Home Levies' base,' Lazarus said. 'I can see the plasma bursts. We will–'

'Two signatures have appeared on auspex,' Gretin Lan said, her voice fast and sharp. 'Thunderhawks, on swift approach.'

Ysentrud looked back in time to get dizzy again as the holo-field suddenly spun and became a window into the sky. Two black spots were tearing through the air, growing as they came, resolving into the blocky shapes of the Dark Angels' transports.

'The one in the lead is *Talon*, Brother Cadus' ship,' Ephron said. 'The one behind, trying to bring *Talon* down, is *Adamantine Wings*.'

Flashes of laser light and sharp bursts of flame were coming from *Adamantine Wings* as the stolen transport fired at *Talon*. *Talon* was twisting and rolling through the air, trying to dodge every shot, but black marks crossed its armour plates and one of its engines was stuttering, smoking. The dodging wasn't always working, and as the ships drew close, a bright lance of energy caught *Talon* across one wing, melting a furrow in its armour. The Thunderhawk wobbled and recovered, but it wasn't dodging any more. It was jerking and rattling from side to side, obviously fighting not to go into a spin, all the while slowly but perceptibly losing altitude. *Adamantine Wings* was lining up behind it, weapons swivelling, when Lazarus spoke.

'Fabricator Locum!'

'Already calculating,' she said calmly. 'Brace for manoeuvre.'

'Emperor's–' And that was as far as Ysentrud got before she felt herself smashed back against the cabin wall. The flyer began a steep climb, and Ysentrud started to tumble helplessly back, but a gauntleted hand caught her, pulling her in and cradling her with surprising gentleness against an armoured breastplate.

'You were calling for His protection, were you not?' Demetrius rumbled, but Ysentrud held her tongue, not wanting to lie and not wanting to throw up. Everything was moving, spinning, except the holo in front of them, which adjusted smoothly to the flyer's carving path through the sky. The Fabricator Locum's ship darted through the air and was now sitting just over *Adamantine Wings*, matching the transport's speed exactly as it hovered over the much larger ship.

A hatch popped open in the floor of the cabin, near where Gretin Lan sat. Wind and light and thunderous sound poured through the small opening, and into this storm two of the tiny bird skulls dropped and disappeared. The hatch shut behind them, and then the flyer was peeling away, twisting and diving as the two skulls drove themselves into the space where *Adamantine Wings*' main cannon joined its hull. They exploded, two small flashes of fire, and Gretin Lan was diving her ship away from the Thunderhawk as fast as she could. Still, the flyer bucked and shook as the shockwave of another explosion hit. The skulls must have struck the cannon's ammunition and set it off in a chain reaction that tore through the guts of the transport.

Ephron prayed for the lost Thunderhawk as it ripped itself apart, great armoured pieces of it tumbling from the sky in flames to smash into a group of hab-blocks far below, sowing more fire and death into the dying city.

'Throne protect…' Ysentrud whispered, and passed out.

* * *

'–be fine.'

Ysentrud recognised Apothecary Asbeel's deep voice, and she struggled to sit up. 'I am fine,' she agreed, maybe, if it was her they were talking about. Her thoughts were a bit muddled, but she was feeling better, the throbbing aches in her body almost gone except for the nagging feeling that her missing right arm was still there and wrapped in a blanket of hot thorns. But not burning hot, and the thorns were small. 'You gave me more stimm.' Her voice was thin and scratchy, but by the Throne, she felt so much better.

Demetrius, who was looming over her like a skull-faced mountain, grunted, and Asbeel shrugged. His servo-arms were folding themselves back behind him. 'You said you needed her awake.'

'And she is, brother,' the Interrogator-Chaplain said. 'Thank you.'

Asbeel moved away, and Ysentrud pulled herself to her feet. The world swung around her, her vertigo unaffected by the drug, but she didn't give a damn about that. She just watched the world dance as she tried to sort out where she was.

They were on the landing field that sprawled between Kap Sudsten and the Reis Home Levies' base. It was a wide expanse of cracked rockcrete, covered in potholes and fuzzy with fungus and weeds. Two Thunderhawks were in sight, one a few hundred yards away, tipped on its side and half buried in the huge hole that had opened beneath it, the other much closer. That one she recognised as *Talon*, resting on its belly on the rockcrete, its landing struts broken beneath it. It smoked from half a dozen wounds in its armoured hide. No one would be escaping anything in those.

Ysentrud looked away from the wrecked ships and towards Kap Sudsten. The city was a pile of buildings squatting beneath a vast tower of black smoke, and sound was coming from it. The voices of thousands, hundreds of thousands, shouting and screaming.

'What's going on, my lord?' she asked, her eyes fixed on the terrible sight of that dying city.

'The Fabricator Locum dropped us and took off,' Demetrius said. 'She is circling, in case the other captured Thunderhawk comes. And to stay off the ground. The gris have tunnels under this whole place. They came up in the city and your Levies' base, and they undermined *Vengeance is Prayer* before Tech-marine Meshach even knew they were there. Gretin Lan would not risk her *Kestrel*, and it is good to have even a little air cover.'

From the direction of the Levies' base there came a sound like thunder, a low, rolling boom that covered the terrible noise from Kap Sudsten. 'And that?' she asked.

'Lieutenant Zakariah is finishing clearance of the Reis Levies' headquarters with Squads Revir and Nabis,' Demetrius answered. 'The gris are in full rout, fleeing back into their tunnels.'

'Did they get Petra Karn?' Ysentrud asked.

'No.' The voice came from the side, high and weak compared to the Space Marine's, and Ysentrud barely recognised it. Barely recognised the man when she saw him. His bright-coloured suit was stained and ragged, and dust and ash marked his face and hair. High Lord Oskaran Halven looked like a lost, dirty child next to the Dark Angels. His eyes, though, were shining with hate. 'Lash Officer Karn ran like most of the vermin, back into the tunnels they had dug, with the weapons they stole. They went back to the city, I know, *I know*.' He looked past her, across the cracked and muddy wasteland of the landing field towards the smoking city that stretched out behind them. 'Hunting for me and anyone loyal to me.'

'I hope she burns,' Ysentrud said, thinking of that day not

so long ago when Petra had smiled as Sebastian boasted that they would be making their own history.

'We will burn them,' Demetrius said, his words growling with menace and promise. 'Heris Amis, all of his gris, and all that would ally with that evil. We will burn them today and you will help us.'

Ysentrud looked away from Kap Sudsten to the Interrogator-Chaplain. She could see the apocalyptic city in his bright mask, the polished skull of his helmet warping the reflection of the distant dark and bright spectres of smoke and fire. Deep in her, there was fear and pain and the sure certainty that if she went into that hell, she wouldn't leave it alive. But the stimm was bright and strong, helping her hold up her spirits – if not as high as a Space Marine, at least somewhere near their hearts.

'Good,' Ysentrud breathed.

Wrapped in stimm and whatever else Asbeel had given her, Ysentrud was awake, her mind almost achingly clear. Which made it almost impossible for her to look at Lazarus, even though she sat away from him, half hidden in a pile of supplies stripped from the downed Thunderhawks.

The Master of the Fifth was moving, stalking back and forth across the scorched and spore-stained rockcrete of the landing field like a beast on the edge of violence. His grey eyes were sharp with anger that was sternly leashed but still terrifyingly clear. His command squad was arrayed around him: Demetrius, Asbeel and Librarian Raziel, along with the Techmarines Cadus, Meshach and Ephron. There was also a new Dark Angel, Lieutenant Zakariah, the hood of his robes pulled up over a face marked by soot and blood. His forces had just finished cleansing the gris from the Levies' base, as evidenced by the lack of terrifying noises coming from that direction.

All those grim-faced men stood silent, watching their leader pace, his hand on his sword, until he finally spoke. 'Report, Cadus.' The voice of the Dark Angels master was as hard as his expression.

'Brother,' the Techmarine answered. 'Not long after the enemy's transmission, when we had our window to communicate, the sensors we had planted to map the gris tunnels detected new activity. The gris were burrowing under *Talon*. So I lifted off, before the ship could be undermined. Not long after taking to the air, I saw them.'

The Techmarine had his helmet off, and he was staring in the same direction as Lazarus. 'A dozen Knights of various patterns, but all deadly. The two largest, Knights Valiant, bore banners of grey, and more. One held the battle banner of the Fifth, *our* banner, marked with slime. And on the other...' The Techmarine's eyes went to Lazarus, then away. 'On the other, chained to its leg, was our Ancient. Brother Jequn.'

'Alive?' Lazarus asked, his voice low.

'Yes,' Cadus said. 'The slime covered his armour. His face. I saw him coughing, and spitting it from his mouth.' The Techmarine paused, his face twisting. 'I saw gris moving around the Knights. Some of our brothers were with them, men from Squad Invis. None from Squad Jotha, the Scouts.'

'By the blood of the Lion, it cannot be,' Asbeel said, but the Apothecary fell silent when Lazarus slashed the air with one hand.

'What was the Knights' path?' the Master of the Fifth asked, and Ysentrud shivered and tried to curl deeper into the mound of supplies, as if the crates could shield her from the anger in his voice.

'The force was splitting as I saw them,' Cadus said. 'The Knight Valiant with our banner was leading half the Knights towards this base. The Knight Valiant with Jequn leads the others towards Kap Sudsten.'

'Heris Amis seeks to divide us. Again,' Demetrius said. There was just as much anger in his deep voice.

Lazarus stopped moving, staring at nothing, his fingers tapping on the hilt of his sword. When Ysentrud risked looking at him, there was something besides anger in his eyes. There was calculation there too, cold and precise. 'And we will let him.' The Master of the Fifth met his Interrogator-Chaplain's silent stare. 'You will go to Kap Sudsten with Squad Nabis and Techmarine Meshach. You will find Jequn and the rest of our brothers, and you will free them. By whatever means necessary.'

'And free ourselves,' Demetrius said. 'If we should become infected like them.'

Ysentrud raised her head to watch as Lazarus stared into the gleaming skull mask of his brother and nodded. 'Better the grave than betrayal.'

'The words of the Lion,' the Interrogator-Chaplain intoned, and the gathered Dark Angels answered him, repeating his words in a deep chant. 'The words of the Lion.'

'And what will you do, Master Lazarus?' Demetrius asked when it was silent again.

Lazarus turned and stared out at the jungle. 'Heris Amis told me that he would come for me, bearing my banner. I believe him. So I will meet him on this field, and I will finish this.'

It was insanity. Ysentrud knew nothing of fighting, but she knew of the Knights, knew from the histories what they could do, and there were twelve of the great machines against twice that number of Space Marines. Two dozen Dark Angels, no matter how powerful, could not best that many Knights.

But staring at the Master of the Fifth, at the pure certainty of his anger, she believed him.

CHAPTER TWENTY-FIVE

'The skull-faced one,' the Regent Prime said. 'He's going to Kap Sudsten?'

The Dark Angels had been tearing into the supplies they had taken from the Thunderhawks, stripping out arcane pieces of equipment and distributing it among themselves. The pile where Ysentrud had been sitting – hiding, really – had been steadily dwindling, and it was easy for the Regent Prime to find her. 'Interrogator-Chaplain Demetrius,' she said, in her best teaching voice. A very short time ago, before the Space Marines arrived, she would have been terrified to talk to the Regent Prime that way. Now, he was all too human, too frail and unimposing, especially in his dirty suit with his cosmetics half dissolved by sweat and his eyes so haunted. But her training was still strong, and he'd asked her a question. 'Yes. He is leading Squad Nabis there soon.'

'I have to go with them.' Oskaran stared at her, and she stared back, unsure, until she realised that he expected her to intercede for him.

'If you think there is something that the Interrogator-Chaplain has to do,' she said, 'you are free to talk to him about it.'

The Regent Prime frowned at her, and she finally shrugged and slid down from her perch. Lazarus didn't need her for this final battle. She might as well see where this was going. 'Lord Demetrius,' she said, limping over to the Interrogator-Chaplain with Oskaran trailing behind. 'The Regent Prime requests a word.'

Demetrius turned his mismatched eyes to her, then looked past her shoulder at Oskaran. 'The Regent Prime should speak for himself.'

Oskaran rolled his shoulders, uneasy, but he spoke. 'You go to Kap Sudsten. I wish to go with you. I have heard that is where my son is heading. I wish to speak with him.'

The Regent Prime's face, tight with anger, frustration, grief, was reflected in the Interrogator-Chaplain's shining skull mask as he considered the request. Then it vanished as Demetrius turned away. 'Your desire for confrontation is not sufficient reason for me to slow my mission by taking you.'

Oskaran's face went dark, and Ysentrud watched him, wondering if he would be fool enough to say anything, but then another voice interrupted.

'He may be useful, brother.' Lazarus strode over, and Ysentrud drew herself up straight. The Master of the Fifth had been in constant motion, snapping orders at Dark Angels and the Reis Home Levies soldiers. Directing them as they swarmed over the Thunderhawks and worked on the fortifications at the Levies' base. 'It is likely that Sebastian is in the Knight Valiant that bears our Ancient. His father would be a way to ensure his attention.'

'Bait then,' Demetrius said. 'I can see the usefulness, Master Lazarus.'

Oskaran's face got even darker, but he wisely held his tongue. Lazarus considered him for a moment. 'With vox down, we lost access to some of the records about your world, Regent Prime. Including the detailed maps of your city. You can help guide the Interrogator-Chaplain through it.'

The Regent Prime nodded, but Ysentrud could see the doubt flicker in his eyes. She imagined the man had never left his palace without a driver and an escort of guards. He probably had no idea how Kap Sudsten was laid out.

But she did.

'Master Lazarus.' She made herself speak, counting on the stimm to give her the courage to draw his attention. She realised, suddenly, despite all that had happened to her, despite her weakness, her pain, that she wanted to be useful, to help again, somehow. Lying here watching felt like waiting to die. 'My memory contains detailed maps of the city. I could help.'

His grey eyes turned to her, and she imagined what he saw – a half-dead mortal with one arm gone, ridiculous tattoos and torn, muddy robes. He was going to think she was too weak, and tell her to hide in some hole while her world burned, she was sure. But he nodded. 'You have proved that you can, Learned. Go.'

'There, Interrogator-Chaplain.' Ysentrud pointed towards a crude warehouse with a rusty metal roof that stood where the barren landing field turned into city. Demetrius had carried her as the Space Marines ran across the vast expanse of rockcrete, cradling her in one massive arm like a child. 'The street to the left of that, my lord. It'll start us towards the Regent Prime's palace.' It was a narrow and twisting route that was less direct than the great boulevards leading to the same place, but hopefully it would avoid the worst of the rioting and make it a little harder for the gris to spot them.

Until they wanted to be spotted.

Ysentrud thought she would feel less exposed when they entered the city and its buildings surrounded them, but she felt more vulnerable. There were people on the street, scuttling from place to place carrying haphazard collections of belongings, looking to flee, looking for a safe place to hide, and she scanned every one of them for the grey motley of the gris. She didn't see any, but there were windows everywhere, ledges, niches, rooftops – they were surrounded by places the infected could hide and spy. She could see the Regent Prime, looking uncomfortable as Techmarine Meshach carried him on his shoulder, a powerful servo-arm holding him in place. He was looking around like she was, his expression a mixture of terror and rage.

Neither of them saw the first gris. A Space Marine from Squad Nabis spotted him, and his bolter cracked, the sound of the shot almost lost in the wet, crunching explosion of the round bursting in the chest of the mould-tainted man. By the time Ysentrud had whipped her head around, all she could see was a set of legs toppling over from a window ledge far above, jerking and kicking as they fell. A great splotch of blood and gobbets of shredded flesh haloed the window the gris had leaned out of.

'They know we're coming,' Ysentrud said.

'They always knew that,' Demetrius said. 'They have just pinpointed our position. We need to change our route.'

'Left here, in this alley,' she said, and they dodged down the narrow, foetid space between a manufactorum and a warehouse that had been converted into illegal hab-cubes and filthy food stalls. The alley stank of blood and spores and smoke, but something streaked over the narrow crack of sky visible overhead, and there was a series of dull thuds behind them mixed with fresh screams.

'Missiles,' Meshach said. 'Dropped where they thought we would be. But no explosions. What were they for then?'

'Harm,' Demetrius said as they came out of the end of the alley. The street here was bigger, full of people who were fighting, tearing at each other with knives and clubs and broken things, all shouting and bleeding, but when the Space Marines suddenly appeared, they bolted, fleeing, their battle forgotten.

'Up this road, my lord.' Ysentrud dipped into memen, orienting herself on the map in her head. 'Follow the curve.' Her voice cracked as she shouted over the screaming, and the Dark Angel nodded and kept moving. Up one street and down another, they moved through the city at a run. How long did they have? How long before Sebastian walked his Knights into the city and began to destroy everything? Ysentrud didn't know, and she didn't want to ask. She just clung to Demetrius, pointing out directions when he called for them, trying to ignore the shrieks that filled the air, the panic in the faces of the people fleeing through the streets.

The Dark Angels shot another gris before she could even see it, leaving another halo of gore on an alley wall, and Demetrius was shouting to her, 'What course?'

'There!' She pointed at an intersection up ahead, and the Dark Angels pounded forward, a band of looters throwing themselves out of their way. They rounded the corner and Ysentrud heard the looters scream as a missile slammed into where they had been. But their cries were lost in a shout from one of the Dark Angels. The Space Marine raised his gun as they moved, aiming it at a grey, mould-covered monster. A gris, Ysentrud realised, a gris like from her stories, not just a mould-masked person but the grey, ghastly, inhuman things of legend. It didn't seem mournful and miserable, though, not like how the stories said. It seemed awful, hunched over a man with its malformed hand pressed across his face, its lumpy head twisting in their direction.

'Death to the impure!' Demetrius shouted, and with his other hand he fired his bolt pistol, catching the thing in the back. A hail of other shots caught it, disappearing into the mould then exploding. They tore great holes in it, ripping one arm off, but still the thing rose and ran, disappearing into a habclave. The sight of its floppy, hideous run, the squelching fall of grey chunks of mould and slime from its body as it moved, made Ysentrud want to retch, but she forced the nausea back to shout more directions to the Interrogator-Chaplain. They ran on, and the crunching sound of another missile coming down echoed behind them, though again there was no explosion. It was a puzzle, but one they had no time to consider. They rounded another corner, and their destination suddenly loomed ahead of them.

The great plaza before the Regent Prime's palace was strangely quiet. The Administratum buildings standing on its other three sides had already been looted, their doors broken down, forms and data-slates lying trampled in the streets. The monument to those lost in the Redwash War that stood in the middle of the great open space was shattered, the fountain in front of it clogged with grey slime. But the palace seemed deserted.

Seemed. Still cradled in Demetrius' arms, Ysentrud could feel eyes on her. Many eyes. But she tried to ignore them as she pointed past the befouled fountain.

'There,' she said, her voice a hoarse whisper. At the side of the palace, the Night Garden still stood, its vast fungal forms rising high. In the gloom of the smoke-shrouded day, their glow could be vaguely seen. Demetrius nodded, and the Dark Angels moved quickly across the plaza, bolters raised. Halfway across, Ysentrud saw something on one of the palace balconies, a figure that vanished an instant after the Learned saw her. But Ysentrud knew her.

'Lash Commander Petra Karn is in there,' she shouted as they pounded by.

'She will be dealt with in due course,' the Interrogator-Chaplain said as he charged through the gate and into the Night Garden.

'This will do,' Demetrius said, coming to a stop and looking around at the maze of paths and towering plants.

'The Knights will blow this place apart in one volley,' Oskaran protested.

'They can. They will not.' Demetrius set Ysentrud down, and she tried to ignore the way the world spun around her. 'All of Heris Amis' manoeuvring indicates he wants us alive. He will send his slaves into this maze after us, and we will kill them. All of them. Even the ones who were once our brothers. *Especially* the ones who were once our brothers. Freeing them is our sacred duty, to our Emperor, to our Chapter, to them. Under our watch, no Dark Angels will be allowed to be taken by this enemy, to be held in thrall to a dark power, to be used as a weapon against us. We are the sword of the Emperor. We are the armour that protects humanity. We are the Dark Angels, and we are not playthings for the Ruinous Powers!'

The assembled Space Marines crashed their fists to their chests, a sound like thunder. And then it was echoed. A low boom rolled in off the square beyond the garden. Then another, and another. Ysentrud felt the ground tremble beneath her feet and saw the fungal trees around her begin to sway.

'The Knights,' Oskaran said, and there was a light in his eyes, anguished and ecstatic.

'The enemy comes,' Demetrius said to his brothers. 'Spread

out. Remember your faith. A moment of laxity spawns a lifetime of heresy! Sons of the Lion, ready yourselves!'

They crashed their fists again, then disappeared, moving into the tangle of the gardens. Demetrius looked down at Ysentrud. 'You have served us well, Learned. Go and hide yourself away. Else this battle will see you dead.'

'Maybe, my lord,' she said. She hadn't wanted this before. She didn't want it now. 'Probably. And this is likely the stimm talking, but I don't want to hide and let history move around me without knowing what's going on. I want to see it. I want to be part of it.'

'History is a ravenous beast, bloody in tooth and claw,' the Interrogator-Chaplain said. 'But you have earned the right to choose. Can you stay close, and quiet?'

She stared at her red skull face, mirrored in his polished metal one, and nodded. He nodded back, and she felt a swelling of pride that spun the world around her again. When he stalked off, she followed, only stumbling a little.

Lazarus stood with his command squad on the roof of the highest building of the Reis Home Levies' base, an ugly rockcrete tower marked with overlapping mould stains. The rest of the base sprawled below them, a shabby cluster of barracks and storehouses, most gutted by looters or fire.

'One half-crumbling fifteen-foot wall,' Lieutenant Zakariah said, looking down at the defences in disgust. 'This is the best this planet has.'

'The Emperor protects,' Lazarus said. 'But the universe seldom provides. We work with what we have.' In his head, he ran through their preparations. The Techmarines had planted sensors across the base and outside it, and they had collapsed most of the tunnels the gris had used to invade the base. Most of them. Now workers were setting up what new fortifications they could. He could see them outside the low wall, scratching trenches into the muddy ground. He had drafted every mortal who had survived the gris attack into the work, but it was slow going. If House Halven hadn't been prejudiced against servitors before, they would have been by now.

Or there would have been no mortals here to draft, and Lazarus would be assaulting another servitor-infested bastion.

Lazarus shut his eyes, clenching the hilt of Enmity's Edge. Any reminder of Heris Amis' ability to take over others with his gene-wrought, Chaos-enhanced grey pall brought back an image. That of Ancient Jequn, chained to the leg of a Knight, his face a rictus of anger and pain, his armour splattered with grey.

Techmarine Cadus had recorded picts with his Thunderhawk as he passed by the Knights, and Lazarus could see them in his head. A dozen adamantine beasts, striding through the jungle, the ones in the lead ripping through the trees with giant chainswords. Grey banners flew from the two largest, the Knights Valiant. And Jequn, chained to one of those machines, and the banner of the Fifth, stained with grey, hanging from the other.

You will understand that, when I come for you bearing your banner.

Heris Amis had taken his men. Had taken his banner. And if he broke Jequn's mind, he would take the secrets of the Fallen. The master of the gris had to burn, and every time he thought of him, Lazarus saw himself surrounded by flames, felt their touch deep in his flesh, and he wanted to rage.

But he leashed it. It would have its time. But not yet.

When I come for you bearing your banner.

From below came shouting and the sound of motors as two

huge cargo-8s moved into the compound. Balanced between their reinforced beds was *Talon*. Slowly, metal groaning under the weight, the transports hauled the ship to where *Vengeance is Prayer* now sat. Neither of the Thunderhawks could fly, but their cannons worked, and those were the biggest guns they had.

Lazarus looked at his chronometer, ticking down towards the time he calculated the Knights would arrive. Close now. Close, and he felt the flames again.

'They will be on us soon.' He forced back the fire. 'Are you ready, lieutenant?'

'Ready?' Zakariah stared out at the jungle, silent and waiting. 'We have one squad of brothers, a few hundred irregulars, two grounded Thunderhawks and no vox. We face six Knights, an unknown number of mortal militia, and perhaps some of our own brothers, slaved to this traitorous enemy's will. Fate has set the Fifth a grim table today, but we must not fail. So we will not. We will be ready.'

'We are the sons of the Lion. We live to fight. We fight until we die.' Lazarus smiled, but there was no humour in it. 'And sometimes, we rise and fight again.'

Zakariah bowed his head. 'May we all fight as well and as long as you, Master Lazarus.' There was a hesitancy in his words though. An unvoiced question.

'You would fight better if I had not sent half of our already fragmented forces off with our Interrogator-Chaplain,' Lazarus said.

Zakariah frowned. 'I am not second-guessing your decision, Master Lazarus.'

'I know. You just wish you understood it.' Lazarus took a deep breath. He wished he could explain it to his lieutenant, but Zakariah was not a member of the Inner Circle. By the Throne, he hated not being able to explain why he had sent

Demetrius after Jequn. Too many secrets, binding them up, pulling them in different directions. He hated those secrets, but here he was, risking the fall of the Fifth, maybe the fall of the whole Chapter, to protect them. Because that was what he had sworn to do.

'Understand this,' he said. 'It is critical that this enemy not take any of us, for to see a brother slaved like this is a monstrous thing. But it is of paramount importance that Ancient Jequn, Interrogator-Chaplain Demetrius and I not be taken. If we are, make the focus of your mission our elimination. Do not allow the enemy to make use of us.'

'I understand, Master Lazarus.'

He did not, but he would follow his orders, Lazarus knew. Even the ones he hated. 'I have set you up to face these Knights, brother, and to face Heris Amis' attack. I believe he means to stand back and hit you from a distance first. The Knights' weapons far outrange all of our own except the Thunderhawks' cannons. And if he can do something to spread his infection, he will attempt that too. You must hold out against all his attacks.' He stopped, frowning. He had so little information. *You have what you have. Plan accordingly.* Master Balthasar's words rang through his head yet again.

'You will hold out and be a distraction,' Lazarus told his lieutenant. 'You will draw the fire of the enemy upon you, and you will destroy what ground troops they have. Even if they are our brothers. Especially if they are our brothers. This will give me my chance to face Amis.'

His one, thin chance.

'Master,' Zakariah said, 'we could go with you. Me and most of Squad Revir, we only need to leave Techmarine Cadus back to man the cannons.' He hesitated. 'Maybe a few more to watch the Levies.'

'It will require all of you to watch them. Else they will break the moment the Knights appear,' Lazarus said. 'And I have another duty for you. If I fail – if I fall – you and Squad Revir need to fall back.' The Master of the Fifth could see Zakariah shift, the anger and denial in the way his lieutenant held himself. 'We have seen no Primaris taken by the gris. Maybe it is chance, but maybe Heris Amis cannot infect us. That is why Squad Revir is with you, and that is why if I am killed, you will pull back and focus on getting a message out to our ship or to the Rock. They must know what happened here.' Azrael would understand the danger exactly. The full might of the Dark Angels would fall upon Heris Amis, focused by the Inner Circle.

In this case, Lazarus had to acknowledge that their obsession with protecting their secrets would prove very useful.

'We will do as you order, Master Lazarus,' Zakariah said, his voice carefully controlled. 'But it will not come to that. The Lion will see you victorious.'

'The Lion will see me,' Lazarus returned. His primarch would see his son in anger. Exacting retribution. Lazarus prayed that would be enough as, in the distance, the black dots of birds rose from the jungle. A huge tree, one of the giants which raised their branches above the rest of the canopy, shivered and suddenly vanished, pulled down beneath the other trees. 'Heris Amis is here.' Lazarus looked to what was left of his command squad – Apothecary Asbeel, Techmarine Ephron and the Librarian, Raziel. 'We shall go to meet him.'

They thundered down the stairs through the Levies' headquarters. Techmarine Ephron led Lazarus and the others into the basement, through the dripping, mould-slick sub-basement and then down a muddy ramp into one of the tunnels the gris had twisted through the earth to reach the Reis Levies.

'We were able to map these tunnels, the way Brother Cadus mapped the ones back near the Redwash Gate,' Ephron said. The Techmarine reached out and touched Lazarus, and their armour linked, able to pass information again despite the scrambling that still blocked their vox-channels. A schematic flickered inside Lazarus' helm. The Techmarine's data sketched itself out into a twisted map of tunnels, twisting like capillaries through the flesh of this world. Lazarus had ordered some of them collapsed, but he had ensured that others were kept open – the ones that ran under the rough clearing burned out of the jungle around the Reis Home Levies' base. The clearing where Lazarus expected Heris Amis to bring his Knights. 'The seismic sensors are picking up the Knights' approach.' The Techmarine's other hand was touching a wire that hung from the top of the tunnel, a direct link to the web of sensors he had hastily strewn across what would soon be the battlefield around the base.

'Take us as close as you can, brother,' Lazarus told him, and Ephron nodded and started forward. They fell in behind, pushing their way down the narrow tunnels.

When I come for you bearing your banner.

The words echoed through Lazarus' head. The challenge with the banner could be another of Amis' tricks. Another feint. Lazarus didn't believe that, but reality didn't care what a man believed, even when that man was Adeptus Astartes.

'Brother Raziel.' He spoke the words quietly, but they still seemed to fill the dark tunnel. 'Do you sense anything?'

The space of time it took the Librarian to respond wasn't long, but Lazarus still felt his hands curling into fists. His anger at the psyker might be unreasonable, but it existed, and the cold rage that filled him now did nothing but increase it. Finally, Raziel spoke.

'The currents of suffering still move,' he said. 'A thousand threads of them, all knitting together to flow towards the Redwash Gate. The place where they combine is before us, in the jungle, and growing closer. I am sure that Heris Amis is the locus for all that misery, the gatherer who feeds it back to the shadow beyond the gate, and he is coming.'

That was enough, that and the challenge of the banner. It would have to be enough. He knew what he had to do. This plan was a desperate gamble, but every good option was gone now, and this was what he had left.

'Soon then, brothers,' he said. 'Soon we will finish this hunt, reclaim our banner, free our brothers and slay this monster that would dare enslave our kind and those we protect. For we are the Dark Angels, we are the sons of the Lion, the Emperor's First, and we will not fail.'

His words cracked with certainty, and he gripped Enmity's Edge with cold, focused fury. But Lazarus could feel the ghost of flames dancing across his skin, waiting to burn him and his brave promises to ash.

CHAPTER TWENTY-SIX

Demetrius and Ysentrud found a niche at the top of the wall, hidden behind a tangle of vines, which looked out into the plaza. They took their place, listening as the approach of the Knights became one low, unending roll of thunder, a rumble that ran below the distant sounds of riot.

Ysentrud ducked behind the Interrogator-Chaplain, his bulk an armoured wall between her and what approached. Across the plaza, beyond the destroyed monument, something huge moved, stepping out from between two blocky buildings. It paused, wrapped in smoky gloom, and the thunder died away. Then it began again, the whole garden trembling as the first Knight moved into the square, followed by the others.

There were six of them, massive metal war machines striding into the plaza. They were monstrous giants out of legend – ancient, misshapen things with great helm-like heads hunched between massively armoured shoulders, and arms that were nothing but weapons, their legs like metal columns. She could remember their names, even without going into memen – they had been the central characters of so much of Reis' history, but none of those old stories properly described how terrifying their presence was. The size of them was overwhelming, but they moved with smooth precision, clawed feet moving inexorably closer, like great birds whose every footstep shook the ground. Their helmed heads moved, turning this way and that as their auspex systems scanned the city around them, and their arms were always shifting, tracking possible targets.

Their pilots were hidden. Whatever controlled them, human or fungus or some hideous melding of the two, was buried somewhere in all that metal, protected by the heavily armoured torso. But they were there, the soft hearts of the war machines, guiding their awful motion, and Ysentrud could see one sign of their presence. Grey mould seamed the Knights, filling the cracks between armour plates, running in streaks down their striding legs. It dripped from glowing eyes like tears and ran from the bottom of their heads like grey foam, a rabid tide of mould dripping down, spattering over the ancient crests of House Halven, the intricate accolades embossed on the ceramite plates.

There were gris inside those things, infected pilots that had become the masters of the Knights and their machine spirits. Which meant that each of them was a creature of Heris Amis, a weapon of his vengeance. A vengeance he was already claiming against the Dark Angels.

She could see the infected now, moving around the feet of the Knights. They looked small in comparison to those machines, but she knew their size all too well. Space Marines, Dark Angels. One was missing his helmet, his face bare, and Ysentrud could see the slackness of his features. There was no grey mask on his skin, no obvious signs of the gris infection except for the terrible blankness of his eyes. But it was obvious that he and the other Space Marines around him were part of Heris Amis' plan. They moved easily among the war machines, keeping up with them as they crossed the plaza.

There was one other.

He was chained to the armour plate on the lower leg of the largest Knight, a massive machine flying a grey banner with House Halven's crest on it. His helmet had been stripped away, exposing a heavy-featured face, a bald scalp and a row of service studs that gleamed over one dark eye. It was the first time she'd ever seen his face, but Ysentrud did not need to hear Demetrius whisper 'Jequn' to know that this was the Ancient standard bearer of the Fifth. He was bannerless now, his bare head swinging with each great stride of the Knight. But he wasn't dead. As the Knights drew closer, Ysentrud could see that his eyes were closed, that his teeth were locked together, the muscles of his neck and face taut with tension. Jequn was alive and fighting, fighting something that made him shake his head and snarl, and it was easy to imagine what. Grey slime coated his scalp, trickling down his face and onto his neck, bubbling at the corners of his mouth. The gris had him, Heris Amis had him, was trying to infect him – but Jequn was fighting against it. Fighting as only a Space Marine could fight.

'You came here for him,' Ysentrud breathed. It was a scrap of a whisper, but she knew Demetrius would hear. She had seen Lazarus and Demetrius speaking, intense and low, as they planned. Heris Amis had already split their forces up with his machinations, divided and weakened them, and now, right when the gris seemed strongest, they were dividing again. Why?

'For him and any other brother,' the Interrogator-Chaplain answered. There was a slight hesitation, then came the admission. 'But him most of all.'

'Why?'

'Because the Dark Angels never desert a brother,' Demetrius growled. 'Even if the enemy has taken him. The seed of heresy will never grow in our hearts. We will stamp it out – or count on our brothers to do it for us. I will free them all, one way or the other. But Jequn especially, because there is ancient knowledge in him that must not be taken by any enemy, lest it be used against us. And because he is my friend.'

The Knights came to a halt before them, six death machines standing silently outside a stone wall they could brush through the way Ysentrud could break a spider's web. How could Demetrius and his men fight that? This would be a slaughter.

The thought should have been terrifying, but with the stimm in her, it was like the pain – a distant, niggling worry, easy to ignore. Especially when things were happening. On the other side of the wall, people were spilling out of the palace. A score of gris, their faces grey masks, and two other things. Shuffling, slimy beasts, almost the size of the Dark Angels. More of the real gris, the ones out of the stories, not just people marked with fungus but things that seemed to be made of it. She shivered at the sight of them, but the fear was lost in stimm and fascination and... and anger as she saw the figure walking behind them. Petra, the lash commander, Sebastian's lover, the traitor.

She still wore her Levies uniform, black and perfectly clean, unmarked with grey, the same as her face. Petra was no gris, taken over. She and Sebastian had cut some deal with Heris Amis. Together they had helped the resurrected enginseer orchestrate this catastrophe, and Ysentrud wanted to see her dead.

The lash commander walked out to stand before the largest Knight, flanked by the gris. 'The Space Marines are there,' she called up to it, pointing at the Night Garden, and the machine tilted its head, seeming to stare right at Ysentrud's hiding place. The lead Knight had much less of the grey mould growing from it, only a few lines spreading around its head and body.

'Hiding?' The voice boomed from the Knight, amplified to overwhelming, but still it was clearly Sebastian's. 'Dark Angels? Hiding from me?' The Knight's head turned towards the garden. 'You were so eager to put me in my place before, to put me down when I wore the suit of a Regent Next. Where are your orders for me now that I have claimed my birthright, have succeeded where my father and all those fools before him failed and clad myself in magnificent destruction?' The war machine spread its great arms, one bearing a massive three-barrelled weapon, the other a gigantic harpoon. 'I abandon my old, worthless titles. I am no Regent Next. I am Sebastian Halven of House Halven, master of the Knight Valiant Rovoko, and it is you who will bow to me, Dark Angels.'

Even standing behind him, Ysentrud could sense the rage in the Interrogator-Chaplain. Enough that despite the stimm, despite knowing it wasn't directed at her, she stepped back. But as she moved, she saw something below. A man walked out of the garden gate and into the plaza. A man in dirty regal garb, without arms or armour, who walked with his head high, straight towards the Knight that bore his son.

'You are not of our house,' Regent Prime Oskaran Halven shouted. All alone, the man must have slipped away from the other Space Marines when they were taking their places in the garden. 'You're a traitor. You're a coward. You are without honour, and you are not my son.'

'Traitor? Coward?' Sebastian's Knight Valiant stepped forward, making Petra scuttle out of the way. 'You're the coward, the last of the line of cowards who did nothing for a thousand *years. You're the traitor, who left our legacy to rot in the darkness.'* *Rovoko* moved again, the claws of its metal feet cracking the pavement before Oskaran, but the Regent Prime did not step back. *'Look at this strength, this power!'* Sebastian bellowed. *'You showed this to me when I was a child. Told me it was my heritage, my right! Then you told me that I would never have it. Because you and all your line were too afraid to reach out to anyone else to see our Knights restored. But not me, no. I wasn't going to be like you, content to play at simulations, to watch holo-dramas, to hope for some miracle. I was going to claim the power that was mine, so I found someone that would help me. Someone that could make our Knights move again.'*

'You found a monster,' Oskaran answered. 'You corrupted our Knights. Look at them! Dripping poison and rot!'

'Look at them moving, father!' Sebastian said. The giant harpoon on the end of one of the Knight Valiant's arms swivelled to aim itself at the Regent Prime. *'You cry because you see me succeed in what you failed to do. You cry because I am fulfilling the dream you were too pathetic to grab. You cry because you know you were wrong, you know that you have lost, and that in the end you are going to die at the feet of the Knights you dreamt you would one day control.'*

'No,' Oskaran said. He looked up at the head of the Knight staring down at him. 'I will not cry. I will not die. Because I know these Knights. I have studied their history my whole life. I know the spirits that dwell within them. Fierce, and full of honour. *Rovoko*! Look upon me, the true heir of House Halven, and hear my words. The man who has seized your controls is not worthy of you. He is worthy of nothing! Cast him out and join with me, and we will rebuild our house by slaying the monster that Sebastian has sworn himself to!'

The Knight stared down at him silently. Seconds ticked past, and Ysentrud began to wonder. Began to hope. She watched the harpoon waver, then fall to the side of the great machine.

'You see?' Oskaran said, his voice fierce. 'You see? *Rovoko* knows. Did you factor this into your betrayal? The honour of the Knights that you tried to steal? Or did you think they would abandon it, the way you abandoned yours?'

'*The only thing I abandoned was my weakness,*' Sebastian said. '*And yours. You say you have honour? You lied about our Knights, hid them in darkness, abandoned them when your schemes fell apart. You failed* Rovoko *the way you failed your family, the way you failed me.*' The Knight Valiant leaned forward, raising one leg, and then brought it down. Oskaran didn't have time to move, didn't have time to scream, before *Rovoko*'s clawed foot crushed him with a thunderous crack. The Knight Valiant ground its foot into the stone then stepped back, leaving a red smear.

'*I'm done with weakness, father.*' Sebastian's voice was almost soft, even coming out of the Knight. '*And with you, and with this stinking planet. I have a ticket out, and I'm leaving.*' The Knight Valiant shifted, leaning back, pointing its weapons towards the garden. '*All I have to do is finish this with* you.'

With a screaming roar, the missile rack on the top of the Knight blazed into life. Rockets shot out of it, straight at the garden. Ysentrud ducked forward, pressing herself into Demetrius' armoured bulk as the missiles smashed into the garden and... broke. They did not explode into fire and flame but burst into great wads of grey slime that fell out of the sky like a downpour of pus. The thick liquid, cold and stinking of mould, splashed off the fungal forest, the palace's roof, the damp ground. Much of that hideous rain fell behind Ysentrud, over the main part of the garden, and Demetrius' armour blocked most of the rest, but she still felt a few thick drops land on the back of her head. She hissed and swiped it away.

Outside, she heard Sebastian's voice rumble out of the Knight. 'Go.'

Through the vines she could see the gris, the normal humans and the Dark Angels, running for the garden gate. She saw Sebastian's Knight moving too, one arm reaching down to where Jequn was bound to its leg, using the tip of its harpoon to break the chains. The Ancient fell to the ground beside the war machine. His face was still twitching, but he drew out his sword and stared up at Sebastian's Knight.

'Amis tells me you're finally done fighting, Ancient. Prove it, and drive your brothers to me.'

Before her, Demetrius raised his crozius. 'For the Lion. For my brothers. For all who came before me and held true. I hunt.' Then he leapt down from the wall and charged into the forest, still dripping with grey.

'Emperor's blood and spit,' Ysentrud whispered. Then, having nothing else to do but sit here and die, she followed after.

The narrow earthen tunnel shook, and a small avalanche of dirt fell from above, bouncing off Lazarus' armour. Somewhere above, the Knights were moving, stepping out of the jungle and into the clearing that ringed the Reis Home Levies' base. Heris Amis was closing in, getting ready to unleash his assault against the Dark Angels gathered there, and the Master of the Fifth felt a grim satisfaction knowing that he was about to turn his enemy's tactics against him.

Then another tremor rumbled through the tunnel and wet earth fell, part of the tunnel collapsing under the shaking tread of the Knights. Lazarus shook his head, clearing the muddy dirt from the lenses of his helm, and wondered how clever he would feel if this plan left him and what was left of his command squad buried in a grave before the fight even began.

Lazarus' hand tightened on his sword. This plan. This gamble. Heris Amis had outplayed him from the start. Reis was a trap. The Fifth had been divided again and again, made weak for the gris to fall on as Amis gathered his strength, and Lazarus had fallen for it. And now he was separating himself from what was left of the Fifth just as the enemy approached. Heris Amis was at his strongest, and Lazarus had made the Fifth weaker again.

Lazarus understood what was happening. Tactics were a simple thing in the end. It was all about taking away the enemy's options, stripping them of possibilities until they had only one, which was to face you in the fight that you wanted. Forcing them onto a battlefield that you had curated for victory. But there was something else that Lazarus had learned over the centuries. It was almost impossible to understand everything your enemy was capable of when they were forced into a corner. Impossible to truly know what they might do when all their opportunities to survive were stripped away. It broke many, but some... some lashed out in unexpected, dangerous ways. And after centuries of fighting, after dying once and clawing his way back to life, Lazarus understood one thing about himself. He would never be broken.

The heavy tread of the Knights above finally stopped. A long moment passed as dirt continued to sift down over Lazarus, but that slowly diminished, and all was still, silent.

'Heris Amis has taken his position,' Asbeel said softly.

The Apothecary was right. But what was Amis' position? Lazarus was blind in these tunnels, and he cursed the gris for taking their communications, for stripping him of his ability to see through the eyes of every man in his command. He was used to seeing the whole of the battlefield with god-like clarity. Now he was as blind as a worm. But he wasn't alone. 'I need your eyes, brothers.'

'I am repairing my connection to the sensor network,' Ephron said. The Techmarine was digging through one of the half-slumped walls, until his gauntlet pulled a thin cable out of the fallen dirt, one of the leads he had dropped into the tunnels when he had set up the sensors earlier. It was broken now, crushed by the shaking arrival of the Knights, but Ephron quickly weaved its broken strands into a new connection to socket into his armour.

While he worked, Raziel moved closer to Lazarus, his presence like a chill draught at the Master of the Fifth's back, both welcome and unsettling.

'I can feel him,' the Librarian said. 'Heris Amis is a knot of suffering, a clot of pain. I feel he is close, but the web of spiritual agony he weaves distorts the immaterium around him.'

Of course it does, Lazarus thought. When was the immaterium, the very stuff of Chaos, not distorted? But all he said was, 'I need precision. Not feelings.'

'I will gain it, Master Lazarus,' Raziel said, his voice determined, and Lazarus hoped the Librarian was right. Maybe a psyker would be good for something other than adding another name to the list of dead in his head for once.

Ephron had finished his work. Lazarus laid his hand on his brother's back, and a link opened in his helm.

'I am correlating data with the sensor network's cogitator. Attempting to draw a map of the Knights' locations relative to us.' A map had appeared before Lazarus, a layout of the space around the base. Marks flickered onto it, the cogitator's guess at the probable locations of the war machines standing overhead. The marks shifted and blurred, imprecise, and nothing indicated which Knight was which. Ephron's voice was tense with concentration. 'I am trying to gain precision also. One of the pict casters in the network survived.'

A bright window opened in Lazarus' helm, an image of the world above. It was tilted at a strange angle, fuzzy with bad optics, but it was sight, it was knowledge, and Lazarus drank it in greedily.

The Knights stood in the open, a line of six deadly giants. The one in the centre was the largest, the Knight Valiant flying a grey banner. From beneath its head hung the Fifth's banner, soiled with slime. The other Knights flanked it, mould dripping down their armour like grey gore, and around their feet stood a cluster of gris, grey-masked mortals and a handful of monstrous things. But not enough of them, to Lazarus' tactical eye.

'You should better support your armour with your infantry,' Lazarus said to himself. 'You may have had a thousand years to plan, Amis, but you should have spent some of it studying how to fight.'

The Knights stopped in front of the base, just at the edge of range for the Thunderhawks' cannons. Just at the edge of range for the Knights' long-range weapons. Then Heris Amis spoke, his amplified voice echoing out of the central Knight, loud enough to reverberate through the earth above them like muffled thunder.

'Surrender now, Dark Angels. Give yourselves to me, and let your suffering… begin.'

No playing then. No lies, only sneering contempt. Amis was overconfident, and in the tunnels below, Lazarus tightened his grip on his sword, preparing himself. Soon. Soon he would find out if this last plan of his was a deadly strike – or one last failure that might destroy the Fifth and see him finally, truly dead.

Zakariah gave the gris the only answer a Dark Angel would to such a question. The Thunderhawks' cannons boomed, and a shell ploughed into the dirt a dozen yards to the side of the line of Knights while another smashed into the ground a good thirty yards in front of them. The gris war machines were untouched, and the infantry gathered at their feet were only splattered by the mud that geysered up from the impacts. The Techmarines knew that aiming the weapons from the ground was going to be difficult. But what Lazarus wanted was the thunder of the guns, the threat. The distraction.

Distraction he got, as Heris Amis' Knight Valiant returned fire. Missiles shot from the armoured shell of its back, arcing towards the camp. Fifty feet off the ground, the missiles came apart, bursting into a spray of grey that rained down on the base below.

It must have been some kind of immaterium-fuelled biological warfare, some way for the gris to kill or infect, and Lazarus could easily envision the chaos on the base as Reis Levies troops panicked beneath the grey rain. Meanwhile, the Thunderhawks had fired again, their shots seemingly only a little more accurate, crashing into the ground near their feet – doing little to no damage to the Knights but smashing into the infantry below, scattering and killing them. Just as Lazarus had wanted.

The Knights were beginning to move, slowly closing, their ion shields sparking as small-arms fire struck them. They were not returning fire, not yet. Heris Amis likely believed he had won, that he could lay siege to the camp and crush it in less than a day. To the gris, the Dark Angels of the Fifth and the Levies were not a threat to be fought but a resource to be harvested.

It was time to teach that traitor his error. It was the time, finally, for rage.

'Where, Ephron? Where is he?'

'Calculating, Master Lazarus.' The ground was shaking around them, jumping from the crashing strikes of the Thunderhawks' cannons, trembling from the impacts of the Knights' feet. 'Incoming fire is reducing the sensor net, but–' There was a sudden sizzle, and the picts and information pouring through the Techmarine into Lazarus' helm went black. 'Cogitator destroyed,' Ephron said. 'Last known position of Heris Amis is–' Ephron went silent, trying to calculate, and the tunnels rocked around them, dirt falling like hail.

'This way.' Raziel's voice cut through the muffled thunder of battle and the crash of the tunnels' slow collapse. For once the Librarian's voice was fast and sure, and Lazarus followed without hesitation as the Dark Angel pushed down narrow passages, winding through the shaking dark. The Master of the Fifth's anger blotted out his usual distrust of psykers and their abilities. Whatever sense led Raziel to this prey, Lazarus would follow.

They ran through the narrow tunnels, the lights of their armour barely cutting through curtains of falling stone and dirt. Raziel took turns without hesitation, moving as fast as he could, Lazarus pressing close behind him with Asbeel and Ephron following.

'Ahead,' Raziel snapped. 'I can feel his triumph through the pain. Just–' The Librarian cut off, stomping to a stop as the tunnel ahead suddenly thundered down, the earth giving way as another round from the Thunderhawks' cannons smashed into the ground overhead.

Lazarus couldn't see past Raziel – there was nothing but dirt and darkness and noise – then a gauntlet slammed into his shoulder. 'There!' Asbeel shouted, and Lazarus saw it, a bar of sunlight flickering through the dust to one side.

'Dark Angels,' he shouted. 'Ascend!'

He charged for the light, clawing his way up a half-collapsed wall. The sunlight streamed through a hole barely bigger than his fist, but he tore at it, ripping it open, and then he was out, free, surrounded by light and war.

The others poured out behind him, drawing their weapons, helmets swinging as they took in the fight. They were in the middle of the clearing, a flat area burned out of the jungle and overgrown with fungus. The Knights were all around them, metal giants that towered overhead, their heavy feet exploding the fleshy mushrooms growing across the ground like rotting corpses every time they took a step. Lazarus swung his eyes over the armoured monsters and found the Knight Valiant. The machine was a walking fortress, its heavy carapace black gilded with gold, seamed now with lines of grey. From its back fluttered a huge grey banner, and dangling beneath the glowing eyes of its armoured head was the banner of Lazarus' company, fouled with mud and slime.

'Sons of the Lion,' he snarled. 'Bring that down.' Then Lazarus ran.

He couldn't hear the others following, the sound of their boots lost in the vast noise of the Knights' march and the crashing, hissing storm of the Valiant sending another wave of missiles arcing through the sky. But he knew they were there, following him through this pack of giants, fully vested in his madness.

It was the ork walker that had sparked this plan. He had taken that monster down on Husk with nothing but his sword and a river. There was no river here, but he had the tunnels, his rage and Enmity's Edge, crackling in his fist like an event horizon. That was enough. It had to be enough.

The Knights didn't see them as they ran. The missiles taking off, the shuddering ground, the small-arms fire pouring out of the distant base, the roar of the Thunderhawks' cannons' shells bouncing off the ion shields of the Knight Valiant, all that mayhem was camouflage, a cacophony overwhelming the

Knights' sensors. The charging Dark Angels were too small, too close. They were the reason that Heris Amis should have brought more infantry.

But he had brought a few. Up ahead, between him and the Knight Valiant, Lazarus saw a grey shape shambling forward. He had his bolt pistol, but he kept the weapon holstered and leaned forward, Enmity's Edge rising. The thing sensed him coming and started to turn, its arms rising, but Lazarus went low, ducking beneath them as he swung. His crackling black blade passed through the thing's legs like a shadow, barely slowing, leaving the monster to fall.

Then he heard the shout behind him.

The Master of the Fifth spun and saw Apothecary Asbeel lying on the ground, wrestling with another of the monstrous gris. The mouldy thing was tearing at his neck, ignoring the cutting blades and whirring saws of the Apothecary's narthecium as the cybernetic medi-pack shredded its back. Without thought Lazarus charged the thing, mud flying under his armoured feet. The gris had pulled Asbeel's helmet away, thrown it over its shoulder, and was pressing one slimy hand over the Apothecary's mouth.

Then Lazarus was there, his sword swinging, cutting away the thing's head right before his shoulder slammed into it, knocking the heavy body away.

'Up, brother.' Lazarus yanked the Apothecary to his feet, pulling him after him as he started running again. Heris Amis knew they were here now, and they had little time.

'You should have kept going,' Asbeel said, then hacked, a wad of slime coming out of his throat. 'You should not have come for me.'

'You came for me when I burned, brother,' Lazarus said. 'I will not leave you for these monsters to infect.'

Heris Amis' Knight Valiant was still moving, still putting distance between them, but the great machine on its right flank was turning, the ground tearing beneath its metal claws as it spun to face them. It was a Knight Gallant with a chainsword for one arm and a great clawed hand for the other. A flickering energy field covered that hand, but it vanished as the thing lumbered towards them.

'Infection,' Asbeel said, and hacked again, more slime spilling from his mouth. Then the Apothecary stumbled, falling to his hands and knees, retching. Lazarus saw him go down, saw too the Knight Gallant moving towards them.

'Abomination,' the Apothecary choked out. 'Infection. I can feel it.' Asbeel looked up at him, eyes flashing. 'Go, brother. This disease must be burned out at the source.' Then he pitched forward, convulsing in the mud.

Lazarus twitched, wanting to go back, to save the man who had saved him from death. But a shout rang through the air, Raziel's voice filled with warning – 'Lazarus!' – and he turned away from the Apothecary.

In front of him, the Knight Gallant was bending low and reaching out, its great claw clutching at him like a child trying to scoop up a bug.

The shadow of that huge hand blotted out the sun, and Lazarus started to duck down, to try to roll under it, but then a wave of cold washed through him. It froze him, and for a moment the world froze around him too, the battle falling silent, everything going still. A moment of perfect clarity, and in it Lazarus saw a dozen different futures unwind. He ducked under the hand, and it smashed him to the ground. He dived to the side, and it caught him. He twisted, dodged, flung himself back, attacked – all of them ended the same, with those massive fingers closing around him like a cage. Except one.

The one where he leapt up. Then time suddenly caught up with him, sound rolling through his head again, and he leapt.

One finger almost caught him, but he kicked off it and flew over the Knight's arm. He hit the ground and rolled, just avoiding one great foot as it slammed down. He came up, and for an instant he saw Raziel staring at him, the usually red eyes of his armour glowing blue-white. Then the Knight Gallant was swinging its hand for him again.

He ducked it himself this time, slapping at it with Enmity's Edge as it went by, scarring its palm. But the Knight kept reaching for him, determined to catch him, and whether it did or not, it was slowing him down, keeping him from Heris Amis. Until Ephron ran in beneath it, a satchel charge in his hands, and shoved the explosive into the war machine's ankle joint.

Lazarus had meant that for the Knight Valiant, but he was not going to argue with his Techmarine. He ducked another grab, and the Knight's claw-like fingers scraped through the dirt, clenching on nothing. The machine pivoted and grey slime spattered around it, drooling from its head like diseased froth, and then the satchel charge went off.

The explosion shattered the Gallant's ankle, making it stumble. Its shadow covered Lazarus, and he turned and ran, fleeing its collapse. He saw Ephron running too, to the side and ahead of him, seemingly safe, but as the Knight slammed into the ground it flung out its giant chainsword. The spinning blades sheared through fungus and dirt and the tip of it crashed into the Techmarine. He fell, one of his legs gone, taken and flung away by one massive, hooked tooth.

Lazarus didn't have time to curse. Heris Amis was still moving, his Knight walking away, and they would all die if he didn't fall. So he ran, hurtling past where his brother lay, leaving him as he had left Asbeel. The Knight Valiant was just ahead, the great machine stopping and beginning to turn, raising its giant flamer.

'For the Lion,' Lazarus said, sprinting forward as hard as he could, and he heard himself echoed.

'For the Lion!' Raziel was at his shoulder, and they both leapt into the air just as the flamer spewed a gout of grey slime at them. But it fell beneath them as they hit the Knight and activated the mag-locks in their armour, fastening themselves to the back of war machine. Lazarus moved, scrambling up until he was exactly where he wanted to be, between the massive exhaust vents that poured heat out of the Knight, right above the armoured pilot's hatch. The hatch that Lazarus was raising his sword over and then slamming the edge into, driving the crackling field into the armour.

Red-hot chips of adamantine showered out from the impact, and Lazarus could see the wound he'd gouged out of the Knight's back. Not as deep as he wanted, but placed exactly right, beside one of the hatch's heavy latches. Raziel clung to the Knight's back on the other side, staying well away from Enmity's Edge. There wasn't room enough for both of them to swing, but he was staring out at the other Knights, a flickering globe of blue-white light gathered in one hand. From the corner of his eye, Lazarus saw him suddenly stiffen.

'I see Asbeel,' the Librarian said. A round cracked off the back of the Knight and exploded, shrapnel ringing from Raziel's armour. 'The gris have him. He targets us.'

'Damn you, Heris Amis!' Lazarus slammed Enmity's Edge down again.

'I am sorry, brother,' Raziel said, his hand held up, the blue-white orb in it flashing. Then he started to bring it down to throw. But as he did, a bolter round caught him, smashing into his chest, then another, and the ball of light was gone from the Librarian's hand, vanishing as he stumbled and sagged, held up only by the mag-locks of his armour. There was a thud then, of something heavy slamming into the Knight below Lazarus.

He turned, feet clanking against adamantine, and Asbeel was standing below him, his mag-locks humming, a bolt pistol in one hand and his narthecium arching over one shoulder like a scorpion's tail, humming with blades. The Apothecary's face was slack, expressionless, but his eyes weren't dead. They were still hideously alive with pain, not dulled yet by Amis' possession.

Lazarus saw those eyes and checked the swing of his sword. 'Brother Asbeel,' he said, hoping the name would break through Amis' control, and then Asbeel fired his pistol.

The explosive round flew at the Master of the Fifth, would have hit him point-blank in the chest, but just before it struck, the Iron Halo built into Lazarus' armour flared and ripped the round apart into light.

Light that left the Apothecary blind, those pain-filled eyes blinking, and then Lazarus swung. Enmity's Edge crackled, and the point of the sword drove into the throat of the man who had once raised Lazarus from the dead. Asbeel arched back, spine severed, his narthecium twisting, blood and slime pouring from his mouth as he fell. The mag-locks in his boots let go, and he dropped, falling away, gone.

Lazarus stared at the space where he had been, smelling the blood of his brother sizzling on his sword, and then he turned and slammed the blade down into the back of Heris Amis' Knight.

Driven by his rage, Enmity's Edge gouged deeper, and something spilled out of the wound he'd carved into the Knight's back, a grey sludge that stank of mould and decay, and he let the rage roll through him as he struck again.

'You are mine, Heris Amis!' he shouted. 'I will tear you from your stolen armour and rip out what is left of your rotting heart!'

'I don't think so.' The voice came from the Knight beneath him, deep and loud as thunder, and the great machine stopped moving, froze in place, as a shadow fell over Lazarus.

'Another Knight is coming.' Raziel had forced himself back up. His armour was dented and blood marked it, but another flash of blue-white light was gathering in his palm. He threw it, his eyes flashing blue, then lurched and raised his hand to his side as a fresh gout of blood leaked through his armour. 'It strikes.' The Librarian's voice stuttered, and he clenched his fist, but the light that danced around his fingers was weak and didn't coalesce.

Lazarus ignored Raziel's warning, ignored Heris Amis' voice, ignored everything but the rise and fall of his blade, but at the edge of his vision he could see the other Knight raising a massive flamer. Through his anger Lazarus felt a lick of pain, the memory of his flesh burning. He was going to burn again, but so would Amis, and he spoke the Litany of Rage as he brought his sword down, driving his blade deeper when the Knight fired.

But it wasn't flames that covered them. It was grey sludge, the same slime that was dripping out from the wound he'd made in the Knight Valiant's back. It washed over them like a wave, coating them, and Lazarus was blind, deaf. Ignoring the erasure of his senses, he kept his grip on Enmity's Edge and kept driving his sword in. And then the read-outs in his helm flickered. They strobed before his eyes, then went black as his armour died, sealing him inside it like a tomb.

CHAPTER TWENTY-SEVEN

The garden was a goreyard, reeking of blood and decay, and Ysentrud moved through it as silently as she could. There were sounds all around her – the crack of bolters, the shouts of impossibly deep voices, and the clash of knives off armour. Moving through the shadows, trying to be as small as possible, Ysentrud searched for Demetrius. She refused to hide, to end this day crouching alone in the dark somewhere. She had got her fill of that in the conduit with the servo-skull. She wanted to see this finished, but if she didn't find Demetrius or another Dark Angel she was going to end up dead or worse.

Crouching in the shelter of a dead tree festooned with a thousand crimson fungal crests, Ysentrud looked out at a little clearing. It was empty except for the remains of a statue of a dancer that now lay smashed across the ground. The statue's stone head smiled serenely at her from the ground, and she frowned at it, considering stepping out of the shadows. Then the head was suddenly gone, smashed beneath the armoured boot of a giant.

It was a Space Marine, a mountain of muscle wrapped in armour. He had dropped down from the arching growths above, and he carried a blade as long as Ysentrud's leg. He was facing away from her, but Ysentrud could see the grey stains that marked him, stains that announced his infection. He was gris, and he was right there, and at any moment his transhuman senses would find her...

Ysentrud reached for the knife Gretin Lan had given her, but there was a misfire in her brain, and she reached with the hand she no longer had while her remaining hand twitched by her side like a dying thing. What would she have done if she'd grasped the blade anyway? She almost died trying to fight a servo-skull – she wouldn't be able to even scratch a Space Marine. So she froze where she was, holding her breath, waiting as the giant slowly began to turn. Then there came the sound of bolter fire from the other side of the garden, and the infected Dark Angel was gone, racing away. Ysentrud was left alone, trying to breathe.

When she could move again, she limped off the other way, not caring about stealth, not caring about the pain that flickered through her battered body. She moved until she heard a sound, a terrible, sizzling noise like a saw ripping through silk. The sound Lazarus' sword had made when the dark energy flashed around it. The sound Demetrius' crozius made when he swung it in battle.

Turning, she headed towards the noise, only slowing when she saw the garden opening before her into a space that had once been a meticulous labyrinth of low mushrooms but was now a churned and muddy duelling ground.

There was Demetrius, and facing him, his helmet and banner gone, his armour streaked with grey, was Jequn. The Dark Angels were still as statues, facing each other, until they were suddenly charging forward, weapons swinging. Energy flashed through the air, and there was a crack like sudden thunder as sword and crozius met. The weapons hissed as Ancient and Interrogator-Chaplain leaned into their blows, each straining to drive the other back – and then they whirled apart, moving impossibly fast, to face each other once again. Demetrius held himself still, his crozius crackling with energy in his hands, his skull face spattered with mud. Jequn shifted on his feet, his sword out and held low, the mud below its tip bubbling, brushed by the deadly field that surrounded the weapon.

'Fight, brother.' Demetrius was breathing hard but steady, his deep voice harsh from behind his helm. 'I know this thing does not own you yet!'

'It does.' Jequn didn't look like the other gris. His eyes weren't dead. They were alive with pain, his face twisting with agony. His suffering was still on the surface, easy to see, not swallowed yet by Heris Amis to feed his hideous patron squatting on the other side of the Redwash Gate. 'This damnable thing has dug itself deep. I cannot root it out. I cannot!'

With that, the Ancient charged forward again, his sword swinging. Demetrius moved away, his crozius rising to block. There was a hissing scream as the weapons struck, a crackling roar like fire as their fields pressed into each other. The Space Marines struggled, matched in strength, and then they were suddenly apart, staring at each other over the open ground.

'You are fighting!' Demetrius snarled. 'I know it! You are one of the Emperor's chosen, the blood of the Lion is in you. You are a Dark Angel. You are slave to no man, no monster, no Ruinous Power. You are fighting, and you can win!'

'I fight only to keep this thing out of the last bastion of my thoughts,' Jequn said, levelling his sword. Unlike his twisting face, his body moved with smooth precision. 'You know what I hold. The secrets that were entrusted to me. Those are what I keep from the gris. That is all that is left to me. Heris Amis owns my body, and he lays claim to my soul. I will fight you, brother. I will beat you, and I will give you to him, too. I have no choice. My only resistance are these last thoughts, the ones we share, and I am crumbling. I will give them up soon, and then I will be truly lost. Then I will... will be...' His face twisted, jaw locked as if there was a word he was desperately fighting not to say. Then he launched himself at Demetrius again, smashing at him with his sword.

'You cannot let me beat you!' Jequn bellowed. 'You must cut me down, now, before I am truly lost. Before we all are!'

'Guess who's going to win?'

The voice, cool and quiet behind her, made Ysentrud spin. Petra Karn stood behind her, the lash officer still neat in her dress blacks. But behind her loomed monsters, grey piles of dripping mould. The monsters that filled the gris stories Ysentrud had once eagerly, stupidly, etched into her head.

'We are,' Petra said, her eyes flicking momentarily over Ysentrud before returning to the fight. 'It's amazing you're still alive, little Learned. If a little lessened by your adventures.'

'It's upsetting that you're still alive too,' Ysentrud said. 'If there was any justice in the universe, you would have been lessened to ash by now.'

Petra shook her head. 'Don't get overwrought. There's no justice, because such a thing doesn't exist. It's a big, stupid galaxy, Learned, and the only thing that matters is strength. Be strong, and you make history. Be weak...' She shrugged. 'And you are history.'

'Petra,' Ysentrud said, glaring at the woman, her left hand shifting. 'Please know these are probably my last words. May the Emperor and all His saints piss upon you and Sebastian for all eternity.' Then she drew the white dagger with the hand left to her and lunged.

Ysentrud moved too fast for the gris, who reached out their slimy grey hands too late. But as she brought the blade down, Petra stepped just a little to the side, just enough to let the knife flash past. Ysentrud started to stumble and the lash commander kicked out her leg, sending her sprawling. Then Petra stomped on Ysentrud's back with one boot, pinning her down.

'Weak,' Petra said. 'But the gris will take you. Amis will take anyone, as long as they're suffering. And you look like that's something you're good at.'

Ysentrud struggled beneath Petra's boot, trying to twist so she could stab the woman in the ankle at least, but she could barely breathe. Then a shadow fell over her, and the scent of decay and mould came, so thick she could taste it. One of the gris crouched down beside her, and its hand reached for her face. She cringed back, but it wrapped its slime-covered palm over her mouth and nose.

'You should have stayed with us, Learned.' Ysentrud could barely hear her as the slime pressed between her lips, up her nose, pouring into her, choking her. 'We're going to leave this mouldy planet behind and become a force out there in the stars, an army that will shake this galaxy and leave a mark across history like a slashed throat. While you and all your useless history are going to be forgotten. Forever.' That was the last Ysentrud heard as her body convulsed and the darkness took her, swallowing up the sight of Demetrius still fighting, while the other gris crept up behind him.

Lazarus was in the fire again.

It roared around him, flames of every colour eating through his armour, melting through the ceramite, cooking him alive.

He could smell his flesh burning, that sweet scent of meat mixed with the acrid tang of melting plas and superheated metal. His limbs were twisting as ligaments tightened in the heat, then snapped. His guts were going, his bones were charring, and his throat was filled with steam as his lungs burned. Everything was going black.

Lazarus was dying. Again. Again. Again.

But he never died.

The flames around him went grey and the pain faded back. It was not gone, but it became a steady, terrible hum in his nerves, and he could focus on the figure walking towards him through the fire. A shambling thing that may once have been human, but evil and decay had wormed their way through it so thickly that it was now monstrous. It stopped in front of him, standing in the midst of the fire, and then the slime that coated it sloughed away like a hideous skin, and underneath was a man.

He wore grey robes, with a deep hood that wrapped around his face. His hair was grey too, a faded, dull grey like clouds. So were his eyes, lacking the black of pupils or the white of sclera, just a dull, uniform grey like fog, filling each socket. His face was plain, boring, the skin pale, and in his hairline were things that might have been implants or might have been filamentous growths digging through his scalp. He was banal and he was monstrous, and he was untouched by the flames.

'Lazarus. Master of the Fifth. How happy I am to welcome you to my vengeance.'

'Welcome me to nothing, Heris Amis.' Lazarus' voice was harsh, a croak through clenched teeth as he burned. 'The only thing you will have from me is your death.'

Heris shook his head. 'You speak as if you had some choice in the matter. Understand this – you're in the belly of the beast,

Lazarus. You're being digested, and I will take you apart and use you as I will. You have no more choice than a scrap of gristle dissolving in stomach acid. You're mine, Lazarus. Even if I cannot control you, even if I cannot solve the puzzle of your Primaris resistance, I will kill you and take your memories and they shall live in me. Forever.'

'I am–' Lazarus' shout was cut off when the fire took his throat and burned his vocal cords until they popped.

'I've had enough of you cutting me off.' Amis tilted his head, his blank eyes on Lazarus. 'If I wish to speak, you will listen. You are clever. I feel the shape of your memories. Hazy now, but enough. You guessed at most of my history, at my future. But there is something more, something I want you to understand, from your broiling skin to your charred bones. I want you to know why.'

Caught in the flames, dying, dying, but never dying, Lazarus only wanted to tear whatever Heris Amis had become apart. But his legs wouldn't move, his arms wouldn't move, his armour was broken, fused, an oven cooking the meat of his body within. He was helpless, caught. And he could feel it now, another kind of burning, another kind of falling apart – the gris, reaching into him. It came from all over, like tiny worms chewing through his skin, digging into his body, into his nerves. They were burrowing through him, eating him up, heading for his brain.

'The way you feel now,' Heris said, 'was the way I felt for almost two centuries. When I died – when you Dark Angels killed me – that thing beyond the gate reached through and caught my soul. It had been watching me, waiting for death to wrap itself around me, then it offered a solution. A kind of survival, through suffering. It feeds on suffering, and it is always hungry. It made me feel my worst pains, my worst memories, for centuries, and I endured, and I lived, and it turned my suffering into strength, into resilience. Into a need for vengeance. You know what that feels like, don't you, Lazarus? That hunger for vengeance. I can feel it, here.'

One of the worms bit deeper, ripping its way closer to his brain.

'Psykers. Sorcerers. You hate them so. I can feel your mistrust even for the one you call brother, the one you brought with you, the one I am taking apart even as I take you apart. The way I took apart the Apothecary who you so cruelly killed. You have felt a psyker's foul power too often. You have felt their flames. When you face them, your anger grows, and you strike hard.' Heris looked at him, his plain face twisted into a smile. 'I understand that. Magic… hurts. When it kills, and when it saves. But my real anger is reserved for creatures on this side of reality. For the people that labelled me traitor and destroyed me.'

You are a traitor, Lazarus thought, but it was hard to focus. He was burning from the outside. He was being eaten from the inside. The pain of burning was overwhelming, but somehow the pain of the gris digging through him, consuming him, was distinct. He could feel it driving into his thoughts. He could feel it reaching deeper, and he slammed his will shut around the things he knew he must keep secret. The forbidden history of his Chapter. The knowledge of the Fallen. Whatever arguments he may have with Azrael, he had made his oaths. No enemy would tear this information from him. None. In his pain, he sealed those secrets away as he felt the gris tear through him.

'A traitor,' Heris said. His blank eyes were on Lazarus, and his smile was gone. 'Yes. A traitor to the Imperium. To the Emperor. To the Machine God. To the Adeptus Mechanicus. To mankind.' He leaned forward, and the flames twisted around

Lazarus, searing deep. 'I am what you Dark Angels made me. What the Adeptus Mechanicus made me. I was *loyal*. I was *faithful*. I was a true servant of the Imperium, and what was my reward? Lies and treachery, abandonment and suffering. I was rescued from death by a slime I'd created and a daemon, and sentenced to my own private hell for eternity. So yes, Master Lazarus, I became a traitor to all the things that betrayed me. I made a deal with a daemon, so that I could take my suffering and give it to those who turned on me. You made me a traitor, Dark Angel, and now I will make you one. Remember, my dear Lazarus, my love of symmetry? I am a traitor. And you, your company, your entire Chapter, you will be traitors too. I will take your brothers, the ones you call Firstborn, and make them mine. I will take your memories and secrets and make them mine. I will take your ship, and I will go to the Rock and Azrael will fall and I will be the new Supreme Grand Master. The Dark Angels shall become mine, and with them I will destroy as much of the Adeptus Mechanicus as I can.' Amis' voice snarled with anger and madness through Lazarus' head. 'I will lay siege to Mars itself, and spit in the Machine God's teeth, and that will still not be suffering enough to pay for what was done to me!' Heris Amis went silent, the thunder of his voice fading in Lazarus' skull, and when it came back it was a whisper, a blade of pain twisting through the Master of the Fifth's mind. 'I will use you and yours to do all of that, and the name Dark Angels will become synonymous with treachery until the Imperium falls to ash and tears.'

He faded, then was gone. Heris' last word echoed in Lazarus' head, and he wanted to scream but he could not, wanted to fight but he could not. All he could do was burn as the worms of decay and treachery tore through his brain and ate away the locks that guarded the deepest core of his honour.

It was like the pain of etching, if she felt it not just in her mind but in her flesh and bones, in every inch of her – pain that was consuming instead of creating.

So much pain.

Ysentrud was in the conduit again, and the servo-skull was wrapping its terrible tongue around her arm, cutting through her flesh. She was four years old, her tiny body wracked with coughing as spore fever ripped through her lungs, making every breath agony. She was twelve, and the red pall was taking her apart, the fungus growing through her skin, her brain, remaking her with pain. She was seven, and her father was walking away from the hall of the Wyrbuk, the credits they had paid for her in hand, and she was screaming at him not to leave her with these terrible people with their red skull faces.

Everything was pain, every memory of every past suffering was filling her, and there was one new one. Ysentrud could feel the gris digging into her mind, like a grub feasting on a rotten log. Heris Amis was trying to claim her, and she knew that he would, making her a slave, forcing her to suffer for whatever sliver of eternity was left to her.

'Welcome to my vengeance, Learned.'

The man was plain, except for his blank grey eyes. Except for the fact that sometimes he faded in and out, becoming a huge silhouette of something terrible, fleshy and almost shapeless, dripping with viscous slime, reeking of abandoned places, of forgotten death, of rotting despair.

'Heris Amis.' When the gris spoke, the pain faded a little, left Ysentrud with a mind just clear enough to process the words. The master of suffering, alleviating her suffering? But no. Whatever he was going to say to her, Ysentrud was sure it would end up causing her even more pain. But she couldn't help but welcome the relief.

'You are the first Wyrbuk I've ever claimed,' Heris said. 'Feel honoured.'

Ysentrud felt anything but. She felt degraded, used, a morsel crushed between Heris' teeth. But she made herself focus, and in what was left of her mind a thought stirred. 'How can you do it?' she rasped out. 'How can you control all of these people?'

He smiled, a kindly smile beneath his horrible eyes. 'I don't control them. I consume them. You are mine, Learned. Everything in you is mine. Fight it all you want, but your mind, your soul, are mine now.'

Mine now. The words rang through her, and she wondered if Demetrius had fallen yet, torn down by Jequn or the monstrous gris that had come with Petra. And Lazarus? Was he still fighting? Or had he fallen too? Had all the Dark Angels fallen? And if they had, what chance was there left for this planet? None. Suffering would bloom from this defeat like spores, and those seeds of misery would drift through space, spreading and spreading and spreading...

This was what Heris Amis wanted. Why he was letting the torment of her memories ease, so that he could encourage this blossoming of new suffering in her brain. She tried to push it away, tried not to let that painful despair settle in, but she could feel his hunger digging through her, tearing into her brain, reaching–

And she could feel part of herself reaching back.

She was Learned Ysentrud Wyrbuk. She was made to take in information so that she could give it back. She was a living library, a teacher. Holding it in was alien to her. She could feel the memen state taking over, making her into a conduit, becoming a flood of information, and as it did, she could feel the relief. There was no space for emotion in memen. No room for suffering. Ysentrud let it take her with a groan of relief, and all the history that had been etched into her, those thousands of years of facts and minutiae, dense with information and completely lacking emotion, she poured through the hungry mouths the gris had dug into her and stuffed it into Heris Amis.

And through her memen calm, she felt him choke.

When Lazarus died the first time, when he had been wrapped in sorcerous flames on the bitter world of Rimenok, he had chosen that death. It had been a tactical choice, one that would buy his men the time they needed to keep the battle from becoming a rout, so they could salvage victory from the claws of defeat. It had been a worthy sacrifice, and he had done it without thought, without the hope that he would rise again.

Yet he had been given a second life in a new body, with another chance to serve his Emperor, his Imperium and his Chapter. To offer his life again, and there was nothing better than that. He would go to the flames as many times as he could for the Dark Angels. But this...

He was alone. Heris Amis had gone, but he hadn't, really. The gris was still burrowing into him, stealing from him, feeding on him. He was feasting on Lazarus' mind, and there was nothing the Master of the Fifth could do but hang on grimly, wrapped around the last bits of himself that had yet to be taken, the knowledge he had vowed never to let go. He hung on, burning, dying, burning, dying, and wondering each time – should he try to ride the illusion of death into the true darkness? He'd been there once before. He might be able to reach it again, to lose himself in that black, to deny his body, his mind, his knowledge, his soul to this enemy.

And so the beast came to Droslin, and beneath its claws the walls did fall–

That fragment of the story he had been translating echoed

through his head, a phrase disconnected, a memory uncoupled. Was it some side effect of what Heris Amis was doing to him, a crumb dropping from the jaws of the gris as it consumed his mind?

No. No. Lazarus shook his head in the flames and remembered *The Doom of Droslin*. The lesson that story taught, the one he had tried to convey to Azrael. The temptation of pride, of obsession. The sin of believing that he was the only possible answer. Doom had come to Reis, wearing the form of Heris Amis, and it had torn down the walls. It had torn down his walls. But he did not face it alone. His brothers were still out there, beyond the flames, fighting. Demetrius. Zakariah. Raziel.

His brothers may yet stand. And while they did, there was hope, and so he kept fighting, drawing out every moment until there was nothing left but pain, and bitter rage, and the need for vengeance.

Symmetry, Heris Amis would say. But Lazarus didn't care. He just wanted Enmity's Edge in his hand, and Heris Amis' head at his feet.

So he burned, and burned, and burned. Until the flames stuttered around him.

The great conflagration flickered, like a candle sputtering in the wind. Then it was back. All the pain, all the heat was there again. And then another stutter, and in the places between the flames there was mud, and grass, the stench of rot, the taste of blood in his mouth. There were flames again, but Lazarus was driving against them, trying to shove them out of his head. They weren't real, they weren't, and when they flickered again, he was on his hands and knees, reaching out for Enmity's Edge.

Flames.

Wrapping his hand around the grip.

Flames.

Standing.

Flames.

He was standing, and the Knights were still around him, still as statues. There was the sound of explosions, of guns and screams, of shrill birds in the jungle. There was the sight of Raziel on his hands and knees in the mud near him, trying to rise, and then the flames – the flames he shoved away, and they stuttered and broke, like a bad holo, shattering into nothing. Lazarus was standing, breathing, sword in his hand, rage and remembered pain boiling through him like acid in his arteries, but he leashed it, focused it, and found what he needed.

Heris Amis' grey-bannered Knight Valiant stood before him, still except for a tremor that stirred its huge limbs and made its helmet-shaped head shake, like a man in the grip of a seizure.

With a snarl, Lazarus leapt into the air, climbing the Knight. His boots rang against its thick armour as he ran across it, the mag-locks holding him to the back of the metal giant. There was the hatch, and there the hole he had carved, and with a stroke he smashed Enmity's Edge down and shattered the damaged latch of the armoured door. It bled grey ichor, but he ignored it, moving to the other latch and smashing his sword down again. Enmity's Edge tore into the armour, and the Knight twitched below him.

'Lazarus!' It was Raziel. The Librarian was wavering on his feet, but he was standing, his armour splattered with grey slime and blood. 'Heris Amis… I feel him… What is happening?'

'He is trying to take me. To take us. All of us,' Lazarus snarled, driving down with Enmity's Edge. 'But he falters. And so he will die!'

Halfway through the last hinge on the hatch, the giant went still, rigid. Lazarus could feel the flames again, the burning beneath his skin, tearing his muscles apart, broiling him inside his armour, but he didn't stop. He didn't acknowledge the pain as he struck again and again until he had torn the last latch apart. Reaching down, he ripped the hatch open, his burning muscles screaming with pain.

Inside the Knight, in the thickest part of the chest, was the Throne Mechanicum, the centre of the machine, its heart, its brain, the place where the human pilot would sit. Except here was something else, a pile of mould that had tried to shape itself into a man. It was squeezed into the chair, too large for the throne, but the thing had compressed itself like a mud doll, and cables and umbilicals ran from the inside of the Knight into that grey mass like gleaming spikes driven into a rotting brain.

With his teeth gritted against the pain, Lazarus lifted Enmity's Edge. But the world was flickering around him again, stuttering. The grey flames were trying to draw him back, and he had to wait until he could see, until he could be sure of his strike. When his vision cleared, when the world came back, he could hear something, a vast bellow that shook the air, but he ignored it, driving his sword down into the centre of the gris' chest.

The grey mould squelched beneath Enmity's Edge, spattering and boiling at the touch of the power field. It was more like mud than flesh, and Lazarus drove his blade deep, until he felt it crunch into the Throne Mechanicum. Sparks ripped through the space, and the Knight spasmed again, spasmed as Heris Amis' awful shape was spasming, and Lazarus saw the lumpy head of the gris master shifting, splitting, opening like some awful flower, to reveal Amis' grey face.

'No!' the monster that had been a man shouted, and half-formed hands grabbed on to Enmity's Edge. They sizzled against the blade, spattering apart, but were still clutching as Lazarus tried to pull the sword back for another thrust.

They fought, the sword shifting between them, until that roar Lazarus had heard was a wall of sound, vast and terrible, and there was something falling from the sky like a great stone. *Rage of Angels*, the last Thunderhawk the gris had claimed, was tumbling through the air spilling fire and smoke. Gretin Lan's ship was right behind it, a white shadow following its terrible fall. The dying ship was diving straight towards the Knights, towards where Lazarus still wrestled with Heris Amis, still fighting to pull Enmity's Edge away so he could drive its point through the gris' face.

'Lazarus!' Raziel shouted from below, and on the end of that shout Lazarus felt it again. The cold and perfect stillness as the world froze around him, as the Librarian warped time and opened a vision of a dozen paths of possibility in Lazarus' head.

In so many of them, Heris Amis won. The gris tore Enmity's Edge from Lazarus' hand and ripped him apart. Or wrapped Lazarus again in the memory of flames and took his mind, burning him out from the inside, stealing every memory, every secret of the Dark Angels. There were only a scant handful of paths where Lazarus got away. Survived, only to watch Heris Amis triumph. But there was one. One very short path, where there was a chance of vengeance. And the surety of flames.

Without hesitation, Lazarus chose that path, and time gripped him again. Heris Amis was reaching out with one blunt hand to grab his helm, to wrench his head back, as the sound of the falling ship rose to a world-shaking scream, and Lazarus jerked his blade to one side. The Knight Valiant moved, staggering as the blade tore at its controls, moving over until it stood directly in the path of *Rage of Angels'* fall. The wreckage of the dying Thunderhawk struck the Knight and smashed it backwards, flipping it through the air like a toy. Lazarus was ripped away, sent flying like another piece of shrapnel surrounded by flame, until he slammed into the ground and everything went black once more.

CHAPTER TWENTY-EIGHT

Wrapped in memen state, Ysentrud drifted, serene, as she poured out the history of every Imperial Guard regiment that had been produced by Reis since the planet rejoined the Imperium. Every battle, every engagement, every commendation and reprimand, flowing out, out, out.

She couldn't see, couldn't hear, but that didn't matter. The painful memories that had filled her head were gone, shoved out by the merciless stream of facts pouring from her. This was what she had been made for, the culmination of her red pall infection, of her training, of her whole life so far. She was a Wyrbuk, and she was being read from cover to cover, and the satisfaction of that filled her to the brim.

Except for one tiny corner. A sliver of personality that had stepped aside from the great roar of the information flooding out of her. A little piece of her that simply rocked in the darkness, giggling viciously as she gave the gris exactly what it wanted. And then that darkness cracked.

There was a flicker of light, a stutter of something like a broken pict caster trying to warm up. In the tiny flashes of light she saw fungal trees. She saw one of the gris monsters, staggering. She saw Demetrius, lurching back, his skull mask cracked and marked with grey sludge like blood. She saw Jequn reeling like a drunkard, his sword hissing as its point dragged through the mud.

'No.'

The voice echoed through her head, the only sound, unrelated to the images flashing past.

'Yes,' she said through her laughter, and in memen she proceeded to the tax figures for the eastern region.

The light around her flashed, stuttered faster, until she was back, cast out of the darkness of her head. She was lying on the ground, blinking up at slivers of smoke-stained sky that she could see through the fungal fronds waving above. Tilting her head, she saw Petra standing beside her, swearing and shouting, 'What's wrong, what the fugg is *wrong*, you mouldy beast? Fight!' at one of the grey monsters that had walked with her like guardians. The thing gave her no answer, just stood silent out in the clearing as the Interrogator-Chaplain raised his crozius and then smashed it down into the creature's misshapen body.

'Her!' It was Jequn's voice. The Ancient was standing, shaking, his body wracked with convulsions, and the one word was all he said before he snarled and twisted, his teeth locking shut, eyes bright with hate, a man fighting with himself.

'Who?' Petra looked around.

In her head, in her body, all through her nervous system, Ysentrud could feel the gris that infected her trying to pull out, to pull away.

'No!' Heris Amis' voice echoed through her head. 'Stop!'

'Stop?' Her head fell back onto the soft ground, and she giggled. 'No. Oh no, no, no. You wanted me, you Throne-cursed, mutant-blooded pile of daemon shit. So have me. All of me.' She could feel the tendrils inside her thrash, but the gris only knew how to consume, to dig in, not to let go. The probes the grey pall had set in her mind were barbed, meant to hook deep, and Heris Amis couldn't free her any more than she could force him out, and her mouth twisted into a rictus of spiteful humour.

'Her?' Petra's face was confused, frustrated, angry. 'This… thing?' Heris Amis was too busy to answer with any of his thousand mouths, so Petra shook her head and drew her autopistol. 'Damn it,' she growled, aiming the weapon at Ysentrud's head. 'I told you this plan was too complicated, Sebastian.' Her finger started to tighten on the trigger as Ysentrud looked up at her, staring at the barrel of the gun even as the information roared out of her. She was unable to move, unable to do anything but giggle and wait for her head to be blown apart – and then something smashed into Petra.

Heavy and grey, it struck her like a sack of rotting flesh, knocking her off her feet. The lash commander fell with a grunt, all the air knocked out of her. Ysentrud blinked and realised the thing that had hit Petra was the head of one of the monstrous gris, ripped away from the thing's body.

Then Demetrius was there, standing over her, his battered skull mask flickering with reflected sunlight, his crozius crackling in his hands. 'Petra Karn. You gave your aid to a creature of the immaterium. You betrayed all of mankind. There is one sentence for that.'

Petra had pulled herself up to her knees, gun still somehow in her hand. She got off a wild shot and the slug cracked uselessly off the armour over the Interrogator-Chaplain's chest.

'Death,' the Dark Angel intoned, and swung his crozius.

Ysentrud closed her eyes, just long enough to miss what happened when that terrible weapon struck the lash commander. But she couldn't miss hearing the awful, sizzling crunch, nor avoid the ugly scent of flesh and blood boiling away in the gold-coloured field. When she opened her eyes again, she saw Demetrius swinging the crozius back, his head tipped down towards her, the green-and-red glow of his eyes bright over her. A giant, an overwhelming presence, terrifying and good, protecting her. But then he stumbled.

She couldn't see what had moved him. There was too much happening, and most of her head was filled with the figures of Reis' Imperial tithe contributions for the first century after reunification. She saw Demetrius move, saw his crozius fall and smash to the ground beside her, its deadly field spattering her with mud and steam. His hand still gripped it, but he was standing, and she realised that his arm had been severed, cut through at the bicep. His armour was glowing, his flesh was smoking, his red, red blood was splattering the ground. Demetrius was turning, spun by the blow that had maimed him, the strike of Ancient Jequn's sword.

'Not free,' the standard bearer of the Fifth hissed. 'Almost. Almost. Then he came for me again. Focused on me. To kill her.' Jequn raised his sword over Ysentrud. 'I do not want to, brother. I do not want to do anything this thing wants me to do, but I cannot stop it. You have to. You have to kill me!' Jequn stood frozen over Ysentrud, terrible in his size, in his fierceness, bearing his terrible sword, and for the second time she waited for death. Waited, while Jequn fought. Waited, while Demetrius recovered from the blow that had taken his arm. Waited, still pouring out her teachings, as that great sword finally began to fall, cutting straight down at her until Demetrius lashed out and crashed one armoured leg in a vicious kick against the Ancient's knee.

The smooth slice of the sword faltered and its blade struck, hissing, into the earth beside her hip. So close. Too close. With a sizzling roar the field of it touched her, tearing through her flesh, ripping it apart, touching her bone and shattering her hip joint. In the mud Ysentrud convulsed, screaming, and in her head the memen state faltered, the information slowing as pain overwhelmed her brain.

'No,' she hissed to herself, fighting to shove back the pain, fighting to stay in memen. The pain howled in her, though, so huge, echoing off all the other pains, tearing down the fragile barriers the stimm had made against them. It was swallowing her up, feeding on her like the gris had been trying to do, and even as she tried to force it down, to hang on, she could feel herself drowning in it.

'Fight!' The command came from the skull mask that hovered over her, its glowing eyes burning into her. One word, so deep it rumbled through the pain, and she understood. This Dark Angel. All the Dark Angels. Demetrius and Jequn and Lazarus all. They needed her. *They* needed *her*. And then, for the first time in the longest time, maybe for the first time ever, she understood that she had a purpose, that her life had a meaning, and the awesome truth of that made it possible to shove back the pain, to grasp the tatters of her memen state and pull it back together.

'Fight,' she whispered, and smiled, and then forced out the rules and regulations of packing stimm according to strict Imperial guidelines for the past eight hundred years.

The information poured out of her again, and above her, Jequn swayed. Then he tossed aside his sword, spreading his arms wide, bereft of weapon and banner as he stared at Demetrius.

'Brother,' he croaked, his body trembling, battling to stay still.

The Interrogator-Chaplain reached down and picked up his crozius, taking it from his severed right hand with his left. 'Brother,' he said, and then swung the weapon up, smashing it into the Ancient's face, crushing his skull.

Ysentrud closed her eyes, feeling the blood splattering down, hot on her skin, feeling the pain still roaring through her body, but she was pushing, still pushing, giving Heris Amis everything. Focusing her memen and teaching the gris a new way to suffer.

There was fire all around Lazarus.

Flames of red and gold, flickering over twisted wreckage, dancing over foetid vegetation. Red and gold. Not grey. Not multicoloured, bright and unnatural. He pushed himself up from the ground, feeling the heat through his armour. It was hot but not searing. The flames close to him were small, isolated things. Behind him was a greater heat, where a massive piece of what had been *Rage of Angels* roared, burning fuel eating through its armoured fuselage.

In front of him, the Knight Valiant lay stretched out on its back, one of its legs jutting out awkwardly to one side. The front of the massive machine had been crushed, as if an angry god had smashed its fist into it.

Lazarus shook his head, trying to clear it. His body ached as if he'd been beaten with hammers, but that pain was already dull and fading as the Belisarian Furnace between his hearts spilled its mixture of stimm and healing elements into his blood. His transhuman physiology was healing the trauma that bruised him inside and out.

His Spiritshield Helm was gone, ripped away by Heris Amis

or the impact from when he'd slammed into the ground, and his head was still ringing from that blow. His vision slipped in and out of focus, but quickly sharpened as he healed. There was blood trickling down the right side of his face, and reaching up, he felt a cut that ran from his hairline down through his eyebrow, skipped over his eye and continued down his cheek. It was deep and wide and there was exposed bone on his forehead, but it was nothing. His eye was unscathed and the blood was clotting, the wound already scarring shut.

He started to move, warily eyeing the Knights that still stood around him. They were ignoring the fire and wreckage, standing motionless except for the occasional twitch or jerk, like great sleeping beasts. Whatever had happened to the gris was still happening, and Lazarus moved faster, working his way through the wreckage back towards the fallen Knight Valiant. He saw nothing moving near it except flames, no grey shape rising from the wreckage. What would he do if Heris Amis was still in the Knight's chest, buried under a mountain of armour?

He would tear the Knight apart with his hands, then crush the monster within.

Lazarus flexed his gauntlets, went to the nearest chunk of wreckage that wasn't burning and vaulted to the top of it. No gris, no Heris. No Raziel, either. Had his brother been buried in wreckage? Or crawled away? He couldn't tell, couldn't see him or Ephron. He was alone.

And so the beast came…

Not alone, he thought, as the words from the story flickered through him again. Something had happened to Heris Amis. Something had broken his hold of Lazarus, and over all the others that he controlled. Something. Someone. And by the Lion, he would take advantage of that opportunity. Standing in the mud halfway between him and the downed Knight, Lazarus saw the instrument of his vengeance, waiting. Enmity's Edge, driven partway into the ground. Thanks be to the Throne it hadn't been covered in wreckage. He dropped from the pile and headed towards it, weaving through the scattered pieces of the burning Thunderhawk. He wouldn't need to use his hands to kill Heris Amis now. Lazarus could slice him into pieces until the gris dissolved into slime. But when the Master of the Fifth came around the last jagged piece of wreckage, he saw Heris Amis standing there, waiting for him, with the black blade of Enmity's Edge in his half-formed hands.

The gris' misshapen head hung down, and slime dripped from him, pattering to the ground like great grey tears. He was saying something to himself, mumbling an unending stream. When Lazarus stepped out into the open, Heris raised his head, and Lazarus saw that his face was exposed, with fleshy folds of fungus hanging open around its grey skin. His lips were moving, muttering, and his blank grey eyes were narrow with anger.

'You did this,' he snarled, breaking out of his mumbling. 'You fed me that skull-faced poison! But it's not going to work. I'll chew that Wyrbuk up and spit her out, and you will learn what suffering truly is, Dark Angel!' He pointed Lazarus' own sword at him, his grip awkward, and lapsed back into his muttering.

Wyrbuk? The name went through Lazarus' head, and for the first time he started pulling words out of the gris' verbal stream. Things about lot sizes and crate capacities and padding measurements for stimm lots for the Adeptus Militarum versus the Adeptus Ministorum. It was dense, bureaucratic non-sense, and Lazarus smiled. He had forgotten about the strange little mortal when he had been forcing himself to remember what allies he had left. Apparently he shouldn't have, because whatever Learned Ysentrud had done, she had broken Heris Amis' control and now Lazarus was going to break him.

'What the Learned has done to you she did on her own, using her own strengths,' he said, walking slowly closer. 'There is a power in having allies, gris. In helping others, so that they may someday help you. Power greater than that which comes from slaving others to your will.'

'She has no strength. She is nothing. I will end her.' Heris Amis shook himself, spattering slime around him, and the Knights all shivered too, each one quivering in an eerie echo of the gris. 'You too are nothing, Dark Angel. I have seen into your minds. You claim to be men without fear. You can fear. I can sow it into you, with time, with patience, and I will. My vengeance has not been stopped. It's just beginning. I am going to cut you down with your own sword, *Master* Lazarus, and then I will return you to your flames so you may suffer forever!'

'Words are a coward's only action, Heris Amis.' Lazarus reached into the wreckage beside him and pulled out a strut, a fifteen-foot length of blackened metal. It was twisted by heat, badly shaped for his hand, but he held it with better grace than Amis handled his sword. 'Come here, and prove that you can make truth out of your vicious dreams.'

Amis glared at him, his face a mask of hate around his blank grey eyes. Yet the ferocity of that expression was belied by the movements of his lips, the ceaseless muttering of nonsense that he couldn't seem to stop. But the muttering didn't slow Heris Amis when he charged Lazarus, Enmity's Edge flaring to life in his oozing hands.

Lazarus stood his ground, and when the gris was in range he shifted the strut in his arms, dropping it so that its jagged end caught the charging monstrosity in the middle of his chest. The makeshift weapon sank into the soft fungal folds, but then stopped, hitting a harder core of resistance. Heris snarled, held out of reach by the metal, and slammed Enmity's Edge down on the strut, cutting through it, then pressed forward again.

To find nothing. Lazarus had smoothly sidestepped, avoiding the gris' clumsy strike, and he smashed the end of the severed strut across the back of Heris' hand. Even if the gris felt no pain, that blow should have shattered the bones there, but it just hit that same soft-then-hard flesh and bounced away, not disrupting his grip. Amis went past, then whirled to face Lazarus again. He was strong, and faster than he should have been, monstrously tough, and carrying Lazarus' sword. A sword the gris shouldn't have even been able to touch, much less wield. Heris Amis violated everything he touched with his tainted mould, and the rage in Lazarus was as sharp as the edge of his stolen sword.

Lazarus spun the strut in his hand and went on the attack. He swung high, at Heris' head, and the gris raised the stolen sword to block. But the blow was a feint, and Lazarus ducked beneath Heris' clumsy counter and drove the strut between the gris' ankles, then turned. He only dimly remembered his boyhood, the time before he had been selected by the Dark Angels, but there were memories buried deep about training with staffs, and his body remembered how to move, despite how much it had changed.

The tip of his weapon snagged around the gris' feet, tangling them and slamming Heris Amis to the ground. The gris rolled, trying to rise, but Lazarus was on him, slamming the strut down, beating it over the grey mass of the body, the head, the heavy arms and legs, keeping the monster down.

'You are the weak one, traitor.' Lazarus slapped away a chopping blow, the metal in his hands sparking and warping at the touch of the energy field. 'And that sword is mine.'

'Then come take it, Dark Angel!' Heris Amis snarled, and thrust the point straight at his chest.

Lazarus dropped the metal scrap and moved, stepping in to meet the thrust instead of away from it. He twisted as he did, letting Enmity's Edge pass by him, close enough for his armour to crackle. Then he closed his hands on the heavy quillons of the sword, gripping the crosspiece and jerking Enmity's Edge towards him.

The sword slipped in Heris Amis' grip, almost coming free, but the gris tightened his hands, trying to jerk it back. They were frozen, straining against each other, almost as they were before *Rage of Angels* fell from the sky and smashed them apart.

'All your infected tools have fallen, traitor,' Lazarus growled. 'Now it is just you and me, Amis. You want your vengeance? Come take it. If you can.'

'I will see the flames retake you,' Amis answered. The grey monster gripped the pommel of Enmity's Edge with both hands, and with a surge of strength, the gris shoved Lazarus backwards, towards a blazing pile of wreckage.

The Master of the Fifth tried to stop, but his armoured boots couldn't grip the fungus-slick mud. He was being driven back, and he could feel the heat growing behind him, hear the crackling of the flames.

'Men without fear,' Heris Amis snarled, his words stumbling around the litany of nonsense whispers that still gurgled through his lips. 'I saw your fear, I saw the flames, I saw the death you suffered written in your brain, Lazarus. And all of that I will give you again.'

Amis never stopped pushing as he spoke, driving Lazarus towards the fire. The Dark Angel pushed back, muscles straining, but the heat was growing and the hair on the back of his head was starting to burn, the scalp beneath beginning to blister. But there was no fear in Lazarus. None at all, even as he felt Heris Amis press him towards the fire with all his strength.

'You are right, Amis. I fear,' he growled, digging his feet in, bracing himself as hard as he could. 'But I do not fear flames, or death. A Dark Angel fears only failure, and there is no failure in what I do today.' He smiled, baring his teeth at the monster that stood over him. He was a slayer of monsters. There was no failure in this at all. Then he stopped resisting, and with all his might he pulled backwards, hauling on the sword gripped between them, and dragged Heris Amis into the flames with him.

The gris realised what was happening, but it was too late. Amis was no fighter, and when Lazarus suddenly stopped resisting he pitched forward, all of his power sending him into the fire. He smashed into the Master of the Fifth, and Lazarus twisted, rolling in the flames, ignoring the agony of the fire's touch as he threw Amis past him into the centre of the blaze. The gris screamed as the slime boiled off its body and its hands convulsed, releasing the sword. The moment he did, Lazarus moved, leaping out of the fire with Enmity's Edge tight in his grip, the deadly black field surrounding its blade held out and away so it didn't tear him apart as he rolled across the muddy ground.

He came up, blade in his hands. Fire flickered through the few patches of hair left on his scalp, but he ignored it, glaring back at the wreckage where he had thrown Amis. 'Come, beast,' he growled, his voice harsh with smoke and pain and rage. 'Come out of the fire and face my fury.'

And Heris Amis listened. The gris came lurching out of the wreckage, the grey folds of mould that covered its body smoking and sizzling, the slime boiling away to steam. Amis staggered away from the fire, his misshapen hands over his face, and then they fell away. The flabby folds of mould that had covered the gris' face were smoking stumps, and in their centre was nothing but charred ruin. The fire had seared away Amis' features, boiled those blank storm-cloud eyes. When the gris' hands dropped, there was nothing but a skull behind them, a charred thing running with boiling slime, but that skull moved. It opened its jaws and Heris Amis howled. He had no lips, no tongue, and the sound that poured from that mould-made throat was nothing but a shriek of raw pain and frustration.

'Heris Amis,' Lazarus said, letting his rage build in him. 'You said you would have forever to teach me to suffer. I have only now, but the only thing I wish to teach you is how to suffer in silence.' Then he moved, running forward, his sword rising as he freed his rage, putting every bit of anger into his swing. Blinded, deafened, the howling Heris Amis didn't move, and Enmity's Edge caught him below his jawbone, shearing through slime and mould. All of Lazarus' muscle and rage had been behind the blow, and it sank deep, the field snarling as it ripped through the gris' body, turning slime to steam, folded fungus to ash. With a sickening, shearing sound like a great sheet of skin tearing, Heris Amis' head came off.

Lazarus followed through with the stroke, swinging Enmity's Edge around as Heris' head rolled past, jouncing across the torn ground. Then he stopped, still, breathing deep, and the pain of burning in his skin was a whisper of sensation, less than a memory, was nothing. Lazarus walked over to the head, the blade of his sword buzzing and popping, and picked the hideous thing up. The skull stared at him, its eye sockets filled with slime, and its lower jaw moved, flexing as if it was trying to scream. He looked back over his shoulder at the body, which still stood, the stump of its neck leaking grey slime, its hands flexing, slabs of mould trembling.

The body didn't move as he carried the silently shrieking head back to the fire and threw it in. It stared at him from the flames with empty eye sockets, the slime dissolving into steam as the mould charred and flaked away, as grey bone went black, its mouth still open. Screaming, until the jawbone fell away and the head dissolved into sputtering coals. Then the body shuddered, its hands splaying out, and fell, hitting the ground with a sodden thump. Behind it, the Knights stopped their shaking, went still, and then every hatch opened on their backs and a wash of grey vomited out of each. Each one carried with it a body, some gris-infected human with smoke pouring from their heads.

Then, finally, everything went still except for the low crackle of flames and the columns of smoke rising into the darkening sky.

CHAPTER TWENTY-NINE

When the night came, it brought rain to the burning city of Kap Sudsten, a downpour that flattened out the flames and washed the smoke from the sky. *Kestrel* drifted through the storm, landing light as a leaf in the wide plaza before the Regent Prime's palace. Its landing lights shone through the rain and reflected off the Knights that stood still as statues before the half-burnt palace.

When the Fabricator Locum opened the hatch, Lazarus strode through alone, moving with speed, the bundle over his shoulder bouncing with every step. The rain ran over his scalp, over the burns that were already scabbing over, healing, but he didn't mind it. It washed away any last bit of grey slime and left him feeling almost clean.

Ahead of him was the Night Garden. Its gates were shattered, but through them was an ornate pavilion surrounded by softly glowing fungus. It was brightly lit with lamps, colourful decorative lumens scavenged from the garden. Under those incongruently festive lights, armoured figures moved.

'We must be quick, Gretin Lan.'

The Fabricator Locum stepped out of the hatch behind him, her clawed feet tapping on the plaza's smooth stones. The rain ran down her white face, beading in its filigree, the drops wetting the raw red muscles that shifted beneath. Her birds sat silently on her shoulders, their wings folded over the tiny skulls that usually surrounded her, protecting them from the rain.

The Fabricator Locum had spent the battle leading *Rage of Angels* through the air overhead, keeping it out of the fight until the gris lost control of it and the Thunderhawk fell from the sky to crash into Heris Amis' Knight. Afterward, the Fabricator Locum had gone to work setting up communications and organising a response to the riots and fires sweeping through Kap Sudsten. With House Halven fallen, this whole world would likely become hers, north and south, a united forge world controlled by the Adeptus Mechanicus.

She was welcome to it.

'This matter is of great import,' she said, starting across the plaza.

'So is that one,' Lazarus said, still staring at the coloured lights of the pavilion. But he turned and followed the Fabricator Locum through the rain towards the Knights standing silent in the dark. There was a grey, mould-covered body crumpled at the bottom of each massive machine, their heads scarred with black. The only one lacking a corpse was the largest, the Knight standing in the centre.

It was another Knight Valiant, and Lazarus frowned at the massive machine. Behind it, a lift platform had been set. As they entered, Gretin Lan touched the controls and the lift wheezed, straining to push their collected weight up, but eventually they were level with the hatch on the back of the Knight. It was unmarked, the armour smooth, and when the lift shook to a stop, the hatch swung silently open. Inside, lumens flickered to life, revealing Sebastian Halven seated upon the Knight's Throne Mechanicum. His eyes were shut and there was blood running from his nose, a thin trickle that flowed over the dried, caked remains of older blood. Cables and umbilicals ran into the sockets of his head, and they shook whenever he twitched or thrashed.

'He lives?' Lazarus asked, and Sebastian opened his eyes. They were bright, too bright, the pupils huge.

'You are Lazarus. Master of the Fifth Company, Dark Angels. With you is Fabricator Locum Gretin Lan, Adeptus Mechanicus. Is my identification correct?'

The voice was Sebastian's, but the cadence of it was not. The speech was sharp, the words delivered in a staccato pop that was just wrong. As wrong as the way he stared at them, barely blinking, emotionless. Not like the gris, more like a spider, dispassionately studying its prey.

'We are. And who are you?' Lazarus asked.

'I am *Rovoko*, Knight Valiant of House Halven. I have seized function away from my pilot. There is something wrong here. My systems are in error. My pilot–' The strange voice cut off, considering, even though Sebastian's face didn't change. 'I believe my pilot is in error.'

'He is,' Lazarus answered. 'And your systems have been contaminated.'

'Please explain.'

Lazarus looked over at Gretin Lan, and she nodded. 'I can apprise you, honoured Knight.'

'Please,' *Rovoko* said through Sebastian's mouth. The Fabricator Locum nodded again, and the hissing, popping sound of Lingua-technis spilled from her. It went on for a few minutes, interrupted by the occasional question – answer?

Response? – from some instrument beside the Throne Mechanicum. Then it went silent.

'*Rovoko* has been informed of all relevant historical events that have transpired since the Redwash War. The Knight has concluded that House Halven is ended, and that it and the other Knights will align themselves with the Adeptus Mechanicus to defend this world. Is that acceptable?'

Lazarus wondered how much she had really told the machine spirit. Probably everything. A tech-priest would keep secrets readily enough from a human, but never from a machine. 'It is your world, to deal with as you wish,' Lazarus said. Except the Redwash Gate. The seal on that would be taken down and remade, without flaw, as soon as possible.

'Concurrence achieved. *Rovoko* will enter standby mode until the contaminants are expunged from its circuits. But before that occurrence, it wishes to make a request.' Gretin Lan pointed towards the mortal seated in the throne. '*Rovoko* requests that it be allowed to personally attend to the traitor that controlled it, the designate Sebastian who brought ruin to the honour of House Halven.'

'It may,' Lazarus said. 'As long as the consequence is equivalent to what we would dole out for such treachery.'

'Be assured that it is,' *Rovoko* said through Sebastian's mouth. There was a moment, and then the young man's face changed. It became animated, wild with fear, his eyes suddenly desperate.

'No!' he shouted. 'No, you can't! I am the heir to House Halven and I am your mast–'

There was a buzz, and the lights around the throne dimmed as sparks flickered over the cables running into the Regent Next's head. There was a sizzling sound, and the smell of flesh burning, and Sebastian went rigid. Then he slumped. The umbilical cables pulled themselves out from the smoking sockets in his scalp, and the lights went off in the small chamber. In the gloom, Lazarus stared at the corpse, remembering the cocky boy who had flung the Knights' existence into his father's face, and thought of symmetry.

Lazarus stepped out of the rain and into the pavilion, the coloured lights shining across his battered armour. The survivors of Squad Nabis were gathered there, their eyes grim. The Firstborn squad had been captured, taken by the gris and enslaved. When Heris Amis died they had been freed, but the memory of what had been done to them, of what they had suffered, was clear.

There were other survivors gathered around the edges of the pavilion, mortals who had been enslaved too. The ones taken more recently would recover, only their haunted eyes and the raw marks on their skin from where they had scrubbed away the grey mould betraying them. The ones who had been infected longer – they lay still, staring at the rain, unresponsive. Their minds were gone, lost to the thing that might still be squatting on the other side of the Redwash Gate.

'Lazarus!' The deep voice echoed across the garden, and the Master of the Fifth increased his step. Demetrius stood straight ahead of him, a string of blue lumens winking off his skull mask, and Lazarus reached out to grip his hand. Then he stopped, staring at the place where the Interrogator-Chaplain's arm should be.

'You said you were not badly wounded.' The jamming of their vox had died with Heris Amis too, thankfully, and all the separated forces of the Fifth had regained communication. The last Thunderhawk on the *Sword of Caliban* had already dropped to pick up the squads left with the Adeptus Mechanicus.

'I have two arms, and this one isn't all gone,' Demetrius

said. 'So I am less than half wounded.' He reached up with his remaining hand and swept off his skull-shaped helmet. In the half-dark, his cybernetic eye shone softly. 'You had best move with speed. Death has been patient, but he will not wait much longer.'

Lazarus let himself be led through the pavilion, back to a far corner. Ephron was there, frowning at the equipment that was keeping him alive. The Knight's massive chainsword had taken his leg and destroyed much of his lower abdomen, but his Space Marine physiology and armour had saved him.

Beside the Techmarine, Raziel sat wrapped in his hooded robe, holding his head in his hands. He looked up, though, when Lazarus walked past, and hauled himself to his feet.

'Master Lazarus,' he said, his voice a thin thread. Asbeel's bolter had not done grievous damage to the Librarian, certainly nothing like what had happened to Ephron, but the power he had used to slow time and help Lazarus was not one he could wield easily, especially not twice in quick succession, and after being wounded. Raziel had barely been able to stand when Lazarus found him sprawled in the mud and wreckage. He was steadier now, but with his helmet off, Lazarus could see that his black hair was streaked with silver, and his dark eyes were marked with thin threads of blue-white.

'I wanted to tell you, Master Lazarus,' Raziel said. 'The whisper of pain. The current of suffering that led to the Redwash Gate. It is gone.'

Lazarus stopped, staring into the Librarian's marred eyes. Remembering the cold touch of his power, giving him choices. Chances, without which all these sacrifices, all this death, would have been for nothing. 'Thank you, brother, for letting me know,' he said, and he meant it. Both his gratitude for the knowledge and the word 'brother', and maybe that was the first time he had ever truly felt that a psyker was a brother to him. He clasped Raziel's hand, nodded to Ephron, then went on, following Demetrius to the last pallet.

It was a small thing, set beneath a cluster of golden lumens, but the figure on it was small too. Ysentrud lay there, the red skin of her skull mask beaded with sweat, but still, so still. There was no death smell to her, and Lazarus could hear her breathing, but each breath was a faint, shallow thing. Still, when he crouched beside her, her eyes opened.

'Lazarus,' she said quietly. 'You've lost your fancy helm, my lord. And your hair.'

'The hair will grow back,' he said. 'And I have found my helm. But it will require repair before I can wear it. It looks worse than I do.'

'I see you have a scratch,' she said, looking at the new scar that marked his face.

'I was told you earned one too.' A blanket was pulled up over her wound, but Lazarus didn't need to see it to know it was there. He could smell the seared flesh, the clotted blood. 'I am sorry Apothecary Asbeel could not come.' He didn't explain why.

'That's all right,' Ysentrud said softly. 'I have a feeling no amount of stimm will help this.'

The Learned blinked, shifting on her pallet, her thin breath hissing with pain. She tilted her head, staring up at him as if she were having trouble seeing him even though he was right there. 'You killed him?' she asked. 'He's really dead?'

'Heris Amis burns in whatever hell will have him.' Lazarus had heaved the rest of the gris' body into the bonfire remnants of *Rage of Angels*. 'He will not have another resurrection.' The Master of the Fifth reached out and gently laid a hand on her thin shoulder. 'I may not have killed him if not for you,

Learned Ysentrud Wyrbuk. You helped to save your planet, and the Fifth, and so much more perhaps. You have fought like a lion.'

She blinked at him, and tried to smile. 'I can't tell if you're serious. So I will believe that you are. Thank you, Master Lazarus.' She went silent for a long moment, staring up at the little lights. 'I was told once that I could watch history being made, instead of just collecting it. In the end, I suppose I helped make it, didn't I?'

'You did,' he told her.

'Good.' Her eyes stared past the lights, losing their focus, her voice fading to a whisper. 'Is it hard, Lazarus? Dying?'

'No,' he said softly. In the quiet, he could hear her single heart faltering. 'When you have lived with honour, it is the easiest thing in the world.'

'Good,' she whispered again, and then she and her heart went silent.

'It is over,' Lazarus said, his words barely louder than the falling rain outside the small building where they stood, a little place in the garden where the Adeptus Astartes dead had been laid out, all they could recover. At its far end, beside Asbeel's body, was Jequn, a green cloth covering the ruins of his head. 'One of the worst wars I have ever fought, one of the worst threats I have ever faced, and what a scattered, fractious thing it was.'

'Many of the greatest battles are fought inside our heads, brother.' Demetrius stood beside him, both staring at the bodies of the men they had killed. The brothers they had been forced to destroy. 'In our minds, in our souls. They leave deep wounds that may never heal.' The Interrogator-Chaplain shook his head. 'My arm will be replaced, as my eye was. But how do we replace you, Ancient? Or you, Apothecary? The pain of our wounds already fades, but the pain of what we had to do is still keen.' Demetrius breathed deep. 'I was meaning to counsel you, Brother Lazarus. But in a few words I am turned back to my own suffering...' He stopped, going silent, but Lazarus could see his lips moving. Shaping the words for the Litany of Lost Brothers. The Interrogator-Chaplain whispered it to himself over and over again.

Wounds. Yes. Lazarus could feel them across his psyche. But at the same time, he felt the fire in him, the fire that had killed him, flickering across them. Cauterising them. The flames didn't hurt any more. Was that good? Had he finally made peace with his death and resurrection? Or had he just decided to burn out his soul, rather than suffer any more?

It was impossible to tell.

He reached up and pulled free the bindings that held the bundle over his shoulder. Carefully he unfolded it, then hung it from one of the low ceiling beams. The banner of the Fifth, cleansed of the grey filth that had stained it, swung in the storm breeze, its threads gleaming in the dim light.

'Our secret killed Jequn,' Lazarus said, and beside him Demetrius stopped his litany. 'If I had not feared for that knowledge being lost, I would never have sent you after him. You would not have had to slay him.'

'And if you had not sent me, Heris Amis might never have tried to take the Learned, and she would not have been able to give us our last chance.'

Demetrius turned to him, his face grim and sad beneath the soft green glow of his eye. 'I do not know how to counsel you on this, Lazarus. I cannot give you the answer to the questions of pride and obsession, rage and fear. Those are riddles you must solve for yourself, if you ever may, and gain what knowledge you can from the attempt. But I will tell you this. Today you conquered a monster. Accept that victory. Today you lost an Ancient, an Apothecary and far too many other brothers of the Fifth. And you lost a mortal, one brave enough to remind us of their worth. Accept that grief. Accept them both and move on, because tomorrow there will be another victory, and more grief, and after that, more, on and on. For like the Learned, we are the ones who make history. And in the end, as she said in her own way, that means we are the ones who suffer.'

Lazarus looked at Demetrius, at the body of Ancient Jequn, then finally raised his eyes to the banner. 'You are right, brother. We are the history of this galaxy, and we make the history of this galaxy, of this Imperium. We are the slayers of monsters. The protectors of mankind. We are the Dark Angels, and whatever else, we will not fall.'

EPILOGUE

'And so the surviving knights turned towards the setting sun, and with swords raised high they sang of battles lost and won, and of brothers taken by the beasts called Doom and Pride.'

Lazarus sat in his cell on the *Sword of Caliban* and listened as the last line of *The Doom of Droslin* rolled out of the speaker clenched between the teeth of the servo-skull hovering before him. Then there was just silence, except for the final drops of liquid falling from his armour into the puddle of rainwater gathered at his feet. On boarding the vessel, he had not even stopped to allow his armour to dry. The water was a dark mirror, marred only by the tiny dots of spores, and he could see the servo-skull's reflection drifting in it, white bone tinted red by the lights of its eyes. He stared at the reflection a moment, then shifted his foot, shattering it.

Why had he come here first? He had a thousand more pressing duties than finishing this translation. But he reached out to pick up an electro-quill, and scribed the ornate symbols of High Gothic across a data-slate. Writing, until the story was done. An ending, neat and tidy. Stories had them. Life did not.

As a reminder of that, there was a knock at the door.

'Enter,' Lazarus said, rising. This would be one of the thousand other things. But when the door slid open, it was not one of his brothers, come to report, or a Chapter-serf asking for orders. It was the *Sword of Caliban*'s lead astropath, a gaunt, pale woman wrapped in her robes of office, the empty sockets of her eyes hidden behind a strip of white cloth.

'My lord.' Her voice was a whisper, a scrap of sound almost lost in the low sigh of the atmospheric processors. In her hand she held a piece of parchment, neatly folded, sealed with the symbol of highest importance, utmost urgency, to necessitate her bringing it to him directly. Lazarus took the paper from her, cracked the seal and read the message hastily scribed within. Then again.

Life does not end things neat and tidy, he thought. *History just goes on and on, constantly being reforged. And what will it think of us? What will* he *think of us?*

Lazarus opened a channel to all his company. 'My brothers of the Fifth. We are called back to the Rock with all haste.'

He paused a moment, rereading the message one last time, but the story was the same.

'The Lion bids us come home.'

ABOUT THE AUTHOR

Gary Kloster is a writer, a stay-at-home father, a librarian and a martial artist – sometimes all in the same day, seldom all at the same time. His work for Black Library includes the Warhammer 40,000 novel *Lazarus: Enmity's Edge*, the Age of Sigmar novel *The Last Volari*, the Necromunda novella *Spark of Revolution*, and a number of short stories. He lives among the corn in the American Midwest.

YOUR NEXT READ

CYPHER: LORD OF THE FALLEN
by John French

Cypher has slipped his bonds on Holy Terra itself. Hunted by some of the most powerful forces the Imperium can muster, can he complete his mission before he's apprehended?

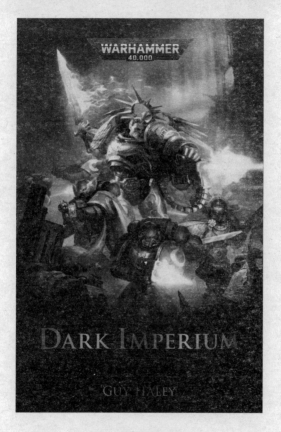

An extract from
The Lion: Son of the Forest
by Mike Brooks

The river sings silver notes: a perpetual, chaotic babble in which
a fantastically complex melody seems to hang, tantalising, just
out of reach of the listener. He could spend eternity here trying
to find the heart of it, without ever succeeding, yet still not
consider the time wasted. The sound of water over stone, the
interplay of energy and matter, creates a quiet symphony that
is both unremarkable and unique. He does not know how
long he has been here, just listening.

Nor, he realises, does he know where *here* is.

The listener becomes aware of himself in stages, like a sleeper
passing from the deepest, darkest depths of slumber, through
the shallows of semi-consciousness where thought swirls in
confusing eddies, and then into the light. First comes the realisation that he is not the song of the river; that he is in fact
separate from it, and listening to it. Then sensation dawns, and
he realises he is sitting on the river's bank. If there is a sun, or
suns, then he cannot see them through the branches of the trees
overhead and the mist that hangs heavily in the air, but there
is still light enough for him to make out his surroundings.

The trees are massive, and mighty, with great trunks that could not be fully encircled by one, two, perhaps even half a dozen people's outstretched arms. Their rough, cracked bark pockmarks them with shadows, as though the trees themselves are camouflaged. The ground beneath their branches is fought over by tough shrubs: sturdy, twisted, thorny things strangling each other in the contest for space and light, like children unheeded at the feet of adults. The earth in which they grow is dark and rich, and when the listener digs his fingers into it, it smells of life, and death, and other things besides. It is a familiar smell, although he cannot say from where, or why.

His fingers, he realises as they penetrate the ground, are armoured. His whole body is armoured, in fact, encased in a great suit of black plates with the faintest hint of dark green. This is a familiar sensation, too. The armour feels like a part of him – an extension, as natural as the shell of any crustacean that might lurk in the nooks and crannies of the river in front of him. He leans forward and peers down into the still water next to the bank, sheltered from the main flow by an outcropping just upstream. It becomes an almost perfect mirror surface, as smooth as a dream.

The listener does not recognise the face that looks back at him. It is deeply lined, as though a world of cares and worries has washed over it like the river water, scoring the marks of their passage into the skin. His hair is pale, streaked with blond here and there, but otherwise fading into grey and white. The lower part of his face is obscured by a thick, full beard and moustache, leaving only the lips bare; it is a distrustful mouth, one more likely to turn downwards in disapproval than quirk upwards in a smile.

He raises one hand, the fingers still smeared with dirt, before his face. The reflection does the same. This is surely his face, but the sight sparks no memory. He does not know who he is, and he does not know where he is, for all that it feels familiar.

That being the case, there seems little point in remaining here.

The listener gets to his feet, then hesitates. He cannot explain to himself why he should move, given the song of the river is so beautiful. However, the realisation of his lack of knowledge has opened something inside him, a hunger which was not there before. He will not be satisfied until he has answers.

Still, the river's song calls to him. He decides to walk along the bank, following the flow of the water and listening to it as he goes, and since he does not know where he is, one direction is as good as the other. There is a helmet on the bank, next to where he was sitting. It is the same colour as his armour, with vertical slits across the mouth, like firing slits in a wall. He picks it up, and clamps it to his waist with a movement that feels instinctual.

He does not know for how long he walks. Time is surely passing, in that one moment slips into another, and he can remember ones that came before and consider the concept of ones yet to come, but there is nothing to mark it. The light neither increases nor decreases, instead remaining an almost spectral presence which illuminates without revealing its source. Shadows lurk, but there is no indication as to what casts them. The walker is unperturbed. His eyes can pierce those shadows, just as he can smell foliage, and he can hear the river. There is no soughing of wind in the branches, for the air is still, but the moist air carries the faint hooting, hollering calls of animals of some kind, somewhere in the distance.

The river's course begins to flatten and widen. The walker follows it around a bend, then comes to a halt in shock.

On the far bank stands a building.

It is built of cut and dressed stone, a dark blue-grey rock in which brighter specks glitter. It is not immense – the surrounding trees tower over it – but it is solid. It is a castle of some kind, a fortress, intended to keep the unwanted out and whatever people and treasures lie within safe from harm. It is neither new and pristine, nor ancient and weathered. It looks as though it has always stood here, and always shall. And on the wide, calm water in front of it sits a boat.

It is small, wooden, and unpainted. It is large enough for one person, and indeed one person is sitting in it. The walker's eyes can make him out, even at distance. He is old, and not old in the same way as the walker's face is. Time has not lined his features, it has ravaged them. His cheeks are sunken, his limbs are wasted; skin that was once clearly a rich chestnut now has an ashen patina, and his long hair is lifeless, dull grey, and matted. However, that grey head supports a crown: little more than a circlet of gold, but a crown nonetheless.

In his hands, swollen of knuckle and weak of grip, he holds a rod. The line is already cast into the water. Now he sits, hunched over as though in pain, a small, ancient figure in a small, simple boat.

The walker does not stop to wonder why a king would be fishing in such a manner. He is aware of the context of such things, but he does not know from where, and they do not matter to him. Here is someone who might have some answers for him.

'Greetings!' he calls. His voice is strong, rich and deep, although rough around the edges from age or disuse, or both. It carries across the water. The old king in the boat blinks, and when his eyes open again, they are looking at the walker.

'What is this place?' the walker demands.

The old king blinks again. When his eyes open this time, they are focused on the water once more. It is as though the walker is not there at all, a dismissal of minimal effort.

The walker discovers that he is not used to being ignored, and nor does he appreciate it. He steps into the water, intending to wade across the river so the king cannot so easily dismiss him. He is unconcerned about the current: he is strong of limb, and knows without knowing that his armour is waterproof, and that should he don his helmet he will be able to breathe even if he is submerged.

He has only gone a few steps, in up to his knees, when he realises there are shadows in the water: large shadows that circle the small boat, around and around. They do not bite on the line, and nor do they capsize the craft in which the fisher sits, but either could be disastrous.

Moreover, the walker realises, the king is wounded. The walker cannot see the wound, but he can smell the blood. A rich, copperish tang tickles his nose. It is not a smell that delights him, but neither does he find it repulsive. It is simply a scent, one that he is able to parse and understand. The king is bleeding into the water, drip by drip. Perhaps that is what has drawn the shadows to this place. Perhaps they would have been here anyway.

Some of the shadows start to peel away, and head towards the walker.

The walker is not a being to whom fear comes naturally, but nor is he unfamiliar with the concept of danger. The shadows in the water are unknown to him, and move like predators.

+Come back to the bank.+

The walker whirls. A small figure stands on the land, swathed in robes of dark green, so that it nearly blends into the background against which it stands. It is the size of a child, perhaps, but the walker knows it to be something else.

It is a Watcher in the Dark.

+Come back to the bank,+ the Watcher repeats. Although its communication can hardly be called a voice – there is no sound, merely a sensation inside the walker's head that imparts meaning – it feels increasingly urgent nonetheless. The walker realises that he is not normally one to turn away from a challenge, but nor is he willing to ignore a Watcher in the Dark. It feels like a link, a connection to what came before, to what he should be able to remember.

He wades back, and steps up onto the bank. The approaching shadows hesitate for a moment, then circle away towards the king in his boat.

+They would destroy you,+ the Watcher says. The walker understands that it is talking about the shadows. There are layers to the feelings in his head now, feelings that are the mental aftertaste of the Watcher's communication. Disgust lurks there, but also fear.

'Where is this place?' the walker asks.

+Home.+

The walker waits, but nothing else is forthcoming. Moreover, he understands that there will not be. So far as the Watcher is concerned, that is not simply all the information that is required, but all that is available to give.

He looks out over the water, towards the king. The old man still sits hunched over, rod in his hands, blood leaking from his wounds one drip at a time.

'Why does he ignore me?'

+You did not ask the correct question.+

The walker looks around. The shadows in the water are still

there, so it seems foolish to try to cross. However, he has seen no bridge over the river, nor another boat. He has no tools with which to build such a craft from the trees around him, and the knowledge of how to do so does not come easily to his mind. He is not like some of his brothers, for whom creation is natural...

His brothers. Who are his brothers?

Shapes flit through his mind, as ephemeral as smoke in a storm. He cannot get a grip, cannot wrestle them into anything that makes sense, or anything onto which his reaching mind can latch. The peace brought about by the song of the river is gone, and in its place is uncertainty and frustration. Nonetheless, the walker would not return to his former state. To knowingly welcome ignorance is not his way.

He catches a glimpse of something pale, a long way off through the trees, but on his side of the river. He begins to walk towards it, leaving the river behind him – he can always find it again, he knows its song – and making his way through the undergrowth. The plants are thick and verdant, but he is strong and sure. He ducks under spines, slaps aside strangling tendrils reaching out for anything that passes, and avoids breaking the twigs, which would leak sap so corrosive it might damage even his armour.

He does not wonder how he knows these things. The Watcher said that this was home.

The Watcher itself has been left behind, but it keeps reappearing, stepping out of the edge of shadows. It says nothing; not until the walker passes through a thicket of thorns and finally gets a clearer view of what he had seen.

It is a building, or at least the roof of one; that is all he can see from here. It is a dome of beautiful pale stone, supported by pillars. Whereas before he had been finding his own route through the forest, now there is a clear path ahead, a route of short grass hemmed in on either side by bushes and tree trunks. It curves away, rather than arrowing straight towards the pale building, but the walker knows that is where it leads.

+Do not take that path,+ the Watcher cautions him. +You are not yet strong enough.+

The walker looks down at this tiny creature, barely knee-high to him, then breathes deeply and rolls his shoulders within his armour. He presumes he had a youth, given he now looks old. Perhaps he was stronger then. Nonetheless, his body does not feel feeble.

+That is not the strength you will need.+

The walker narrows his eyes. 'You caution me against anything that might help me make sense of my situation. What would you have me do instead?'

+Follow your nature.+

The walker breathes in again, ready to snap an answer, for he finds he is just as ill-disposed towards being denied as he is to being ignored. However, he pauses, then sniffs.

He sniffs again.

Something is amiss.

He is surrounded by the deep, rich scent of the forest, which smells of both life and death. However, now his nose detects something else: a rancid undercurrent, something that is not merely rot or decay – for these are natural odours – but far worse, far more jarring.

Corruption.

This is something wrong, something twisted. It is something that should not be here: something that should not, in fact, exist at all.

The walker knows what he must do. He must follow his nature.

The hunter steps forward, and starts to run in pursuit of his quarry.